"Child, there is no room for your wayward ways in this. What you study is magic. Will you have a lesson now from me?

"Know this of investiture: You have been told it is hard, and that those who fail that first attempt die, for those who free their luck cannot live without it. But on the birthday when you make your try, you will call up the luck out of you, to place it in the vessel of your choosing. And you will find that you have called an angry sea, a shark pack, a mountain to fall on you. Untrained luck is a wild force, stronger than you will ever believe until you summon it into your hands and find out for yourself. When you do, you will need all your training, not just what you find it convenient to remember. You will need discipline, to set your will as an inflexible barrier around the luck you've called. And you will need patience, for all that you do must be done again and again. Investiture is a battle of many hours, and a novice must use every moment of it if she is to cheat death and become a magician."

edited by
Will Shetterly
and Emma Bull

ACE FANTASY BOOKS
NEW YORK

"Badu's Luck" copyright © 1985 by Emma Bull
"The Green Rabbit From S'Rian" copyright © 1985 by Gene Wolfe
"Ancient Curses" copyright © 1985 by Patricia C. Wrede
"Birth Luck" copyright © 1985 by Nancy Kress
"An Act of Contrition" copyright © 1985 by Steven K. Z. Brust
"The Inn of the Demon Camel" copyright © 1985 by Jane Yolen
"The Hands of the Artist" copyright © 1985 by Kara Dalkey
"The Green Cat" copyright © 1985 by Pamela Dyer–Bennet
"A Coincidence of Birth" copyright © 1985 by M. Lindholm Ogden
"Bound Things" copyright © 1985 by Will Shetterly
"The Fortune Maker" copyright © 1985 by Barry B. Longyear
"A Tourist's Guide to Liavek in the Year 3317" copyright © 1985 by Emma Bull and Will Shetterly
"A Magician's Primer" copyright © 1985 by Emma Bull and Will Shetterly
"Liavek: A Creation Myth" copyright © 1985 by Emma Bull and Will Shetterly

LIAVEK

An Ace Fantasy Book / published by arrangement with
the editors and their agent, Valerie Smith

PRINTING HISTORY
Ace Original / July 1985

All rights reserved.
Copyright © 1985 by Will Shetterly and Emma Bull
Cover art and frontispiece by Gary Ruddell
Maps by Jack Wickwire
This book may not be reproduced in whole or in part,
by mimeograph or any other means, without permission.
For information address: The Berkley Publishing Group,
200 Madison Avenue, New York, New York 10016.

ISBN: 0-441-48180-9

Ace Fantasy Books are published by The Berkley Publishing Group,
200 Madison Avenue, New York, New York 10016.
PRINTED IN THE UNITED STATES OF AMERICA

For Terri and Val. It's their fault.

ACKNOWLEDGMENTS

The editors would like to thank Robert Asprin and Lynn Abbey for their advice and encouragement on this project, and for breaking ground for all shared-world anthologies. Thanks are due also to Bill Colsher, who told us what they eat in Liavek, and Nate Bucklin, who discovered the practices of the Faith of the Twin Forces.

Contents

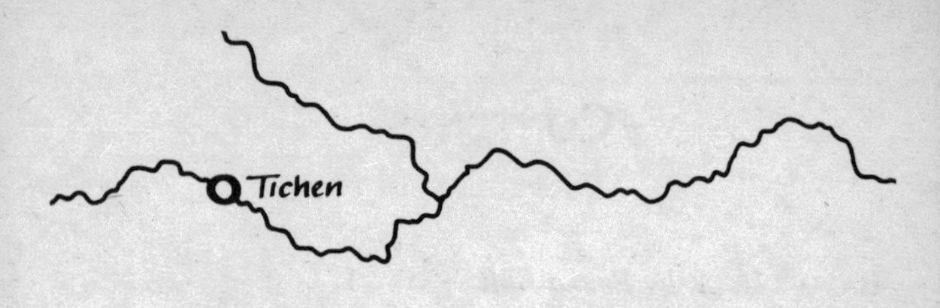
Tichen

EMPIRE OF TICHEN
THE GREAT WASTE
Trader's Town
SILVERSPINE
Liavek
Saltigos
Ombaya City
Hrothvek
Crab Island
Gold Harbor
Ka Thow
Ka Zhir
THE SEA OF LUCK
N

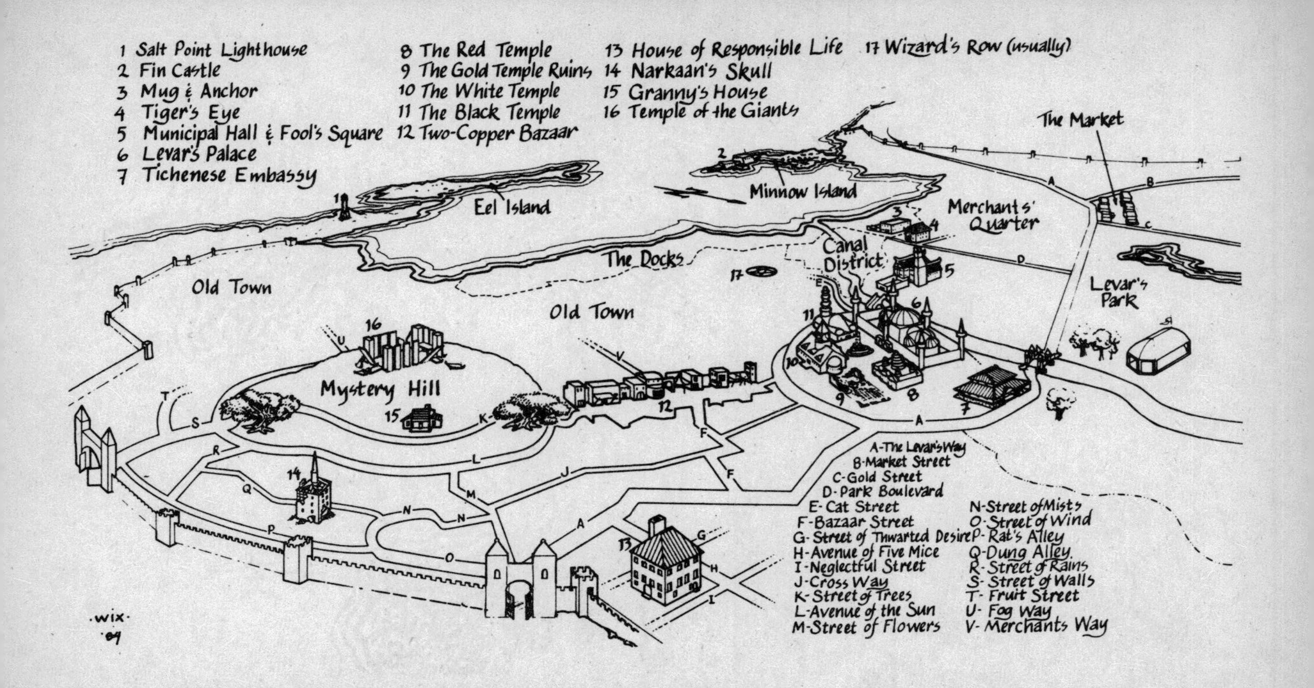
1 Salt Point Lighthouse
2 Fin Castle
3 Mug & Anchor
4 Tiger's Eye
5 Municipal Hall & Fool's Square
6 Levar's Palace
7 Tichenese Embassy
8 The Red Temple
9 The Gold Temple Ruins
10 The White Temple
11 The Black Temple
12 Two-Copper Bazaar
13 House of Responsible Life
14 Narkaan's Skull
15 Granny's House
16 Temple of the Giants
17 Wizard's Row (usually)
The Market
Eel Island
Minnow Island
Merchants' Quarter
Canal District
The Docks
Old Town
Old Town
Levar's Park
Mystery Hill
A-The Levar's Way
B-Market Street
C-Gold Street
D-Park Boulevard
E-Cat Street
F-Bazaar Street
G-Street of Thwarted Desire
H-Avenue of Five Mice
I-Neglectful Street
J-Cross Way
K-Street of Trees
L-Avenue of the Sun
M-Street of Flowers
N-Street of Mists
O-Street of Wind
P-Rat's Alley
Q-Dung Alley
R-Street of Rains
S-Street of Walls
T-Fruit Street
U-Fog Way
V-Merchants Way
·wix·
'09

LIAVEK

Badu's Luck

by Emma Bull

The Tiger's Eye was neither the richest nor the largest shop in Liavek, but its many customers agreed that it was one of the most interesting. It was two stories high, stucco-flanked in blinding white, with door and window frames painted bright rust and teal blue. Along the side of the building, on the Street of the Dreamers, firethorn grew to the roof, and at its feet peonies bowed like perfumed courtiers.

Awnings in the intricate patterns of Ombayan weavers shaded the front windows, and by extension, bits of Park Boulevard. But it was the contents of the windows that told the shop's character. There, depending on the whim of the proprietor or her assistant, one could admire a Saltigan crystal decanter threaded with gold, or a flintlock pistol and dagger with matching lapis inlay so handsome that their deadliness went unremarked.

If one were to push open the brass-studded door, making the porcelain bells above the lintel sing like spirits, one would find the promise of the windows richly fulfilled. The door opened on an airy, high-ceilinged room, enticingly scented.

Vivid textiles, glassware and ceramics, metalwork, leatherwork, the arts of gunsmiths and blade-crafters, jewelers and cabinetmakers—all these were represented in the wares of the Tiger's Eye. There were children's toys and antique amulets, embroidered slippers and Zhir hammered-harps, and, shining on the back wall like a lamp, an oval mirror framed in silver and sapphires.

The proprietor, whose name was Snake, was hardly less exotic than her goods, though she was a native Liavekan. She was tall, which was power at the Freeladen ships' auctions and the meetings of the minor merchants. Her dress was often foreign, from the loose ankle-length abjahin of the desert nomads to the sleeveless linen tunic and tight trousers of the Ombayan lancers. Her mother had said, in a fury long past but never forgotten by either party, that she dressed like "a brawling caravaneer." It was not true; or at least, it was only true when she drove a caravan.

Not the least exotic of her attributes was her skill with the long whip of the caravan driver. Unlike the dress, the tool came with her when she left the trading routes. But away from its natural place, the whip became a tool of a different sort, and when asked about it, Snake would turn the subject.

Snake was slouched in one of the two wicker chairs near the little tile-fronted fireplace that warmed the Tiger's Eye in the cooler months. A low brass table next to her held a painted porcelain pot of kaf. Her hands held the matching cup. *"Isn't* it beautiful?" she said, and not for the first time. The object of her gaze and her approbation was the silver-framed mirror.

"Yes, very," said Thyan, also not for the first time, and with even less inflection than the last. Thyan was Snake's assistant, fifteen years old and Tichenese. "And you're the only importer in Liavek fool enough to bring a mirror all the way from Ioros Jires by land."

"No, my little raisin. With vision enough."

"Vision. All I see in the thing is myself, and I look the same in any hand glass."

Snake smiled, leaned back and closed her eyes. "You have the soul of a Zhir marine."

"So who will pay you what it cost to transport?"

"Thyan, Thyan, there's more to our business than squeezing a half-copper 'til your fingers meet in the middle. There's beauty. There's art."

"There's camel dung by the shovelful," muttered Thyan. She applied herself to dusting the glassware, chanting the purchased spell that sent little dust devils flying across the shelf.

Snake only smiled, sipped her kaf, and looked at the mirror. The detailing wasn't clear from where she sat, but she remembered it. The oval frame told a story in pictures, cast and sculpted of silver: A merchant, leading an ass heavy-laden with fruit, stopped to rest beneath a coconut palm. Two monkeys in the tree began to pelt him with nuts. But as the nuts struck the ground they became sapphires, large as the merchant's head, and he left the ass behind and fell to his knees to gather the gems. The monkeys descended on his unattended fruit and carried it up the palm. The ass found itself untethered and ran off. When the merchant turned, his possessions were gone, and worse, the sapphires in his arms had turned to hairy coconuts once again. In the leaves above, the wizard-monkeys clutched their bellies and laughed.

It was, Snake reflected, an old lesson, but the elegance of the work, the sense of loving humor, and the sheer singularity of the thing elevated it beyond craft. She would find someone who saw that when he looked at the mirror, who could likewise afford to own it. Then Snake would have the satisfaction of her customer's pleasure. Until then, the pleasure was her own.

"Ah, I have caught them in sloth and self-indulgence," said the woman who stood in the doorway of the Tiger's Eye. She was tall as an afternoon shadow, hard edged as marble, and dark as a ripe black plum. Her hair was cut close to her head, which made her eyes seem even larger and brighter than they were. She was beautiful and terrible as any goddess, and her laughter made the hangings sway and the porcelain chime.

"Badu," Snake said smiling, and Thyan regained control of her slack jaw and whooped, "It's Badu!"

"Indeed," said the tall woman, as she stepped into the shop and swung her pack up onto the counter in front of Thyan.

"And what's self-indulgent about dusting?" Thyan said.

"I have heard you say, oh, many times, that to pay for such a spell when the work can be done by hand for free is a costly indulgence."

"Only when it's Snake's turn to dust," Thyan explained.

Badu laughed. "Perhaps, little woman, you should spend less time in the study of magic, and apprentice yourself to a Council member. *Do* you continue to study?"

"Lessons three times a week."

"Ah, but do you learn from them? Recite to me, something recent."

"Now?" Thyan said piteously.

"What good is magic if it will not come when you call? Now."

Thyan sighed and squeezed her eyes shut, and after a moment, began.

"Sweet Illusion's balm for weary hearts
And potent season for the jaded eye.
Transformation feeds the hungry mouth
With wood and stone made flesh and fragrant fruit.
But nowhere is there wizard with the will
Or wit to make, where nothing stood before,
A thing, a true Creation, that will last
When wizard and his power both have passed."

Thyan's shoulders dropped with relief, and she grinned. "Splendid!" cried Badu, and Snake applauded.

"But surely," Badu continued, "that's none of Silvertop's teaching. There's too much of humanity there, and too little of theory."

Snake stood and stretched. "I asked Marithana Govan, the healer, to teach her when Thyan and Silvertop, ah, had a difference of opinion."

Badu turned to Thyan with an expression that would have daunted a roomful of large adults. There was no sign that it worked on Thyan. "Indeed?" Badu was forced to say.

"He was making a spell-web that he said would keep itself working without any attention from him, but all I could tell that it ever did was stink 'til the neighbors complained. And I told him so."

"Which, of course, he appreciated," Snake muttered.

But Badu shook her head and looked solemn, and put her hands over Thyan's where they lay on the counter's polished wood. "Woman-child, there is no room for your wayward ways in this. What you study is magic, not sewing or gardening where all that is at risk is a seam or a melon vine. Will you have a lesson now from me?"

Thyan nodded, her eyes very round.

"Then my lesson is this. Until you have learned enough to

invest your luck you will be a student and no magician, for your magic will come to you only on your birthday, in your birth hours. Yes, I know you know this already. It has made you impatient, and so has placed you in danger."

"Danger?" Thyan squeaked.

Badu nodded. "Know this of investiture, child. You have been told it is hard, and that those who fail that first attempt die, for those who free their luck cannot live without it. But on the birthday when you make your try, you will call up the luck out of you, to place it in the vessel of your choosing. And you will find that you have called an angry sea, a shark pack, a mountain to fall on you. Untrained luck is a wild force, stronger than you will ever believe until you summon it into your hands and find out for yourself. When you do, you will need all your training, not just what you find it convenient to remember. You will need discipline, to set your will as an inflexible barrier around the luck you've called. And you will need patience, for all that you do must be done again and again. Investiture is a battle of many hours, and a novice must use every moment of it if she is to cheat death and become a magician."

Thyan studied the floor for a moment, then raised her head and grinned and said, "All right."

"All right?"

"I'm scared enough to make my stomach bounce, and I promise to be as patient as . . . as you."

"Oh, flattering girl. Open my pack, then, and take your reward for learning your lessons."

Thyan untied the pack eagerly. Ten peaches, fuzzy and golden, rolled out and jostled themselves into an untidy line on the counter. They were as ripe and unbruised as the day they were picked, in spite of the long, hard journey they'd made, and more beautiful than any other peaches in Liavek; for they were from Ombaya, where farming was a high art. Their fragrance was intoxicating.

"Eat one," said Badu, and one of the peaches leaped into Thyan's palm.

"Eeek. I'm not sure I can, now." But of course she did, and was plainly delighted with it.

"That was also a bit of bribery," Badu continued sheepishly. "You see, I must ask Snake to send you away."

"What?" chorused Snake and Thyan, both quite shocked.

"Oh, not far, and not for long—only until tomorrow."

"Tomorrow?" said Thyan, implying by her tone that she did not consider the word "only" to apply in this case.

Snake added, "Why?"

"I . . . can't say." Badu shot a look of great significance at Snake. Snake frowned, since, for all its weight, the look explained nothing.

It was Thyan who responded. She cocked her head, stared hard at Badu, and said at last, "Magic and politics." Badu looked surprised. "And since I don't know the one yet and don't care for the other, I'll go. Marithana will let me sleep on her roof."

"You are a woman of kindness," Badu said seriously.

Thyan turned by the hanging that curtained the back door of the shop, her arms full of peaches. "But if this has anything to do with *adventure*, I'll never forgive you." They heard her thump up the stairs.

Badu collapsed into one of the wicker chairs, poured fresh kaf into Snake's cup, and gulped it. "Ah, Name of Herself," she sighed, resting her head against the chair back, "would the child call this an adventure?"

"As long as she didn't have to get up early for it. What's got you in such a state?" Snake said, as she dipped water from a sweating jar into an earthenware cup. She offered this to Badu, who smiled sheepishly, poured a few ceremonial drops on the hearth, sipped, and handed it back to Snake. Snake did the same, and emptied the cup. "Did you walk all the way from Ombaya?"

"I came on a walleyed camel of abominable disposition. My first act in Liavek was to go to the market and sell the monster, and I can only hope that he was promptly boiled down into soup."

Thyan thundered down the stairs again, and poked her head through the curtain. "Is midday tomorrow late enough?" she asked.

"Excellent," said Badu.

"Okay. I'll go out the back door."

Snake called, "Take a peach!"

"I took two!" Thyan's voice drifted back. The back door thumped closed.

"Now," Snake said, turning back to Badu, "are you going to try to tell me that a camel is the source of all this fuss?"

"No, I think not." Badu sprang from the chair and began to stalk through the store like a restless panther. "My fancy runs to shopping. What have you that's new, and small?"

Snake stared at her. "Do you want me to humor you, or call a doctor?" she said at last.

"Humor, please." Badu fingered a silk sash, then shook her head. "Too fragile. Jewelry would be wiser." She crouched and peered through the glass that fronted a display case.

Snake sighed, went behind the case, and pulled from it a tray and several boxes. She snapped one open and pushed it forward. Inside was a brooch in the shape of a dragon, made of silver and peridots. Its finny tail seemed to wave with the winking of the yellow-green gems, and silver waves licked at its belly.

"Splendid," said Badu. "The sort of piece I would expect only at the Crystal Gull. But too rich for this application."

"If you would *tell* me—" Snake began, but Badu silenced her with a wave and a frown.

"What's in this one?" she said as if to herself, and opened the lid of a box of carved wood.

It contained a pair of earrings of gold-plated brass, set with teardrop-cut jade of respectable quality. Snake was consequently startled when Badu flinched away from them.

"No," said Badu. "Too much nonsense in these already. I'd sell them soon, were I you."

"So buy 'em."

"Not I. Ah—" Badu's hand hovered over the tray, "May I?" Snake shrugged, and Badu lifted a hammered gold leaf, delicately veined, from off the velvet. "Perfect. It suits me, it goes with everything, and it does not catch the eye."

"Why, by Herself, do you want to wear jewelry that doesn't catch—" Snake suddenly thought of a purpose for unobtrusive jewelry and let her sentence fall.

"So, how much will you ask for the bauble?"

"Nothing," Snake said, watching her. "I think I'm making you a birthday gift of it."

Badu smiled hugely. "Your quick wits more than make up for your flaws."

To Badu's clear disappointment, Snake ignored that. "You're finding a vessel for your luck. That means your birth hours are near, when your luck has to be reinvested. But you're looking for a *new* vessel. Two possible reasons for that. Either your old one was destroyed, which would rob you of your magic until your next birthday—and those peaches wouldn't have wandered so freely around the counter—or someone knows what your old vessel is. Even that wouldn't matter, if the someone didn't wish you ill. Boil that, and what floats to the top is: you're in trouble."

"Well, yes," said Badu.

"And, since you told Thyan she could come back at midday, you must be expecting the worst either this afternoon or tonight."

"Both, in fact."

"So you've brought the whole poisonous mess to my doorstep, with the assumption that I will help you deal with it."

Badu nodded.

Snake grinned and pressed both palms to her forehead in salute. "I'm honored."

"I thought you would be," said Badu.

They sat at the little brass table and Snake poured kaf for both of them. "Aren't you even a little worried about me knowing your luck time?"

Badu shrugged. "Who else do I trust so?"

Snake looked at her cup. "I *am* honored."

"We've saved each other's lives a few times. We're neither of us so wasteful that we'd want the other dead now."

"It's a killing matter, then?" Snake asked, alarmed.

"It may be. If they're wise, they would see me dead, and some other blamed. Their last best chance is tonight, for I meet with the Council representative tomorrow."

"Would you mind terribly starting from the beginning?"

Badu did not mind. "Among the Matriarchs of Ombaya, there is a faction alarmed at Ka Zhir's growing strength and recklessness. Zhir pirates have crossed the Sea of Luck to plunder the little coastal towns to the south of Ombaya. These I speak of, among the Matriarchs, know that only fear of Liavek and her navy keeps the Zhir from striking for control of the whole of the northern seacoast.

"These Matriarchs seek to forge a military alliance between Ombaya and Liavek. The Zhir would hesitate to harry our settlements if they knew that Liavek helped defend them."

Snake poured herself more kaf. "What does all this have to do with reinvesting your luck?"

"Patience, patience, dear friend. You did ask for the beginning, after all. I have many times served as go-between for traders in various lands who needed a fair negotiator in business matters. My skill in such things brought the Matriarchs of the alliance faction to me. They wish me to establish contact with the speaker for a like faction in the Levar's Council. It seems that certain Council members have independently reached the same conclusions and would seek a military agreement with Ombaya. Liavek, they reason, needs Ombaya's exported grain, livestock, and lumber—and more particularly, would suffer if Ka Zhir controlled them in Ombaya's stead. Such an alliance could also better protect the farmsteads, both Liavekan and Ombayan, on the western plains."

"You sound convinced," said Snake.

"Only, perhaps, convincing. I cannot in honor choose a side until my role in this is done." Badu frowned down at her long fingers. "And there is, indeed, another side. In the Levar's Council, there are those who say that Liavek has enough to do, keeping the Zhir shark from her own coast and shipping—there is no strength left to offer Ombaya. In the Matriarchy, many hold that if the Liavekan military is free to move in Ombaya, it will overrun her, in however peaceful a fashion, and Ombaya will end as nothing but a chick to Liavek's hen, like Saltigos and Hrothvek." Badu shook her head at Snake's look of mild outrage. "Can you say, my friend, and believe it, that Liavek would never do such a thing? She is a fair city, as moral and honest as any that ever was—but she is a living city as well, and like all that lives, her first concern is to keep it so. To annex Ombaya . . . will you not eat a trout, though the trout may have thought itself your equal while it lived?"

"Hmph. Thank you, at least, for not calling the cursed fish 'she.'"

"When I speak Liavekan, I find my thoughts seduced to Liavekan ways," Badu laughed.

"So, you suspect that one opposing side or another is trying to stop you from making your contact?"

"It could be that. It could also be the Zhir themselves, who would fear a Liavekan–Ombayan union, did they know of it. It might be the proalliance factions, one or both, who fear that I am not so neutral after all. It would be a clever ploy, could the alliance's opponents trick those I serve into thinking that I secretly work against them. It might even be that Tichen is alarmed by the possibility of Ombaya and Liavek united and strong to the south of her. In short, I have the spectres of countless enemies, and the substance of none."

"Then how do you know you have any?" Snake asked.

"Ah, forgive me. I do have a substantial foe, but still a faceless one."

"Now we're getting to it."

"It was *you* who asked for the—"

"—beginning, I know," sighed Snake. "Go on, before I foam at the mouth."

Badu steepled her fingers under her chin. "The first was at an inn, a day's ride from Ombaya. I had stayed the night, and was preparing to ride out, well before dawn; my camel was brought from his stall, and I had strapped my pack to the saddle-frame and mounted. Then one of the strap buckles broke off and rolled across the stable floor and into a crack. My annoyance distracted me—I had to make the beast kneel again, so that I could dismount and fetch the buckle. Then I would have to wait for the stable master to mend or replace the strap. I could foresee hours of delay. What I failed to see was the ready way in which an irregularly-shaped buckle had made its way across the rough floor, and how securely it had been stitched to the strap only minutes before, when I had fastened it.

"So I dismounted and thrust my right hand into the crack where the buckle had gone. Immediately, my fingers were seized in a grip so fierce I thought the bones would break. Then I forgot my pain, for the ring that holds my luck was being drawn from my finger."

Badu raised her right hand. Three of the fingers were ringed, but she tapped one, a gold band set with black stones. "I called fire to my fingertips. I heard a gasp, and my hand was freed. I ran from the stable and around the side, but quick as I went, I was not in time to catch my attacker, and with the dark and the distance, all I saw was a figure in many robes, the muffling garb of the desert folk."

Snake took advantage of Badu's pause to weigh the details of the story. She knew Badu well; she did not need to question her observations. If a strong grip and loose clothing were all she described, then they were all the identification that could be had. "You said the first. There was another attack?"

Badu nodded. "Last night, on the Farmers' Road. The first attempt had made me wary, and I spent little time in posting-houses and inns. Last night I camped in the lee of a hill, off the road, and lit no fire. Perhaps it was the same person. If it was another, then he knew of his partner's failure, though I traveled as fast as ever I have. I had set guarding spells and placed a few warnings of more humble nature. He avoided the magic and all but one of my other warnings."

"A good one, then."

"Very good," Badu agreed. "And clever, or well-instructed. Instead of falling on me immediately, he began to work a spell to stop my breathing from within. I would have seemed to die in my sleep, unmarked, and no one would connect my death with the alliance proposal. Had I still been asleep, he would have succeeded. But I countered his magic. At that, he switched to a physical attack, and we wrestled. I seized the eventual opportunity to throw him over my hip, and he fled into the night."

Snake frowned. "You say 'he' this time. Are you sure of that, or are you only thinking in Liavekan?"

"Language may seduce my thinking, but not so much as that! I have wrestled with men and with women, and though it's true that I might have been fighting a well-muscled woman with very little fat, I suspect still that my attacker was male. And there were other indications. I have rarely met a woman so big-boned in the wrists, and when I threw him, he threw like a man, as if the center of his weight was high on his body."

"Was he armed?"

Badu rose and went to her pack. From it she drew a felt bundle which she unwrapped. The contents gleamed softly on Snake's counter: a long knife, slightly curved, its hilt wrapped with many bright colors of leather. The weapon was particular, though not exclusive, to the nomadic tribes of the Great Waste.

"This one also wore desert gear," Badu said. "And his face was covered, so that I could be sure only that he had two good eyes of uncertain color."

"Unfortunately, there are a great many men with two good eyes. When are your birth hours?"

"From four-and-a-half hours after midday, until a quarter-hour into tomorrow."

"And you think someone will try to strike at you here, tonight."

Badu smiled wolfishly. "He would be a fool not to, and I

would hate to think I am hunted by fools."

Snake rubbed her forehead. "So my job is to keep you safe while you invest your luck?"

"That's more succinct than I would be, but yes."

"The entire Society of Merchants is more succinct than you'd be. Any hope of some help from you, or is it to be my strong right arm and nothing else?"

"Until I have invested my luck, I cannot help you. As I told Thyan, investiture requires complete concentration. Nor can I supply you with magical defenses, for when my birth-hours begin all my luck will return to me, and any spells that I have made will disappear."

Snake looked down at her right arm. "Just you and me against the hordes of evil," she said. Then she turned again to Badu. "You can use the living quarters upstairs, anyplace you're comfortable. I'm going out, but I'll be back before you have to begin. Set a warding spell or something around the place until then."

Badu smiled, gathered up her pack, and made her way upstairs.

Snake took her caravan driver's whip from behind the counter and hung its coils over her left shoulder. Then she set out the "momentarily closed" sign and headed for Silvertop's.

Silvertop lived on Street of the Dreamers, which Snake had always taken as proof that the universe was well-ordered. She met the caretaker on the stairs, and they each touched their foreheads in greeting.

"Ah, Madame Snake," the little man beamed. "You visit your Farlander friend?"

Snake nodded. "Is he well?"

"I think he is never not well. And all else is much better, for there is not anymore the smell."

"Ah," said Snake faintly. "I'm glad to hear it."

"Have the good visit," he said, and trotted down the stairs.

Snake knocked on Silvertop's door and received, as usual, no answer. She went in cautiously.

The room had been intended by the builder as a parlor or sitting room. Its present function would not have been completely described by any word that Snake knew in any of several languages. One wall supported shelves untidily filled with bound books, papers, and scrolls. A badly-stuffed peacock was hung from a beam by one brittle foot. The center of the room was crowded by a long table, its scarred top cluttered with objects: feathers, broken pen nibs, a goblet on its side (indications were that it had tipped over and spilled its contents some time ago and the fact had yet to be discovered), a ball of string the size of a small dog, and other things less easily recognized or coped with.

Silvertop sat hunched over this intricate chaos, on an upholstered stool from which stuffing leaked intermittently. He was small and slight and bleached-looking, with his pale Farlander skin and silvery-blond hair. When Snake cleared her throat he glanced up from a random-seeming construction of brass wire, bits of wood, and strips of fabric.

"Oh, it's you," he said cheerfully, and returned his concentration to the table. "Come hold this, will you?"

"Not for the Levar's own treasury," Snake replied. She spotted the back of a chair, resolved to excavate its seat, and moved parchment, boxes, and sheets of copper until it was unearthed. She sat down.

"Have a seat," said Silvertop.

Snake didn't bother to respond.

Silvertop frowned at the ill-assorted mess before him. "Up," he said to it, and the whole thing rose, trembling, to a handspan above the table. From out of an empty space in the middle of the object, a curl of smoke rose. Suddenly every knot and weld and wrapping seemed to give way, and wood and brass wire and fabric strips showered the tabletop.

"Beautiful!" said Silvertop, and turned grinning to Snake. "Did you see that? Beautiful!"

"I'm, ah, glad to find you in such good spirits," Snake said weakly.

"Yep, the best. What can I do for you, Snake?"

All of this made Snake not a little dizzy. Silvertop coherent *and* accommodating? There was not a moment to lose. "I need a guardian spell, for the Tiger's Eye."

He blinked. "I thought you only bought housekeeping spells and things that kept sparks from getting out of the fireplace."

"Special occasion."

He turned and began to scoop through the mess on the table with both hands. "D'you want to keep out everything?"

"No," Snake said, trying not to notice the mummified orange

that rolled mournfully off the table in front of her. "I want a spell that will keep anyone from entering the shop by magical means."

He looked disappointed. "That's been done before."

"Yes," Snake sighed, "but not for me."

"Wouldn't you rather have—"

"No."

"Oh, all right. Ah, perfect!" Silvertop held up an old grey glove with all the fingertips worn through. "How long do you want it to last?"

"Make it ten hours," Snake said.

Silvertop held the glove under his nose and began to mumble at it, scowling fiercely. He traced the seams of the glove with a fingernail as he chanted; when he came to the glove's missing finger-ends, his tracing continued, as if to fill in the missing lines of stitching. He groped among the table's contents for a moment without raising his eyes from the glove, bumped into a little stoneware dish and pinched something out of it. (Snake wondered if he had any idea what it was he'd grabbed.) He dropped the powder into the palm of the glove, folded it over, and scrubbed the surfaces together. Suddenly he flung the glove into the air. It glowed blinding blue for an instant, then dropped back into his hands, as grey and gnawed-looking as before.

"There you go," he said, and held it out to her. "Tack it up over the front door, inside."

"And hope no one looks up," Snake muttered. She took it by the cuff, gingerly. It was stiff with age and dirt. "Well, thank you. How much do I owe you?"

"It was pretty easy, that specific and that short a time. Call if a half-levar."

Snake pulled out the pouch and counted a half-levar plus a little, which she knew Silvertop wouldn't notice, into his hand.

"Can you bring the glove back when you're done?" he asked her at the door.

"I wouldn't think of keeping it," Snake said fervently.

"Oh, and—" he said, and stopped.

"Yes?"

"Um, tell Thyan that the . . . um, the spell didn't work. And I guess you should tell her she was right, too."

Snake laughed. "If I don't, she'll say it herself."

"And it's okay if she wants to come back." He looked embarrassed.

"I'll tell her."

"Thanks, Snake. G'bye." And he shut the door behind her.

Out in the street, she steeled herself and tucked the obnoxious glove in her sash. Late afternoon pedestrians eddied past her. Food cart owners hawked meat rolls, fruit tarts and stuffed dates to tide their patrons over until dinner. From somewhere around the corner she heard street musicians, fiddle and baghorn and drums. A redheaded woman selling half-copper scandal sheets shouted her tease, which mentioned the names of a famous nobleman and a notorious artist in interesting conjunction. There was something encouraging, Snake found, in the way that Liavek ignored her incipient crisis. She strode back to the Tiger's Eye feeling strengthened.

The shop door opened to her pull, and she felt a sudden fear. Badu hadn't barred it behind her. She stepped forward—and thumped painfully against a barricade of perfect transparency and Badulike contrivance. "Ouch," Snake said. "It's me."

The barrier began to change at once, from iron to pudding to air, under Snake's hand. She rubbed her nose and went in.

Badu was in the parlor upstairs. The room occupied most of the front half of the second floor, which made it more or less square. The walls were panelled in scrubbed pale pine to about hip height; above that was rough whitewashed plaster, relieved by a very few carefully chosen woven hangings and other bits of art. Badu sat on the red patterned rug at a low table, setting out sausage, golden cheese, and two of the peaches.

"The last of the travel food," she said with a wave at it. "Have you any bread?"

Snake fetched it from its box in the little kitchen and settled down across from Badu for a hasty picnic. "Anyone come calling while I was out?"

"Either two people, or the same one twice. The first very nearly did what you did, at the front door. The second tried the latch on the back."

"You didn't get a look either time?"

"It didn't seem prudent to stick my head out the window."

"Mmm." Snake gathered up a second helping of everything to take downstairs. "Here's my plan. I assume you'd be better able to do what you were hired for if you didn't have to dodge assassins while you did it."

Badu nodded.

"Then I'm going downstairs and opening the shop. I can't

catch the fellow if we barricade him out."

Snake had made sure to say this when Badu's mouth was full, and she ignored the resulting strangling noises that followed her down the stairs.

As she nailed the revolting glove to the lintel next to the bells, she considered her chances. She was not as confident as she had given Badu to think; still, the assassin would very likely underestimate her and her preparations when he found she'd opened the shop. If she simply kept him out for the night, he would make another attempt on Badu's life soon after, and Snake did not care to live with the burden of unpaid debt that would be hers if he succeeded.

Reasoned arguments aside, she felt a stubborn unwillingness to bar the doors and hide in her own house. Had she wanted to live as a cloistered woman, she would have moved to Ka Zhir and bought a veil.

When she stopped hammering, the noise continued. Someone was pounding on the door. Her whip was still over her shoulder, and she judged the hammer in her hand a nice touch. She unbarred the door.

"Your pardon, sir," she said to the man on the other side, and dipped him a shallow but formal bow. "I was closed for . . . repairs. Be pleased to honor my shop."

He was shorter than she was, but if he found her height disconcerting, he showed no sign. His features, as well as Snake could see, were Liavekan. He had a thin, high-bridged nose, prominent cheekbones, and clear, penetrating black eyes; in combination they reminded Snake of the eagles that swept down on occasion from the Silverspine. The lower half of his face was hidden by a short black beard that looked, somehow, unintentional, as if its owner were not quite aware it was there, or hadn't yet decided what to do with it. He was deeply tanned, and creases fanned from the outer corners of his eyes. Snake found him handsome and immediately suspect.

He wore a high-necked, long-sleeved blouse and loose trousers the color of sand, and over these a sleeveless coat that reached to midcalf made of black felt richly embroidered. Snake recognized the clothing as bits and pieces from several nomadic tribes in the Great Waste. She speculated on the weapons that could hang from his belt under the coat.

His step over the threshold managed to convey disdain.

Snake wondered what he would think if he looked up and saw the abominable glove. "I wish to see Badu nolo Vashu," he said in tones of polite command.

Snake heard the little clock on a shelf behind her chime midhour, and realized it was half-past four.

She tilted her head to one side. "I beg your pardon?"

"Badu nolo Vashu," he repeated, and frowned at her. Snake had the irksome feeling that she was being taken for a servant.

"Very sorry. She's not here."

He raised one eyebrow. "I'm afraid I don't believe you." His voice was chilly.

"What a pity."

"I'm prepared to see for myself, Madame . . ."

"Snake," she said with a polite smile and a little nod. "And you, sir?" She was suddenly and perversely reminded of her presentation party at the age of fifteen.

His eyes narrowed, and he seemed to study her face. She returned the stare. "Koseth," he said at last. Snake smiled in what she hoped was a skeptical fashion. It was a fairly common surname. "May I sit down?" he added.

"I thought you were about to push past me and search the house."

"I changed my mind."

"Good." She stepped aside, and he went to the hearth and sat in one of the wicker chairs.

"Can I help you find something?" Snake asked, gesturing vaguely toward the merchandise.

Koseth, narrow-eyed and smiling, leaned back in the chair until the wicker creaked. "So, you say Badu nolo Vashu is not here?"

"I said that."

"Does that mean you're here alone?" he said softly.

"Why do you ask?" At half-past four, Badu had begun the rite of investiture. Could magicians sense these things? Was Koseth a magician? Snake wished mightily that she could ask Badu.

His reply, however, was simply, "To find out how you'd answer. The reason behind any question. And I think I shall be satisfied with 'Why do you ask?'"

Snake wished that he would do something decisive, if he was indeed Badu's nemesis. If he wasn't, she wished he'd quit behaving suspiciously and go away. "I'm sorry, sir, but if you've come neither to look nor buy, you can go to a café to sit. I've work to do."

"No doubt." Clearly, he was not easily provoked.

But she was so startled by his next words that she almost forgot Badu. "Did you know Siosh Desoron, before he died? He had three sons and two daughters. The sons learned their father's trade, the outfitting and managing of caravans, out of duty. But he taught his youngest daughter, Galeme, as well. It was said that she could bring a 'van through the Waste in midsummer, with robbers thick as flies in a barn, and never so much as a broken goblet in all the load.

"Now all that is said of someone named Snake, and the Desorons claim that Siosh had only one daughter. Are you, perhaps, *that* Snake?"

Snake replied, with corrosive emphasis on every word, "What business is it of yours?"

He shrugged.

"There's no secret of it, however much my mother may wish there was. But Snake is quicker to say, so for your convenience, you may leave the Desorons out of it."

He rose and made her a bow. There was a great deal of self-congratulation in his smile, and she felt a surge of anger, at him and at herself. Why had she taken his bait, and what possible good could he get out of it?

She stepped out into the aisle, placing herself where he had to confront her or turn toward the door. He chose the latter. So they both saw the flash of gilded red swoop toward the opening. It was a finch, one of the multitude that lived half-tame on the city's accidental bounty, bright fluttering ornaments on roof peaks and windowsills. It was nearly within the door frame before it beat its wings furiously, veered, and was gone upward and out of sight.

The face that Koseth turned to her was bland and unreadable; but she had caught a glimpse of it before he'd turned, and his look had been black as the bottom of the sea.

After he left, the shop had a breathless quiet about it. The finch, Snake knew, could have been quite ordinary. She'd had to catch birds before that had gotten in a door or open window and forgotten how to get out. Its sudden change of direction might have come when it saw the two humans blocking the doorway.

Or it might have been a magician, wearing bird-shape to enter the Tiger's Eye, who'd discovered the effect of Silvertop's glove. (Which made her wonder, what *was* the glove's effect? Was it a barrier, like the one Badu had made? Did it return a disguised magician to true shape? Snake wished she'd asked.) If it was a magician, was it an ally Koseth had summoned, or was it the true danger, and Koseth no threat at all?

The third possibility Snake liked even less: that Badu had two enemies.

It was Snake's custom to keep the Tiger's Eye open until seven o'clock on business days. She managed to hold to that, though seven had never seemed so late. The traffic was lively as people came in to browse before continuing on to their dinners. Many ascended to the status of customer: A young man with curly black hair bought a coverlet woven in a rare antique pattern called Palm Leaf Shadows known only to an old woman who lived on the Street of Trees; an elegant-looking man in his thirties knocked over a fat little brass bowl and bought it by way of apology; and a shaven-headed ship's captain, who laughed often and without humor, bought herself a large copper earring.

The little clock chimed seven times, and Snake slumped forward over the counter. Her vigil, she knew, was far from finished. But now she could bar the door and make the Tiger's Eye a fortress. She felt a fleeting longing for previous visits from Badu, when at seven o'clock Snake and Thyan would go upstairs and make dinner, and Badu would entertain them with Ombayan gossip.

Or further back, when Snake was sixteen, and she and Badu had been herd guards one summer in Ombaya. . . . It was dangerous work, and the two of them had worked and fought well together. Snake wished Badu could be at her back now.

She had just slid the bar home when she heard a sound behind her. She turned.

The elegant man, the one who had knocked over the bowl, stepped from behind a tall mahogany cupboard. In his hand was a flintlock pistol, its single barrel pointed unwavering at Snake. He cocked it ostentatiously.

"And now," said Snake, "I suppose you're going to tell me all about how you did it."

He flung back his head and laughed. "I confess, that was my intention. Would you prefer me reticent?"

"Not at all," said Snake. She leaned against the door, trying to look off balance. "Would you mind starting with who you work for?"

"Ah, no," he said sadly, "I cannot oblige. If you knew that, I would have to kill you. As it is, if you will stay sensibly out of the way, you need take no harm from this at all. My business is with the Ombayan woman upstairs."

"I'm nothing if not sensible," Snake nodded. The whip was heavy on her left shoulder. "So, how did you get in?"

"Just as you saw, when I came in as a customer. Your spell kept me out in bird-form—yes, that was I, and quite a setback you gave me then, too." Snake looked at his red-and-gold patterned half-robe. The finch had been a reasonable match. "I made other, more subtle attempts, and found that the spell was proof against them all. I was driven at last to make a dangerous experiment. I came in and, after a suitable time, knocked down the charming brass bowl. Your attention was drawn away from me for barely long enough. I was able to duck behind the cupboard and leave an illusion of myself in my place, which then went through the motions of buying the bowl and left the shop. Had that most excellent spell worked both ways, allowing no magic to cross the boundaries of the house, my illusion would have melted in the doorway, and my last hope for subtlety and stealth would have been gone."

"At the very least, an aesthetic defeat," murmured Snake.

"Now I must ask you to unbar your door, if you please. A representative of . . . my employer will be along presently to verify the fulfillment of my commission." He spoke as if the words tasted bad. "Those without honor assume everyone else to be without it, as well."

"How true," said Snake absently. Inwardly, she rejoiced. The man who stood before her was only the arrow; the archer was on the way. And it was the one who drew the bow that she wanted to trap. She turned and pulled the bar back, keeping her hands always in sight of the man with the flintlock.

"I don't believe we've introduced ourselves," she said when she turned back.

He looked startled, but made her a sketchy bow. "You may call me Yamodas, Madame, if it please you."

"Not your real name, I assume."

"Alas, no."

"My name is Snake," she said, and began to uncoil the whip from her shoulder.

He frowned. "Madame—Snake—as I told you, you have nothing to gain and your life to lose by opposing me."

Snake smiled and flicked the whip hissing along the floorboards.

Yamodas pulled the trigger.

Into the silence that resulted, Snake said, "I once lost a valuable piece of porcelain in an accident involving a drunken Scarlet Guard and a pistol. I then found that a spell can be bought that will prevent small quantities of gunpowder from igniting. It takes a long time to prepare and only works in an enclosed space, but the cost is really quite reasonable. I have it renewed annually."

Yamodas sighed, looked regretfully at his pistol, and thrust it into his belt. "I suppose you have a surpassing skill with that whip."

"I do. I could put your eyes out with it, or break your wrist, or strangle you. But I'd rather extend to you the courtesy you offered me. If you swear to give up your present, ah, commission, effective immediately, and if you follow the instructions I'm about to give you, you'll go free and unharmed."

He looked at her measuringly. "I am an honorable man, and I am under a previous agreement."

"Mmm. I'd hate to have to shame an honorable man in the sight of so dishonorable a slug as your employer sounds. But if you don't cooperate, I'll truss you like a chicken and hang you from the ceiling to greet him when he comes in."

"On the other hand, I *have* been paid in advance. . . ."

Not long after, there was a harsh knocking at the door of the Tiger's Eye. Yamodas opened it and bowed low to the man who crossed the threshold. The newcomer had the meaty fatness of a wrestler, insufficiently disguised by a saffron-yellow robe and a long blue overvest with a pleated back. He wore an abundance of jewelry—necklaces, pins, bracelets, and earrings—and even sported a gold fillet that bound his red-dyed beard just under his chin.

"Have you killed the Ombayan?" he snapped at Yamodas.

"I have not. I was delayed with the shop owner."

"Hah! The deadly Yamodas, tussling with a shopkeeper?"

"She was rather more than that. I should have been warned."

"We knew nothing about her. If you can't do your own research, you're not worth your price."

"Enough. The Ombayan has had no warning. We will go upstairs now, and you may have your proof firsthand."

The fat man snorted. "'We' will go nowhere. You were hired to take the risks, and you will take them. I will come nowhere near the Ombayan until she is dead. Go up and do what you were hired for, and call me when you're done."

"As you will," Yamodas said, and went to the back of the shop and through the curtain.

From behind that curtain came a muffled thump, as of a door closing, and the fat man's eyes narrowed with suspicion. He hurried toward the back of the shop.

Snake rose up from behind a display case and snapped out with her whip. It coiled around the fat man's neck and bit deep when she pulled it tight.

He grabbed at the whip with both hands, and Snake prepared to resist his pull. It didn't come. Instead, the leather began to writhe and twist under her hands, and the hard, heavy butt end flexed and fastened itself to her forearm with a many-fanged lamprey mouth.

The fat man uncoiled the lash end from his neck, showing an angry wine-red line where it had cut. He whispered to the end he held and tossed it casually toward Snake. It lashed itself around her knees and clung there.

Laughing, he walked toward her. Snake's hands were still clenched together around her animated whip; she swung them like a club at his temple and connected hard. He staggered back against the display case, which tipped over, spilling jewelry and her attacker onto the floor with a crash. Snake grabbed a small bronze fencing shield off the back wall next to her and jumped at him, hoping to bring the edge down on his throat. But before she could reach him, he raised his arms and shouted. A hail of jewelry pelted her face. The shield was wrenched from her hands.

He pulled her up by her hair, which was painful, until she was standing. "You sow!" he screamed at her. "You are the offspring of a goatherd and his favorite nanny!"

"Make up your mind," Snake said through clenched teeth. If she lived through this, she would have to see if Silvertop knew a charm to keep anyone from ever again enchanting her whip. It had let go its grip on her forearm and twined itself around her wrists. She was beginning to lose the feeling in her fingers.

"You have turned my assassin away from his target, and you have marked me—" He jerked her head around, and she could see, in the beautiful silver-framed mirror set with sapphires, his face behind hers. His left cheek was cut open and bleeding, probably from the edge of the display case. "You shall watch yourself die, and know that the Ombayan woman will die next, and you could not protect her!"

He began to chant. Snake cursed at him, struggled, tried to kick and would have bit, had there been anything before her but the silver mirror. She could not break his concentration. He raised his right hand before her face, the little finger delicately extended. The fingertip began to shine like a polished knife. She watched in the mirror as he set the fingertip to her throat and began to draw it across the skin with creeping slowness. A drop of blood welled and trickled down where the finger touched, and the fat man's face behind her, shining with sweat and blood, beamed.

Behind him in the mirror she could see the Tiger's Eye, its precious contents glowing like a loving portrait in the lamplight, the front door open on the empty indigo darkness of Park Boulevard. She couldn't scream—probably part of the fat man's chanting. She hoped Thyan would take good care of the shop.

Then from behind them, where the mirror showed empty air, a voice said, "Ahem."

The fat man dropped her and spun to look, and got Koseth's fist in his face, with the rest of Koseth behind it.

Snake's whip suddenly became a whip again, and fell to the floor around her feet. The fat man, his nose bleeding and his face contorted with fury, flung both arms around Koseth and lifted him off the floor.

Snake vaulted over the fallen display case and rammed both her heels into the fat man's kidneys. He went down. Koseth rolled clear and squatted on the floor, clutching his ribs and looking pale.

"Watch him," he gasped. "He's not done yet. . . ."

Koseth was right. The fat man half-rose and gestured fiercely, screaming something. Snake turned and found the silver-and-sapphire mirror flying off the wall at her. She caught it without bending or breaking the fragile silverwork frame, but it continued to press forward, forcing her slowly toward the fat man.

Then at the edge of her vision she saw Koseth stagger to his feet, raise both hands above his head, and begin to whistle. A ball of black smoke formed between his palms. He flung it at the fat man, and it streamed out from his hands like a veil and wrapped around the fat man's head. The fat man cursed and gestured, and the smoke became a veil in truth, made of black gauze which tore easily in his fingers.

All the force went out of the silver-framed mirror. Snake looked from it, inert and shining in her hands, to the fat man, who had begun to chant at Koseth, and felt hot fury begin to rise in her. He couldn't be troubled to defend himself against her? She set the mirror down against the wall, snatched up the broken-off leg, long as her forearm, from the display case, and advanced upon the fat man.

He was chanting steadily at Koseth, who had dropped, white-faced, to his knees. The room smelled of lightning. Snake jabbed the man in the ribs with the leg. "Hey," she said. He turned.

She clubbed him, and he slid gently to the floor.

After a few moments, she heard Koseth clear his throat. "Not a moment too soon. Oh, I hurt. Did you kill him?"

Snake knelt and rolled the fat man over. There was blood in his hair, but he was still breathing. "No. What shall we do with him?"

"Disarm him." Koseth stood up slowly and limped over to Snake. "Help me strip him."

"Strip him?"

Koseth nodded at the man on the floor. "Something he's wearing or carrying is the vessel of his luck. Do you want him to wake up with his magic to hand?"

They stripped the fat man and piled his clothing and jewelry in a heap in the middle of the shop. Koseth bent over it and began to sing. With one finger, he traced a circle around the pile; when the circle was closed, he straightened up and clapped his hands. With a crack! and a rush of air, the fat man's belongings were gone.

Snake said, "Where—?"

"They're on your roof," said Koseth. "I'm afraid I didn't have the strength to send them any farther, but that should keep them the necessary three paces away from him."

"My roof." She shook her head. "Come on, let's tie him up."

Once they had, Koseth ventured out into the night and returned with four uncommonly deferential soldiers of the Levar's Guard and a donkey cart. It took all six of them to hoist the unconscious assailant into the cart.

When the soldiers had gone, Snake went back in the shop and dropped into one of the wicker chairs. She looked up, and found Koseth watching her closely.

"No hysterics?" he said.

"The time for that was when he was killing me."

"I find that's exactly when there *isn't* time for them. I like to have mine later."

Snake laughed weakly. "Let me know when, and I'll join you."

"I would be honored," he said, and bowed.

"Now, make kaf and tell me who you are."

Snake watched him dip water from the jar and set the kettle heating on the hearth brazier. To her surprise, she didn't resent the easy way that he found and used her things—she was content, for now, to sit quietly and be catered to, and Koseth seemed content to cater.

When he at last sat down across the brass table from her he said, "I didn't lie to you, you know. My name is Lir Matean Koseth ola Presec."

She blinked at him in dawning comprehension. "Which means that you're . . ."

"The Margrave of Trieth," he finished apologetically.

"The Desert Rat," she said, then added quickly, "Sorry, Your Grace."

He laughed. "Well, I am—or was, until I had to take my seat in the Levar's Council. That was when I became involved with a group of councillors who favor alliance with Ombaya."

Snake sat up in her chair. "Are you telling me you're the person Badu was to meet?"

"I beg your pardon? Oh, yes. I am."

"Why, in the names of any of a hundred gods didn't you just *say* so?"

"Don't shout. We knew there was opposition to the proposal in the Council. We also suspected that one of those opponents was spying for the Zhir, but we had no way to be sure. I was chosen as the contact since I wasn't yet publicly associated with the proalliance group, and was thus least likely to lead the spy to the Ombayan emissary, or to be a target for him myself."

"You haven't answered my question."

"Madame," he said, exasperated, "how were we to know you weren't in the pay of the spy?"

Snake stared at him. "I think I'm insulted."

Koseth—the Margrave of Trieth—shrugged. "Oh, when I realized who you were, I knew you were no spy. But by that time, I had other things to think of."

"The finch?"

"Exactly. But I could do nothing except keep a watch on the shop front, and as far as I could tell, all was quiet. Until our fat friend strolled down the street and knocked at your door."

"When you very kindly followed him in and got me off his hook. But why didn't you show up in the mirror?"

"Once, in my misspent youth, I tried to creep up on someone who was standing in front of a mirror. It's made me wary. I cast an illusion, causing the mirror to show everything in the room but me. That's a loophole in your guardian spell, by the way—though you can't enter the house by magic, you can cast illusions back and forth through the doorways."

"I know," Snake said, grinning.

He raised an eyebrow, but went on. "And I needed the element of surprise. I'm no match for the likes of Borlis in a head-to-head duel."

"Borlis?" she hinted.

"Our fat friend is Borlis iv Ronwell, the Count of Seagirt, and a Council member high in the opposition movement."

Snake nodded slowly. "And a Zhir spy," she said.

"Exactly. You smoked out our rat. With my testimony, and yours, if you're willing, the opposition will be discredited, and the alliance proposal will be approved by the Council and sent to the Levar."

The kettle began to rumble on the hearth, and he fetched it back to the table. He poured boiling water over the ground beans, fine as powder, and the thick brown smell of kaf rose into the air between them as it brewed. Then he filled two cups and offered one to her. His hands were large and brown, clean, but calloused and broken-nailed—very much like her own, she realized, after a trading trip.

He looked at her over his cup. "And I suppose that Badu *is* upstairs."

"Mmhm." He opened his mouth, and she continued quickly, "And if you're going to ask why she didn't come down when she heard the fight, the answer is, 'None of your business.'"

"Oh," he said.

"I suppose she'll want to know why we couldn't have saved her life a little more quietly."

He stretched his legs out before him. "A good question. An insightful question. Why couldn't we?"

"If all I sold was rugs, I'm sure we'd have had no problem," Snake said, eyeing the smashed display case ruefully.

"Would it be at all helpful," he said, studying his cup, "if I were to stay around—to help you explain it all to Badu?"

Snake shot a look at him. She rather thought she recognized that tone of voice. "To leave before then, in fact, would be unforgivable," she said at last.

He smiled. "Then I'll be courteous and stay." He lifted his cup. "To a remarkable woman," he said, watching her face.

She smiled. "To a charming rescue."

The porcelain cups chimed like bells.

The Green Rabbit From S'Rian

by Gene Wolfe

CAPTAIN TEV NOEN took off his gilded dress helmet and scratched his shaven head—not because he was puzzled by the sight of two of his best hands nailing up a placard at the mouth of Rat's Alley, but because it had occurred to him that the placards might be ineffective, and he had not yet decided what to do if they were. He had composed them himself that afternoon, and Ler Oeuni, his first mate, had lettered them with sweeping strokes of the brush.

JOIN THE LEVAR'S NAVY!
THE GALLEASS *WINDSONG*
IS NOW ACCEPTING RECRUITS!
THREE COPPERS A DAY
PROMPTLY PAID AT EVERY PORT!
AMPLE FOOD, DRINK, AND CLOTHING, AND
GOOD TREATMENT!
SIGN TONIGHT AT THE BIG TREE!
FIVE COPPERS WHEN YOU SIGN!!
PRIZE MONEY COULD MAKE YOU RICH!!!

It was a simple appeal to self-interest, and Noen wondered whether sounding the trumpets of Liavek and Her Magnificence, as most captains did, would not have been better. He thought not. In his experience, recruits did not care about such things.

The hands drove home their final nails with resounding whacks and turned to face their captain, touching their foreheads with all fingers. Automatically, Noen replaced his helmet and returned their salutes. "Good work. Now we'll rejoin Lieutenant Dinnile and see if these have brought anyone yet." Recklessly he added, "I'll buy you each a tankard, if there's a good hand already."

The sailors grinned and took their positions like proper bodyguards, the woman ahead of him and the man behind him. Noen tried to recall their names; they pulled the first (that was, the rearmost) starboard oar—Syb and Su, of course. Each wore a sharply curved cutlass in a canvas sheath now, although the hammers they carried would be nearly as effective.

He himself was far better armed, with his sword and double-barreled pistol. Not that swords or "villainous saltpetre" should be needed for the drunken sailors of Rat's Alley, or its cutthroats either—Naval officers were notoriously savage fighters and just as notoriously broke.

If they were attacked, it might even be possible to carry the fellow—undamaged, Noen hoped—aboard *Windsong*. There he would sign on or chase a sack of ballast to the bottom.

"Why, if we were attacked by fifty or so . . ."

"Sir?" Su looked over her shoulder at him.

"Talking to myself," Noen told her brusquely. "Stupid habit."

There were always the judges. A judge could pardon an offender willing to enlist. And judges *did* pardon such offenders—for well-connected captains, and for captains who could offer rich gifts in return. Not for Tev Noen, to be sure.

A rat scampered across Noen's boots, and he kicked it. It sailed past Su's head, and in the darkness of Rat's Alley someone swore and spat.

"Good 'un, sir," Syb whispered diplomatically.

Noen had recognized the voice. "Is that you, Dinnile?"

"Yes, sir. Some filthy devil just flung a rat at me, sir."

Inwardly, Noen damned his luck. The story would be all over the ship by morning, and such stories were bad for discipline. Aloud he said, "Officers who leave their posts have to expect such luck, Lieutenant." Or perhaps they were good for discipline after all, or could be made to be. Syb and Su would be the cynosures of the main deck, and he himself shouldn't come off too badly.

"I didn't leave my post, sir." Dinnile's brass breastplate gleamed now in the faint light. He spat again and wiped his mouth on his sleeve. "I got 'em."

"Got what?"

"Fifty-two rowers, sir. You said not to take no more, remember? No use payin' more than's authorized."

Noen squinted at the dim column that trailed after Dinnile in the dark. "You got fifty-two in a couple of watches?"

"Yes, sir! They come together, sir. They're nomads from the Great Waste." Dinnile halted before his captain and touched his forehead. "There's been a drought there, they say, so it's worse than usual—cattle dyin', and all that. They come to Liavek to keep from starvin', and somebody that saw one of Oeuni's placards sent 'em to us."

Noen nodded. It seemed best to nod in the face of Dinnile's enthusiasm. "That's a piece of luck."

"For us and them—that's what I told 'em. We'll sail tomorrow with a full complement, sir."

Noen nodded again. "They're strong enough to pull an oar, you think?" Dinnile was not the most brilliant officer in the fleet, but as a judge of what could be extorted with a rope end, he had no peer.

"Give 'em a little food and they'll do fine, sir. They spent their five coppers on ale and apples and such at the Big Tree, sir. And I promised 'em, too, a good feed when we get to the ship."

"Right," Noen told him. Anything to keep them from deserting on the way. "We'll go with you."

Away from the beetling structures of Rat's Alley, there was more light, and Noen counted the recruits as they filed past. Forty-nine, fifty . . . he held his breath . . . fifty-one, fifty-two. Then the pair of crewmen he had assigned to help Dinnile. All present and accounted for. It was beyond belief, too good to be true. For a dizzy moment he wondered if it were his birthday—could he have forgotten? No. Dinnile's perhaps. No. Or—of course—one of the nomads'. What better luck could the poor devil have than seeing himself and all his friends fed and safe aboard the *Windsong?*

Or what worse?

Noen asked one of Dinnile's sailors if there had been fifty-two exactly.

"Oh, no, sir. More like to a hundred, sir. The Lieutenant picked out the best, and let them sign."

Let them sign! It was a night to remember.

Ler Oeuni touched her forehead as he came aboard. Noen touched his own and said, "We'll put off for Minnow Island as soon as Dinnile has the new hands at the oars."

"There's a bit of night breeze, sir."

"Under oar, Lieutenant, not under sail." Oeuni was sailing officer (and gunnery officer); Dinnile rowing officer. Ordinarily it would be best to spare the rowers as much as possible, but the new hands had to be taught their job, and the sooner the teaching began, the better—tomorrow they might have to ram a pirate.

Noen mounted to *Windsong*'s long, lightly built quarterdeck and watched Dinnile shoving the new hands to their places, most to forward oars from which they would be able to watch the trained rowers at the aft oars and would be caught up in the rowing rhythm that was almost like a spell. "See that there's at least one experienced hand at each oar, Dinnile."

"Aye, aye, sir." The tone of Dinnile's response managed to imply that the instruction had been unnecessary.

"Do they speak Liavekan?" Noen cursed himself for not having found out sooner.

"Some do, sir. Some don't."

"Then *talk* to them. They've got to learn, and quickly."

"Aye, aye, sir."

"Foreigners?" Oeuni ventured to ask.

"Nomads from the Great Waste," Noen told her. She would have to deal with them, after all, as they all would. Eventually, she would have to train them to reef and steer.

"They're subjects of the Empire, then."

Noen shook his head. "They're not Tichenese, if that's what you mean. And whatever they were, they became subjects of Her Magnificence when they signed with us."

Dinnile had pushed the last of the nomads into place. Noen

cleared his throat. "Listen to me, you new hands! I'm Tev Noen, your captain. Call me Captain Noen. This is Ler Oeuni, our first mate. Call her Lieutenant Oeuni. Lieutenant Beddil Dinnile signed you—you should know him already, and the petty officers you'll learn soon enough. You'll be treated firmly on this ship, but you'll be treated fairly. Do your best, and you'll have no cause to worry.

"You've been promised a good dinner tonight, and you're going to get it. There are navy kitchens at the base on Minnow Island, and they'll have hot food for you." It was probably better not to tell them they would not be permitted to leave the ship, that the food would be carried on board. "When I give the order 'out oars,' watch the trained hands and do as they do."

Noen glanced at Oeuni. "You may cast off, Lieutenant."

"Stand by to cast off!" she shouted at the sailors stationed fore and aft. They leaped onto the wharf. "Cast off!"

A few moments more and *Windsong* was under way, her oars rising and falling awkwardly, but more or less together, in a beat as slow as the timesman at the kettledrums could make it.

A fresh wind touched Noen's cheek as the dark wharves and warehouses of the waterfront vanished in the night. Little cat's-tongue waves, the hesitant ambassadors of the lions in the Sea of Luck, rocked *Windsong* as a mother rocks her child.

"Not so bad," Oeuni said.

Noen answered with a guarded nod. How hard were a nomad's hands? Not as hard as a sailor's, certainly. These men would have blisters tomorrow, if the wind failed, and—

On the main deck, Dinnile's rope end rose and fell. There was a shout that sounded like a curse, and the flash of steel. Dinnile's big fist sent someone reeling over the next oar. Something—a knife, surely—clattered to the deck. Noen called, "Tivlo! Bring that to me." Tivlo was the petty officer in charge of the mainmast. "Dinnile! If he's conscious, put him back to work." Attacking an officer was punishable by death, but Noen had no intention of losing a hand this early.

Tivlo handed up the knife, hilt first. Its blade was curved and wickedly double-edged.

"We'll have a shakedown as soon as we tie up," Oeuni said.

Noen nodded. The cresset burning atop the highest tower

of Fin Castle was already in plain view. The nomads would need their knives to cut rope and do a thousand other tasks. But they would need nothing more, and there was no telling what else they might have.

Oeuni had lined the new hands up and hoisted lanterns at the ends of the main yard when Syb came to the quarterdeck, touching his forehead. "What is it?" Noen asked.

"About Su and me, sir."

"Yes?"

"You promised us a tankard each, sir, if there was a hand signed."

"So I did." Noen bent over the quarterdeck rail. "Would you as soon have the money?"

"No, sir. Perhaps, sir . . ." The words trailed away. Hands were forbidden the quarterdeck, except upon order. Noen said, "Come up."

"Thank you, sir!" Syb mounted the steps. "I thought it might be better to speak more private-like, sir. Su and me—well, her folks and mine live here on the island."

Noen shook his head. "I can't let you go ashore. We'll be sailing at dawn, and perhaps before dawn."

"Sir . . ."

Noen knew he should cut the man off, but there was something in his face that forbade it. "Yes?" he asked.

"Let us go just for this watch, sir. If we're not back when it's over, you can put us both in the irons. It's not to drink or nothing like that, sir."

"What *is* it for?"

"They're fisherfolk, sir. It's not no easy life, sir, and now we've got our pay, and . . ."

"I see," Noen said.

"A prosperous fishing village, sir. That's what they call it, those that don't live there. It means they've generally got enough to eat, if they fancy fish, and maybe enough to mend the boat or buy the twine to make a new net. But it's a terrible hard life, sir."

Noen began, "If I gave you leave, I'd have to give it to others who have just as good a—"

He was interrupted by a touch at his elbow. It was Dinnile, now officer of the watch. "A sojer, sir. Got a letter for you."

When Noen had carried the note to the binnacle light, he

announced, "I'm going ashore, and I'll want bodyguards. Syb, you and Su did well enough last time. Dinnile, see that they're issued cutlasses."

"For goin' ashore on Minnow Island, sir?" Dinnile was utterly bewildered.

"You're right," Noen told him. "Their sheath knives should be enough, and there's no time to waste."

Fin Castle rose from a rocky headland at the easternmost tip of the island, where its great guns commanded the principal entrance to the harbor. Noen dismissed his "bodyguards" at the castle. "I'm going in to see Admiral Tinthe. I don't know how long I'll be, but when I come out, I expect to find you waiting here for me. Understand?"

They muttered their aye-ayes, touched their foreheads, and hurried away.

Noen needed no guide to direct him to the admiral's chambers. High in the keep and facing south, they permitted Uean Tinthe to scan the Sea of Luck. As Noen climbed stair after weary stair, he wondered how often the old man did so, and when he would decide the price of his view was too high.

Noen's knock brought a gruff invitation. He ducked from habit as he entered, conditioned by *Windsong*'s low cabin. Admiral Tinthe was in his favorite spot by the window; beside him sat a distinguished-looking woman of middle age.

"Captain Noen, Serkosh," the admiral said, returning Noen's salute. "Noen, Serkosh the Younger."

Noen bowed. "A great pleasure, Lady."

She nodded stiffly.

"Told you to be ready at sunup," Tinthe continued.

"Yes, sir."

"You're undermanned like the rest. I can send you a scant half dozen."

"*Windsong* has a full complement now, sir," Noen said.

For an instant, the admiral studied him. "Sailors?"

"Landsmen, sir."

Admiral Tinthe turned to the woman beside him and winked. She smiled; he had been a handsome man once, and traces of it still remained in his scarred old face. "Recruiting practices," he told her. "Best left to the young ones. Best not to know too much."

"All signed in due form, sir," Noen told him. Inwardly, he blessed his foresight in inspecting Dinnile's roster book.

"Good. Sail you will. Course south and a point east. That's the best of them, and your crew's earned it for you."

Noen forbore asking what made it the best. "Pirates, sir?"

The admiral shook his head. "You'd better hear the story. Know what you're up against. Tell him about the green rabbit, Serkosh."

The woman said, "Perhaps you might ask him to sit, first."

When Noen was settled in a chair, she continued, "I am a jeweler, Captain. I own the Crystal Gull—possibly you've seen us? We're situated near the Levar's Park. The next time you've need of a gaud for some young woman, perhaps you'll stop in."

"I'd like to," Noen told her, "if I had the money."

Serkosh nodded. "And if your mission is successful, you will. I've promised to pay twenty thousand levars to the captain who returns the green rabbit to me."

Noen said nothing. It was a fortune, a prize so great it stunned the imagination.

"You're aware, I'm sure, that there was once a city called S'Rian on the hill overlooking our bay."

Noen nodded.

"Occasionally—very occasionally—something is discovered there. I do not say something of value, because they're very seldom of value; but something of interest to collectors and antiquarians. Perhaps once a year. Perhaps less. Do you understand?"

Noen nodded again.

"Such things are invariably brought to me. My reputation for honesty is second to none, and I pay the highest prices—often a good deal more than the item is worth."

Noen said, "I'm certain you do," trying his best to keep any note of sarcasm from his voice.

"Such a find was made last winter by men digging a well. It was—it is—a crouching rabbit carved in jade." Serkosh used her hands to indicate the length of the rabbit, then its height. "About half the size of a living rabbit. The size of a very young rabbit, if you wish to think of it so."

"I understand."

"We often have to hold such things for years. In this case several noble collectors were interested, but we had not come to an agreement about terms." Her face hardened. "Three days ago, the rabbit was stolen from my vault."

Noen asked, "Someone broke in?"

Serkosh shook her head. "It seems the thief was an employee. My assistants are allowed to enter the vault. My apprentices are permitted to enter when accompanied by an assistant. Nothing else was taken. That suggests, to me at least, that the thief supposed that the absence of the rabbit would not be noticed, as the absence of a diamond—"

Tinthe cleared his throat.

Serkosh glanced at him, then back to Noen. "Your admiral and I differ in our interpretation of the crime, though we are both determined that the thieves be brought to justice. He will give you his own view, I feel sure."

Noen said, "A jade rabbit the size of a rat isn't worth twenty thousand levars."

Serkosh shook her head. "Of course not. But the security of the Crystal Gull is worth much, much more. If we are robbed successfully just once, there will be a hundred more thieves eager to try. But if you, Captain, can intercept the ship carrying the rabbit, it will be seen that the thieves were *not* successful."

A massive brass telescope stood on the admiral's work table. He picked it up, sliding its jointed sections in and out. "There's something more, I'm afraid, Noen."

Serkosh exclaimed, "That absurd story!"

Tinthe closed the telescope with an audible click. "Absurdity doesn't matter if people believe it. And they do—maybe I do myself. Know what a magic artifact is, Noen? A magician puts his luck into something. The thing's magic then, and it doesn't matter if the magician lives or dies."

"And this rabbit—" Noen began.

Serkosh cut him off. "Nonsense! I had it tested by a competent professional. He conjured it, instructed it, burned incense, sacrificed, did everything! It's no more magical than your shoe."

Tinthe smiled and opened his telescope again. "But there's a rumor it is."

Noen asked, "What is its function supposed to be, sir?"

"Nobody knows. Or anyway, nobody agrees. Brings you women. Brings women children. It's a rabbit after all. Should be something like that, eh? But there are S'Rians living in the city. You probably know that. And they say it's magic. Serkosh's magician said he found nothing. Suppose he did, returned it, stole it himself by magic?"

"I see, sir."

"Or suppose it brings women. Would he tell? Or would he think it his own doing? Suppose it's wealth. He got a good big fee. And you'll get twenty thousand if you bring it back here, Noen. That's wealth, wouldn't you say?"

"Do you know it left the city on a ship, sir?"

Tinthe nodded. "We thought it might. That's why I had every ship here make ready. Report reached the Guard tonight. There's a lip in Old Town. Always is. *Zhironni,* big carrack, sailed yesterday. Probably making for Ka Zhir, though we can't be sure." Tinthe leaned forward. "Noen, maybe the rabbit's a magic artifact. If it is, and the Zhir get it . . ."

"I understand, sir."

"Wish I had a magician to send with you. I don't. We've got them looking for the rabbit, but no one available to go to sea." The old admiral hesitated. "Serkosh's professional may be on board—the Guard can't find him. All this is under seal, Noen. Very much so."

Day had dawned with a weak breeze that soon died, leaving *Windsong*'s triangular sails flapping against their masts. Noen had ordered them furled and put the oars out. A few moments ago Oeuni had cast the log, and now her face was grim. "A scant two knots, Captain."

"They'll get better," Noen told her.

"They'd better, sir."

Though the air was dead calm, there was a nasty chop; the galleass, long-bodied, narrow-waisted, and shallow-keeled, rolled in it like a belaying pin. The new hands were sick at their oars. Dinnile had four sailors filling buckets and swinging swabs, and *Windsong* left a trail of filth behind her that would have done credit to a garbage scow.

Noen squinted at the horizon, then at the sun. "Oeuni, how much do you know about magic?"

"Not enough to make sailors of Dinnile's recruits."

"We'll do that. How long would you say it would take a good magician to raise a wind?"

"You're serious, aren't you, sir? I have no idea. I suppose it would depend on the size of the wind he wanted—longer for a storm to wreck a ship than for a zephyr to cool a garden."

Noen nodded to himself. The wind had been gentle yesterday when the *Zhironni* sailed—a big ship wouldn't have gone far on those light airs; and now *Zhironni* was probably as becalmed as they were. Worse in fact, because they were at least making two knots. A carrack would be drifting with the current. Perhaps *Zhironni* had no magician after all.

"Look at that! You served on one once, didn't you, Captain?" Oeuni was pointing aft. Barely visible, the triple-banked oars of a trireme rose and fell like the wings of some enchanted bird.

"Yes," Noen said. "They must have got under way a good deal later than we did." That was a little consolation at least. He turned away to look at his own ship once more. Like most galleasses, *Windsong* had only a single oar bank; but five rowers pulled each of her enormous oars. Four rowers, or three, Noen reminded himself, when the crew was understrength.

With his telescope trained on the trireme, he tried to guess how many of its oar ports were empty. How beautiful she was! They had put up the mast, and it pointed to the heavens like a single white arrow.

But why? A trireme under oar normally shipped its mast, laying it flat in two cradles on the narrow storming deck that ran all the way from the quarterdeck to the gun deck on the forecastle. And why did it look so white? Could the captain of the trireme, still far behind him, see something he could not?

He turned to Oeuni. "You're supposed to be keeping a weather eye out, Lieutenant."

"Yes, sir." Her face puzzled, she scanned the horizon.

"Try northward," he advised her.

She squinted, shading her eyes with one hand.

"We're in for a blow, Lieutenant. A carrack's wind."

And a soldier's, as it proved, a wind that blew from dead astern and sent *Windsong* flying under reefed sails, pitching as if to shatter her flimsy hull each time her great bronze ram smashed into a wave.

"Pass the lard bucket, Lieutenant Dinnile! The new hands will need it."

"Tev Noen," Oeuni asked at his ear, "what are we after?"

Surprised, he stared at her.

"I know, the *Zhironni,* and the rest is secret instructions. But what if you're killed? I'll be in command, and I won't know what our objective is." Her hand touched his, as if to remind him of how desirable she was.

He knew what she was offering him, and knew he must

refuse. The price of love bought with secrets would be his self-respect. He said, "I'll try to tell you before I die, Lieutenant," and she turned away.

Another watch, and stinging hail pelted the ship. Noen pulled the hood of his sea-cloak over his head, wondering if he should have his steward bring his helmet. They would be fighting soon anyway; he could feel it. Armor might save an officer's life, but it endangered it as well. Many a captain, many a lieutenant, had gone to the bottom weighted with armor. Noen found that he was thinking of Oeuni drowned, helmetless, the green sea-light shining on her shaven head, arms and long legs tossed in death's parody of swimming. Oeuni whom he would never possess, drawn down to the dark by her cuirass. Ler Oeuni lost.

The lookout in the maintop shouted something that was blown away by the gale. Noen went to the quarterdeck railing. "Lookout! I can't hear you!"

"Sail! Point to starboard!"

"Point to starboard," Noen told the woman at the wheel, and vaulted the railing. Dinnile was still supervising the distribution of lard, seeing that each rower who needed it used it and that none took too much. Hands with infected blisters could not row; heavily greased fingers could not hold an oar, if rowing should be necessary again.

"Can they fight, Dinnile?" Noen asked as softly as the wind allowed. "Will they?"

Dinnile shrugged. "I dunno, sir."

One of the nomads appeared at Noen's shoulder, still rubbing his palms together. "Yes, we fight. Give us swords."

Dinnile roared, "Stand to attention there!"

The nomad had better sea legs than most of them, and he stood as he must have seen the sailors stand, his brown rags flapping about him.

It was the first time, Noen realized, that he had looked at one of the new hands as an individual. Like all of them, this one was small and wiry—dark, though not so dark as a true Tichenese. Every line of his skull showed in his face, and Noen might have thought a candle lit there from the fire that burned in the bony sockets of those yellow eyes.

"Sir, we will fight. With our knives if we must. With our hands."

"I think you will. Dinnile, break out the arms. Everything

we've got." Noen turned back to the nomad. "What's your name?"

"Sir, Myllikesh."

Oeuni was on the gun deck, checking *Windsong*'s main battery. When Noen put his telescope to his eye, she told him, "*Zhironni*."

"Thank you," Noen said, his voice expressionless. He forced himself to add, "Lieutenant."

"You must have seen her at the docks. Fifty guns at least."

"Mostly rail pieces." On the pitching gun deck, it was hard to keep his telescope trained on *Zhironni*, but Noen glimpsed figures on her quarterdeck with their own lenses trained on him.

"And what have we got, aside from Poltergeist here?" Oeuni patted the big culverin affectionately on the muzzle. "Four basilisks and a couple of sakers. If those aren't rail pieces, what are they?"

"And the ram," Noen told her, shutting his telescope.

"Ram that? It will damage us more than it will them."

To himself, Noen admitted she was probably right. Aloud he said, "Have the crew stand to quarters, Lieutenant."

She shouted the order to the timesman aft. "Are we going to attack her straight out, sir? Shouldn't we give them a warning shot—"

A smudge of black appeared at the carrack's taffrail, instantly whisked away by the howling wind. The boom of the gun—a long basilisk much like the two on his own quarterdeck, Noen thought—was nearly lost.

"Waste your powder," Oeuni told the Zhir. "You couldn't hit Kil Island at this range."

Noen wondered. *Zhironni* was a far more stable gun platform than *Windsong*.

Aft, the timesman had begun the long, fast roll that called every sailor and officer to fighting stations. The gun crews boiled out of the forecastle below the gun deck, some carrying baskets of the premeasured charges Oeuni liked, others shot and slow match. Just one of Poltergeist's big iron balls was a load for any sailor—in so rough a sea, almost too much of a load.

The tompions were jerked from the muzzles of Poltergeist and the two swivel-mounted basilisks, powder and shot rammed home. (Privately Noen regretted the loss of the old system, in which the powder was poured down the gun bores from a scoop; then at least a captain could note its condition.)

The gun captains had kindled their slow matches at the galley firebox; they spun their glowing tips to keep them alight in the wind-blown spray.

Zhironni's sternchaser spoke again, a bit more loudly this time. An instant later the port forestay parted with a snap. The bosun and his mate hurried forward to repair it.

"They're rigging boarding nets, sir," Oeuni reported.

"So I see," Noen told her. "We won't be going over the side anyway. Bosun! You've seen a xebec?"

Surprised, the bosun turned, touching his forehead. "Aye, sir."

"You know how they slope the foremast forward to give the foresail more room? I want *Windsong*'s foremast to look like that. Tighten those forestays and slack off the backstays until the masthead's raked as far forward as our ram. And I want ratlines from the deck to the masthead."

Dinnile was at the aft gundeck railing, touching his forehead. "Oars, sir?"

"No. Just have them ready to board—old hands first." It was not necessary to tell Dinnile to lead them. He would anyway—probably would, Noen reflected, even if he were ordered not to. "Oeuni, see how that gallery overhangs at her stern? I'm going to bring us in under it. Disable the rudder as we're coming in."

As Noen spoke, one of the many-paned windows of the carrack's stern cabin swung wide. The black muzzle of a gun emerged from it like the head of a snake as the other window opened.

"You can fire when ready."

As Noen reached the lower deck, the port basilisk went off with a crash. The foremast was lurching toward the beakhead, and Dinnile had his boarding party mustered forward of the mainmast. Looking at him, Noen realized the burly mate must be as frightened as he was, but like himself would rather die than show it. "Good luck, Beddil," he called. Then, "A place ashore!" It was something one said; the "place" was the grave, which could never be mentioned directly.

"A place ashore," Dinnile responded cheerfully.

The port corner of the quarterdeck exploded in a cloud of splinters. "Steersman!" Noen yelled. "Port a point. We're coming in the back door."

The steersman's "aye, aye," was strangely muted; when Noen reached the quarterdeck, he saw that a splinter had laid her cheek open, baring white molars in a misplaced grin. One of the starboard sternchaser crew was ripping up her shirt to staunch the bleeding.

The sternchasers would be no use in this fight. He sent the rest of their crews to join the boarding party.

The two sakers had already been shifted to the port rail. They would not be able to fire without damaging *Windsong*'s rigging until they were very close, he thought, but they might get a chance then.

Oeuni's hail came faintly from the gun deck. "She's luffing!"

Noen nodded to himself. *Zhironni* would try to turn in order to present her broadside to her attacker. But imposing though they were, carracks were notoriously unhandy, and now the wind made every plank in her towering freeboard work against her.

Dead ahead, a leviathan rose from the sea, golden-scaled, with eyes like pale moons and teeth like the blades of cutlasses. Poltergeist fired with a roar that shook the ship, and the giant fell backward in a welter of blood. Noen braced himself for the shock when the ram struck its body, but there was none; it had sunk too quickly, or perhaps disappeared.

Somehow the culverin's roar had reminded him that he had not yet wound the wheellock of his pistol. He got out the key and did so. A pistol with a tight lock was always dangerous, and if the lock were wound too soon, the spring might break or lose its strength. But shapes like horned Kil were clawing at *Windsong*'s racing sides with crimson hands, and it seemed to him that the time to wind it had come.

"Magic," a crewman at one of the sakers wailed.

"Illusions," Noen told him, shouting against the whistling wind. "He hasn't had time for something new."

Poltergeist and the gun-deck basilisks went off together; *Zhironni*'s rudder flew to bits, and ragged holes gaped in her transom. An unlucky roundshot cut through the boarding party, leaving a dozen hands writhing on the reeling deck. They were close now, so close Noen could see the dark faces of the gun crews through the sterncastle windows. He fired at one, not with much hope of hitting him, but because it was bad tactics to permit your enemy to fire without being fired upon.

Zhironni's stern loomed above them. Noen felt they were hurtling toward a cliff, and it was no magical illusion, but the effect of the carrack's sheer size. The sakers banged like hammer blows, scouring *Zhironni*'s sterncastle windows with harquebus balls and scrap metal. Noen shoved his pistol back into his belt and grabbed the quarterdeck railing.

The ram struck with a shock that nearly knocked him off his feet. Only weakly braced by its angled backstays, the foremast snapped, fell against the carrack's stern, slipped, miraculously caught on the gilded molding. As Dinnile's boarding party swarmed up the ratlines, a Zhir with a petronel appeared at the taffrail. Noen fired the remaining barrel of his pistol at him, shouted for the sakers' crews to follow, and leaped to the maindeck.

The ratlines were slack and thus hard to climb, lying almost against *Zhironni*'s stern gilding. Shattered window casements hung in shreds of iron, glass, and lead. A dead man slumped over the breech of one of the sternchasers. Noen hesitated, hardly daring to believe his eyes, put one foot on the gun muzzle, then the other. Half falling, he caught the window frame and swung into *Zhironni*'s stern cabin.

Outside, it had seemed impossible; but it was there. A circular, inlaid table was bolted to the floor in the center of the cabin; on it a small jade rabbit slid restlessly with the rolling of the ship, confined by the table rim. Only when he reached for it did Noen see the delicate girl who sat in shadow beside the cabin door.

"It is mine," she said. "But it could be ours."

The rabbit felt as cool as any river-washed stone.

"There are many isles—" She had risen and was coming toward him; her fingers toyed with a white rose. "—even in this little Sea of Luck. And there is the ocean beyond. We might master an isle and rule there together." Her face had a delicate beauty that made Oeuni and every other woman Noen had ever seen seem like a man. No, a beast.

The cabin door flew open, kicked by a nomad with a knife in one hand and a cutlass in the other. Noen said, "This woman is a prisoner, Myllikesh. Take her to our ship and put her in the wardroom. See that she's well treated."

The nomad pointed to the rabbit with his cutlass. "Sir, move away your hand."

Noen picked up the rabbit.

"Sir, I do not desire that I kill you. But you must give that to me."

"You knew what it was," Noen said. "That was why so many of you signed on. You heard it had left Liavek by ship, and you knew our ships would be sent after it."

Myllikesh took a step nearer. "We told your stupid Guards of this ship, so your ships would be sent. Sir, I can kill you most easily before your sword is out. Put the rabbit down."

Noen did.

The girl said softly, "Do you know its secret, brave man of the wastes? Tell me."

Myllikesh turned to her, eyes flashing. "Yes, we know! Long ago our fathers were driven from S'Rian, but we remembered. Friends told us it was found, and we came!"

"Tell me. Now you will be a king." Her great eyes were fixed on Myllikesh; Noen was surprised at the pain that gave him.

"I am a king! Now I shall rule a rich land." The nomad laughed. "Rushing streams for us. Fruiting trees and fields of wheat! A great mage made this so S'Rians might have such a land, though the city was lost. But it was left behind, lost too. You must throw it down. That only! Then even rocks and sand will blossom."

The white rose flashed forward and vanished in the nomad's chest, then reappeared a red rose. He gasped and dropped his cutlass.

Noen hit the girl in the face with the twin barrels of his empty pistol. She staggered backward; when she struck the canting cabin wall, she was an old man who grasped a scarlet dagger.

Myllikesh was half out the cabin window, one hand pressed to his wound, the other clutching the rabbit. Noen caught him by the neck and wrist, and the rabbit fell from his hand, tumbled down *Zhironni*'s towering stern, dropped between *Zhironni* and *Windsong*'s bow, and splashed into the sea.

When it touched the water, it seemed to bounce—the upward bound of a hunted hare who tries to sight its pursuers. It struck the water again running, jumping and skipping from wave to wave, racing across the restless sea as if the sea were an upland meadow.

Behind it, seals lifted sleek heads and a thousand dolphins bowed. The sea itself grew dark with the tiny creatures on which the smallest fish graze, and the great whales; fish surged in silver shoals, swirling and leaping everywhere after the rabbit for as far as Noen's eyes could follow it, until the sound of their swimming entered *Zhironni*'s timbers and filled the cabin like the humming of bees.

"Wasted," Myllikesh whispered.

Noen thought of Syb and Su, of the unpainted fishing cottages on Minnow Island and the wretched shacks on Eel Island. "No," he said. "Not wasted."

But the rattle of the last breath was in the nomad's throat.

From *Windsong*'s taffrail, *Zhironni* seemed a seaworthy ship. Her mainsail, maintop, and mizzen were all drawing, and though she listed a bit and the twin streams of water spurting from the lee side showed where Dinnile had prisoners at work on the pumps, Noen decided *Zhironni* might well limp back to Liavek even if they met with squalls. A captain's share of prize money was a full quarter. That would not come to twenty thousand levars, he thought, but it might come close. Even damaged as she was, the big carrack should be worth sixty thousand at least.

"Rekkue!" he called to the midshipman of the watch. "Make signal: 'reducing sail for night.'"

"Aye, aye, sir."

"Tivlo! Reef the mainsail. We don't want to lose her in the dark."

"Aye, aye, sir!"

The big triangular mainsail dipped. It was a great advantage of the lateen rig, Noen reflected, that the crew did not have to go aloft to take in sail or let it out. Some of the hands Tivlo was directing had been Myllikesh's nomads; some were former slaves from *Zhironni*.

Rekkue told him, "*Zhironni* acknowledges, sir."

Noen nodded. "I'm going below to write my report. In my absence, you're officer of the watch. You're to call me if anything happens. *Anything*, understand? Call me at the end of the watch and I'll relieve you so you can get some sleep."

"Aye, aye, sir." Rekkue touched her forehead.

She would be an officer soon, Noen thought. She was fit for one already. As he went down the steps to the lower deck, he decided to announce her acting promotion to third mate in the morning, if everything went well that night. He ducked automatically as he entered his cabin, pulled out his chair and seated himself before his little writing desk.

Ler Oeuni said softly, "I hope you don't mind, sir."

He spun around. She was in his bunk, her face, her bandaged arm, and one bare shoulder visible above the blanket.

"It was lonesome in the wardroom with Dinnile gone," she whispered, "and I wanted to tell somebody how brave I was."

When he had kissed her, she added, "I'll bet you were brave too, Noen."

Ancient Curses

by Patricia C. Wrede

THE OLD WOMAN stood on the moonlit hilltop, leaning on a heavy walking stick. Around her rose the homes and shops of Liavek's Old Town. At either end of the street stood an ancient cypress, visible only as an enormous silhouette against the stars. The street was silent, and empty except for the wind and the woman. The night had a feeling of strangeness in it, and those who lived on the Street of Trees had learned to stay indoors at such times.

The old woman tilted her head back and took a deep breath, tasting the wind. It was dry, dry as ashes, despite the nearness of the sea. Her lips tightened, and she darted a glance at the giant cypress ahead of her. Not a leaf stirred, despite the steady breeze. Bad, she thought. Very bad.

A cloud passed in front of the moon, plunging the hilltop into cold shadow. The old woman looked up. "All right, that's enough!" she snapped. "I can take a hint."

The air shivered and seemed to grow warmer. The moon came out, throwing silver shadows all along the edges of the street, and the leaves on the trees began twisting and rustling in a damp, salty breeze. "That's better," the old woman muttered. She snorted and started toward a small, neat house near the center of the hilltop. Omens could be useful, in their way, but they seldom conveyed much real information. Lot of fuss and bother, and what did you end up with? Vague forebodings and rheumatism.

Inside the house she paused, considering. Something was happening, or would be soon—something with a wrongness about it. That description, however, could fit anything from an attempt to assassinate the Levar to a plague of aphids on her prized azaleas. She snorted again, wishing, not for the first time, that the gods could bring themselves to be a little more specific. Well, she would have the details eventually. The gods seldom made mistakes when they sent omens to a particular person. A smile touched her thin lips. If they had, they would hear about it.

The following morning, as she was sitting at her loom, there was a light rap at the door. When she did not answer at once, the rap was repeated with more insistence. The cats, all eight of them, looked up, affronted by the disturbance.

"Just a minute," the old woman called. She rose and started briskly toward the door, then paused and picked up her cane. Tapping it loudly, she walked slowly to the door and opened it.

The girl outside started as the door swung inward. She was dressed in a brief, sleeveless blue tunic and a pair of worn leather sandals. Her dark brown hair was cut short and held back with a faded ribbon that had once, perhaps, matched the color of the tunic. She looked about seventeen, but she might be younger. Her eyes were brown, and her skin was dark, even for a Liavekan. A touch of the old blood there, the old woman thought, and her eyes narrowed. "Come in where I can see you properly," she said, and swung the door wider.

The girl entered and looked around uncertainly. Her eyes came back to her hostess, and the uncertainty increased. "Granny Carry?"

"I'm called that, among other things," Granny said. "And who, exactly, are you?"

The girl flushed. "I'm sorry, Granny. I'm Jin Bennel."

"Ah. One of Marra's girls, then?"

"I'm her granddaughter."

"Been a bit longer than I thought since I saw her last. Did she send you?"

Jin hesitated. "She told me once to come to you if I ever needed help."

"Hmmph. Marra always did take a bit more on herself than she should have."

"I don't want to disturb—"

"Then you shouldn't have come at all," Granny said tartly. "But as long as you're here, you might as well sit down and tell me what you're after."

Jin looked at her doubtfully. "It's just that I don't know why you would be willing to help, or what you can possibly do about it."

Granny pressed her lips together, and her eyes narrowed. Was this chit of a girl deliberately trying to play on her curiosity? She thought about it, and, reluctantly, her lips twitched. If the girl *was* doing it purposely, she was succeeding quite well. She studied Jin, then said, "Think of me as a great-aunt, if it will help you decide what to tell me. If not, I'll get back to my weaving."

Jin sighed, shifted, and capitulated. "It's my brother, Raivo," she said. "He's . . . Do you know much about magic?"

"Quite enough for your purposes," Granny said dryly.

"Well, Raivo's always wanted to be a magician. But he's never found anyone who would train him. His Time of Power isn't very long, you see."

"You mean your mother rushed it when he was born," Granny said. "Silly wench. Why doesn't he try something he's more suited to?"

Jin flushed. "It's not Raivo's fault that he only took four hours to be born! He has more than enough luck to be a magician!"

"But he only has access to it for four hours a year," Granny said. "That's not much time to invest it in something, especially the first time. Still, I've known magicians who were no better off."

"Then why wouldn't any of them teach Raivo?"

"At a guess, he's like his mother—in too much of a hurry. No one wants to have a half-trained apprentice get himself killed trying to invest his luck too soon. It's bad for a wizard's reputation."

"I suppose so. But Raivo's finally found someone. Only . . ."

"Well?"

"I don't trust her!"

Granny studied her. "Why not?"

"I don't know. She just gives me shivers. And why would a wizard work as a stage dancer?"

"Wizards do unlikely things. Have you told this brother of yours about your worries?"

Jin looked down. "I've tried, but Raivo won't listen to me."

"Mmmm." Granny looked at her sharply. "Your luck time is longer than his, I take it."

Jin looked up, startled. "How did you know?"

"Talent." Granny saw no reason to point out that most Liavekans had a luck time of more than four hours. Some women even paid midwives to prolong their labor, in hopes that their children would have a better chance of becoming wizards. Midwives seldom hurried a birth unless something went wrong—or unless the mother was fool enough to request it. "Tell me about this magician."

"Her name's Deremer Ledoro, and she works at Tam's Palace, down by the Levar's Park. That's where Raivo met her. He helps serve the patrons, and she . . . entertains. She calls herself The Black Swan. I'm told she's very good."

"And she's offered to train him?"

"Yes. He didn't even have to ask! That was a month ago, and now he spends nearly all his time with her. But he can't have learned much yet, and his day of luck is next Moonday, and I'm afraid—"

"If your brother wants to be a wizard, you shouldn't go around telling people when his luck day is."

Jin flushed and nodded. "But if Deremer lets him try to invest his luck this year and he's not ready . . ."

"He must know the risks. And if she's going to let him invest, she must think he can succeed."

"After only a month of training? And why is she so determined to have him summon Rikiki *before* his day of luck?"

Granny's eyes narrowed suddenly. "What's Rikiki got to do with this?"

"I don't know. But Deremer's been pestering Raivo about it for weeks." Jin made a face. "I can't imagine why she's so interested in a blue chipmunk."

"He's a god," Granny said dryly. "Some people think that's important."

"I didn't mean it that way! Rikiki's a nice god, but he isn't exactly . . . bright. So why does Deremer want Raivo to call him?"

Granny could think of several possibilities, none of which pleased her. She kept her misgivings to herself. "Hmmph. Silly situations you young people get yourselves into. Well, I'll see what I can do for you, but I make no promises, mind!"

"Thank you," Jin said doubtfully. "Uh, when will you do whatever it is? If you do it."

"I'll have news for you in a fiveday or so. Be off with you now! I've weaving yet to do this morning."

But when the girl was gone, Granny did not return to her loom. She shooed the tortoiseshell cat from her favorite chair and sat thinking for a time. There were four days before Raivo's day of luck, but Deremer wouldn't wait until the last minute to summon Rikiki. She would probably try it Tenth Day evening; the moon would be in the right phase then, and she would want to have every advantage she could. Two and a half days, then. Granny sighed, then rose, picked up her cane, and left the house.

The Merchant's Bazaar was a colorful, lively place. Granny picked her way through its ever-changing fringes, where the newcomers set up their tents for a week or a month. As she passed one of the newer booths, a camel coughed at her. She turned and glared. The camel caught her eye and pursed its lips as if to spit, but before it could complete the gesture, Granny's cane flicked up and rapped it smartly on the nose. The camel grunted in surprise and settled back to await a different victim.

The camel's owner, mindful of a possible customer, called out, "You've quite a way with animals, Grandmother!"

"Hmmph. You'd best learn a bit of it yourself, young man."

"What?" The man, who looked around fifty, seemed confused.

"I mean that if you don't teach that camel some manners, you're going to regret it some day," Granny said acidly, and walked on.

The fringes of the Bazaar gave way to more permanent booths and stalls, and then to brightly painted wooden buildings. Granny found the shop she was looking for, and noted with pleasure that it had grown. Danesh must be doing well for himself. She went inside, and in a short time was ushered into a private room with Danesh himself.

"Granny Kahri," Danesh greeted her. "It's good to see you." He was a short man, still lean despite the temptations brought by years of successful trading. His dark hair was shot with grey, and he watched her with wary respect.

"And you're wondering what I'm here for and how long it will take me to get to the point," Granny said. "And probably how much it will cost you."

Danesh spread his hands. "I'm a merchant."

Granny chuckled. "I should keep you in suspense for a while, but I'm in a hurry. I want some information about the People."

Danesh's eyebrows rose. "I'd think you would know more in that regard than—"

"I've been out of touch," Granny interrupted. Her voice was curt, because he was right. She should have known more than anyone about the doings of those of the old blood, the remnant of the people left when Liavek was built on the ruins of S'Rian nearly seven hundred years before. But things had been going too well, and she'd gotten lazy these past few years. That would be fixed, but Granny couldn't attend to it while there was the slightest possibility of a threat to Rikiki.

"I see. What information, then?"

"I want to know who might be foolish enough or desperate enough to sell Rikiki's story to a wizard," Granny said bluntly.

"What?" Danesh looked shocked; Rikiki held a special place in the hearts of the S'Rians.

"You heard me. Some time within the last year, I would say, though it might be any time in the past five."

"Luck of a little pig! You're sure about this? No, of course you are. I don't suppose you can narrow it down any further?"

"Someone who ought to know better, and definitely of the old blood. Beyond that, I've no information."

Danesh sighed. "You don't come up with easy problems."

"Easy problems you can find for yourself," Granny replied tartly. "Can you do it or not?"

"I'll know the answer to that by Tenth Day. Should I send a message, or will you be favoring us with your presence again?"

"A message will do. I'll expect to hear from you in two days, then."

• • •

Outside, Granny hailed a footcab and started for home. As they crossed the river, she remembered yet another visit she ought to pay. She leaned forward and called, "Boy! I've changed my mind."

The young man pulling the cab stopped and turned. "Where to, then, mistress?"

"Wizard's Row."

The man stared. "Wizard's Row? You're sure?"

"Are you deaf? Go along; I haven't got all day."

"Uh, yes, mistress." He turned and started off again, muttering under his breath.

Wizard's Row was being difficult; half an hour of traveling up and down the three streets which sometimes intersected the Row failed to produce any results. Finally Granny halted the footcab and paid the driver, then began walking determinedly down the street herself. Halfway between the Street of Scales and Bregas Street she stopped and looked around. Buildings rose on either side, without a sign of a cross-street.

"Lot of childish shenanigans," she muttered, and closed her eyes. She gripped the worn brass head of her cane more tightly and drew on her power, then muttered a brief spell. When she opened her eyes, a street led off to her left. She nodded in satisfaction and started down it.

The houses she passed were large, imposing structures of white marble and gold, shining impressively in the hot sun. Several had the feel of illusion, but she did not bother to penetrate the spells. Let them show off; they'd at least chosen a harmless method. She found the house she sought, a modest wooden building near the middle of the street, and went up to it. The brass gargoyle on the door appeared to be sleeping. She pulled the tongue with unnecessary vigor.

"Mlrb, mlff, mlff," the gargoyle said without opening its eyes.

"Speak plainly if you insist on speaking at all," Granny snapped.

"Go 'way," the gargoyle responded. Its voice was faintly metallic. "No visitors allowed."

"Open your eyes and behave yourself." Granny rapped the door smartly with her cane, barely missing the gargoyle's head.

The gargoyle gurgled and opened an eye. The eye focused on Granny, and the other opened with an audible snap. "Oh, it's you," the gargoyle said in a disappointed tone. "It's been a long time."

"Quite so. Are you going to let me in?"

It considered for a moment, then sighed. "I suppose so." It shut its eyes, and the door swung reluctantly open.

The hall inside was dark, but as she crossed the threshhold a series of silver lamps along the walls flashed into fire. The floor glittered in the sudden light, as though it had been sprinkled with gold dust to make a carpet for a queen. "A bit overdone," Granny muttered, pleased in spite of herself.

She went briskly down the hall. She nodded greetings to the two cats standing outside the door at the far end, then went in. The room beyond was a comfortably furnished parlor. The man known to all Liavek as The Magician sat in a large, carved chair on the opposite side of the room. He still looked about twenty, as he had when she'd last seen him thirty or forty years before.

As she entered, he rose and bowed. "Tenarel. It's been a long time."

"That it has." She studied The Magician. He was at least as handsome as she remembered.

"May I offer you refreshment?"

"Pretend you already have, and I've declined, and we've talked about the weather and the policies of His Scarlet Eminence regarding trade with Ka Zhir."

The Magician sighed. "I take it this is not a social call."

"At my age, I don't have time to waste on such nonsense."

He laughed. "That can be fixed."

"I still wouldn't have the time. And I don't notice *you* traipsing around the city visiting people, Trav."

"The disadvantages of fame."

"You chose your way of living," she pointed out.

"And you chose differently. I don't suppose . . ."

"No." Her voice was firm but unusually gentle. "I have responsibilities."

"Well." He looked at her. "What *can* I do for you, then?"

"There's a wizard who may be getting into something that's of interest to me."

"And since I keep track of wizards the way you keep track of S'Rians, you came to me for information." He studied her for a moment. "I usually charge for this sort of thing, you know."

"Hmmph. In that case, you still owe me for that time down in the Levar's Park, when—"

"All right!" He sighed. "I will never be rich. Who is it?"

"A dancer down at Tam's Palace. On stage she calls herself The Black Swan or some such thing; off it I'm told she goes by Deremer Ledoro."

He frowned in brief concentration. "Ledoro . . . Ah, yes. One of the Golden Branch school's better students."

"She's a true wizard, then?"

"Oh, yes. She's the daughter of old Emarati Ledoro, who was killed dueling with Aritoli ola Silba about fifteen years ago."

"Ola Silba, the art advisor?"

Trav nodded.

"Deremer's father was a painter?"

"No. He was high priest of the Shrine of Irhan. Very devout, I'm told."

"He'd have to be, to serve a god that's as minnow-brained as Irhan. If he wasn't a painter, what did ola Silba do to him?"

"The cause of the duel was Deremer's mother. Or rather, the exact paternity of the child she was carrying at the time."

"Hmmph. Sounds like a nice mess."

"It was. The only surprising thing about it is that Emarati would challenge a man thirty years younger than himself. He was apparently . . . unduly overconfident."

"Just so," Granny said dryly. "What about the mother?"

"She miscarried and died of it shortly after the duel. Deremer was about ten at the time, and took the whole thing very hard. She had some sort of argument with the new high priest about it, and left the Shrine."

"And since then?"

"She took up wizardry a year later. She was younger than usual when she succeeded in investing her luck for the first time."

"She's good?"

He nodded. "She even studied in Tichen for a while. She has a reputation there as a rash experimenter, but the way the Tichenese feel about progress . . ."

"And how long has she been back in Liavek?"

"Fourteen months," he responded promptly. "She's living in the family home, on Pine Street in Old Town."

Granny raised her eyebrows. "You're keeping closer track than usual. Is there a reason?"

"A feeling, nothing more."

She looked at him narrowly. "Tichen has a reputation for subtlety."

The Magician gave her a small smile. "So have I."

Granny snorted and climbed to her feet. "I'm more concerned about her methods than her politics. Is there anything else I should know? Then I'll be going; I've a lot to do in the next few days."

The Magician rose and bowed. "It has been a pleasure to deal with you again, Tenarel. You should drop by more often."

"Not until that sentient doorbell of yours learns a few manners. But thanks for the offer."

His laughter followed her down the hall, punctuated by the tapping of her cane.

Danesh's messenger arrived early on Tenth Day morning bearing a sealed note. Granny thanked him and shooed him off before opening the missive. It was a list of six names, each followed by a brief description. She frowned; it was better than she'd expected, but it might take longer to find the right one than she'd hoped. She started down the list, then stopped suddenly. The third name was Giresla Bennel, daughter of Marra Bennel. Jin's mother.

With a sigh, Granny set the list down. It was inevitable, she thought; Deremer was involved with the whole family. And it was certain to make the matter awkward. Well, at least she knew where to start looking. She picked up her cane, paused to check the directions, and left the house.

She found the building without difficulty. It was a rattling old structure near one end of Rat's Alley, untouched by the recent prosperity that had brushed other stretches of the street. The steps were split, and they creaked as she climbed them. The door sagged on its hinges; when she rapped it with the head of her cane, rotted splinters broke away and fell at her feet. Her lips thinned; then she heard shuffling sounds from the house's interior.

The door opened, revealing a heavyset woman with tangled dark hair and bloodshot eyes. Her face wore a hard, suspicious expression that changed to frightened astonishment as she recognized Granny. "Granny Karith!"

"Of course," Granny snapped. "Are you going to stand there all day?" She leaned heavily on her cane, and the wooden step creaked ominously.

"Oh, uh, no, come in," the woman said. She opened the door wider, and Granny followed her into the dim interior of the house.

The place stank of sweat, smoke, and cheap wine; Granny's nose wrinkled in spite of herself. The windows were partially hidden by the filthy rags of what had once been curtains. The furnishings consisted of a broken-legged chair, a pile of dirty straw in one corner, and a rickety round table holding up a litter of mismatched plates and cracked cups.

Granny's lips tightened in disgust. "Giresla Bennel, you know why I've come."

"N-no," Giresla said. "I never expected—"

"Poppycock. You've been afraid I'd come ever since you started dealing with Deremer Ledoro."

Giresla looked startled, then angry. "How did you . . . Jin! Jin told you, the sneaking little—"

"Nonsense. And you'd do better to tell me about it, instead of wasting my time abusing your daughter."

The anger vanished suddenly, and was replaced by fear. "I didn't mean anything," she whined. "And it won't do Ledoro any good; she hasn't a drop of the old blood in her. All I wanted was a place of my own. That's not so much to ask, is it?"

Granny glanced around again and snorted. "It certainly isn't. How much did you tell her?"

A cunning look came into the woman's eyes. "I didn't tell her anything, Granny. Truly."

Granny rapped her cane sharply on the wooden floor, and the other woman jumped. "I've no time for this," Granny said irritably. "I don't care whether you spoke to her or wrote her a note or gave her your grandmother's diary! You know what you've done. What was it?"

"I-I gave her Mother's copy of the *Book of Curses*."

There was a brief silence while Granny controlled her temper. The *Book of Curses* contained the most ancient writings of S'Rian, including many of the most powerful spells and curses. And among them were the details of a spell that might actually be the curse afflicting Rikiki. If Deremer intended to tamper with *that*... "Of all the fools in Liavek," Granny said finally, biting off each word like a chip of flint, "you are the worst."

"But she can't use it for anything! There can't be any harm..."

"She can learn a lot from it. And even if she can't use it, she can get help from those who can."

Giresla whitened, but rallied quickly. "Who'd help her? No one of the old blood would—"

"Oh, hush. It doesn't matter anyway; you're my concern at the moment. And you know the penalty for what you've done."

"Service to the gods, for a year and a day. That's not so bad," Giresla said, but her chin trembled.

"Not quite. Rikiki's involved; it will have to be a Change Price."

Giresla's face turned a sickly yellow. "Granny, no! Please, I—"

"The time will be the same as for service: a year and a day," Granny went on implacably. "And you're lucky it's no longer."

"A year! I'll never last that long! Deremer's the one you want! She—"

"She isn't S'Rian. You are. The penalties don't apply to her."

"That's not fair!"

"You don't have a choice, and neither do I," Granny said tiredly. "And you may make it through. Meanwhile..." Her right hand made a pass in the air, cutting short Giresla's protests. The woman's eyes glazed, and her face became expressionless. Granny sighed again, and turned to leave.

As soon as she arrived home, Granny propped her cane in its usual place by the door and led the still-ensorcelled Giresla down into the cellar. At her bidding, a section of the cellar floor vanished, revealing a rough stone staircase, and they continued their descent.

The stairway ended in a large cave. Long shelves had been carved into the stone along one wall, and they were crammed with boxes, bags, pots, and strange-looking implements. At the near end of the shelves was a wine rack, half-full of neatly arranged bottles. Granny crossed to the shelves and began selecting the items she wanted, while Giresla stood watching blankly.

When the circle of enchanted silver wire had been carefully laid, and the candles and straw positioned properly around the tiny, empty gold bowl, Granny paused. She surveyed the circle grimly to make certain nothing was out of place, then led Giresla to its center. Returning to her position outside the ring, she said formally, "You are S'Rian, and you have tried to work harm against the gods of S'Rian. You owe a Change Price for a year and a day. And may Rikiki's appetite be satisfied elsewhere until the price is paid." Then she began her work.

The chant was long, and the gestures that accompanied it were complex, but though she had not needed it in years, Granny had not forgotten the smallest detail of the spell. As she neared the end, she saw Giresla's eyes widen. Granny threw up her arms and shouted the last three words of the spell.

The straw burst into flame, and Giresla vanished behind the resulting cloud of greasy smoke. A single scream echoed through the cave, then chopped off. It was followed closely by a pinging sound, like a pebble dropped on a metal plate. Granny winced, and settled down to wait.

Slowly the smoke cleared. Only when the last wisp had thinned and vanished did Granny reach down to touch the circle of silver wire. It was thin and brittle; at her touch a piece snapped away and the rest crumbled into dust. Granny straightened and stepped toward the golden bowl.

The bowl now held a medium-sized hazelnut, which seemed to have a faint, silver sheen. Granny looked down at it a little sadly. The transformation was temporary; in a year and a day, Giresla would resume her usual form. Unless, of course, something else happened to the hazelnut first. And with Rikiki involved . . .

Granny shook herself, bent, and picked up the hazelnut. She pocketed it carefully, then went to the far side of the cave. She took a small broom from a hook on the wall. Frowning, she set about sweeping up the silver dust and the ashes of the burned straw. The incident with Giresla had delayed her; she'd have to hurry to get to Deremer's house before the best time for Deremer to work her summoning spells.

The streets were not busy in midafternoon. Most people

preferred to do their business in the morning, before the heat of the day reached its height, or in the evening, when it had passed. Granny simply ignored it and walked on.

Outside Deremer's house, Granny paused. Deremer might well be out gathering materials for the summoning. Perhaps it would be better to wait and catch her at Tam's Palace in the evening, or . . . Granny's eyes narrowed suddenly, and she muttered a word. Yes, there it was; a subtle spell of avoidance, guarding the house. Her lips tightened. The girl was as good as Trav had hinted. Frowning, she went up the steps and tried the door.

It was locked as well as warded, but she had expected that. She placed her palm flat against the door, just above the lock, and whispered a brief spell. A moment later, the door swung inward. She went in, and closed it softly behind her. As she did, she heard voices coming from a room just down the hall. She went quickly toward them.

"—still don't know, Deremer. I mean, I don't even have my luck yet." The voice was a rather whiney-sounding male.

"Dealing with gods isn't the same as doing ordinary magic," answered a woman's voice, rich and smooth as cream. "You have nothing to worry about."

"That's easy for you to say," the male voice grumbled.

"We can stop now, if you'd like," the woman said with deceptive casualness. "Of course, that would mean postponing your investiture another year. At least."

"No, no, I'll do it. I just—well, I'm still not sure."

"You've said that twelve times if you've said it once. Either begin now or go away, but for Irhan's sake stop dithering."

"All right, all right. Which one do you want first?"

"Rikiki. I'll call Irhan myself, later."

"Are you sure about this? Without my luck—"

"Will you stop whining about your luck!"

The argument sounded as though it might continue for hours. Granny pushed the door of the room open and stepped inside. "And just what do you think you can do with them once you have them?" she said.

During the instant of stunned silence that followed, Granny glanced quickly around the room. A tall, carved wardrobe stood against the wall beside the door. In the middle of the floor lay a circle of silver wire, in the center of which was a small golden bowl full of nuts. A little table just outside the circle held an unlit candle and several bowls of herbs, laid out ready for use. A dark-haired man stood beside the table. His resemblance to Giresla was obvious; somehow he managed to look startled and sullen at the same time. Seated in a silk-draped chair next to him was a beautiful woman with light brown hair. She held a worn book with a green leather cover, and Granny smiled grimly when she saw it. "It appears that I've arrived just in time."

Raivo was gaping like a beached fish; Deremer recovered more quickly. "Who are you?" she demanded, rising. "How did you get in here?"

"Most people call me Granny. I walked."

"You can just walk right back out again, then," Deremer said angrily. "This is my home, not a public dining place!"

"More shame to you, then. There's a mouse's nest behind your wardrobe that should have been cleaned out a month ago." She pointed in the general direction with the tip of her cane.

Deremer looked bewildered. Before she could reply, Raivo found his tongue at last. "Now, Granny, you don't want to get mixed up in this," he said coaxingly.

"Don't patronize me, you young clamhead. Hush up and answer my question."

"Question?" Raivo looked as bewildered as Deremer.

"Just what do you plan to do with Rikiki and Irhan once you've called them?"

"Nothing harmful, you may be sure," Deremer said soothingly. She shot a glance at Raivo, who had opened his mouth to speak, and he closed it again quickly. "But I agree with Raivo; you really ought to leave." She gestured gracefully with her free hand, and light glinted on a heavy gold bracelet.

Granny felt a pressure like an invisible hand, pushing her toward the door. Automatically, she recited a counter-charm in her head, and broke the spell with ease. She leaned on her cane as though she had noticed nothing, and said pointedly, "If there's no harm in it, why do you need the *Book of Curses*?"

Deremer's eyes narrowed. "You seem to know quite a bit about my business."

"As long as it involves Rikiki, it's my business as well, young woman. Answer the question." Granny added a magical shove to the command.

"For my revenge on—" Deremer stopped, and her eyes widened. "How dare you!"

"As I said, it's my business." Granny eyed her thoughtfully. "Revenge. I see. And you certainly wouldn't need such an elaborate scheme to deal with Master ola Silba."

"Ola Silba can wait! It's Irhan I want now."

"Why?"

"He agreed to protect my father, and he broke his word."

"I'm not surprised. Irhan has never been the most reliable of gods. Good-looking, but not dependable."

"Then it's time he was taught a lesson. My father died because of him!" Deremer paused and looked speculatively at Granny. "I don't suppose you'd care to join us? I'm willing to pay quite well."

"Deremer!" Raivo sounded appalled. "You can't—"

"Don't be tiresome, Raivo. Your grandmother is a bit of a wizard herself, or she wouldn't be here. She could be very helpful."

Granny suppressed a snort. Deremer had plainly been studying the *Book of Curses* with care. The rites for summoning Rikiki could be performed by anyone who knew them, but they were most effective when performed by a woman of S'Rian blood. A male S'Rian was a distinct second choice, and Deremer herself would have only a small chance of success.

"I'm too old to buy a fish in a flour sack," Granny said. "Perhaps you'd explain your proposal in more detail?"

Deremer hesitated, and Raivo jumped in again. "It's quite easy, Granny. We'll summon Rikiki, and Deremer will cast a spell to hold him. Then she'll summon Irhan and we'll duplicate Rikiki's curse on him."

"You make it sound simple. These are gods you're dealing with."

"Well, neither of them is a very powerful god. And all the spells we need are in the *Book of Curses*."

"Then what do you need Rikiki for?" Granny demanded, though she was afraid she knew already.

"We can't get all the ingredients for the ritual," Raivo said reluctantly. "So we need Rikiki as a model, to get the new spell started. It won't hurt him."

"That constitutes tampering with Rikiki's curse," Granny snapped. "Which would force him to spend another hundred thousand years as a chipmunk. I won't permit that."

"It's not like that, it—"

"It doesn't matter, Raivo," Deremer said, giving him a significant look. She waited until he stepped aside, than moved toward the silver circle and looked at Granny. "Do you truly believe you can stop me? How? You don't really think I'll waste all these preparations, do you?" She waved her left hand in a sweeping arc, and ended with a chopping motion. Light gleamed on her golden bracelet, and the wood of Granny's cane shattered.

"Now, Raivo!" Deremer shouted. "That was her luck-piece; she can't stop you without it!"

Raivo started forward, and found himself looking down a long, thin swordblade. "Sorry to disappoint you," Granny said acidly, "but it's not my luck that I stored in my cane." She shook a few remaining splinters from the gleaming metal, and Raivo backed away.

"You're lying!" Deremer cried. "I saw you use—" Her right hand clenched on the *Book of Curses,* and she made another sweeping gesture with her left.

Granny shifted her attention away from Raivo long enough to dispel the attack, and Deremer's eyes widened. "Impossible!"

"Nonsense. Now, if you'll just—"

"Nuts?" a bright, high-pitched voice piped from the floor behind Granny. "Where nuts?"

Granny turned, appalled. She had been so concerned with stopping Deremer's summoning spell that it had never occurred to her that Rikiki might notice the preparations and simply show up. In his human form he would know better; but then, as a human he would have no difficulty handling a minor threat such as Deremer Ledoro. The mental limitations inherent in his present shape were one of the main reasons behind the creation of Granny's position, so long ago. She thought of the silver hazelnut in her pocket; if she fed it to Rikiki, he would regain his human form for a few minutes, long enough to deal with Deremer. But there had to be a way of getting him out of danger without sacrificing Giresla. "I have nuts at home, Rikiki," she said. If she could persuade him to leave before Deremer had a chance to begin her spells . . .

"Home?" Rikiki's black eyes stared up at her. "Where home? Want nuts!"

As Granny started to answer, a flicker of motion beside her caught her attention. She dodged, but not far enough. A heavy wooden club landed on her shoulder, knocking her to the floor.

Rikiki gave a startled squeak and ran under the wardrobe. Half stunned, Granny brought up her sword, sparing a brief mental curse for her own carelessness. Before she could use it, the spell of immobilization struck.

It was a good spell; she could hardly even breathe. She heard Deremer say coaxingly, "Nuts, Rikiki! See? Nuts!" Hurriedly, Granny cast her counterspell.

Nothing happened. Shocked, Granny shoved at the spell. It gave a little, but not enough. She studied it, and saw the difficulty. Deremer had clearly prepared well for the appearance of the two gods she planned to summon. The enchantment had been cast earlier, with all the care and subtlety possible in a ritual spell. All she had had to do was set it in motion at the right moment.

She could break the spell eventually, Granny decided, but was there time? Rikiki was already sitting beside the golden bowl, stuffing nuts in his cheek pouches. Deremer opened the *Book of Curses* and ran a finger down the page, while Raivo moved closer to watch. Granny took a breath and closed her eyes, visualizing the pattern of the spell she wanted as she mentally recited the words. She felt the paralysis weaken again, but the counterspell did not have the power that came from a full ritual. All she could move were her fingers. She still held the sword, but Deremer was well beyond its reach.

Deremer started to chant, moving her left arm in a rhythmic motion in front of her. Granny's eyes narrowed suddenly. She flicked the tip of her sword in an intricate pattern, hoping her guess was correct. Deremer cried out and dropped the *Book of Curses* to clutch at her left wrist. She was too late; the gold bracelet was dissolving. In a moment more, all that remained was a fine gold dust, sifting slowly to the floor. Deremer paled and swayed as though she had been struck, then collapsed.

The spell holding Granny dissolved, and she started forward. Raivo lunged for her, but another gesture froze him temporarily motionless. She took a moment to catch her breath, then went over to Deremer and examined her. She straightened with a satisfied smile. The bracelet *had* been Deremer's luck-piece, and the shock of its destruction had made her collapse. Granny made certain Deremer would sleep for a while, then looked around.

Rikiki had finished the nuts and disappeared, she noted thankfully. She picked up the *Book of Curses* and stowed it safely in the pocket of her skirt. Rapidly, she scanned the room, searching for the threads of other spells. She found two more paralyzing spells and a death curse and unraveled them all. She turned to the circle of silver, then paused.

Raivo was S'Rian, one of the old blood. He had knowingly threatened Rikiki's welfare; by the ancient laws, he owed the same price Giresla had paid. Granny glanced at the table of herbs; yes, the proper ingredients were all there. Her lips tightened. Pity she couldn't do the same to Deremer, but Deremer wasn't S'Rian. Well, perhaps being sick for a week from the sudden destruction of her magic-source would teach her a lesson. Being magicless until her next birthday might do her good, too, though it was too much to hope that the destruction was permanent.

Granny made the arrangements quickly, then left the circle and began the spell. When it was over, she pocketed the hazelnut with a grimace. Rikiki would likely get indigestion from that one, if it were ever used. When she turned back, Deremer was watching her.

"Who are you?" Deremer whispered at last. Her voice was ragged.

"Tenarel Ka'Riatha."

Deremer's eyes widened in fear. "Ka'Riatha—the one the *Book of Curses* calls the Guardian of the S'Rian Gods? You're that old?"

"Don't be ridiculous. I'm hardly the first to hold the title since S'Rian fell," Granny snapped. Which was true, as far as it went; she saw no reason to mention her real age.

"What are you going to do with me?"

"Nothing whatever."

"I don't believe you." Deremer's eyes shifted toward the empty bowl in the middle of the floor, then turned quickly away.

Granny sighed. "You're not S'Rian and you didn't actually succeed in doing anything. As long as you don't try it again, I'm through with you. And I think you've been given sufficient warning."

Deremer looked down, and the fingers of her right hand circled her other wrist. Granny almost felt sorry for her for a moment; it was not easy for a wizard to live without magic, however short the time. "How did you know?" Deremer asked.

"That the bracelet was your luck-piece?"

Deremer nodded. "I used protections; not even you should have been able to tell . . ."

"Hmmph. The way you were waving it around, I'd have been blind not to guess. You young people have no appreciation of the value of subtlety."

"I'm not giving up, you know." Her voice grew stronger as she spoke. "Irhan will pay for what he did to my family! You can't stop me."

"I could, but I won't bother. Unless you try involving Rikiki again." Granny paused. "I wouldn't recommend it."

"I'll bear that in mind," Deremer said coldly.

Granny nodded. "Mend your manners," she advised conversationally, and left. Outside, she turned wearily toward the Street of Trees and home. It wasn't the most satisfying conclusion, and it was going to be a bit difficult to explain to Jin what had become of her mother and brother. Granny sighed. At least she'd recovered the *Book of Curses*. And Raivo might learn something from being a hazelnut for a year. Deremer, though, would almost certainly try to make trouble again as soon as her day of luck came and she could invest her magic once more. It was almost a pity that she wasn't S'Rian. Well, Granny could handle Deremer.

She stopped a street vendor and bought a bag of nuts. A few blocks further on, she found one of the small bowls of nuts Liavekans sometimes set out "for Rikiki, for luck." She filled it to the brim, and went on her way, humming.

Birth Luck

by Nancy Kress

ONE OF THE three had left the window open. Noises drifted into the attic room—late-night noises, muffled noises, floating up from the late-night and muffled activities in Fish Alley below. Footfalls, murmurs, a woman's too-shrill chuckle. Then a sudden ring of crystal, piercingly sweet, followed by the yowl of a cat.

"The bell hawker," Reykja whispered. "She must have finally thrown a glass bell at that orange cat!"

The other girl, the white one, nodded. Her eyes met Reykja's and Reykja giggled, a high nervous giggle unexpectedly sweet, like the thrown bell. Sallow and intense, with black brows like angry wings, Reykja did not look like a girl who giggled. The boy sitting cross-legged in the middle of the floor glanced at her in annoyed surprise.

"Sorry, Kalum, I didn't mean to laugh," Reykja said, all in a rush, and laughed again.

"You're just nervous, dear heart," the white girl said in her quiet voice. "She's just nervous, Kalum."

"We're all nervous," Kalum said, not angrily. His gaze sought

Reykja's. She reached across the boundary of the chalked circle in which he sat, a circle splintered by the rough attic floor, and grasped his hand. Brother and sister exchanged a long look from eyes of the same black, excitement rising in each like tide against dark glass.

"Nearly time?" Kalum said huskily. "When should I start?" Although of course he knew, had known for years, could not have even begun the chalked circle in this tense attic room without knowing.

"Six minutes after midnight," Reykja whispered. She let go Kalum's hand, sat back on her haunches, and pushed the thick dark hair, sweaty at the hairline, back from her face. "Her birth labor started at six minutes past midnight."

"And only three hours of it," Kalum said. "So little time—I wish I had taken twice as long arriving in the world!"

"Perhaps your mother did not," the white girl said dryly. She was truly white: hair, skin, fingernails, eyes, a smooth slim whiteness traced with blue veins so delicate they might have been shadows, as unlike Reykja and Kalum as moonlight is unlike the rough bark of trees it touches with mystery. Yet Kalum loved her and Reykja trusted her. All three had come to Liavek as bond servants, all three were barely grown, all three wore the patched rags of a mean household meanly run. But still Reykja felt the wordless differences that lay among them in Ondur's whiteness, and in her unnatural silences. The differences did not chill Reykja because they were not her nor Kalum; instead they excited her, because they were not Liavek. Ondur was the white strangeness in a gray life, the grasped-at largeness in a small one. Sometimes in the dusk Reykja watched her friend's profile, and regretted fiercely that it was not quite regular enough to be beautiful.

"Two minutes more," Reykja whispered. "Again today I made certain of the sandglass against the clock at the Fountain of the Three Temples, and once more at sunset against the sandglass at the inn, and—oh, Kalum!"

"It will be fine," Kalum said. "All will be fine. We just breathe deeply and leap."

"You leap, dear heart. The risk is all yours, the gain all of ours."

"Camel dung," Kalum said. He spoke with difficulty; his dark eyes gazed fixedly at the garish cheap colors of the sandglass in his sister's hand. "Is it time yet?"

"Not quite. Can you feel the birth luck stirring?"

"No. Not before the time. Reykja—remember not to cross the circle until the three hours are done. You too, Ondur. No matter how the investiture fares—no matter *how*. Stay out of the circle."

"I'll remember," Reykja said. "Ondur?"

"You can still turn back," Ondur said.

Shocked out of their excitement, brother and sister swung their heads to stare at her, Kalum wrenching his gaze from the sandglass and Reykja from Kalum.

"Turn back!" Reykja cried aloud.

"Hush!" Kalum hissed. "They will hear downstairs! Oh, gods!"

The three held their breath; no one of family or servants in the huge shabby house heard. A night breeze blew in the window, smelling of flowers and garbage, ruffling the candle flame in its holder on the floor. The sandglass trickled without noise.

Kalum said evenly, "I will not turn back," at the same moment that Reykja hissed, "Why would you even *say* such a thing, Ondur!"

"I have said it before. Investiture is dangerous."

"Stealing to pay for a magician's lessons is also dangerous," Kalum said, "and I will have you two doing it no more. Look what happened to you last month, Ondur, when that corporal at the Pickerel caught you picking his pocket and the bastard—I've had enough lessons. I'm ready. Tonight I invest my birth luck in a vessel, and tomorrow all three of us leave this dung heap of a city. Not one day longer—not one, Ondur. I will be a wizard, and a wizard cannot be held by bond."

Ondur said quietly, "Our bondship will end of itself, in time."

"Now," Reykja said.

Kalum closed his eyes. A sudden swallow worked the flesh on his throat, and for a second he looked as young as he was, as young as he would have been without the hard gleam on his dark face. From his sash he drew a seal ring and laid it before him on the rough floor. The ring, the sort favored by unskilled artisans or farmers, was large and light, fashioned of gilded copper pretending to be gold. The seal was bent in on the left side, and part of the finger guard had turned green.

"Into this unity whole. Into my grandfather's ring," Kalum chanted, his face flushed with effort. "Into my grandfather's ring—Reykja—"

"You have three hours," Reykja said. "Go slowly, Kalum, you have all the time you need!"

"Into this unity whole, into my grandfather's ring . . ."

In the alley below, the cat yowled.

The night flew. Reykja, bloodless of face, stared at the sandglass, shook it, hurled it, finally, against the wall. It shattered, a few shards of glass bouncing into the chalked circle. As soon as they crossed the chalk the shards glittered brilliantly and viciously, like knife points, and vanished.

"No, ah no, time does not pass that fast, it does not, Ondur stop it *stop it*—"

"Into this unity whole! Into my grandfather's ring!" Kalum chanted desperately. "Into my grandfather's *ring*—gods, Reykja, I can feel the birth luck here in my hands. I can feel it, but it won't leave, it won't *invest*—"

He could not sit upright. One arm trailed along the floor, fingers limp, dangerously close to the chalked circle. Kalum's face, ravaged with the effort of hours that should not have passed so fast—*could* not have passed so fast, gods *no*—had gone nearly as white as Ondur's. His glance scuttled from Reykja to Ondur, Ondur to Reykja, pleading for help they could not give. The attic room reeked with the smell of sweat gone wrong, acrid and unnatural.

"Into my grandfather's ring—help me, Ondur!"

Ondur gave a soft, anguished whimper. Reykja threw back her head and, beyond all thought of those downstairs or those anywhere but this desperate place she had not foreseen, howled like a dog in pain. Ondur threw herself across the other girl and clapped both hands over Reykja's mouth.

"Hush, Reykja—you'll bring the master! Kalum has a few minutes still—a few—"

"Into this unity whole. Into my grandfather's ring . . . *into my grandfather's ring*—"

The three-hour labor of Kalum's mother, fifteen years dead, ended.

For a single shining moment, the last moment, it seemed the investiture had succeeded after all. The cheap ring began to glow with a tentative, flickering light. The chalked circle smoked and quivered on the floor. Kalum's face somehow expanded, as if his exhausted skin were floating off his face, or if something behind the skin were floating away from it in hard and bloodless sheets. But the moment collapsed; the ring dulled; the circle merely twitched, imprisoned still on the splintered wood. Kalum howled the same howl as his sister had, grabbed at his forehead with both hands, and toppled sideways.

Reykja screamed. Clawing at Ondur, she tried to scramble from the white girl's grasp and hurl herself on Kalum. Ondur held her fast with more strength than that slight body could have contained.

"Reykja, no—not yet—it is dangerous still, no, the magic is not finished with him yet—"

Footsteps pounded up the stairs. The attic door flew open and the room was full of people—people, shouting, the brightness of torches, curses and gasps. Someone knocked against the window shutter and it banged closed; Reykja, tearing herself free from Ondur—or perhaps released—threw herself across Kalum. The master of the house burst through the door. Huge and bearded, red-faced with outrage, he bellowed something no one heard and tried to seize Reykja by the hair to pull her off the still form of his other bond servant.

He had thrust one hand over the circle, had actually felt the brush of coarse dark hair against his palm, when his hand jerked to a halt. It was held immobile by the pressure of slim white fingers, and through the chaotic gloom Ondur gazed at him from eyes white and cool as moonlight on untouched snow.

"No," Ondur said. "Not yet." The master felt his hand pushed slowly backwards. He stared at her in fear and outrage, both too sudden to permit words, although his red face grew even redder.

"No," Ondur repeated, and now she stared at the two figures on the floor, her voice white with emptiness.

Later the master, recovered from the queer moment of paralysis and all the angrier for it, flogged them both. Reykja screamed and howled, thrashing so hard from side to side under the whip that her wrists, chafing against their bonds, ended as bloody as her back. Ondur held both her hands over her face and shuddered, noiseless, and even the master averted his eyes from the red welling on the white skin. Kalum was not beaten. He sickened rapidly, as do all who fail at the investiture of birth luck into a vessel of magic. On the second day he died.

"But he was *ready,*" Reykja said, for perhaps the hundredth time. "He *was.*"

The two girls huddled in a hidden cranny on the roof of the master's house, sheltered between twin squat chimneys. Below them Liavek shimmered like a bright mosaic in the brilliant afternoon sunshine. It was the month of Wind; Kalum had been buried for a month, and Reykja sat facing the distant graveyard, unseen beyond the Cat River, where he lay. Before them to the north the roofs of Old Town glittered in whorls and swirls around the green copper of the Levar's palace; from behind them came the salty smell of the sea. The city below teemed with color, with movement, with life. Ondur's white hair blew free above the roof, without ribbon or veil. She never sunburned.

"Kalum was ready for the magic, Ondur. He was!"

"No," Ondur said patiently.

"By all gods, don't keep *saying* that! I told you—I told you the little magics he could do each year in his birth hours. More each year. Just last year, remember—no, it was a few months before you came, you didn't come until after my birthday—what was I saying? Kalum! He made that mirror reflect the cottage where we were born—I *told* you. He was ready."

"No, dear heart."

"And the ring, the vessel—it was a unity whole, it was strong enough to bear the investiture, it would have held the luck for a year until it was freed on his next birthday. He talked about investing it in something else next year, something richer, we might have been able to buy something rich next year—he was ready!"

Ondur put her arms around Reykja.

"It was the magic," Reykja cried passionately. "Kalum was ready for investiture, I know he was! It was the magic that betrayed him!"

"Oh, Reykja—"

"Don't talk to me like that!" Savagely, not knowing what she did, she pushed away Ondur, whom she had been holding fast, and turned upon her because there were no tears left and she must turn on something or feel she was going mad. "'Oh, Reykja'—little mincing protests, as if I were a baby who had lost a sugarfruit! I was his sister, his *sister* damn you, and you were only the latest girl he bedded—Ondur, I didn't mean that! I didn't!"

Ondur had begun to weep. Reykja seized her friend and held on tight. She suddenly felt that the whole world was whirling around her, the terrible bright sky had fallen below her and the roofs of Liavek twirled giddily above; her soul was falling right through the hole torn in the whirling world by Kalum's death. Terrified, furious, hating herself for having hurt Ondur out of her own hurt, Reykja grabbed wildly for something to hang on to in the whirling. Something, anything . . . if she did not grab hold of something she would be sucked into the sky below, smashed against the roofs and alleys above—something, anything! Anything to make sense of the senseless, to invest the whirling anger, because if she did not the tears were surely going to drown her and the choking and raging anger would tear her apart bodily, limb from limb, something, anything . . .

She found it.

"But it *was* the magic, Ondur! Hear me—it was. That's what killed Kalum, that's what brought him and me here—I've told you the story, the magician uncle of ours who sold us into bond after my aunt died—don't you see? All this," she waved one hand over the city below, "what does it do but serve all the evils of magic? It's the magic that causes the suffering. It's the magic that is the enemy!"

Ondur grew very still in her arms. Reykja, plunging on, did not notice. Her voice was feverish now, frenzied, the voice of someone grasping at the door out of pain.

"The magic is the enemy, Ondur. Liavek is rotten with it. Even the Levar herself, the stories of the way her first regent died—and the houses on Wizard's Row that appear and disappear, what are they hiding? Where do they go? Nowhere clean, nowhere alive—ah, Ondur . . ."

Ondur shuddered in Reykja's arms, her face hidden against the coarse blackness of unbound hair. But Reykja sat up straighter and her eyes gleamed as if with fever. "It's true, Ondur, you know it is. Liavek is built on blood and magic, both! The S'Rians who were here first and enslaved, and the horrible magicians of the Church of Truth squatting all over the city trying to lure victims inside, victims like Kalum—gods! It is magic that is the enemy, lying in wait to suck in Kalum, unnatural, *unclean*."

Ondur gasped as if she were drowning. "Marithana Govan, on the Street of the Dreamers . . . She uses her magic for healing. . . ."

But Reykja was beyond hearing. She spoke in a rush of new-minted hatred, on and on: all the old stories of pain in the world. And in her telling, invested luck and the wizards who used it were the cause. Deformed infants, pestilence, murderous priests, children sold into bond, all the cruelties of men to men. She could not stop herself. The words poured out like molten glass, settling around her, solidifying in the air into shards hard and brittle and bright. In her arms Ondur cowered. Reykja ranted on, and with each word Ondur could feel the hard glassy brightness grow sharper, while sunlight danced on the mosaic of colored buildings and green copper roofs of Liavek below. Minutes passed, more minutes, nearly an hour. Still the two girls remained rigid on the roof, Reykja bolt upright and ranting, ranting, Ondur shuddering in her arms, every word a jab. Magic evil. Magic greedy. Magic twisted, magic enslaving and devouring, magic that had killed Kalum.

"It was the magic," Reykja said finally, hoarsely, hard with glassy brittleness. "The magic."

Ondur whimpered. Kalum's grandfather's ring, on its string around her neck, lay crushed against her breast by the rigid grip of Reykja's arms.

Reykja's birthday fell on a Moonday in the month of Buds, six weeks and a day after Kalum's. Her mother's labor had started at dawn and been long and hard; in the end she had died of it, moments after her squalling bloody girl infant had kicked into the world feet first. All this Ondur knew. She had heard Kalum and Reykja speak of it often. It was the reason, Kalum had whispered to Ondur as she lay with her head pressed against his chest, that he was studying the magic, and not Reykja. He was afraid for her to do it. A mother's death is a fearful price for birth luck. And Reykja, he had said painfully, was too . . . flighty. She was like a dark bird. Even for a wizard standing within the required three paces of his vessel, magic was mostly a question of strength of will, of stubbornly fastening onto an outcome and holding on. Reykja, Kalum had said, skimmed along, always in flight. She could not have become a magician.

Ondur wondered how Kalum, whom she loved, could not

know that the strongest talons belonged to the birds with the highest flights.

"Stay indoors today," Ondur said when Reykja came into the kitchen on her birthday. It was a little past dawn. Ondur had been doing the breakfast work—both their work—for nearly an hour.

"So no ill luck will befall me in my birthday hours?" Reykja said mockingly. She wore boots and the loose, concealing cloak which both of them had worn to steal coins for Kalum's lessons.

"So no ill magic will befall you, yes," Ondur echoed.

"Camel droppings. You're afraid of the luck I may cause, not the luck that may happen to me. Aren't you, Ondur?"

"I feel ill, Reykja. Stay here and help me with this work."

"You are never ill. Why is that, Ondur? Why are you never ill?"

Ondur did not answer. She bent over mortar and pestle to grind more breakfast grain, and her white hair fell forward over her face in a thick veil.

"I asked you a question, Ondur. Did you hear me ask you a question? I asked why you are never ill!"

"I am sometimes ill," Ondur said from behind her hair. "I am ill now."

"No. You are not."

"Stay indoors today, Reykja."

"What do you think I will do, burn down Wizard's Row?" She laughed, a sudden glittering sound, sharp as broken glass. "Do you fear that for me, Ondur? That I will try to set fire to Number Seventeen Wizard's Row? Me, a bond servant with neither money nor magic? Me?"

"It is your birthday, Reykja."

"Then perhaps I'll find a two-copper on the street for my birthday luck. Eh, Ondur—a two-copper, as a token of what magic can do for such as me? Why are you never ill, Ondur?"

Behind the curtain of hair, the pestle rose and fell in the mortar.

"I heard in the Market," Reykja said in the same glittering voice, "that someone in Liavek seeks a white girl, all white. Someone is asking questions about a white girl."

The pestle stopped.

"Why are you never ill, Ondur?"

With one quick motion Ondur flung the white hair back from her face. Her colorless eyes met Reykja's, and they did not flinch. "Stay indoors, Reykja."

"Are you a magician, Ondur?"

Ondur put both hands over her face.

"Are you a magician? Is that why you are never ill? Answer me!" Reykja pulled Ondur's hands away from her face—not roughly, but with a kind of coiled intensity that was almost pain. The slim white hands came away easily. Under the hands, Ondur was laughing.

"Ondur!"

"I can't help it," Ondur gasped. She could not. It was helpless laughter, without mirth, and she could not get her breath.

"Are you a magician?"

"No," Ondur gasped out. "I am not a magician!"

Reykja let her go. Ondur spoke the truth, and even in the brittle glassy state to which Reykja had come, she could see that it was the truth. She hissed in frustration, and in relief, and in the sharp restlessness that never left her alone now, never, not for a moment.

"Stay indoors today, Reykja."

"No." She flung open the kitchen door. Outside, it rained. Rain dripped from the eaves of the house, the leaves of the straggly vegetable garden, the loose stones in the crumbling garden wall. A gust of wet air blew into the kitchen, bringing with it the smells of ashes and dead fish. Reykja pulled her hood over her uncombed hair and slammed the door behind her.

Birth magic tingled along her arms, sparked at her wrists, danced at the tips of her fingers. She had never felt it before, not like this. She could not keep her fingers still: they curled of themselves into fists. Reykja let them, clenched hard, thought suddenly of Ondur's thin white fingers pushing the white hair off her face. *I am not a magician.* Reykja pushed the picture from her mind.

Liavek was full of magicians.

She slipped noiselessly, muffled in her cloak, along the streets of Old Town, along Bregas Street, along Wizard's Row itself. The Row was here today, although Reykja could not have said what it looked like. At the end, where Wizard's Row joined Cheap Street, stood the tiny house where Kalum had taken his lessons in investiture. She had never gone with him, never seen the magician—but Kalum had shown her the house. It faced not the Row but Cheap Street, and the house itself was a little hard to see through the mist. The magician, who, now that she thought of it, had never been named directly by Kalum—how could she not have noticed that Kalum never uttered the wizard's name?—might also have been a little hard to see. Or might not. Kalum had never said what he looked like, and why had she never noticed that either?

But Reykja knew what he looked like, what he must look like. Out of bitterness, out of the need for enmity fit for Kalum, she knew what he looked like. Tall. Gold. Icy, powerful, glittering . . . Yes.

She paused at the tiny arched door set in the wall. Rain trickled under her hood and down her neck. She had one moment of fear, but only one. The glassy shining hatred was thick within her, and with it the birth magic, that once-a-year intensification of chance and will that is not true magic but is the closest thing to it, luck strengthened in payment for maternal pain. The luck could be for good or ill, tiny or not so tiny, quirky, unreliable. Untrained and uninvested, it was only chance. Only luck. Reykja laid her hand on the knob of the arched door.

Someone had left it unlocked.

Ondur drooped with exhaustion by the kitchen fire. Breakfast, dinner, a light supper, fetch and carry, hot water, sweep and scrub, wash and bake. "Reykja is busy emptying the slop jars, Master, what do you need?" "Reykja has gone to borrow another bucket, Mistress, I will do this." "Reykja is tending the pot-boil lest it burn, scrubbing the hearth and filthy with ashes, coming in another moment or two." And all the long day the rain had fallen, drop after monotonous drop, and in the dank stones of the windowless kitchen, Ondur had smelled dread.

It was nearly dark.

A noise at the door—no, just a mouse in the corner, scrawny and ill-fed, with bright mean eyes. Undoubtedly hungry—in this house, a small creature would go hungry.

Ondur folded her hands over her belly and drooped in her chair. The hearth did not give much warmth, not against the chill damp of rain. Poor firewood, poorly cured. The single candle sputtered.

Where was Reykja? What had she done? She had done something, that Ondur knew. She had done something. . . .

"Ondur!"

Ondur woke with a start. Reykja knelt on the stone floor before her, hood thrown back from wet hair, eyes glittering and feverish. She held something clenched in her fist. Mud smeared onto the floor from her boots and the hem of her cloak, and the candle she held in the other hand sent shadows leaping to the smoke-blackened ceiling.

"I did it, Ondur. *I did it.*"

Reykja opened her fist. On the palm lay a small wooden cat, a child's toy, carved neither well nor badly. It had once been painted in bright, childish colors: yellow, with a blue collar. The yellow had soiled to dun and the blue faded to a tired gray. But the wooden cat tingled with power. Ondur could feel it. She closed her eyes and wrapped her arms tightly across her breasts.

"How?"

"The gate was unlocked. The one Kalum used to use. The house was locked, but I hid in a bush and waited. All day I waited. It felt—eventually two servants came out, and I heard one tell the other that the master would not be home till dark. And one of the servants left open a window—"

"In the rain?"

"In the rain. The cat was on the table—"

"No," Ondur said. Her eyes were still closed. "No. A wizard would not leave it behind when he was from home. Not the vessel of his investiture, all his magic—"

"I tell you he did!" Reykja shouted. She leaped angrily to her feet, paced the length of the room, turned to smile at Ondur with a brilliant, spangled smile. "I tell you," she said softly, "he did. He left it. Perhaps he thought he had it with him, perhaps a spell protecting it faltered just one second, perhaps . . . I don't know. It was my luck, Ondur. My birthday luck."

"There's nothing you can put it to. It's his birth luck in there, and only he can use it. You can't put it to any use."

Reykja went on smiling. "Yes, I can. There's a use. Oh, yes, I can."

Ondur shuddered.

"Stop that, Ondur. Why are you shaking? You said you were not a magician. Are you a magician, Ondur?"

"No."

"Then stop shuddering. Birth luck was what killed Kalum, wasn't it? And that is what is in this vessel—birth magic. I can put it to use. Magic can only be vested in a unity whole—remember? We chanted that over and over, the night he died. A unity whole."

Dropping to her knees, Reykja set the wooden cat before her on the stone floor. She seized a brick from the hearth, a sooty misshapen stone Ondur had used to weight bits of straw for kindling. Raising the brick over her head, she brought it down with all her strength on the cat. The moment it struck—or perhaps the moment just before—the cat flared brilliantly, a sudden rush of light so strong Ondur flung up one hand to shade her eyes. There was a sound like a note of music that was not music. As soon as the brick struck the cat, the light vanished and the cat shattered in two. Reykja swept together the two pieces and went on striking, again and again, as if she could not stop, until the wooden fragments became splinters on the stone floor.

"An unchanging vessel," Reykja said, gasping from exertion. To Ondur's eyes she glittered, encased in the bright shining hardness brittle as glass. With huge effort, Ondur wrenched her gaze away.

"A unity whole," Reykja said. She dropped the brick and bared her teeth in a smile.

Ondur thought desperately: *Once a year. A birthday comes only once a year.*

Until her next one, Reykja would have no power to slip through the falterings of spells, seize unlocked doors, have anything at all to do with birth luck. Until her next birthday, Reykja was safe. Until her next birthday—

But Reykja did not wait.

"This is Sorel," she said to Ondur. "His birthday falls tomorrow."

Sorel looked about twelve, a skinny and needle-eyed twelve, with a furtive glance and a skinny swagger. The expensive silver knife stuck through his sash matched neither his age nor the state of his sandals. Ondur had seen many such boys. They slept on the ground at the Two-Copper Bazaar, carried notes at the docks when an illiterate messenger was desirable, made themselves available at Rat's Alley for whatever was nocturnal, stealthy, and dangerous. But beneath the dirt and above the wicked gleam of the dagger, Sorel's cheek curved plump and smooth. Ondur could see clearly the child Sorel had been, and even more clearly the man he would become.

"Reykja," she whispered. "What are you doing?"

But Reykja only laughed, and turned away. And two days later she brought to the kitchen a brass earring, so nondescript it might have been any of a thousand brass earrings from any of a thousand ears in Liavek, except that light flared brilliantly when she smashed it into a brass lump against the stone floor. Sorel left with a five-levar gold coin from behind a brick that the mistress had no idea anyone knew of. Ondur shuddered whitely, and held her arms across her belly. And Reykja, at the moment of the light's flaring, spat out "Into a unity whole," and looked up at Ondur, and smiled.

"Are you a magician, Ondur?"

"No. *No*. But no more, Reykja, no more—"

"Liavek reeks with luck," Reykja said, and the glass around her glittered and shone as hard as petrified light.

But that night Ondur heard her in the attic room, weeping.

The next evening, Ondur and Reykja sat hemming a blanket by the last of the light from the open kitchen door. It had stopped raining; beyond the crumbling garden wall the rooftops of Liavek shone purely against the dark blue sky, like gems against silk. One side of the rough blanket flowed over Ondur's lap, the other over Reykja's, and both their heads were bent over the stitches. It was tedious, soothing work; both master and mistress had gone out for dinner. Halfway down her side of the hem Reykja, never a good needlewoman, had pricked her finger, leaving a flat smear of blood. She had sucked the finger a moment, then gone on working.

Ondur said suddenly, "There is a wizard in the house."

Reykja's head jerked upwards. "A wizard!"

Ondur sat unmoving, her profile white and strained over the sewing. Reykja's eyes narrowed. "How can you know that? Ondur, how can you know that?"

Ondur did not answer.

There were slow footsteps on the stairs.

Reykja sat staring at the doorway that led from the house above to the kitchen. She held her needle before her and a little to one side, like a sword. To Ondur the glass that encased her sprang suddenly into sharpness, glittering shards poised outward. A small smile came and went on Reykja's lips, and it too glittered. Ondur, who could stand in full sunshine despite her white skin, shrank back.

"A wizard," Reykja said, and the smile was gone. She sat waiting, armored, absolutely still. But when the door opened and a figure stood there, framed by the rough doorjamb, even Reykja blinked.

An old woman, a countrywoman from her clothing, with wrinkled sad eyes and the strong smell of fresh-dug potatoes. She walked with a limp, leaning upon a cane, and peered into the kitchen as into a root cellar—a dim craning peer from eyes gone dim—while her fingers tightened on the head of her cane to keep them from trembling. Her face and neck were thick bundles of dirty cords, and she wore one brass earring.

"Reykja?"

Reykja only stared. She had gone nearly as white as Ondur.

"Reykja," the old woman repeated uncertainly. Her voice was a pleading whine, a voice already grimy with the disappointment of other whinings, other pleas. "I need back my earring. My vessel of luck, I need it. Please."

Reykja rose and took one step forward. The old woman stumbled backwards a step. "I need it, please. My vessel of luck. I need it for the potatoes."

"Potatoes!"

"They won't grow," the old woman said desperately. "Not without my vessel of luck. Please. Please."

Reykja took another step forward. Ondur, watching her, drew the edge of the blanket to her mouth.

"A boy told me someone took it," the old woman whined. "A boy in the city bazaar. I paid him and he told me your name, and I came here, and the potatoes won't grow without it! They won't!"

Ondur saw the glassy hardness around Reykja begin to burn. No mere glittering, this, but a hard glow, scarlet and maroon. Reykja's jaw clamped tight, and her black eyes snapped. Ondur tried to look away, and could not, and bit down on the edge of the half-hemmed blanket.

The old woman quavered, "For the *potatoes*. I ask for the potatoes. My birth luck—"

"You are not a wizard!" Reykja spat.

"Yes. Oh, yes. But only for the potatoes. My earring—"

"You did not invest your birth magic. *You*—No!"

"The potatoes—"

"No! How dare you!"

Reykja's strong hands curled into fists. The old woman glanced around the room, a horrible glance of desperation and fear. She found Ondur's face, white above the blanket.

"A wizard, yes, I am . . . tell her, child, *you* can see. You are—"

Ondur dropped the blanket to grip Reykja's arm. She felt only hardness, hot to the touch and already beginning to smoke. But the old woman seemed not to see it; she gazed instead at Ondur—at her whiteness in the twilight, at her face and body—and the old jowls drooped even more.

"Aaaahh," she said softly, a dry desolate sound like the fumblings of stiff leaves.

Ondur said, "Reykja . . ."

"How *dare* you!" Reykja shouted. She shook off Ondur's arm and lunged toward the old woman. "You—with invested magic! And this is what I've stolen from, this is what Kalum . . . Potatoes! You!"

The old woman shrank back against the doorjamb. "They won't grow. A unity whole—"

"Curse your potatoes! For this Kalum . . . this—"

"Don't hurt me, for earth's sake, don't—"

Reykja raised both fists and advanced on the old woman. Her breast heaved, and fury twisted her face. Beneath the fury Ondur saw the panic, roiling and heaving against the hard glassy hatred—*this,* the enmity that should have given dignity to Kalum's death, *this*—and she cried out, "No, Reykja. No!" Reykja did not hear her. The panic beat against the smoking glass, and the hard glass would shatter and explode, Ondur could see how it would explode, hurtling shards outward to impale them all.

"Reykja . . . *no* . . ."

"Don't hurt me, I'll go away, don't—"

"Investiture—magic! This!"

"Not entirely," said another voice.

He stood in the garden doorway. Tall, angular as crystal, with crystal's cold clarity, he looked down at them from an unsmiling height. His loose clothing was of dull gold silk, his loose long hair white, his eyes the purple of the deepening sky behind him. At his waist coiled a whip with a handle of gold and a thong of such light, unbraided fiber that it could only be there as a boast of how little he would ever need it. Rings gleamed on every finger; rings of opal and bloodstone and sardonyx. Beside his still figure the kitchen looked even meaner, shabbier, and dirtier, and even the white of Ondur's hair was greyed by the shadow where he blocked the light.

Ondur put her hands over her face. The old woman, face knotted in terror, sank to her knees.

But Reykja whirled to face the wizard like a drowning man seizing land. Gazing at the arrogance of that whip—soft, gossamer, by all the gods *useless!*—her fists unclenched, flexed, clenched again, not in panic but in a fierce and unholy joy. Her dark eyes blazed. Color rushed back into her face, deep rich blood color; here the enmity, gorgeous enough, strong enough, *here*—

The wizard did not even glance at her. "Breliniparr," he said.

Ondur, hands before her face, shuddered.

"It's destroyed!" Reykja cried fiercely. "The wooden cat is destroyed, gone forever. Your magic has been freed, you won't have it until it returns to you at your next birthday! It's gone, and I am the one who destroyed it!" Her eyes blazed in triumph.

The wizard ignored her. He said again to Ondur, "Breliniparr. Come."

"Don't you hear me?" Reykja shouted. "I destroyed it, your vessel of luck. I! And your magic is gone!"

The wizard walked toward Ondur, who did not move. In the dusky air the light fibers of the whip rippled gently.

"Not her!" Reykja screamed. "I! *I* did it! I did it for Kalum!"

The wizard stopped within three paces of Ondur. He glanced down once, a quick cold glance, as if to be sure of the pacing. He did not touch Ondur. But the brilliant clarity of his face sharpened, and almost he smiled.

"Did you think, Breliniparr, that I could not find you? You?"

Then, finally, Reykja understood.

"Ondur, *Ondur* . . ."

Ondur said from behind her hands, "I am sorry, Reykja, I couldn't tell you, I couldn't tell Kalum, oh by all gods, Jalampar, let me go."

Reykja said slowly, "You are a vessel of birth luck. You. His magic is invested in you."

At last Ondur pulled her hands from her face. "Not by my choice!" she cried desperately, but the desperation did no good, did not even dent the glassy smoking shield around Reykja.

The dark girl's face twisted in fury, in hatred, in an agony of betrayal. It seemed to Ondur that the glass glowed red, then yellow, then a bright blinding white like a burst of light. At that blinding, Ondur threw up one hand. Reykja launched herself, fingers curled into claws, through the hand and at Ondur's face.

She caught a fistful of white hair. Ondur had dodged sideways, but the force of Reykja's attack knocked her down and they both fell heavily to the stone floor. Reykja pulled back her fist and struck Ondur in the mouth, wildly but with deadly accuracy.

"A vessel of luck, you, *a unity whole*."

Ondur cried out, dodged a second blow, somehow rolled free. Blood welled from the corner of her mouth. A fistful of the white hair lay scattered on the stone. She scrambled to her feet and backed away from Reykja, crying words Reykja didn't hear. Ondur backed to the garden door, but then abruptly turned, eyes huge, and sprang forward again. But the wizard had already stepped between the two girls. With one hand he seized Ondur and held her, the source of his power, in a fierce grip. With the other he had pulled the gossamer whip from his sash. Uncoiled, the silky fibers floated free; they were strands of Ondur's white hair.

Almost casually, unsmiling still, he flicked the end toward Reykja on the floor below him.

In the long, long moment while the magic thong floated toward her, while she scuttled uselessly on the floor to escape it, Reykja's eyes met Ondur's. Against the doorjamb the old woman yowled in fear, and Reykja saw again the attic room with Kalum in his chalked circle, heard again the orange cat yowl beyond the window, felt the sandglass heavy in her hand. The whip was ritual magic: It would kill her, as Kalum had been killed. The sandglass ran out, the circle smoked on the floor, the room reeked with the acrid smell of sweat gone wrong. In the wizard's grasp Ondur squeezed shut her eyes, and her eyelids were shadowed moonlight. Reykja felt the magic all around her, pressing in and piercing her, sharp as Ondur's pain. In the second before the whip struck her, she heard again the sound of shattering glass—*she must have finally thrown a bell*—piercingly sweet.

Ondur's eyes flew open. She seemed to see, as Reykja could not, the bright hard glass shield shatter and the grieving girl crouch, freed, the moment before the gossamer thong struck her face.

The thing struck.

Reykja screamed, but only in surprise. She did not smoke or shrivel, she did not collapse in a vicious burst of light. The bright glassy light had shattered, and she crouched in ordinary twilight in a mean kitchen, and the thong caressed her cheek light as air.

The wizard stared at his whip. He jerked his glance to Ondur, who looked as dazed as he. Again he flicked the whip at Reykja; it slid over her upturned face without effect: like moonlight, like a blown lock of Ondur's hair. Reykja's mouth gaped; Ondur stood as if she had been struck; the wizard glared without comprehension. None of them spoke.

It was the old woman who said finally, in her quavering voice, "She is not a unity anymore. A vessel must be unchanged to hold magic, a unity whole, or the magic is freed. But now, see, there are two. She and the child. Two."

The others stared at her.

"A unity whole," the old woman repeated, and now the quaver was gone from her voice.

Reykja groped her way off the floor, toward Ondur. "You didn't know . . ."

Ondur whispered, "Not that it would free the birth luck . . . *birth luck . . .*"

Suddenly Reykja giggled, a high nervous giggle, shocking the room. Ondur gasped. The giggle became a whimper and then a yowl. Then Reykja was crying, tears for Kalum coursing down her face, and Ondur sat with her arms fiercely around her and cried as well. The wizard, looking suddenly less tall, less gold, scowled and strode away; there was nothing here for him now. But the ancient countrywoman crept closer and sat near them, a gnarled dim shape, no longer afraid.

"I bore six children," she said pensively, to no-one. "And all six died."

But the two girls did not hear her. They went on holding each other in the blue dusk, clinging tightly between life and death, and there was nothing bright, nothing glassy, in Reykja's messy tears, and nothing of unity at all.

An Act of Contrition

by Steven Brust

STANDING IN THE Tiger's Eye was, among other things, a relief from the heat. How its proprietor kept it cool was a small mystery, but one to be appreciated rather than solved. Dashif certainly made no effort to solve it. He kept his eyes on the owner's back as she dealt with a customer, showing him a decanter of cut glass imported from Ka Zhir, then a goblet made in Tichen with a glaze found only in the Great Wastes. Dashif was patient. For the past two weeks he had felt as if he were walking about naked, and this would end soon; he could afford a little patience.

Eventually the customer left, promising to return when he had thought things over. *He's lying, of course,* Dashif decided. *Poor bastard couldn't afford anything.*

The owner stood behind the counter and looked at Dashif. They were the same height—nearly six feet—and so stared straight across at each other, an effect neither was used to. "Good afternoon, Count Dashif," she said. "They're ready."

"That's well, Snake."

Snake pulled a heavy box from under the counter, set it next to her, and rested her hand lightly on it. Dashif found a five-levar coin and flipped it onto the counter. Snake, without touching the coin, pushed the box across to him. He removed the wooden top, set aside the oiled cloth within, and picked up one of the two weapons.

"He added about a quarter of an inch to the flint-cock, to allow your thumb a purchase," said Snake.

Dashif nodded. "And the mechanism?"

"Loosened a bit. Not too much, or it would start misfiring."

The flint had been carefully replaced, he saw. He picked up the other pistol with his left hand, his fingers caressing the gold inlay work on the ivory butt.

"Try it," said Snake, who had still made no move to pick up the coin.

Dashif nodded almost imperceptibly and swung the pistols until they pointed at Snake. *Ca-click, click, click,* and all four mechanisms were cocked.

"Fine," said Dashif, still pointing them at her stomach.

She did not seem to be impressed. "They aren't loaded," she said.

"I would hope not."

He set one down and used both hands to release the double mechanism of the one pistol, then repeated the process with the other. He opened the pair of pouches at his right side and went through the ritual of loading the guns. He had bought the pistols through this very shop a few years before. The mechanisms were made by Tichen locksmith Erigo Niola, the barrels by metalsmith Fereth Loyale, and the stocks and grips, at Snake's recommendation, by master jeweler Kentanno Reffina of Trader's Town. They were far more reliable than the more common wheellock or matchlock; he could expect at least three of his charges to go off when firing all four. The only drawback had been, up until now, the need to use both hands to cock one. Now this was solved.

After loading both pistols, he stuck them into the wide black leather belt that supported his rapier and knife. "They'll do," he said, adjusting the red cloak over his white blouse.

Snake took the coin. "Thank you, Count Dashif."

He nodded and walked back into the heat. As he stepped through the door, four others entered. They were young, raffish, and looked as if they couldn't afford even to look at most of what the Tiger's Eye carried. Troublemakers, of course. It occurred to him that quite a bit of Snake's merchandise was breakable, which must make her susceptible to such as these. He wondered how she'd deal with it. He could offer his help, of course. He shrugged. Either she could handle it or she couldn't. None of his concern. He resumed walking. Behind him, from inside the shop, he heard the crack of a whip, followed by a scream, and the sound of several persons making a hasty retreat to the street. He smiled to himself.

The walk back to the Levar's palace took him through the Merchant's Quarter near the canals. He passed a fruit stand and took an apple, paying for it with a half-copper. A beggar-child, recognizing his red cloak, low black boots, and long dark hair, hastened out of the way. A trader's camel, not recognizing him, spat on his cloak. The trader tried vainly to suppress his mirth, but didn't quite succeed.

Dashif pulled one of his pistols from his belt and cocked it. The trader's laughter died at once. Dashif caught the trader with his eyes and raised the pistol. The trader licked his lips, but the pistol didn't come to rest aimed at him. Still looking at the trader, Dashif held it against the head of the camel. The camel started to swing its head to bite. Dashif fired the first barrel, then the second. The animal fell at their feet, and began jerking spasmodically. The trader's expression turned from fear to anger. Dashif allowed his left hand to rest on the butt of the second pistol. The trader turned away.

Dashif resumed his walk to the Levar's palace. Behind him, he heard faint mutterings, but ignored them.

He knew several of the names he was called when he wasn't around, but they didn't bother him. Hate was preferable to contempt, and contempt preferable to pity. The only name he dreaded hearing was "Dashif the Luckless," but few knew enough to call him that. Of the people who could have done so, one was his wife, who had long ago left him and was now, probably, in Tichen, living with his children—he hoped. Probably as someone's pet. That would suit her.

Dashif's master, His Scarlet Eminence, knew enough to add "the Luckless" to his name, but wouldn't. It was in His Eminence's interest to keep that story hidden—at least for now. Later would take care of itself.

Only one other could ever have told the story. Erina. His slim, tall, lovely Erina of the smooth, dark skin, and the long, dark hair, and the sad, dark destiny. His witch from Minnow Island. She could have told the story; she had been the cause, she had done it—stealing his magic forever. From before the time his ancestor became the Count of Dashforth, the family had been wizards. Now, thanks to Erina, he was wizard no more. Erina the enchantress, Erina the thief. She could have told the story of how he had left her to marry the bejeweled bitch. She could have told how she, Erina, had robbed him of magic in revenge. She could have told it all, if she were alive, but four lead balls in the back of her head had guaranteed her silence. Foolish, sentimental Erina; she shouldn't have taken his magic and then left him alive. Or maybe she had done the smart thing after all; perhaps hers was the best revenge.

Count Dashif, who would never be called Dashif the Luckless, entered the palace of the Levar, to wait once more upon his master. The Regent, Dashif hoped, had luck enough for them both.

If not, the gods help Liavek.

One carefully measured powder charge, a bit of wadding, and a lead ball, rammed in tightly enough but not too tightly. Repeat for the second barrel. A little powder in the touchhole, and the spark from the flint would ignite the charge. He admired the beauty of the weapons once more.

Dashif was a fair swordsman, but sorcerers fought from a distance, and one must respond from a distance to match them. He took out a polishing cloth, and—

"Good afternoon, Count Dashif." He looked up, saw the lanky figure of Pitullio in front of him, and nodded. Pitullio continued, "His Scarlet Eminence would like me to fill you in on the background, then he'll see you himself."

Dashif nodded once more and put the pistol back into his belt. From His Eminence's waiting area, Dashif followed Pitullio into the latter's small, comfortable office. Pitullio flopped himself into a chair and heaved a sigh. "He's in one of *those* moods today, Count Dashif. Better tread lightly."

"I always do, Pitullio. What have you to tell me?"

"I have to give you a history lesson," he said, "though Rikiki alone knows why."

"Let's have it, then."

Pitullio stretched out and locked his hands behind his head. "You two are just the same. Always in such a bloody hurry."

He sighed. "All right. What do you know of the Gold Priesthood, the Seekers of the Light?"

"They were destroyed about seventeen or eighteen years ago, just after the destruction of the Blue Priesthood."

"Do you know who destroyed them, or how?"

"No," lied Dashif.

"We did." Pitullio waited before continuing, but if he had expected some reaction he was disappointed. "They had gained a great deal of influence by then, and Those In Power decided they had to go."

"How?"

Pitullio chuckled. "The Gold high priests all had overlapping Times of Power each year. Do you know what that means?"

"Go on."

"Having one's Time of Power at the appropriate time of year was a requirement for the high priesthood. That way, the high priests could unite to bind their magic into their altar. I take it you are familiar with the binding of magic, as distinct from investiture?"

"Theoretically," said Dashif, carefully keeping his voice neutral.

"Whereas, in a normal binding, anyone may use a bound object, but only for a particular task, the Gold priests wanted to bind their altar with the power of their entire high priesthood, so that one particular person, the high priest, could use it for any task."

"How?"

"It took the Gold priests a long time to build up a sufficient number of high priests. This gave us time to plant an agent among them. At the moment of binding, our agent twisted the spell in such a way that no one would be able to use the bound power. It's still there, locked up in the altar, but they can't touch it."

"I see. And the priests?"

"A few of them survived. But, of course, they will not be able to use their magic unless the spell in the altar is unbound, which is ever so slightly impossible. Nothing has been heard from them since then. I expect they've died out."

"Of course," said Dashif. To himself, he added, *Once again, Pitullio, you act the fool. If they'd died out, and the altar cannot be unbound, it wouldn't be necessary for you to give me this history, would it?* "Did the agent survive?"

"Yes," said the Eminent Pitullio, "I did. Questions?"

"Where is the altar now?"

"In the ruins of their temple. We keep a small guard there in case anyone shows up to worship the dead, as it were. You are aware, I'm sure, that there is almost no way to destroy such a thing. Any other questions?"

"No."

"Very well." Pitullio pulled himself out of his chair and showed Dashif out.

"Luck," said Pitullio.

Dashif had no response. He returned to the waiting room and polished his pistols for a few more minutes. Finally, a servant announced, "His Scarlet Eminence will see you now."

Dashif replaced his pistol, made sure the smudge had been thoroughly cleaned off his cloak, ran a hand through his long black ringlets, and followed the servant. When the door closed behind him, he was in a plain, bare office with two chairs and an oak desk. His Scarlet Eminence looked up from the papers he was signing and nodded. Dashif bowed. "I am ready, Your Eminence."

"Several Gold priests have been trying to gather funds," said the other, with no preamble. "If they gather enough, they may be able to buy the services of a wizard powerful enough to release the magic bound in their altar. There are indications that they have found a wealthy backer. We cannot tolerate civil disturbance of any kind at this time. A resurgence of the Gold Faith could be disastrous for the city. You will prevent this, without involving the Levar or the Faith of the Twin Forces in any way."

"Yes, Your Eminence."

The Regent handed him a heavy purse. "That is all."

Dashif tucked the purse into his cloak, bowed deeply, and backed out. Once out of the door, he touched the butts of his pistols for comfort and the hilt of his rapier for strength. Then he set out through the labyrinth of the palace. He returned to his chambers long enough to write a note, seal it, address it to His Scarlet Eminence, and set it out on his bureau. Then he found his favorite small side door and stepped back into the heat of the late afternoon.

Wizard's Row consisted of two long blocks of short, squat houses, garishly painted, set in a wide street in Old Town, near the canals. Number 17 was taller than most and identifiable by the huge wooden door, bound with strips of iron, with a doorbell in the form of a brass gargoyle head.

Dashif found the house with no trouble, and pulled the tongue of the gargoyle. When he released it, it snapped back into the mouth. The eyes opened and the mouth moved, emitting a deep, metallic, yet faintly feminine voice.

"Yes?"

"You know who I am, Gogo. Tell your master who is on your doorstep. I have money."

"Yes," said Gogo, and the doorbell became a mere doorbell again.

Today a man opened the door. He wore the subdued colors and subdued manner of a butler, and today the hall was narrow and dark. Today The Magician's office was the last door on the left, and today the office was small and bare. The client's chair, the only constant item, was just as soft and comfortable as ever. The servant bowed him into the room and Dashif turned his attention to the man who sat behind the desk.

The Magician kept his own looks constant. He appeared to be in his early twenties—a small fraction of his true age, which Dashif could only guess at. Two hundred? Two hundred and fifty? More? Probably more.

"Please sit down, Count Dashif. What may I do for you?"

Dashif seated himself and readjusted the position of his pistols so they didn't press into his legs or stomach. After that, he was careful not to allow his hands to come anywhere near them; The Magician was sometimes touchy. He dug into the purse given him by His Scarlet Eminence and placed two ten-levar pieces on the desk. "Information," said Dashif.

The Magician nodded and pointed at the coins, which promptly vanished.

"That should be sufficient if it's something I already know," he said.

"It probably is," said Dashif. "I have heard of a group gathering money to buy a major spell. You are the only wizard I know of who can work it. I want to know who you're dealing with, and where I can find him or her. If you are not the one, you may earn more money by finding this information any way you can."

The Magician nodded. "The nature of the spell?"

"Releasing the binding on the altar of the Gold priesthood."

"I . . . see."

"Well?"

The Magician chewed his lip. "You're right. I've been asked to set a price for that task."

"By whom?"

"I'm truly sorry, Count Dashif, but that *is* a confidential matter. Now, unless there is something else, my man will show you—"

"My dear wizard—"

"It will be useless, I'm sorry to say, to offer me more money."

"If you would—"

"You certainly aren't about to ask for a refund, are you? I thought you knew me."

"I do," said Dashif.

There was a moment of silence, during which Dashif made no move to leave.

"Well?" said The Magician at last.

"I would like this information, wizard."

"I'm sorry. I would rather not have to ask my servants to—"

"There is no need to play that game with me, wizard. You have one servant in addition to Gogo, whatever the tales may say. I know a shapeshifter when I see one, and I can recognize the soul behind the multitude."

The Magician shrugged.

"I imagine," Dashif continued, "that you would be sorry to lose your butler. And your cook. And your errand boy. And—"

"What are you talking about?" asked The Magician, his eyes narrowing.

"I would also imagine that, even if you kept him, you would just as soon knowledge didn't come out about his nature."

"You're playing a dangerous game, Count."

"It gets more dangerous, wizard."

"With what can you threaten my servants?"

"Servant. Have you ever heard of His Excellency, the Chancellor of Colethea?"

The Magician showed no reaction, not that Dashif had expected one. "Perhaps."

"His body was found floating in the canal two and a half months ago."

"How does this—"

"His heart had been pierced by a single blade thrust. He seems to have fought a duel, despite the ordinances. We know this duel was fought with your servant, wizard. And we can prove it."

"I doubt that," said The Magician.

Dashif shook his head. "Oh, you can force your way into my mind if you choose, find out what the proof is, and dismantle it—"

"I can do more than that, Count Dashif."

"Yes. You can kill me. But then the note that I left explaining all the details of this will come to the attention of His Scarlet Eminence, who thoroughly disapproves of dueling, not to mention the killing of his servants."

"Before killing you, Count, I could compel you to destroy this note."

Dashif looked him in the eye. "I doubt it."

They studied each other for a moment, then The Magician grunted. "Perhaps not. But evidence—"

"Yes, you can destroy it. But I would like to point out a few things. Item: Even if you save your servant from the law, the news will come out about his nature. I think you would prefer it didn't. Item: You would have to put yourself to a great deal of trouble without recompense, a practice I know you find distasteful. Item: You would lose, at least, the Levar's future business, and you might find yourself harried and attacked. The former will cost you money; the latter will be a nuisance. Item: If, instead of all this, you cooperate, you will be serving the Levar, doing me a favor, and I will add another forty levars to what I have already given you."

The Magician shifted in his chair. "You build a strong case," he said.

"Thank you."

"I will be helping the city, you say?"

"Yes."

Another pause. Then, "You should have said so at once."

"My apologies. Thoughtless of me."

"The money, please."

"The information first."

"The money first."

"Very well."

• • •

Dashif walked out of Wizard's Row and found a footcab. "The Red Temple," he said.

"That will be three coppers, please, my lord." said the cabman.

"You should be a wizard," said Dashif.

The main entrance to the Temple of the Faith of the Twin Forces was gaudy, huge, impressive, and always open. Dashif avoided it, as he avoided all main entrances whenever possible. The entrance on the east side was seldom used, but still a public access. It led, more or less directly, into the presence of the beadle, a prematurely balding man of about two and twenty.

"Yes, my lord?" said this worthy young man. "Do you wish a consultation?"

"Precisely."

"Have you a particular priest with whom you wish to consult?"

"Yes. Narni."

The beadle gestured disdainfully. "My lord, the Lady Narni is a high priest. She cannot spend her time . . ." His voice trailed off as Dashif held up the ring on the third finger of his right hand, bezel turned out. The beadle swallowed and said, "Up the stairs, my lord. The second door on the left. I'll send for her."

Dashif went up to the indicated room. It was a simple audience chamber, intimate but plush. He stood in the center of the room and waited for about five minutes before the door opened.

The woman who entered was small and seemed to be about sixteen or seventeen. She was buxom, and her hair was darkish blond. Her eyes were an innocent, merry blue. She was dressed in the red robes of the priesthood, but the clothing was of a far tighter fit than that of most priests.

She saw Dashif and squealed. "Count Dashif," she said breathlessly. "You wanted me? Oh! I'm *so* happy to see you. Why don't you ever *visit* me? I get so *lonely* here all alone, without anyone to talk to or, or *anything*."

Dashif said, "Save it, Your Grace."

Her face took on a sudden wry cynicism. "If you like, my lord," she said coolly. "What do you need?"

"His Scarlet Eminence would like a service."

"Oh, would he indeed? Then, no doubt, I should go see him, shouldn't I?"

Dashif shrugged. "If you like. But Pitullio says he's in one of those moods. Still, it's up to you. I can tell you what it is, if you'd prefer."

She gave him a dry chuckle. "What a surprise. Very well, then. Let's hear it."

"The Emissary from Ka Zhir."

"I see. Information."

"Yes. He's been scheming with a group of Gold priests. Who and where are they?"

"How am I to find out, my lord?"

"Do as you think best, Your Grace. You know where your skills lay. Excuse me, lie."

She sighed. "Why am I only used for my body? When will I find a man who wants me for my money?"

"You have three days."

"I'll need one night."

Dashif took the short walk to the Levar's palace, returned to his chambers, and carefully destroyed the note about The Magician. He'd never expected to need it anyway. He undressed, set his pistols next to his bed, and prepared himself for sleep.

As he closed his eyes, an image appeared before him. Tall, slim, with smooth, dark skin, and long, dark hair. Erina. Erina, Erina, Erina.

He sighed. It was going to be a long night.

The next morning a note appeared with Dashif's breakfast tray. He broke the seal, and read, "The basement of a newly-abandoned inn, in Old Town, Number 61 on the Street of the Dreamers.—N. P.S.: He wasn't half-bad. You should try him."

Dashif first destroyed the note, then ate his breakfast. He cleaned and carefully reloaded his pistols before leaving his apartments in the palace and finding a footcab to take him to Old Town.

It would, he decided later, have been too much to hope for that they would all have been sitting there discussing the scheme to free the spell in the altar. But they were certainly present, and they were certainly Gold priests, and that was enough. He crouched in a dark corner of the basement. They were all in gold robes. There were nearly a score of them facing the front of the room, about equally divided between men and women. There were nine in the front, facing the others, in fuller, richer robes. The ones facing forward all seemed to be in their twenties. The ones facing the back seemed to range in age from forty to sixty.

Nine of them, Dashif observed. *Hmmm. If I had a score of guards . . . no, that would involve the Levar directly. I'll have to think of something else.*

They appeared to be concentrating intensely on their activity. So much so that Dashif had had no trouble penetrating the basement. Dashif had never seen such a thing before, but he'd heard enough to be able to tell what they were doing. They were praying.

"Good afternoon, Count Dashif. Is there a problem?"

"Not at all, Snake. Merely something I wish to buy."

"Always glad to help. What is it?"

"How much is that cut glass decanter worth?"

"What will you . . . Never mind. Thirty levars."

"What about that gaudy saber in the corner?"

"Even more, I'm afraid. Forty-five."

"Hmmm. The looking glass, against the back wall?"

"The silver-framed one, with the jewels?"

"Yes."

"Those are sapphires, Count Dashif. Six hundred levars."

"I'll take it."

"I . . . all right."

"I'd like it delivered, if you please. To me, personally; no one else."

"Of course."

"I may be forced to have someone inspect it first."

"Inspect it?"

"That is correct. But you needn't worry. You must await me in the square near the Old Town Farmer's Market, at the third hour, tomorrow."

"About this inspection . . ."

"As I said, you needn't worry. Someone may wish to see it, but that is all. Allow it, but be certain to hand the package over to me personally."

"Very well."

"Until tomorrow, then."

"Until tomorrow."

Narni frowned in concentration. "Would you mind telling me, my lord, what the significance of the water is?"

"You have no need to know, Your Grace," said Dashif. Her eyes narrowed and a storm quickly began forming on her brow. He chuckled. No sense in baiting her too much, he decided. "Never mind. The messenger is a follower of the Way of Herself. When she is offered the ritual, she'll assume the priest is, also. Remember, she won't know he's a priest."

"What's the point?"

"To alleviate her suspicions. The package is worth six hundred levars—she isn't going to take her eyes off it without prompting."

Narni nodded. "All right. I can do my part well enough. But tell me, why are you making everything so complicated?"

Dashif paused, looking for an answer. "You have no need to know," he said at last.

The priest wore baggy blue pants, a light green tunic, and a wide hat of bright yellow. He looked nothing like a priest. But he couldn't afford to look like a priest—yet. Soon, with the help of the God, he would wear his gold robes before the world.

Once more he thanked his God and, quite literally, counted his blessings. Eighteen years after the catastrophe—eighteen years of thinking that all was lost forever. Then, only a few months before, (1) the foreigner had come as if sent by the God Himself (and strange were His ways that He would send a Zhir to help them in Liavek!). The Zhir had explained that the altar could be unbound, what monies would be required, and who to see when the monies were available. He had even (2) promised to supply the money when the time came.

And now, (3) apparently the time had come. How mysterious are thy ways, Lord. That fair lady, serving as a priest (as if they deserved the word, the murderers!) for the Red ones, waiting to serve the God in her way. She had appeared from nowhere, frightened but determined, and told them when and how they would receive the money.

He recited her instructions to himself once more. The time,

the place, the woman with the package, the contents of the package, the long series of passwords and countersigns needed to verify who they were.

Around him walked the other high priests, equally disguised. As they neared the appointed place, he turned to them and said, "Wait here for the signal. You remember the plan?"

"Yes," said a sister. "We are to walk in front of the messenger, jostling her and getting in her way."

"That is correct. Don't worry; she won't be trying any harder than she has to, to make it look good. And if anything happens to me—"

"Brother!"

"If anything happens to me, take the parcel, whatever it is, and *keep going*. If we should happen to meet any guards, use your knives."

"I don't know if I can, brother."

He looked fully into her face. "I hope we don't have to, sister. But if we do, you'll be able."

She nodded. He took a deep breath, and a last look at his friends, his comrades through the long years of waiting.

The old East Wall was in sight. The sun told him that the third hour was near. His friends lounged around the small farmer's market, unobtrusively mingling with the customers and merchants. He breathed deeply and settled down to wait.

He'd only been there a matter of moments when she appeared—dark and willowy, just as she'd been described. He was startled for a moment when he recognized . . . what was her name? Serpent, or something? The owner of the Tiger's Eye. Was she one of the Faithful, or merely fulfilling a commission? Well, best not to take any chances. She had the package, that was all that mattered.

He approached her. "Excuse me, but are you looking for the Count?"

She nodded. "I suppose you wish to inspect the parcel." There was the faintest bite to her tone, as if she thought this exchange to be so much foolishness.

"Yes."

As he'd been told she would, she scrutinized him carefully. Apparently satisfied of his harmlessness, she nodded and said, "Very well." Then she peeled back the cloth covering.

He gasped. It was a looking glass in a silver frame with impossibly intricate detail work. The silver alone must be worth a small fortune, not to mention the sapphires clustered at the top and the bottom. But more, the whole of it was a work of art. This would certainly pay for that wizard the foreigner had told him of. He felt his pulse racing as he silently thanked the God for their fortune.

"By the . . . Levar," he said quaveringly, prudently amending his oath. "Hide it away, quickly!"

She nodded and covered it, but from her expression, he guessed that she was pleased that he understood its worth and its beauty. For an instant he regretted the need to dispose of it, but the God came first, always. He bowed to her, not trusting himself to speak. He stood there for a moment in silence, then noticed that she was looking around the market area. Almost choking, he remembered that he hadn't yet completed the code. The last part bothered him a bit, for he knew it to be the ritual of another faith, but those were his instructions.

He reached into his pocket and produced a vial of water. He carefully poured some on the ground, swallowed a mouthful, and handed the vial to her. Her face lit up, and she took the vial. One final countersign . . . Yes! She completed the gesture by pouring a small amount of the water onto the ground. Quivering with relief, he took the parcel from her now-relaxed hand and stepped back. His comrades, who had begun moving as soon as he had given her the vial, surrounded him as they sped down the street. He looked back and saw that the messenger was, indeed, in pursuit. She would drop back soon. Her expression, he noted with satisfaction, was quite genuine. She could have been a fine actress. Anyone who didn't know better would think the parcel had been stolen from her.

Narni came running up breathlessly to the two guards. The wiry, red-haired one with the blue sash over his gray vest saw her first.

"Narni!" he said as she reached him.

"Oh, Lieutenant," she sobbed, clutching him around the arm and pressing herself against him. "You have to help me!"

"What is it, Narni? What are you doing outside your temple?"

"Never mind that," she said. "Do you know Snake?"

"Huh? Of course."

The other guard, a large man with his dark hair tied back,

who wore a corporal's badge, said, "Uh, Rusty, isn't Snake that nice lady who—"

"Shut up, Stone. What about her, Narni?"

"She's over at the Farmer's Market, and she's been *robbed*. Nine of them came and took something she was delivering. She's chasing them, and they're headed this way. I'm *so* glad I found you, Lieutenant. Ohhhhh, it was *horrible!* They . . . *There they are!*"

And, in fact, nine men and women appeared in a group. The one in the middle did, in fact, seem to be carrying a parcel. And behind them, Snake—running, her whip uncoiled, her lips drawn back in a snarl.

The one called Stone said, "Uh . . . should we stop 'em, ay, Rusty?"

"Right, Stone," said the other, already drawing his short sword and moving to cut them off. Stone ambled after.

"Halt in the name of the Levar!" called the lieutenant from twenty feet away. His voice had the ring of power and authority; everyone around stopped at least long enough to see what was going on. Then they quickly moved out of the way. Neither of the guards noticed Narni duck behind a farmer's stall.

To the lieutenant's surprise, the nine of them actually did stop. But then one said, "We've been betrayed! Run, we'll hold them." Then he turned to the lieutenant and said, "We won't halt for murdering Red priests or their lackies, dog!" By the time he had finished speaking, his knife was in his hand. Five others had drawn weapons; the remaining three, also with their knives out, were running back up the street the way they'd come.

The lieutenant met the quickly-formed line of three men and three women. "Put down your weapons, please," he said.

The one who'd spoken before said, "And be handed over to your murdering masters? Never!"

From back up the street, the lieutenant heard what sounded like a crash, an oath, and a whip striking, followed by screams. His forehead was suddenly drenched with sweat.

"Please," he said. "Stand aside, or I'll have to force my way past you."

"Do your worst," said the man. On the faces before him, the lieutenant read determination and defiance, but no fear. He could still hear screams and oaths from up the street.

"Damn it," he said, and strode forward. A knife flashed toward him. He dodged it and struck the man's head with the flat of his sword. Then there was another knife, and he repeated the process. Then there were two more knives flashing and he had no time to be careful. Next to him he heard Stone saying plaintively, "Aw, nuts, Rusty," and felt rather than saw Stone going into action. Stone, peace-loving though he was, knew only one way of fighting.

A few seconds later the lieutenant stepped over four corpses and two stunned prisoners, yelling over his shoulder, "Hang onto them, Stone." He raced up the street after the three who had fled.

He saw the woman first, on her back, her head at an impossible angle. One of the men was also on his back. There was nothing odd about his position, but he wasn't breathing, and, in any case, the lieutenant had seen enough death to recognize the condition. Of the other man, there was no doubt. There was a gash across his throat and a deep cut in his chest. Next to him was a flat bundle of cloth. Bits of broken glass lay next to it, and he caught the glint of blue gems from an exposed corner. Snake still held her whip and her knife, but now looked drained and sad.

He considered the situation for a moment, and said, "Why is it, Snake, that I always find you . . . Never mind. I saw enough. If you can prove ownership of that . . . whatever it is, you won't be in any trouble. And we still have two of them."

And, in fact, Stone came up with them at that moment. The woman was moaning and leaning on the guard for support. The man was held by a tight grip around the neck.

The lieutenant glared at them. "Damn you, why didn't you surrender?" They looked back defiantly but didn't answer. "All right," he continued. "Let's all go . . . you!"

"Good afternoon, Lieutenant," said Dashif, appearing from nearby. "Hot, isn't it?"

Dashif walked up to the others. Snake was just beginning to put the pieces of the puzzle together when she realized that his hands were concealed under his cloak, and that his pistols weren't in his belt.

"Dashif, *no!*" she said, and he raised his hands. Barrels thundered, in a steady rhythm of chick-*crack,* chick-*crack,* chick-*crack,* chick-*crack*. Each of the prisoners gave two jerks and one scream; then the woman collapsed. The man would have done so had Stone not automatically prevented it by tightening his grip. Silence settled like a blanket over the market. Four distinct puffs of dark grey smoke rose above Dashif in the still air. An acrid smell filled the market area.

Dashif coolly replaced his pistols. "I had expected you to kill them all," he said.

Rusty, the first to recover, suddenly roared. "You sonofacamel! They *surrendered!* I'll have your bear-buggering arse for this! By the Levar's future tits, you're under arrest, you—"

He stopped. Dashif, who had made no move or gesture, was looking steadily at Rusty with no more expression than a blank wall. Rusty didn't complete his sentence. There was still another moment of silence, then Dashif turned away. As he passed in front of Snake, who was still too stunned to move, he dropped a purse on top of the remains of the mirror.

"Six hundred levars," he said. "As agreed."

Then he caught a footcab back to the Levar's palace. On the way, he reloaded his pistols, just as a matter of course. Back at the Farmer's Market, nine bodies slowly stiffened on the street.

"His Scarlet Eminence will see you now, my lord."

Dashif entered and found the Regent studying a map hung on a wall of the office. The Count stood quietly for a moment. Without looking at him, the Regent said, "Is that your idea of not involving the Levar or the Priesthood?"

Dashif shrugged, and decided not to ask how His Eminence had heard the news in the quarter of an hour it had taken the footcab to arrive. Maybe he hadn't but was only guessing. It didn't matter. "The way the lieutenant carried on, Your Eminence, everyone will know he wasn't involved. No one saw the Margrave of Narnitalo except the guards, who won't want to talk about it, I think."

The Regent made several marks on the map. Then he turned and faced Dashif fully. "I almost wish I couldn't protect you," he said. Then he sighed. "Very well. It is done; that's the important thing."

"I learned something else, Your Eminence," said Dashif. "The entire affair was set up by the Zhir."

"Yes," said His Scarlet Eminence. "That will be all."

Dashif stood for a moment, then bowed and left. As the door swung shut behind him, he said under his breath, "Someday, you son of a bitch, I'm going to make you admit that you're surprised about something." He was almost out of the palace before he realized that the map the Regent had been facing was of the area around Ka Zhir, and the marks had been plans for a naval blockade.

She was waiting for him right outside the palace. He approached her, stopping about eight feet away. His arms stayed at his sides, his rapier and his pistols stayed in his belt. There were, if not crowds, at least good numbers of passers-by in the area, who saw the two of them looking at each other and made a wide detour around them.

A pair of corporals in the City Guard approached them. One started to speak. Dashif spared them a look and they backed off. He turned his eyes back to her.

She spoke a single word.

He chuckled without mirth. "At least," he admitted.

Then the whip was in her hand. She cracked it once, and spoke a different word.

"Yes," he agreed. "That, too."

"You used me," she said, in a deadly, calm voice.

"Quite."

She stared at him a moment longer, then her great whip writhed out. A long welt appeared on Dashif's right cheek, just below the eye, blood flowing from it to blend with the red of his cloak. Still, he didn't move. The whip cracked once more. Another welt appeared, this one beginning just below his left eye. Still, they waited and looked at each other. Then Dashif gave an almost imperceptible nod, turned, and started back for the palace.

He stopped after five paces and looked back. The two Guards were advancing toward Snake. He caught them with his glance and said, "Don't." They froze, then backed away.

Dashif continued toward the palace, wondering, himself, just why he had done it that way. He hoped he'd still be able to use Snake. His pistols would need repair from time to time, and she managed to get things done efficiently and quickly.

Besides, she was pleasant to look at: so tall, so slim, her smooth dark skin, her long dark hair.

The Inn of the Demon Camel

by Jane Yolen

It was in this very place, my lords, my ladies, during the reign of the Levar Ozle the Crooked Back, two hundred years to this very day (the year 3117 for those of you whose fingers limit the counting), that the great bull camel, afterwards known as The Demon, was born.

Oh, he was an unprepossessing calf, hardly humped, and with a wandering left eye. (You must remember that eye, Excellencies.)

The master of the calf was a bleak-spirited little man, an innkeeper the color of camel dung, who would have sold the little beast if he could. But who wanted such a burden? So instead of selling the calf, his master whipped him. It was meant to be training, my Magnificencies, but as any follower of the Way knows, the whip is a crooked teacher. What that little calf learned was not what his master taught.

And he grew. How he grew. From Buds to Flowers, he developed a hump the size of a wine grape. From Flowers to Meadows, the grape became a gourd. It took from Meadows all the way till Fog and Frost, but the hump became a heap and he had legs and feet—and teeth—to match. And that wandering left eye. (You *must* remember that eye, my Eminences.)

Without a hump he was simply a small camel with a tendency to balk. With the grape hump he was a medium-sized camel who loved to grind his teeth. With the gourd hump, he was a large camel with a vicious spitting range. But with the heap—O my Graces—and the wandering eye (you *must* remember that eye) the camel was a veritable demon and so Demon became his name.

And is it not written in *The Book of the Twin Forces* that one may be born with a fitting name or one may grow to fit the name one is born with? You may, yourselves, puzzle out the way of The Demon's name, for I touch upon that no more.

It came to pass, therefore, that the innkeeper owned a great bull camel of intolerably nasty disposition: too stringy to eat, too temperamental to drive, too infamous to sell, too ugly to breed. But since it was a camel, and a man's worth is measured in the number of camels he owns and oxen he pastures and horses he rides, the innkeeper would not kill the beast outright.

There happened one day, this very day in fact, 195 years to this very day during the reign of Levar Tinzli the Cleft Chinned (3122 for those of you whose toes limit the counting), that three unrelated strangers came to stay at the inn. One was a bald ship's captain who had lost his ship (and consequently his hair) upon the Eel Island rocks. One was a broken-nosed young farmer come south to join the Levar's Guard. And one was an overfed mendicant priest who wore a white turban in which was set a jewel as black and shiny and ripe as a grape.

Was not the innkeeper abustle then in the oily manner of his tribe! He bowed a hundred obeisances to the priest, for the black jewel promised a high gratuity. He bowed half a hundred obeisances to the farmer, for his letter of introduction to the Guards promised compensations to come. And he bowed a quarter-hundred obeisances to the ship's captain because riches in the past can sometimes be a guarantee of riches later on. Thus did the innkeeper count his profits, not into the palm but into the future. As you know, Graciousnesses, it is not always a safe method of tabulation.

They ignored the innkeeper's flatteries and demanded rooms, which he managed to turn up at once, his inn being neither on Rose Row nor favored by such worthies as yourselves. He served his guests an execrable meal of fishless stew and an excellent mountain wine, the one cancelling the other, and so they passed the night, their new-forged friendships made agreeable by the inn's well-stocked cellar. Thus lullabied by strong drink, the three slept until nearly noon.

Now perhaps all that followed would not have, had it not occurred on the seventeenth day of Buds, for it was the very day on which four of the five mentioned in our story had been born, though they recognized it not.

The captain, who had been birthed that day forty years in the past, did not believe in such birth luck, trusting only to his own skill—which is perhaps why he had fetched up so promptly on the shoals of the Eel.

The young farmer was an orphan who had been found on a doorstep some twenty years past, and so had never really known his true birth day. His foster parents counted it five days after the seventeenth, the morning they had tripped over his basket and thus smashed the infant's nose.

And the priest, who had been born some sixty years in the past, had been given a new birth date by the master of his faith who had tried, in this way, to twist luck to his own ends.

So that was three. But I *did* say four. And it is not of the innkeeper I now speak, for he knew full well his luck day was the twenty-seventh of Wind. But he had forgot that the bull camel, The Demon, humped and with the wandering eye (you *must* remember that eye, Exultancies) had emerged head first and spitting five years ago to that very day.

An animal casts no luck, neither good nor bad, you say, my Supremacies? And where is that bit of wisdom writ? Believe me when I tell you that the seventeenth day of Buds was the source of the problem. I have no reason to lie.

So there they were, three birth days sequestered and snoring under the one inn roof and the fourth feeding on straw in the stable. Together they invented the rest of my small tale and invested it with the worst of ill luck, which led to the haunting of the place from that day on.

It happened in this manner, Preeminencies and, pray, you *must* remember that wandering eye.

The sun glinting on the roof of the Levar's palace pierced the gloom of the inn and woke our five on that fateful day in Buds. The camel was up first, stretching, spitting, chewing loudly, and complaining. But as he was tucked away in the stable, no one heard him. Next up was the innkeeper, stretching, grimacing, creaking loudly, and complaining to himself. Then in order of descending age, the three guests arose—first the priest, then the captain, and last the farmer. All stretching, sighing, scratching loudly, and complaining to the innkeeper about the fleas.

They gathered for a desultory breakfast and, as it was a lovely day, one of the lambent mornings in Buds when the air is soft and full of bright promise, that meal was served outdoors under a red-striped awning next to the stable.

The camel, ignoring the presence of ox and ass, chose to stick his head into the human conversation, and so the concatenation began.

The three guests were sitting at the table, a round table, with a basket of sweet bread between them, a small crock of butter imprinted with the insignia of the inn to one side, and to the other a steaming urn of kaf, dark and heady, and a small pitcher of milk.

The talk turned to magic.

"I do not believe in it," spake the captain.

"I am not sure," said the farmer.

"Believe me, I know," the mendicant priest put in and at that same moment turned his head toward the right to look at a plate of fresh raw shellfish that had been deposited there.

Now that placed his head—and atop it the turban with the jewel, black and shiny and ripe as a grape—slightly below the camel's nose, and it, great protuberance that it was, sensitive to every movement and smell carried by the soft air of Buds.

Well the turban tickled the nose; the camel, insulted, spat; the priest slapped the beast who snapped back at the priest's hand.

But you did not—I hope, Ascendencies—forget that wandering eye?

For the camel's eye caused him to miss the offending hand and snap up the black jewel instead.

At which the priest fainted. Then rallied. Then fainted again, clutching his chest and emitting a scream rather like that of a Tichenese woman in labor: *"Ee-eah, ee-eah, ee-eee-ehai."*

The captain leaped to his feet, upsetting the table, bread, butter, shellfish, milk, and kaf, and drawing his knife. The farmer simultaneously unsheathed his sword, a farewell gift from his parents. The innkeeper hovered over the priest, fanning him with a dirty apron. And the camel gulped and rolled his wandering eye.

At that, the priest sat up. "The jewel," he gasped. "It contains the magic of my master."

To which sentence the captain responded by knifing the camel in the front. This so startled the farmer, he sunk his sword into the camel up to its hilt from behind. The priest fell back, screamlessly, into his faint. The innkeeper began to weep over his bleeding beast. And the camel closed his wandering eye and died. Of course by his death the luck—such as it was—was freed.

And do you think, Extremities, by this the tale is now done? It is only halfway finished for, in the course of the telling, I have told you only what *seemed* to have happened, not that which, in actuality, occurred.

The priest at last revived and offered this explanation. The master of his faith, a magician of great power but little ambition, had invested his luck in a necklace of ten black jewels which he distributed to his nine followers (it was a *very* small sect). He kept but one jewel for himself. Then each year, the nine members of the faith traveled the roads of Liavek letting the master's magic reach out and touch someone. But now, with a tenth of his master's luck swallowed and—with the camel's death—freed, there was no knowing what might happen.

On hearing this, the innkeeper began to scrabble through the remains of his camel like a soothsayer through entrails. But all he could find in the stomach was a compote of nuts, grains, olives, grape seeds, and a damp and bedraggled feather off the hat of a whore who had recently plied her trade at his hostelry.

"No jewel," he said at last with a sigh.

"Probably crushed to powder when the luck was freed," said the farmer.

"Then if there is no jewel," said the captain, "where is this supposed luck? I told you I did not believe in it."

At which very moment, the severed remains of the camel began to shimmer and reattach themselves, ligament to limb, muscle to bone; and with a final *snap* as loud as a thunderclap, the reanimation stood and opened its eyes. The one eye was sane. But the wandering eye, Benevolencies, was as black and shiny and ripe as a grape and orbited like a malevolent star 'round elliptic and uncharted galaxies.

The four men departed the premises at once in a tangle of arms, legs, and screams. The innkeeper, not an hour later, sold his inn to a developer, sight unseen, who desired to level it for an even larger hostelry. The priest converted within the day to the Red Faith where he rose quickly through the ranks to a minor, minor functionary. The farmer joined the Levar's Guard where he was given a far better sword with which he wounded himself serving the Levar Modzi of the Flat Dome. And the captain—well, he sold the jewel, black and shiny and ripe as a grape, which he had stolen from the turban the night before and replaced with an olive because he did not believe in magic but he certainly believed in money. He bought himself a new ship which he sailed quite carefully around the shoals of the Eel. There had been no luck in the jewel after all, for the priest's master had had as little skill as ambition, no luck except that which a sly man could convert to coin.

Then what of the camel? Had his revival been a trick? Oh, there had been luck there, freed by his death which had occurred at the exact day and hour and minute five years after his birth. But the luck had been in the whore's feather which she had taken from a drunken mage who had bound his magic in it, creating a talisman of great sexual potency. So the demon camel, that walking boneyard, ravaged the inn site and impregnated a hundred and twenty local camels—and one very surprised mare—before the magic dwindled and the ghostly demon fell apart into a collection of rotted parts. But those camels sired by him still haunt this particular place; spitting, chomping, reproducing, and getting into one kind of mischief after another.

And each and every one of those little demons, Tremendousies, is marked by a wandering eye.

The Hands of the Artist

by Kara Dalkey

"IT'S QUITE SIMPLE, really," said Aritoli ola Silba. "I believe I might be of great service to you."

"Is it so? I thought the only thing art critics do is insult artists," said Sheyn. Although his Liavekan was good, he spoke with a heavy Zhir accent.

Aritoli held up a slim, elegant hand—his fingernails painted gold to suggest the promise of wealth—saying, "If you please, I consider myself an Advisor to Patrons of the Arts."

"I see," said Sheyn. "In Ka Zhir, we do not have such. Critics, yes, but not advisors. At least, I did not know of them."

Of course you wouldn't, thought Aritoli, *You were the Royal Portraitist at the court of Prince Jeng. You had no need of an advisor then.*

"Hmmm." Sheyn ran a hand through his short, black hair. He was large, for a Zhir. As tall as Aritoli, but much heavier. Sheyn's hands, Aritoli noticed, were graceful in movement, and his fingers smooth and tapered. *The hands of an artist.* The advisor smiled inwardly in appreciation as Sheyn continued. "And what can you do for me?"

"For one thing, I can put your work in a better light—" Aritoli flicked his fingers toward a nearby painting, showering it with a silvery, sorcerous glow. The painting, a stormy seascape, for a moment seemed almost real. "—So to speak."

"Ho ho! That is funny! A wizard art critic. What else will you do? Make my canvasses go flying around the room?"

Aritoli laughed. "No, sir, my wizardry is limited to working with light and color, shape and shadow. Oh, I have had occasion to be a spell-breaker when a patron finds the work he commissioned to contain something he didn't pay for—a curse, or a hidden command to give the artist a million levars. You are not a magician, I assume?"

"What? Oh. No, I have not learned magic." Sheyn gave a regretful shrug and looked at his lap, absentmindedly massaging the back of his right hand with his left thumb.

"Well, that's nothing to be ashamed of. Just because Liavek is called the City of Luck does not mean all of its residents must be wizards. Though, I admit, it may sometimes seem that way."

Sheyn pointed at the short walking stick leaning against the chair beside the advisor. "Is that where you keep your . . . how do you say, luck?"

Aritoli's black-mustached lip twitched into a semismile. Stroking the golden raven's head of his cane, he said, "Among wizards, it is not good form to admit one's luck-piece. And as long as we are on personal questions, may I ask one?"

Sheyn shrugged again. "Ask."

"Why did you leave Ka Zhir?"

The big man frowned and shifted in his chair. "I . . . tired of doing portraits. Always the same sort of portrait. Always the same people. I wanted to try something different."

"And I would say from your beautiful landscapes that you have succeeded. But could you not have accomplished this in Ka Zhir?"

"No!" Sheyn looked momentarily surprised at the vehemence of his denial. He looked down at his hands. "No. I'm sorry. There are . . . bitter memories."

"Then I shall not pry further into the matter. I apologize if I have upset you. To return, then, to the reason for my visit: Have I your permission to speak at your showing at the residence of Count ola Klera?"

"You will have to ask the Count for permission to attend."

"I did. He suggested I ask you."

"Oh. You know him?"

"Yes." Rapid visions of a pair of startling green eyes, a well-muscled torso . . . "I know him. I'm acquainted with many of the noble families of Liavek—another avenue through which I could help you, I might add. Come now, Sheyn, what possible reason could you have for denying me?"

The artist rubbed his chin and frowned slightly. "Well, you write articles for the street papers. You have ruined careers that way, I hear."

"Only for those who deserved it. And as I've stated before, you're hardly one of them. In fact, I can already tell you what I will write. Ahem. 'Sheyn fills his landscapes with all the awe and majesty of nature, yet adds a touch of otherworldliness, as if what the viewer sees is a dream more beautiful than reality.' And this, by the by, is a third way in which I might aid you. What say you?"

Sheyn twisted his hands in his lap. "I . . . I would like to think about it."

"Take your time."

"Could you not come back later for my answer?"

"The showing *is* tomorrow, sir."

"Oh." Sheyn stared at the floor.

Now the man seems positively nervous, thought Aritoli. *Does he worry about how his new style will be received? Am I that intimidating?* Aritoli slumped down in his chair and stretched out his long legs, trying to look more relaxed and less threatening.

Glancing around, the advisor noted that Sheyn's apartment was simply furnished, small but tidy. Not a speck of paint anywhere. No lingering odor of turpentine and oil. No canvasses stuck in odd corners. Very unlike the homes of other painters he knew. Aritoli nodded approval. *A professional. He keeps his work separate from his living quarters.* The advisor looked back at Sheyn's hands. No specks of paint under the fingernails. No stains on the skin. "You are a fastidious man, Sheyn."

"What?"

"Never mind. I should like, sometime at your convenience, to see your studio. I get my best feel for an artist when I see the atmosphere in which he works."

"No!" said Sheyn half-rising out of his chair. Then he sat

again suddenly. "No one sees my studio."

A professional who is used to getting his way. "Forgive me, sir. I shall withdraw that request. But as to my first . . . ?"

"Eh?"

"May I attend your showing?"

Sheyn looked embarrassed for a moment, then gave an awkward laugh. "Hah. So be it, by Thung! Do your worst! It matters not to me."

"Sir, I intend to do my best, if you please. And I trust you will find my presence to be to your advantage."

"Ah! You will seduce all the patrons so they will like my work, yes?"

Aritoli paused, not sure if he had just been insulted or if this was merely an example of Zhir humor. The advisor chided himself for failing to research Zhir customs, particularly before approaching such a potentially valuable client. With a tight smile, he responded, "Of course, Sheyn, that will not be necessary. Your work is sufficiently alluring on its own. Now, if you will pardon me, I have other matters to attend to. Thank you for your kind patience, and I look forward most eagerly to your showing." Aritoli picked up his cane and headed for the door.

"Thung kwas jhieng fa choh," said Sheyn.

Aritoli turned. "Eh?"

"Is Zhir. It means 'May Thung shield your eyes from evil.'"

The advisor smiled and bowed and took his leave.

The townhome of the Count and Countess ola Klera of Richgrove was elegantly furnished: carved wood paneling from Ombaya, crystal wall sconces from Saltigos, and carpets of intricate design from Tichen. When Aritoli entered the entertaining salon on the night of the showing, it seemed more elegant still, filled as it was with attractive men and women of wealth. Aritoli's sense of aesthetics was pleased.

He paused before a gilt-framed mirror to admire himself. *Yes, the black silk blouson definitely adds the right touch.* He smoothed back his loose, wavy black hair, and noted with satisfaction that his fingernails were just the right shade of reassuring blue. Raising his chin in hauteur, Aritoli sauntered into the salon.

"Aritoli Montanija Galifavi ola Silba, Vavasor of Silversea," announced a servant. The advisor looked around the room for his host. Spotting a tall, dark man with green eyes in a knot of guests, Aritoli went to him.

The Count ola Klera was conversing with a merchant in gaudy brocade, who was saying, "So this fellow in the red cape, see, he takes out his pistol and shoots the damn camel right in the head! In the middle of the Market, in front of everybody! And the camel owner didn't do a thing. The caped fellow just walks away. Strangest thing I ever saw."

"Perhaps the pistoleer was in need of target practice. Ah, Master ola Silba! What a pleasure to see you. We feared you might not come."

"Formality, Meceno?" Aritoli said softly. "I thought we knew each other better."

"For the sake of the guests, Ari," said the Count, taking the advisor's arm and drawing him away from the others. "The Countess and I are the brunt of enough gossip already."

Aritoli laughed. "Gossip? In Liavek? Does the sea mind a spoonful more salt?"

"I have a chance at a council seat next year, so I must be careful."

"Ah, I see. Then I shall behave myself. And how is Her Grace this evening?"

"Quite well, thank you. She should be joining us shortly."

"Good. And Sheyn, has he arrived yet?"

"Yes. In fact, he came somewhat early. As you can see, his paintings are already on display."

"Tell me, does he seem at all nervous to you?"

"More awkward than nervous, I would think. No doubt he is not yet used to our informal Liavekan ways. And, though the Countess has done her best in designing this place, it is hardly the Jeng Palace."

"Ah, here comes Her Grace now."

The Countess Siena ola Klera, a lithe woman whose ebony hue suggested noble Tichenese heritage, came up to them and smiled.

Aritoli bowed, saluting with three fingers, saying, "And am I to be formal with you also, Your Grace?"

"Not necessarily," she replied, kissing his cheek. "I'm not seeking a seat on the council . . . just yet. Have you heard about the surprise?"

"Surprise?"

"Yes. Sheyn has done a painting especially for this showing.

He says he worked on it day and night this week to finish it in time."

Ahhh. That explains Sheyn's behavior yesterday. He was anxious to return to his work. "I look forward to seeing it."

"Excellent," said Her Grace. "I believe all our guests are here. We can begin whenever you are ready."

Aritoli bowed again and looked around the room. Each of Sheyn's paintings was surrounded by a small cluster of admirers, except for one which was hidden beneath a cloth of green silk.

The surprise, thought the advisor. *I shall save it for last.* Aritoli went to the painting furthest from the covered one. As onlookers gathered around him, he drew power from his cane and prepared to speak.

"This first work, my lords and ladies, is an excellent example of Sheyn's talent." The painting showed a jagged mountain sierra just touched by the rays of a rising sun. "The Silverspine? Perhaps. But where in those great mountains could one see such delicate rock formations? Trees shaped like the temples of Tichen? A sky of that hue? These are the mountains of dreams and myth, the place one longs to see, but will never attain."

Aritoli let sorcerous power flow from his fingertips in the form of glistening light motes that he flung onto the canvas. The painting seemed to absorb the light and reradiate it, enhancing the illusion that the gilt frame was actually a window, and the scene beyond it real. The peaks glowed in the pale pink sunlight. One could almost catch the scent of pines in cold mountain air.

There came sighs of approval and scattered applause. Aritoli smiled. He loved working with truly fine art. It made critiques so much more pleasant for all concerned.

He moved on to the next painting. This was a rural scene that could be the lands near Ombaya. But not even there could one find fields of such intense green, or such an atmosphere of serenity.

The next work was the wild, stormy seascape Aritoli had seen before. After it came a scene of a starkly compelling desert, and a cloudscape in which one of the clouds resembled a floating castle. Each seemed like a dream brought to life on canvas, and each was hauntingly beautiful.

At last, Aritoli came to the covered easel. From beneath the cloth came an odor of fresh paint. As was traditional, the count and countess, as hosts, had the honor of unveiling it. The onlookers, including Aritoli, could not help gasping in awe as the green silk was raised.

The painting was a vista of the city of Liavek, but as none of its citizens had ever seen it. The copper-green domes and spires of the Levar's palace shone with splendor, and the surrounding streets seemed to glow with an aura of magic. Aritoli felt his embellishments were hardly necessary with this one.

The advisor bowed to Sheyn, who smiled, looking . . . surprised? *Did he think we could possibly not appreciate such a masterpiece?* "A most fitting finale to this showing, my lords and ladies. This painting is a superb example of the best of Sheyn's talent. A scene that would be ordinary from anyone else's hand, takes from Sheyn's brush the power of emotion and the vividness of dreams." Aritoli could not resist a final flourish of sorcerous light.

But instead of enhancing the painting, the light danced on the surface of the canvas for a few moments, then rushed to the lower left-hand corner. There, it swirled and formed first the word "help," then the number "3," then the form of a fish, and last the form of a knife. Then it vanished.

Aritoli blinked, taken aback, and bent to examine the corner closely. Sheyn walked up to him. "What is it? What are you looking at?"

"Er, I was . . . just examining the fine detail, sir." If this was another joke of Sheyn's, the advisor was not about to admit its presence until he understood it.

"What were you doing with that light?" the artist asked suspiciously.

Aritoli glanced at Sheyn. The artist's face held no sign of hidden glee. *He honestly doesn't know what it was*. The advisor bowed, smiling. "A mistake, sir. In my excitement, I threw the wrong spell. Give it no thought. I am deeply impressed with your work."

Sheyn seemed confused, but mollified, and Aritoli stepped aside to give him time to calm down. The countess took Aritoli's arm and guided him to an empty corner of the room.

"A mistake, Ari? I've never known you to make mistakes at a showing."

"Shhh," Aritoli cautioned, "There is more to this than I implied, but I'd rather not speak of it until I'm certain. Could, perhaps, Your Graces distract Sheyn for a while so that I may ponder this?"

"Of course, Ari. We need to discuss our patronage with him anyway."

Aritoli watched as the count and countess drew Sheyn aside. Then the advisor strolled back to the painting of Liavek. Surreptitiously, he tossed another light spell at the canvas. It behaved normally—illuminating the work, nothing more.

The effect could only be triggered once, then. Aritoli closed his eyes. He could still clearly visualize the "help," the 3, the fish, and the knife, as if the images had been imprinted on his mind. *Yet Sheyn is no wizard,* he thought. *Could someone have tampered with the painting?* He visualized the images again and realized that the energy that formed them had flowed throughout the work. *No. Whoever planted the spell painted the picture. And it is Sheyn's style exactly. Yet Sheyn is no wizard.*

The 3, the fish, and the knife were a puzzle. They had been placed on the part of the painting representing the Canal District—near the wharfs, an area generally inhabited by poor sailors and dockworkers. Suddenly, it all clicked. *There is a Street of Fish Knives in the Canal District.*

With word to the servants to give his regrets to his hosts, Aritoli gathered up his cane and cape and departed.

This portion of the Canal District was not considered safe for a nobleman alone on a warm night. Even the footcab runner was grateful to take his few coppers and depart quickly. Aritoli was glad he had chosen to wear black that evening.

It took him but a minute to find a beggar willing to guide him for an exorbitant sum, and soon he was led to a rotting door beside which a painted 3 was peeling off the wall. The reek of oil and turpentine confirmed that he had come to the right place. Aritoli rapped on the door with his cane.

"Who is it? Sheyn?" came a faint, female voice from behind the door.

"I am Aritoli ola Silba. I believe someone within requested my assistance."

The door opened a crack and a small face peered up at him. "Are you . . . are you the wizard art critic?"

"I am."

The face disappeared and the door opened wide. Aritoli stepped into a tiny room lit by a sputtering oil lamp. Canvasses, rags, and paint pots cluttered the room, and the smell of paint was nearly overwhelming.

Turning, Aritoli saw a girl of perhaps sixteen, painfully thin, with skin the color of kaf when too much goat's milk has been added. Her matted hair framed a bruised and grimy face in which two eyes gleamed with triumph. "I hoped you'd come."

"It was you who summoned me?"

The girl nodded.

Aritoli shut the door behind him and looked once more around the room. Some canvasses held unfinished paintings clearly in Sheyn's style. "This is Sheyn's studio, then?"

"You could say that, sir. He pays for it. But I do the work here." There was an edge of defiance to her voice.

Aritoli turned back to her and examined her hands. The skin was blotched and stained with paint. Paint also lay deep under fingernails that were cracked and torn. There were calluses on fingers bent from holding brushes for hours. These were the hands of an artist.

"So, you paint Sheyn's work for him?"

"Aye, sir." The girl shifted and something metallic clicked and clinked. Looking down, Aritoli saw one of her bare feet was chained to the floor.

"What is your name, child?"

"Vetzah."

"How did this happen, Vetzah?"

"Sheyn said he'd teach me. He found me on the street where I'd draw on the sidewalks with chalk and people would toss me coppers if they liked it. He said I was good and ought to have lessons."

"His training seems rather harsh."

Vetzah lowered her gaze to the floor and nodded. "It sounded so nice, so I let him bring me here. He feeds me and teaches me. Brings me lots of canvas and paint. But he put this chain on me to make sure I stay at my work."

"Did you know he takes the credit for your paintings?"

The girl nodded again. "Old beggarman Rog came by and told me. I got mad at Sheyn when he came in. But he beat me, tellin' me folks would know they're my paintings when

I'm ready. Says it's bad if folks know it's mine before I'm good enough. What do you think? Am I good enough to take my own credit?"

Aritoli solemnly took one of her paint-stained hands and kissed it. "My dear Vetzah, your paintings should decorate the Hall of Arts in the Levar's palace. You have exquisite talent. But, clearly, you have magical talent as well, else you could not have summoned me as you did. Couldn't you have escaped this fate with that?"

"I'm not a wizard, sir. But today's my birthday, and this morning was my birthing-time. I could feel it, all bubblin' and burnin' inside me while I was finishin' the city painting. So, while Sheyn was sleepin', I put that feelin' into the painting. He warned me you were gonna be at the showin', so I just thought how I could tell you to help me and where I was and all. And I just put those thoughts into the painting."

"And you've had such practice at putting your feelings into your work that it no doubt flowed naturally. It is no wonder your paintings are beautiful fantasy landscapes. They were your only avenue to escape this dreary reality. But, never fear, I—"

The door slammed open and Sheyn stood in the doorway, breathing hard and sweating, face pale with fear and rage. "So," he growled softly. "You come to my studio, though I warn you not to." Sheyn took two steps into the room and slammed the door shut behind him.

"Ah! Just the person I wanted to speak to," Aritoli began.

"What do you want?"

"I want to know why, Sheyn. Your reputation was unequaled anywhere. Why . . . this?"

The Zhir said nothing, but walked around the advisor to a table on which lay palettes and brushes. Sheyn reached out slowly to one of the brushes and grasped it as if it were an animal that might escape. Raising it, his hand began to shake, the tremors becoming more and more violent. He grasped his right wrist with his left hand to try to still the trembling. But it continued until, with a gasp, he had to drop the brush.

Sheyn's face contorted as if he were about to cry, and he slammed his fist into the table. "You see?" he whispered. "You see?"

"Disease?" Aritoli asked softly.

"A curse. I did a portrait for Prince Jeng that he did not

like. He thought I insulted him. He asked Shzafakh, court wizard, to curse my hands so I could do no more 'insulting' paintings. Then I was banished. So long as I am cursed, I cannot paint."

"Why didn't you ask someone for help? There are wizards here in Liavek who—"

"I knew no one here! And the shame . . . I could not bear the shame. I hoped if my name was still good, I could borrow a set of hands and earn enough to buy countermagic. Then I would return to Ka Zhir and use my uncursed hands upon Shzafakh's neck!" Sheyn raised his face, his eyes sad and begging. "Please, Master Critic, you will . . . forgive my deception? Tell no one? Let me be, and in time I can repay you—"

Aritoli shook his head. "I'm sorry. I cannot condone what you have done. For one thing, although slavery may be common in Ka Zhir, it is illegal in Liavek. But the greater crime to me is denying this woman the attention she richly deserves. I cannot pretend that I do not know, or forget what I have seen."

"In that case, Master Aritoli," Sheyn said, stepping forward, "I must ensure that you cannnot speak of this to anyone." The artist's fist plowed into Aritoli's middle, knocking him against the wall.

"Stop it, Sheyn!" cried Vetzah.

Desperately trying to regain his breath, Aritoli watched Sheyn advance on him, preparing to strike another blow. Suddenly there came a loud snap, and Sheyn fell to the floor. Vetzah had pulled taut her leg chain, tripping him.

The Zhir picked himself up and snarled at Vetzah, "You! You are street filth! You are chalk dust and lost coppers without me. It is for us both that I do this. Shut up and keep to your place!" Sheyn backhanded Vetzah, sending her crashing against an easel.

Recapturing some air, Aritoli pushed himself up against the wall, knocking over canvasses. As Sheyn came at him again, Aritoli readied himself, briefly wishing he had thought to bring his rapier.

With a quick shift to the left, he managed to dodge Sheyn's fist and struck out with his cane. Sheyn gasped as the beak of the raven's head struck just above his right elbow. As Aritoli hoped, the arm dropped limp to Sheyn's side, temporarily paralyzed with pain. As Sheyn grabbed his right arm with his left hand, Aritoli twisted and struck with the cane again, for the left arm. Again, Sheyn's arm dropped to his side. With a shove of the cane into Sheyn's stomach, Aritoli pushed the artist into the wall, where he sat with a thud.

"Now," said the advisor, "I shall take Vetzah and—"

"How? She is in irons. By the time you find a blacksmith to free her, she and I will slip away like bats on the night wind. There are cities other than Liavek."

Aritoli paused a moment, then opened his hand to show a small, iron key. "Not quite. You see, I have found her key."

Sheyn's eyes flicked instinctively toward a patch of bare bricks high on a wall. Then he frowned, confused, at the key in Aritoli's hand.

"That is to say," the advisor continued, allowing the illusion in his hand to disappear, "that I have found it *now*." He went to the wall and felt for a loose brick. Pulling one out, Aritoli discovered a niche containing a small bag of coins and a key.

"A trick!" snarled Sheyn. "Cursed to Thung be all wizards!"

"With that attitude, you'll never paint again," said the advisor, unlocking Vetzah's leg iron. He helped her stand, then reached inside his shirt. He pulled out a coin purse and added its contents to those of the purse found with the key. This the advisor then tossed into Sheyn's lap. "Number seventeen, Wizard's Row. If you cannot find help there, you'll find it nowhere else." Without another glance in Sheyn's direction, Aritoli took Vetzah's arm and guided her out into the warm Liavekan night.

"I can hardly believe this, Ari," said the Countess ola Klera. "This young woman is the real painter of these beautiful scenes?"

"Yes, I am, Your Grace." Vetzah had only just been brought from Sheyn's rathole of a studio, and she was clearly overawed by the luxury surrounding her.

The countess laughed. "Well, Vetzah, although you are not quite what we expected, under the circumstances it would be unfair of us not to offer you the same patronage we offered Sheyn. Though I'm not sure how we'll explain this to our friends."

"You need only hedge the truth a little," suggested Aritoli. "Say that Sheyn declined your offer of patronage, instead recommending his promising student, Vetzah."

"Yes, I think that will work," said the countess. "Then there will be no surprise at the 'similarity' of their styles. Thank you, Ari. Once more you prove your skill at gracious solutions."

"I thank you, too, sir," said Vetzah. "Can I do anything to repay you?"

The advisor kissed her hand, saying, "You owe me nothing, my dear, save to fill the world with your exquisite art. Oh, and you might, at some point, look to taking lessons in magic. You have talent there too strong to ignore."

The artist nodded, gazing at Aritoli with admiring eyes.

"As to . . . anything else," Aritoli said, raising an eyebrow, "we'll see."

"You are no doubt weary from your ordeal, Vetzah. Come, and I'll see that you are bathed and given fresh clothing. If you will excuse us, gentlemen." The countess nodded to them and led the artist away.

The count stepped closer to Aritoli and said, "Another conquest, Ari? She hardly seems your sort of challenge."

"Actually, I'd rather she spent her emotional energy on her painting. Still . . . we'll see what she looks like when she's cleaned up, eh?" Aritoli winked.

The count sighed and shook his head. "Sometimes, Ari, you make me think the rumor about you is true."

"Which rumor is that?"

"The one that claims whatever god or goddess made you put your heart in your eyes."

Aritoli shrugged and smiled. "It is possible."

"But what of Sheyn, Ari? He did defraud the countess and me, though we lost little—thanks to you. And he did enslave Vetzah. Shouldn't we report him to the Guard?"

"I beg your forbearance in this instance, Meceno. I have given Sheyn the means to regain his own talent, if he will but use it. And if he succeeds, he will be worth more to the world than if he is sent to languish in a cell, or forced into labor to pay off heavy fines."

"I see. But are you certain he will not simply find another talented beggar to be his 'hands'?"

"He knows I will be watching for him. He can no longer trade on his name as he did. Not until the work is indeed by his own hands." Aritoli chuckled. "You know, that is what should have given me the clue in the first place—his hands were clean." The advisor raised a finger to stroke his mustache and noticed that his nail-paint was chipped and flaking off. Examining his palm, he found smudges of paint and dirt from Vetzah's studio. "Speaking of which, Meceno, could you tell me where I might get a good manicure?"

The Green Cat

by Pamela Dean

9 Buds, Rainday, 3317

The first task Verdialos gave me was to keep a journal. That was a year ago, and I have not done it. Whatever troubles drove him to the Green priests, prying and tattling sisters cannot have been among them. The second task was to write down what drove me to the Green priests. I have not done that, either. Since he has trusted me, I had better do both now.

I have been a very long time planning the end of my life. Even before I met Verdialos, this seemed just. I am the last of eight children, and any week-guest in the house can discover that everybody concerned wishes there had been only six. My brother Deleon ran away when he was twelve and I was ten, so they are no longer troubled with him. If I knew where he was, I would have gone to him long since. But he never sent me word. If he is dead, you may say I am going to him soon.

This will have to be translated for its inclusion in the Green Book. I am writing in the Acrivannish of the ninth century—Liavek's thirty-second; unwieldy numbers do not trouble the

Liavekans—which they call Farlandish. They call all the true kingdoms the Farlands and all the languages, old or new, Farlandish. In fact, there are several dozens of countries and more languages, any of them a far more reasonable place to be and a far more melodious sound in the ears than Liavek and its language.

My family all come from there, but none of them can read the older language. My grandmother taught it to me when I was little, so we could have a secret. She, too, thought that eight children were too many, but it was the first six she disliked. She died when I was eight. My diction in this language is limited, because I stopped learning it so young; but I remember it well enough, seven years later. My sisters will think I have secrets, when they find this, but they think so already.

So, then, I am obliged to say what has happened to me this twelvemonth, and what my life was like before to make this twelvemonth happen so. Verdialos and The Magician and I will do the ritual tomorrow, by which time this must be finished. Like my brothers, who went to college to become even sillier than my sisters, I'll stay up all night, swearing and scribbling and drinking bitter tea.

Floradazul just thudded in and thumped onto my cot. She can walk as if she were not there, when she chooses. But because my room is over Livia and Jehane's, and I don't want them to wake up, Floradazul chose to walk as though there were fifty of her.

I hope she will not mind the ritual. Verdialos swears it won't hurt her. If we fail, she will remain only a cat; and I will have peace, however inartistically achieved. He takes her very seriously. She is the responsibility I must not shirk—a thing that has caused the Green priests considerable trouble over the years.

I met Verdialos because of a game Deleon and I used to play. It pleased us to think that, if we sickened and died, or fell into the Cat River during the spring rains, or ran beneath the wheels of a cart while on some distasteful errand, our parents would be sorry they had not loved us while we lived. We pictured gleefully the grief of our mother and father, and the consternation of our brothers and sisters. Even the hopeful imagination of youth could not see our brothers and sisters grieving for us.

We haunted a healer called Marithana Govan, who lived in the Street of the Dreamers and patiently answered all our questions day after day. Then we would go home, and one of us would be afflicted with all the diseases Mistress Govan knew of, while the other played a distraught parent or a jealous brother. During the summer drought, we flung ourselves into the shallow river and were dragged screaming under the raging waters. In streets deserted during the heat of afternoon, we fell shrieking in the dust and were trampled by horses or oxen.

I can't remember exactly when or how these games became serious; or rather, since they were always serious, when they became insufficient. Sometime in the summer of Deleon's eleventh year, we began the ranging about Liavek that I have kept up ever since. We were looking for places in which, rather than having a good chance of being killed, we could kill ourselves. We would look in the early morning, come home to write reproachful notes during the heat, and go back in the evening meaning to do the deed. But there was always an argument, over who went first, whether it would be possible to go together, whether one would die from jumping or merely break a leg, whether the notes were after all written exactly as they ought to be.

It is hard for two children in Liavek to find certain death. The consequences of failing to kill ourselves we did not care to contemplate. We did not think our parents would love us better for causing the neighbors to think we had been made more miserable than parents may rightfully make their children. We had always planned to leave the notes where only our parents could find them: A secret reproach might have softened their hearts, but a public one would have made them glad we were gone.

Verdialos has pointed out to me that it was only after the worst pain of Deleon's absence was past that I turned fourteen—old enough to buy poison. If I had been able to get it one year sooner, I would not be writing this. When I could get it, the pain had lessened, and I had been given Floradazul, who not only loved me but, unlike Deleon, would have been lost without me.

I met Verdialos in the month of Buds in the Liavekan year 3316, on my fifteenth birthday, in the late morning, on the east bank of the Cat River under the Levar's Bridge. I was trying to discover the depth of the water; he was watching for people who thought they had discovered it already. He says that after fifteen years of looking for people who mean to kill themselves, he can tell them by the way they walk.

I had had no luck with long sticks or rocks tied to strings. I had decided that my choices were to find someone, a riverman perhaps, who knew the depths of the Cat River (which would be difficult and oblige me to talk to strangers), or to dive (which would be immodest if I took my clothes off, or drown me before I was ready if I left them on). I could not decide whether to go or stay, and I was furious. I did not hear Verdialos making his way down the bank.

"A good death to you, little sister," he said behind me. He has a light voice that causes people to think him of no account, but he could not have startled me more if he had boomed like a City Guard.

"And a bad one to you!" I snapped, as if he were in fact one of my sisters, jumping out at me from under the stairs.

Although I did not know it then, this is the worst thing you can say to a Green priest, but from being so long among the uninitiated he had grown accustomed to it and was not much shocked.

"And what is a bad death, little sister?" he said.

"Long and painful," I said, happy to be furious with him rather than with the river, which was unreasonable, or with myself, which was unrewarding.

My fury did not vex him. He looked at me thoughtfully, as I have seen Floradazul look at a beetle she knows will taste vile. He was not very tall, like most Liavekans, and had big brown eyes and a hopeful face. He wore a green robe and no jewelry. His hair needed cutting. I wished he would go away.

"But if you chose the pain?" he said.

"Who would do that?" I said, as rudely as I could manage. He seemed to take no notice.

"Perhaps one who thought it would strengthen him for the trials of the afterlife," he answered, just as if we were two men in a tavern discussing philosophy.

"I don't think there is an afterlife."

"But if there were, and it had trials, and pain in this life strengthened one for them, then would not a long and painful death be a good death?"

"Well, I suppose."

"What death are you seeking here?"

"I dropped my necklace in the water."

"I think you must have thrown it," he said, smiling. After a moment I realized that he had seen me fishing further from the shore than one could expect to drop a necklace.

I looked at the ground. After a moment he said, "Why would a man who, not believing in the afterlife and thinking thus to have only this one, hasten to end it?"

I had had the healer on my mind as I went about the city in search of death, and I said to him something I had once heard her say to her assistant. "As a man who has only pain will take a drug to stop it, though it gives him a sleep so deep he cannot even dream, and in time will kill him."

Verdialos opened his eyes very wide, as if someone had dropped a piece of ice down his back. He does this when something startles his mind. (If you drop ice down his back, he hardly moves.)

"This drug," he said, "will dull the senses without killing the pain. It is very shallow to drown so tall a girl."

"What do you recommend, Master?" I said, meaning to show him his presumption.

But he told me: The Green priests are an order of suicides. This idea amused me greatly at first, because it seemed to me impossible. If all of them killed themselves, where was their order? But Verdialos explained to me about the responsibility one must not shirk.

I was walking along a wall once, in the Canal District, talking to Deleon over my shoulder, and he yelled at me to stop, and I did, and just where my next step would have been was a missing stone; and the canal fifteen feet down on one side and a forest of young trees twenty feet down on the other. I felt that same squeezing of my heart now. I might have killed myself one fine day and left Floradazul to be spoiled on Luckday and neglected the rest of the week, never knowing why I had not come back.

There was a great deal Verdialos did not tell me then. But he promised me a certain and beautiful death once I had shown his order that I had no obligations except to myself, and that those I labored under when I met him on the riverbank had been honorably discharged. He gave me a square of paper that had written on it, in an upright hand, an address in Old Town; and scrambled back up to the bridge, smiling at me over his shoulder as if the two of us had just contrived a way to confound the wickedness of Ka Zhir for all time.

I went home feeling as if we had accomplished this. I had only one obligation. In the lightness of the first hope I could remember since my grandmother promised I should come to live with her one day, I thought this obligation would be easily dealt with. It was not.

My parents, who have no use for cats, had allowed me mine on the condition that I would take all responsibility for it. My brothers all affect to hate cats. I think Gillo likes them in his heart, but he would never show this to the others. My sisters are too timid to look after any animal, except Jehane. She truly loves Floradazul, though she will call her Flossie and coo at her as if they were both imbeciles. But she would spoil her for six months, then forget to give her water and go into a decline when she died.

Besides, none of them would take the cat while I was still living in the house; and if I asked any of them to promise to care for her should anything happen to me, either it would be laughed off, and when the time came no one would care for her because everyone thought someone else should do it, or else they would begin to watch me. Given their other faults, it is a great pity that they are not stupid as well.

When I came home they were all sitting in the parlor, reading or knitting. To the despair of our mother, Livia and Jehane and Isobel are no good at embroidery. I cannot even knit. I would have been scolded for going immediately upstairs, so I waited for a moment to pay my respects, rubbing Floradazul's ears.

"Nissy," said my brother Givanni, "that cat of yours has been at my bowstrings again. I'll wrap them around her and choke out all her nine lives if I catch her at it."

"Don't scold your sister on her birthday," said my father.

"Furthermore," said my mother, "if you must solace yourself with superstitions, let them be Acrivannish; don't dull your mind with the fancies of Liavek."

"Separate body and soul and burn the soul, then," Givanni said to me. Watching me, he added, "And make a hat out of the body."

Isobel shuddered, Jehane cast her eyes up, and Livia said, "Who'd wear a fur hat in this climate?"

"You won't catch her," I said.

"Well!" said my father. "If one can believe this highly-colored and dubiously-intended literature, Ka Zhir and Liavek are at each other's throats again."

My mother looked up. "Could you take advantage—"

"We don't want Liavek," said my father, tiredly. "We want to go home. Let Liavek stew; let Liavek rot."

"Not," said my mother, "so long as we have to live in it."

"But it won't be much longer," said Jehane, placidly.

"It's been too long already," said Isobel. "I will not marry a Casalena, and none of the Leptacazes will marry me. And if we all marry here, who'll be left for Nissy?"

"I'm not getting married, so save your worry," I said, startling myself.

"Nissy, what nonsense," said Livia.

"Thank you. I'm glad you approve."

"Nerissa, don't be rude to your sister."

"She was rude to me first."

"What you said *was* nonsense."

"That doesn't mean it's polite to say so!"

"What *are* you going to do, then?" said Jehane.

I picked up Floradazul, who in the sensible manner of cats was about to flee the battlefield, and said the first thing that came into my head. "I'm going to have nine cats and a good library."

"Who is going to pay for them?" asked my father. "I can give you a respectable dowry, but not for cats and books."

"You set Gillo up in trade!" For some reason, men are allowed to be vulgar at certain times and in certain ways. Trade is vulgar; making and selling wine is a trade; yet my parents were pleased when my brother proposed to do so. He was not allowed to have Isobel help him, and was scolded for suggesting it. Remembering this made me angrier.

"Nine cats and a good library," said my father, "are not a trade."

"I'll breed the cats and sell kittens."

"Master Benedicti," said my mother, "I told you we had lived here too long."

"We have nowhere else to go," said my father.

"This child must not ruin what marriage prospects she has with this babble of setting herself up in trade—and such a trade."

"She can hold her tongue when it suits her," said my father, "so you had best see that it suits her."

"I'll go practice now," I said, and went up the stairs, quickly.

Floradazul sat in my lap, purring, while I tried to think of how to provide for her, and worried instead about how my family was likely to provide for me. I had always known that things could only get worse, but from time to time I had forgotten how quickly it was likely to happen. In a year I would be old enough to marry, by our laws; I was already old enough by Liavek's. The boys of the other exiles had been all very well to play with when Deleon was sick or sulky, but they had no real thoughts in their heads and had once thrown a kitten into the river to settle a bet over whether cats could swim before they were grown. That one could not.

I had not met all the exiles, but I was not going to marry any of them. Liavekans were worse, having no manners and being generally either vulgar or inexplicable in their ways. I hated my family, but at least I was used to them. The idea of changing to a new hate was distressing. It was time to be gone.

The matter of Floradazul occupied me for three days, until I remembered from whom I had had her. Granny Carry's house had been crawling with cats, though how she kept them out of her weaving was a mystery to me. My sisters used to get out of doing their needlework by claiming that Floradazul would give them no peace when they tried to work at it, which was perfectly true, if they were foolish enough to try doing it in the same room with her. In any case, Granny would hardly notice one cat more or less; and she was much too busy to ask awkward questions.

I was so pleased with this solution that, it having come to me in the early morning, I called Floradazul at once. She always comes when I call; she comes when the others call if she thinks they have food or feels I've been too long away. I packed her into her basket and ran quickly out the back door before anyone should ask where I was going.

Granny Carry lives on the Street of Trees. Although she is a blood-relation of my mother, Granny is not my grandmother, and I am not sorry. My mother finds her exasperating, and this is perhaps the only matter in which my mother and I agree. She does not visit us often, and some of us always visit her briefly on the great festivals—Liavek's, not ours. I had not seen her since she gave me the kitten; Jehane, who likes her, has gone in my place since then. I am surprised Jehane likes her. She speaks so freely, and Jehane is so easily shocked. I do not care to argue with Granny: When dignity and decency are upset, it is never she who is discomforted.

Thinking of that as I walked along the Cat River heading

for the Levar's Park, I felt less pleased. If for any reason she would not take the cat, what could I say to her? I remembered that, whenever she saw me, she used to give me a sharp look, as if I had said something under my breath and she knew it was cheeky. I wonder now whether she knew, long before I thought of it, what I meant to do.

The street was so quiet I could hear the clack and thud of the loom inside the house. Her azaleas were shiny and smug-looking. Mine had died last year. I knocked on the door. The loom stopped, and after a moment a shuffling and tapping came close, and she opened the door.

She looked the same as she had when she gave me the kitten: brown and wrinkled, with very bright eyes, her white hair braided and wound around her head in the style Isobel called "snakes," before she became so foolish that merely to hear the word sends her into a faint. Granny was not much smaller than I. She wore a robe of her own weaving; it had been on the loom when she gave me the kitten, unbleached cotton with an intricate border. I would have given a great deal to have woven it myself.

"Are you a Benedicti, or a Casalena?" she asked, when, lost in thought, I did not greet her. She might have been asking whether I was a thief or merely a beggar. "Or are you pale from the heat?"

When she looked at me, I remembered that I had told the maid to go away when she offered to dress my hair, that there was cat hair on my tunic and skirt, and that I had mended my left sandal by tossing the cracked wooden buckle into a drawer and replacing it with a gold one from a worn-out pair I had not liked to throw away. Well, at least she would think badly of my upbringing when I told her my name.

"I'm Nerissa Benedicti." She did not look welcoming, so I added, "I've come about my cat."

"I suppose you'd better come in before you do faint."

I followed her in and opened the basket. Floradazul, who has very good manners, did not jump out before she was invited, but made an inquiring noise. I wished she were less endearing.

"Greetings, Floradazul," said Granny Carry, smiling for the first time. Floradazul jumped straight into her lap and began her best purr. I could not tell whether I was more put out by that, or by Granny's remembering the cat's name when she had forgotten mine. Sometimes Floradazul's judgment is not what it might be. At least she should be glad to live with Granny again.

"Is she sick?" said Granny, rubbing her between the ears. "She doesn't look it. Pregnant?"

I was shocked, but hoped not to show it. "She's very well. I want to give her back to you."

"Why, what's this? Does she scratch your sisters?"

"Serve them right if she did. She's a very good cat; but I can't do with a cat anymore."

"And why not?"

"I'm too busy."

She looked at me as if I were about to eat an azalea. Then I saw I ought to have said that Floradazul scratched my sisters, or that my parents didn't like finding a pile of dead rats on the doorstep once or twice a week. In fact they did not, but I would never have given away the cat for any annoyance she was sensible enough to cause my family. And now Granny knew that. Yes, I was stupid.

"She's no trouble," said Granny, "but you're tired of her."

"Yes."

Floradazul chose this moment to jump to the floor and push the top of her head against my ankle. For the first time in her life, I ignored her. If I could treat my only friend like this, it would certainly be better to die.

Granny seemed to agree with the basic sentiment, if not with the particulars. "Young woman," she said, "one does not give a cat away. Ever."

"You gave her to me!"

"She wasn't mine. She lived in my house because her mother did. You accepted her; you took her home; you have lived with her these four years. This is your cat."

"But I can't—"

"You must. I certainly can't take her back. She'd pine for you. And it would spoil you for life, letting you get away with giving a cat back. Murder and blackmail and marrying for money would be nothing to it."

I decided that she had gone mad, being so old and living by herself with only a loom and some cats and azaleas. I could hardly leave my cat with a crazy woman. I got up, and Floradazul jumped into the basket, making a few remarks about my sudden haste.

"I'm sorry to have taken your time." I picked up the basket.

"I'd have been sorrier to have taken your cat." She stood up and saw me to the door.

"Fare well," I said politely.

"Mend your ways," she said, as if it were a common courtesy, and slammed the door.

I felt bruised in my mind and therefore tried not to use it. Not using it, I thought suddenly that I might leave the cat with Snake. I was halfway to the Tiger's Eye already. It would be a long walk home, but later was always better for going home.

I knew Snake's name because I had heard an occasional customer, and later her assistant Thyan, call her by it. I had never spoken to her. Isobel tells me that when there were fewer children in the family, my mother used to take the elder girls there to buy gifts for our festivals. She says Snake was gracious but did not smile much, which is still true. Isobel (who was the best of us at listening on the stairs after she was supposed to be in bed, and who has kept it up the longest) also tells me that Snake is one of the Liavekan nobility. It is just like them to let someone of that class keep a shop.

I have never bought anything at the Tiger's Eye myself: Not only are the prices high, but one must bargain down even to those, and bargaining is not a skill in which any of my family has been instructed. In the true kingdoms no citizen would stoop to argue with a shopkeeper.

I haunted the Tiger's Eye when I was younger, pretending to look at the merchandise and looking at Snake. I can hardly remember, now, what fascination she held for me. There was a time when I wished earnestly to be a Liavekan, and perhaps she is the sort of Liavekan I wished to be, in her slender dark solemn looks and her conduct if not in her occupation. I do remember the deadly jealousy that gripped me when Thyan came, although considerable thought never produced a clear idea of what, exactly, I was jealous of. I did not want to be a Tichenese bond servant; I did not want to work in a shop, being pleasant to strangers, or even being acerbic with them in a way they could not dispute; I did not want to work with beautiful things. Servitude is disgraceful and trade vulgar, I am afraid of strangers, and beautiful things are afraid of me, knowing that having once come into my hands they are not long for this world.

The Tiger's Eye, as always, was shockingly cool and instantly overwhelming. In truth, Snake's shop is spacious. But I feel there, always, as though the merest breath could knock something priceless into rubble.

I felt this more strongly with a basket of cat on my arm. I looked around. Snake was not there. Thyan, behind the counter, was eyeing the basket, so I went up to her. I thought her raisin-colors of cats. Most people would have said grey and white. but they look more natural among the Liavekans than my flour-like face and hair like old butter.

"Do you think I could leave this here while I look?" I said.

"I was hoping you'd ask," she said. "Will it fit under the window?"

I set it down and propped up the lid. Floradazul put her nose out and looked inquisitive.

"Rikiki's nuts!" said Thyan, violently. I looked to see what I had broken, but she was staring at the cat.

"It's all right, she won't jump out unless she's asked," I said, but a feeling of vast defeat had settled on me. No one can own a cat and a shop full of breakables. I had been mad to come here. In my disappointment, feeling nothing mattered, I found my tongue loosened.

"I'm sorry, I should have thought just to measure her neck with a piece of string. But she's quite safe."

Thyan was still staring, now at me, so I plunged on. "You do sell collars for cats?"

"I think they're for monkeys," said Thyan, "but we might find one that would do. What color did you have in mind? What is she—blue and cream, with green eyes. Green, do you think?"

I was impressed that she knew the proper words for the colors of cats. Most people would have said grey and white. But I only said, "Yes, and simple, so she won't catch it on something and choke herself."

Thyan led me to the back of the store.

"Do people ever bring their monkeys to be fitted?" I asked her. I could not seem to keep quiet. Perhaps I was afraid she would ask me something.

"Thank all the gods they don't," she said over her shoulder. "People who own monkeys delight in mess."

She opened a carved wooden box about the size of a cradle and began taking out collars. They came in every color, and most of them were gaudy with jewels and bangles and bells.

Thyan grinned at me. "You see?" she said.

"No bells, either, I think." I got down and helped her rummage. After considerable giggling and exclaiming, which ought to have disgusted me by its similarity to the behaviour of my sisters, we found a green leather collar with three opals and a plain silver buckle.

"That," said Thyan, dropping it into my palm and beginning to pile the other collars back into their box, "is probably the mistaken work of some apprentice who hasn't learned how to attach these abominable bangles."

"Well, the stitching is perfectly regular. How much is it?"

"A half-levar."

"Thyan," I said, forgetting myself entirely, "those are opals."

"My dear Mistress Benedicti," she said, "they are not good opals. The shape is wrong."

"Well," I said, furious for forgetting my manners and calling her by her name when she had not even told it to me, "you should know." Then I thought, we are bargaining backward; it is I who must denigrate the collar and make her lower the price. Are we both mad?

"It will be a little more," Thyan said, slamming the box shut and taking the collar to the front of the shop, "if I have to exercise my rare skills and bore another hole in it. This looks a little large for a cat."

She held her hand out to Floradazul, who was sitting bolt upright in the basket with her nose quivering. I wondered if there were mice in the store. Thyan, I noticed, held her hand properly below the cat's head. Floradazul sniffed briefly and rubbed the side of her head against Thyan's first finger. Thyan held the collar out and let her sniff that, too. It was a great pity I could not give her the cat; she knew just how to treat them.

"But then, this is a large cat," said Thyan, fastening the collar. Floradazul twisted her head around several times, trying to see what was around her neck, and then gave up the attempt as lacking dignity.

I felt in the pocket of my skirt for the money I had saved to join Deleon when he sent me word, and then brought along to give Granny to help pay for the cat's board. I counted out half a levar in coppers and half-coppers.

"Lovely," said Thyan, "we never have enough coppers."

I thought that if I told her my given name, it would not

have been so rude to call her by hers, but that took more courage than I had.

"Thank you very much," I said, and picked up the basket.

"You're both welcome here any day," she said, and turned to deal with two young boys who seemed torn between buying their mother a bracelet and wrestling among the Tichenese glassware. I went out into the blazing afternoon.

I came home with a headache and the beginnings of a sunburn. The usual dull weight of hopelessness was back, and seemed heavier for having been away.

The household was in an uproar. All my sisters were crying in the hall; Marigand had come with her husband so she could cry with them. Her husband and my father and brothers were talking furiously in the parlor. The maid and the cook were wailing in the kitchen. My mother was sitting in the parlor, looking as she had when Isobel refused to marry Hanil Casalena: as angry as it is possible for someone to look who refuses either to frown or to throw things. It occurred to me, not for the first time, that though all the things my mother taught my sisters, and tried to teach me, make a girl insufferably silly, my mother is not in the least silly herself. If she had not tried to make me so, I might be fond of her.

Floradazul leaped out of the basket the moment I opened it, and streaked up the stairs to my room to be out of the tumult. I would have liked to follow her. I went out to the courtyard and found Cinnamon, who does errands for the cook and the maid when he is not learning carpentry from his master. He refuses to tell anyone his Tichenese name or choose a Liavekan one, so he is called for the color of his eyes. He always knows what is happening, although it doesn't do to let him know you think so.

"What is the matter with them?" I asked him.

"All the pale ones have gone back overseas," he said.

"Well, we haven't."

"You and the Casalenas. The new king pardoned everyone else, but not your father, because your father killed his father; and not the Casalenas, because your sister married one."

He looked at me to see how I would take it, but he did not seem altogether pleased with his news.

"Thank you, Cinnamon," I said, having been taught to be polite to servants, and I went back into the house and upstairs.

Floradazul was washing herself but chirruped at me as I

came in. I felt as though someone had told me that water was no longer wet. My father had been the leader of the exiles. That they would so much as consider a pardon that did not include him—that they would consider any pardon rather than waiting until they could bring sufficient force to establish themselves in the thrones and council of Acrivain—was impossible. This was also the first I had heard of my father's having killed the old king. It did not make me like him any better.

"Well," I said to Floradazul, "that was the last dream."

She yawned at me as if to say she had thought very little of it all along. I wondered what I had meant, and then I knew. Returning to Acrivain, had we accomplished it soon, might have been an escape. My mother's rule might have been less oppressive, my father's prejudices more harmonious, my family's foolishness almost sensible, in their proper setting. There might even have been some young man who had manners but had not, in his boyhood, thrown kittens into rivers.

Well, I would never meet him now. I found the scrap of paper Verdialos had given me and went out by the back way.

The Green priests have a house rather than a temple, in the extreme northeastern tip of the Old Town on the Avenue of Five Mice. Verdialos says the name refers not to actual mice, but to some political satire wherein five officials of the old Green Temple were likened to mice.

The House of Responsible Life is large and square, three-storied, and plastered a pale green half grown-over with ivy. It takes up the entire eastern side of the block between Neglectful Street and the Street of Thwarted Desire. It has many small doors, but at the middle of the block a double wooden one stood open, so I went up the three green steps and inside.

It felt, that first time, like a warehouse, or some similar place where business is done with a great deal of mathematics.

Two young Liavekan women, perhaps a year or two older than I, sat at a table to the left of the door. One of them wore a green robe, and the other an exceedingly immodest green tunic. They looked at me unsmiling, but with a sort of welcome.

"Good death to you," said the immodest one. "May we answer your questions?"

"Good death to you," I said, suppressing a foolish urge to say, "and the sooner the better." This first greeting felt strange on my tongue. "My name is Nerissa Benedicti, and I've come to see Verdialos."

"He's waiting for you," said the modest one, "behind the fifth door to your right."

I did not like what she said—whether she meant that he had been waiting since he met me on the bridge, or that he had known when I was coming. He never would tell me which, if either, was the case. When I told him he had too great a sense of fun for a confirmed suicide, he promised me that, once my death was determined, I would have one myself.

At that first meeting, as at all the others, he gave me tea and honey-cakes and melons the Green priests had grown themselves. Once he made it clear to me that it was my duty, however painful, to talk to him, and to tell him all about my family and myself, I found it much pleasanter than anyone would have imagined. Well, anyone besides Jehane, I suppose. She will talk to anybody about anything; I once heard her telling Cinnamon what she remembered about Deleon. She got most of it wrong.

I had hoped Verdialos would offer to take the cat himself, or say he knew an old woman with five cats who would gladly take another. But he only sat there nodding and grimacing and running his hands through his shaggy hair while I told him of everything I had tried and thought of. He was not impressed, either. He seemed to think anybody would have done the same thing, tramping all over Liavek in the heat and talking to strangers.

"So I don't know what to do," I told him at last.

"I will tell you this much," he said. "You are made for this order. I have never heard of someone starting so young."

"Perhaps all the rest of them succeeded," I said.

"Ah, but that is why you are made for this order. You were not content merely with success. We can give you success with honor and elegance."

"As soon as I provide for the cat."

"That is true."

"Well, then, I must leave it to luck." This is an Acrivannish saying, which means "leave it to chance." But in Liavek, luck means magic. Verdialos leaned forward and spilled his tea.

"Nerissa, have you invested your luck?"

"No. Holy Sir, what if I were to invest it in the cat? Then I would die when she did!"

"Perhaps in the Farlands you would," he said. "Here you would merely sicken, and your luck would be lost."

"But I might die?"

"You might. We cannot deal here with might."

He looked as if he had made a joke, but I did not know what it was. I was sure he was wrong. "Cook told me a story once," I said. "About a magician who invested his luck in a magic ring, and because his luck was in it, it could not be hammered or melted or in any way destroyed. But his enemies labored long years and they made a potion from the most fiery parts of the venom of the most venomous of snakes and spiders and the little mouse no longer than your finger that lives at the borders of Ka Zhir. And they suborned his gardener—"

Verdialos spilled his tea again. "Wait," he said. "Wait. That was Tellin. His luck was not invested, Nerissa. It was bound. And that is why the ring was so hard to destroy. And why, when they did destroy it, he died. Not invested. Bound."

"Well, then!"

Verdialos put his empty glass out of harm's way and looked at me with his hopeful eyes. "Only master magicians can bind their luck. You had better begin soon."

I almost said, "Yes, Holy Sir," and went away. But something in his face made me think first.

"No," I said. "It's not certain. I might die investing my luck or in studying along the way, and then what would happen to the cat? How can I even think of doing something as dangerous as studying magic, until she is safe?"

"How can she be safe," said Verdialos, "unless your luck is bound to her?"

"But, Holy Sir—"

"My name is Verdialos." When I did not answer, he added, "Or Dialo, if that's easier. It's what my wife calls me."

"Your *wife!*" I wished I had not talked so freely to him.

"Well?"

"How could anybody marry a committed suicide!"

"She is one also," said Verdialos. "Our deaths are tied to one another—in ways I am not allowed to speak of."

"Dialo. If I could bind my luck to my cat, so I would die when she did—would your order accept that?"

"Our order would be honored."

"Perhaps we could consult some magician."

"I think we could," said Verdialos, in his unemphatic voice. "The Magician, in fact."

I looked at him. "You knew all along!"

"But you did not."

"You ought to have been a philosopher."

"I am one," he said. "And being one, I think it better to visit The Magician after we have set matters in order here. I am required to see you five more times. When can you come again?"

When I came out it was close to supper time. I was so far north that to use the Levar's Highway would take me twice as far as I needed to go. I did not know the streets here. Deleon had known a shortcut from Drinker's Gate to the Levar's Park that would take me in the proper direction, but I was not sure I could remember it. Besides, someone might have built or taken down a wall or terrace since then, or the people with the fishpond might, since our last visit that way, have gotten a large dog.

While I hesitated in the street, and the shadows grew longer, an enormous voice called, "Hey, ghostie!"

This is what the Liavekans call us. It used to make me furious, but I do not think they mean much by it, except that we are lighter than they are. I used to think they were mocking our downfall in Acrivain, but they do not even know about it. Most of them are more stupid than cruel.

Certainly this was true of the one who had yelled at me. He is called Stone and looks like a statue carved by an apprentice gifted with too much granite and too little sense of proportion. He is a corporal in the Levar's Guard. I have never seen him without his lieutenant, who is called Rusty. Rusty is not stupid, and if he is cruel he has never shown it. They know me from my wandering days with Deleon, when they often shooed us out of dangerous places and occasionally took us home. Deleon hated them, even when I told him that they were only doing for us what most children would have liked.

They stopped a decent distance away from me. Liavekans mostly stand too close to you, and Stone sometimes still did if Rusty didn't prevent him, but Rusty seems to understand how things ought to be done.

"What are you doing way up here?" Stone asked me.

"Up where?" I said, before I thought.

Stone looked confused, and Rusty gave me a perfect you-ought-to-know-better look: My mother would have envied it.

"Is it very dangerous?" I asked Stone, to make up for confusing him.

"No," said Stone, "but the priests are crazy."

"They find us a lot of runaways," said Rusty.

"Who won't go home," said Stone, morosely.

"Well, I'm not a runaway and I am going home."

"How's that cat?" asked Rusty. He might stand where he belonged, but he would never let you leave when you wanted to. On the other hand, Floradazul liked him.

"She's well, thank you." I looked at him with sudden hope. Perhaps he wanted a cat.

"I've been thinking," said Rusty, and I almost took him by the hand, "that when I've lost an arm or a leg and retired, I'd like a cat."

If I could have chewed the arm or the leg off then and there, I would have done it. It did not help that he was looking at me as if I ought to have liked what he said.

Stone snorted. "You'd have to lose your head," he said.

We both stared at him.

"Good evening," I said, and hurried off in the wrong direction, towards the Street of Thwarted Desire. Stone's laughter followed me around the corner.

Deleon and I had occasionally had a fancy to kill ourselves in Wizard's Row, but had never found it by looking for it. We had found ourselves passing through it once or twice, and I promise by any god you care to name that the very pavement was soft to the feet. We might have contrived to smother ourselves in it, but that was the only form of death its cushiony appearance left us. Usually it was not there at all.

With Verdialos, I saw it as we came along Healer's Street. It sat between Bregas Street and the Street of Scales, just as it ought, looking solid and a little dusty. I supposed that, when it was not there, the spring rains could not wash the dust off.

"It's not very impressive," I said, more to my anxious heart than to the priest.

"Be flattered," he said dryly. "They do not think us impressionable."

We trudged along. I left the looking to Verdialos, since he had not seen fit to tell me to which house we were going.

"Or perhaps they do," he said.

He stopped, so I did too, and we looked at the house on our left. It glowed a brilliant and pulsing green. Its window frames were warped; I looked more closely, and saw that they were made of bones. Skulls sat on the gateposts. Little skeletons of gargoyles grinned from the roof. The gutters held themselves to the walls with bony hands. The house number squirmed and writhed, but remained 17. I did not look too closely; I was afraid that it was made of worms. I knew only a few of the plants growing in the front garden, but these persuaded me that every one of them was poisonous. The hedge was of yew, which startled me. In Acrivain, we plant this tree in the graveyards and make much of it. In Liavek, it is just a tree.

"Trav, it isn't funny!" said Verdialos.

The house made no reply. Verdialos put his hand on my shoulder and we went up the cracked walk to the door. All the flagstones were carved with names, dates, bad poetry, and an occasional startlement: "All things considered, I'd rather be in Ka Zhir," or "I told you I was sick!" I decided that I would ask the Green priests to cremate my body. The two urns on either side of the green door were not half as disturbing as the gravestones.

There was a brass gargoyle head in the middle of the brass door. Both were badly tarnished: that is, they were green. Verdialos jerked the gargoyle's tongue, and I jumped backwards off the porch, because it opened its eyes and made a face worthy of Isobel at her most malicious.

"He doesn't like girls," it said melodiously.

"That's not true," said Verdialos, "nor is it relevant. I am not bringing him one."

"What's that, then?"

I had never seen Verdialos flustered. Perhaps he, too, had disliked the worms.

"Can't we go to the back door?" I whispered.

"On no account. The one there is worse." He thumped the gargoyle atop the head and said, "I'm bringing her to talk to him, Gogo. Now let us in."

"He doesn't like talking."

"Does he like money?"

The gargoyle was silent.

"I'm bringing him a great deal of money, and he knows it, or he wouldn't have gotten himself up like this."

"He hates women who walk backward," said the gargoyle, but it flattened itself back into the door, which opened.

I had expected the inside of the house to be worse than the outside, but it was spacious, light, and airy. There was a great deal of marble and polished wood, but not much ornament.

"Trav!" said Verdialos. "Must I jingle the coins for you?"

A man came down the long central hall. He wore a green robe and tarnished brass bracelets. He looked remarkably like one of my brothers: He was darker than they, but much lighter than most Liavekans. He had pale brown hair like theirs, and was much the same height as Givanni. He seemed about Gillo's age, except for something in his eyes. He looked like a clerk for the Green priests, which would have explained what was in his eyes, and he looked nothing whatever like a wizard.

"Nerissa," said Verdialos, "this is Trav, The Magician, whose fame meets itself on the other side of the world. Master, this is Nerissa Benedicti. Together, I think we bring you a challenge."

I spread my dusty skirts and bent my knee to him, as I had been taught when I was little. He bowed to me, in the manner of Acrivain. I thought of the yew hedge, and wondered how he knew. Anyone can guess where my family comes from, but very few care to know which kingdom thereof, or its customs. The Magician looked at Verdialos.

"I thought your order forbade magical suicides."

This was the first I had heard of that, and I felt as if someone had hit me over the heart.

"This one," said Verdialos, "has such a high degree of originality that we have made an exception."

I stared at him in outrage, of which he took no notice. I had told him everything, and he had allowed me to believe that, except for the death-tie with his wife, he had done the same for me.

"You will also make a precedent," said the Magician.

"It would be worth it."

The Magician smiled. "Tell me about it, then."

Verdialos explained the matter.

"Have you invested your luck?" The Magician asked me.

"No, my lord." We have few magicians overseas, and this is what we call them. My father says it is to make up for causing them so much discomfort in other ways.

"Have you practiced magic at all?"

"Well, I used to play jokes on my sisters, or try to cover up my scrapes—you know how children do on their birthdays, my lord." He did not look as if he did, so I went on, "But I've never practiced it seriously, thinking to become a magician; I haven't done even a joke for years. It's a great indignity to be sent to bed without your own birthday dinner."

He looked less than understanding; it occurred to me that Liavekans might have some other method of celebrating their birthdays. They are peculiar folk. I wished I had not said so much. Verdialos was making me forget how to hold my tongue—and holding his all the while!

"How long is your luck period?"

"Four and a half hours," I said, bitterly. This is what comes of being the youngest. Marigand, with twenty-eight hours, might have made a splendid magician, but she preferred giggling and marriage.

"When is your birthday?"

"Buds tenth, my lord."

"And this but the fifteenth of Wine. Well." He looked vaguely around the hall and beckoned to us. "Come and sit down. This is not a standing matter."

We followed him into a room little less bare than the hall, with a fountain in the middle. We sat on ivory benches. Each seemed to be all of a piece, and I wondered what beast they were the bones of.

The Magician looked at me. "I have never bound luck to a living thing," he told me. "There is no intrinsic reason that it cannot be done, barring the fundamental and idiotic danger, which is just what you want. Now. Four and a half hours is sufficient time for me to bind my luck, supposing I should wish to do so. The question is whether, in four and a half hours, I can bind yours."

"I was not certain a method existed," said Verdialos.

"A method exists for doing most things," said The Magician, dryly. "Most of the methods, however, have as their incidental results occurrences rendering the original object useless. A method does exist whereby a master magician may bind another's luck for him. It is seldom attempted. Its nature is to destroy both parties. In fact, it usually destroys the younger, because the elder's instincts provide a protection the younger cannot yet command. If the elder were exceedingly strong and insanely unselfish, he might protect the younger and be destroyed himself. I am strong, but far from unselfish. However, you wish to be destroyed, so all will be well regardless."

"Trav," said Verdialos, "she must not be destroyed except in the manner of her choice. How great is the risk?"

"Considerable," said The Magician, "but why should not this, as well as the other, be the manner of her choice?"

"It lacks elegance," said Verdialos. "I am afraid, Nerissa, that you must take the long road, learn magic, and do the binding yourself."

"I can't wait that long!"

"We have ways to make it easier."

I was still outraged at his having kept things from me. "Dialo, I'll be perfectly happy to go back to the old way and throw myself off a bridge."

"And what would happen to your cat then?"

We glared at one another; for the first time, I hated him.

"I'll take the cat," said The Magician, "if I fail to protect you."

"You!" said Verdialos. I wasn't sure whether he was surprised, or just calling The Magician the worst thing he could think of.

"I have two of my own," The Magician told me. "Come, see if they have been beaten and starved."

He whistled. Two cats darted into the room, skidding a little on the polished floor.

"This is Chaos," he told me, "and this is Disorder." Chaos was black; Disorder was every color a cat can be, in wild combination.

They sniffed my outstretched hand politely and jumped into The Magician's lap. I saw that he understood the scratching of ears and chin, and how to disengage an inadvertent claw from one's garment.

He scooped up Chaos and put him into my lap. I stroked him, and he looked uncomfortable.

"Thump him lightly with the flat of your hand," advised The Magician.

"That's for dogs, isn't it?"

"He isn't a smart cat," said The Magician.

I beat lightly on the cat's flank, as if he were an extremely sensitive drum. He began to purr.

Verdialos, who must be excused from not liking cats, because they make him wheeze, stood up and said to The Magician, "Well?"

"Jingle your coins, then," said The Magician.

"Ten levars."

The Magician's eyebrows went up, but he said, "Fifteen."

"Thirteen."

"You're mad."

"Thirteen and a half."

"You're madder. Done."

"Why mad?"

"What do you hope to accomplish?"

"Intellectual beauty," said Verdialos, quite soberly.

"That may be had for less."

"Not in material accomplishment," said Verdialos.

I was rapidly failing to understand what they were talking about. I had begun by thinking that they liked one another, but I was no longer sure.

The Magician put Disorder on the floor and stood up. "When is your natal period?" he asked me.

"From just before midday."

"And your birth-moment?"

"Half past the fourth hour after midday."

"If you and your mentor would oblige me by being here an hour before midday on the tenth of Buds, I think we shall do very well. Now. At what are you talented?"

"Nothing," I said, glaring at him, "or I would not be here."

"Can you dance or sing?"

"No, my lord."

"Sew? Weave? Paint? Sculpt?"

"No!"

"Invent stories?"

"Well—"

"Do so, then. Invent one about a cat, if you please." He gave me a piercing look. "Have you younger sisters?"

"I am one."

He gave me another look. I felt turned inside out. "Invent a story about a cat that you would like to have had one of your sisters invent for you."

"What must happen, my lord?"

"Nothing. But as you invent, consider in your mind what you wish this ritual to accomplish. There must be a cat in it."

He thought for a moment. I was grateful that he looked at his hands while he did it.

"There must be mice in it also," he told me, "also a ball, a camel, a gun, and someone who cuts his hair."

"What!"

"And what do you wish to be the purpose of the magical artifact?"

"My lord?"

"What do you wish the purpose of the cat to be? You are creating a magical artifact; it must be able to do something for you that neither you nor it—nor she—could do alone."

"It hardly matters." I wondered how he knew Floradazul was she.

"Certainly it matters. We must provide for all contingencies. Suppose you were to die before the cat does. She is, after all, a very young cat."

And how did he think he knew that? "She's four years old, my lord."

"Only once," said The Magician.

"Once is enough to be young," I said, wondering why we were suddenly philosophical.

"Well," said Verdialos, "what are cats good for?"

"Cats are good spies," I said. "Could I be able to see what she sees, and hear what she hears—and understand it as I would if I were there, instead of however she understands things?"

The Magician frowned. "The seeing is easy; the understanding I will endeavor to contrive." He stood up. "One hour before midday, six months hence. My duty to you," he said, which is the farewell of an artist to his patron in all the true kingdoms.

He strode out the room's opposite door, and Verdialos and I returned the way we had come, through the arch of bones and along the walk of tombstones. We were not comfortable with one another. We had entered this place allies, and I did not know what we were now.

The week after we had struck our bargain with The Magician, I went to work for the Green priests, to pay them back the thirteen and a half levars.

They gave me the job of copying their old and crumbling manuscripts in a clean and modern hand so they could send the matter to the printers without being first cursed and then charged a fee comparable to The Magician's. They did not mind my bringing Floradazul with me. She caught the mice that chewed on the scrolls, and even the unfortunate old woman whose desk she chose to pile the bodies on thought the mess a fair payment. Once a week or so Floradazul would rampage around the building with her tail fluffed up, knocking flat the tottery bamboo shelves they kept the scrolls on, tripping up the unwary clerks on the stairs, and pretending to mistake someone's sandalled foot for a mouse. She never attacked a booted foot, which circumstance cast doubt on my assertions that she meant no harm. Whether her depredations among the mice were worth this periodic disturbance was a matter for much debate, but it had not been settled when the time came for Verdialos and me to make our visit to The Magician.

I finished the story three days ago. I have called it "The Green Cat." I wrote it about a little girl who cut off her long hair to make a bed for a kitten, and found that for this gift the kitten, who was a young woman enchanted into this form by a magician for refusing his suit, would bring her news she could profit by. I had some trouble fitting in the camel and the gun, especially since I know nothing of guns, but I managed in the end.

Jehane found the story yesterday. She said she was looking for a bracelet she thought I might have borrowed. I do not wear jewelry, and if I did would not keep a borrowed bracelet in a box of old sandals and outgrown hats. That she liked the story and wished I would write another did not make me like her any better.

Floradazul has jogged my arm for the fifth time, to tell me that I must come to bed so she can sleep on my feet. It is best not to deny a cat.

11 Buds, Sunday, 3317

I thought that remark a fine one to be my last, but it was not my last, and it seems unlikely that I will ever again be in a position so to plan my final words. I am at the mercy of a cat I could not deny if I would. This comes, I suppose, of not thinking things through, a thing my mother has often chided me for.

I slept very well, probably because I thought it would be my last chance to do it and I have always loved to sleep. Floradazul woke me at the usual time (two hours before noon) and in the usual way (by biting my nose).

"I'll wager," I told her, "that The Magician does not suffer his cats to bite him on the nose when he has been working until the crack of dawn." She returned me a thoughtful and ambiguous remark.

I got up and dressed in a green tunic that was too long and a green skirt that was too short, the former having belonged to Isobel until she grew too wide for it, and the latter having belonged to Livia until she spilled wine on it and decided that I had bumped her elbow.

Verdialos was walking furiously along Bregas Street when I saw him; as I watched, he turned the corner onto Healer's Street with a vicious flapping of his robe. I floundered after him and caught him on his way back. His mouth was set.

"I can't find it!" he greeted me. "For the first time since—well."

I looked over my shoulder and there it was, in its squat and dusty guise.

"The Magician has taken a fancy to you," said Verdialos.

"I can't help that. Anyway, what does it matter?"

"It will matter if you survive the ritual and continue to work for us."

I shrugged before I thought, and Verdialos scowled at me. "I have taught you badly," he said. "I thought you so well suited in your nature that I neglected to properly inform your thinking."

"Well, maybe you'll have lots of time to inform it."

"And maybe not. I do not like to think of you going to your death in this frame of mind. It will not help your case with the gods."

"Which god do you believe in, Verdialos?"

"I have seen Irhan and Rikiki," said Verdialos, slowly, "and I have not studied any of the others so well as to be able to say I believe or I do not."

"Well, we've only one in Acrivain, and I don't believe in it. I don't think my mother does, either. She has more sense than my father."

"None of us has half so much sense as the cat," said Verdialos. "How in all our talking could I have taken your knowledge of the gods for granted?"

"It's time to go in," I said, and started down Wizard's Row.

Verdialos followed me. Number 17 had a yew tree in its front garden, but was otherwise undistinguished. We went up a cracked green marble walk, and Verdialos pulled on the gargoyle's tongue.

"You who are about to die, salute me," it said.

Verdialos drew back his hand as if he would strike it, but I was amused, and bent my knee to it as well as I could in my too short skirt.

"Verdialos," said the gargoyle, "you are too proud."

"That," said Verdialos, sounding caught between anger and laughter, "is what the camel said to the Empress."

"What Empress?"

"Let us in, and I'll ask your master to tell you."

The door swung open, and The Magician's cats walked away from us down the long central hall. From the basket, Floradazul made a low snarling sound, like the grate of stone on stone. They took no notice. We followed them into a little room, where The Magician stood wearing white and strewing dried green leaves in a circle. Besides him, the cats, and the leaves, the room held only dozens of green candles, still unlit.

"You come most carefully upon your hour," said The Magician.

Verdialos snorted. "Master," he said, "if we were to say to you, we have changed our minds, this ritual is needless, what portion of our money would you return to us?"

I was outraged.

The Magician looked at him with a sort of alert amusement, and said, "Return to you?"

"Our minds are as they were," said Verdialos.

I wondered if I should be even more outraged. Was Verdialos playing some game with The Magician, or in sober fact was my favor with the gods not worth, to Verdialos, the money he had paid?

"Nerissa," said The Magician, "leave the basket in the hall, if you please, and bring the cat and the story here into the center."

I did this. Floradazul hissed at Chaos and Disorder and walked in circles in my lap. The Magician whistled, and his two cats left.

"Will you administer the last rite, priest?"

Verdialos looked at him in uncomprehending annoyance. I wondered how he knew that our Acrivannish god wanted its priests to say a ritual over the dying so that it would know they were coming. Perhaps he knew everything.

The Magician knelt on the floor next to me. "How long is your story?"

I showed him the four thin sheets. I can write very small. He turned them over in his hands, settled back, and read through them. Floradazul climbed into my lap, wound herself into a circle, and put a front paw over her face. She was bored.

The Magician looked at me. His dark eyes had gold specks in them, and there was a small round scar above his right eyebrow.

"During the time of your mother's labor," he said, "you need not do anything, except to keep quiet and to stay in this circle of leaves. I will be lighting candles, and perhaps muttering from time to time. When I say to you, 'In this manner must these things be accomplished' begin to read your story aloud. Kindly disregard what goes on in the room, and don't worry about the cat. She may run about if she pleases. If you feel sick, use this," and he put a large brass bowl before me. "When you come to the end of the story, say, 'Thus must it happen.' Do you understand?"

I nodded.

"Verdialos, shut the door, if you please," said The Magician.

He took a long taper from his sleeve and waved it in the air, whereupon it lit. He began lighting candles. The walls of the room were green marble, highly polished, and as each yellow flame sprang up they reflected it smudgily. The air itself seemed to sparkle. I made sure I could still read my handwriting. The whole room danced and glittered, but the words of my story were steady.

I began to feel most uncomfortably that someone was looking for me and that I should not let him find me. Perhaps, in whatever way wizards accomplish these things, The Magician was drawing near to my luck, if there is a near and a far to luck.

The Magician, in an enormous ringing voice, said, "In this manner must these things be accomplished." I began to read.

"Before Meadows was a month, because all the world was trees; when the sun was a golden coin and the moon a marble amulet; a little girl lived in a large house."

I liked the story better than I had before, and this was good because as I went on I found it increasingly difficult to attend to my reading. I was being pulled at, assaulted at the center of my being: Something was being stolen from me. I read on. I finished. "Thus," I said with the last of my breath, "must it happen."

And then I did feel sick. I remembered, long ago, fighting with Jehane for possession of a cloth camel. She was stronger than I and would get it away from me in the end, so I had decided to hold onto it until it tore. She divined my plan and, instead of holding onto its head and pulling until the neck divided, she kept moving her hands along the camel, gathering in more and more of it until I had only one leg and she could bite the fingers that held it and I had to let go. I felt like that now. Something was pulling away from me, thread by thread. I tried to let go of it before it tore, but some part of me wanted it to stay. This is my life leaving me, I thought, may it go quickly.

It went slowly, but in the end it went. I fell sideways, as I once had when Isobel and I were fighting over a piece of rope and she let go of it suddenly. Floradazul gave the squawk of a cat startled and annoyed, but not hurt, designed to strike guilt into the heart of an owner. It struck something else into mine.

I was still in The Magician's house.

The candles were all out. The leaves were crisp and blackened. The air was full of smoke. Verdialos was coughing. The Magician stood against the far wall, looking a little shaky and extremely smug, like Floradazul after she had fallen from a high shelf bringing the jar of fish stew with her.

I hoped he found the flavor to his liking.

27 Buds, Moonday, 3317

My mother has often told me that I lack steadiness, that I never finish what I begin, and that this is why I think I cannot do anything worth the time it takes. The progress of this narrative, which I was told to write day by day, and every day, seems to bear her out. Yet here I am, writing again, and out of what if not habit and duty—in a word, steadiness? I think I have done with the Green priests, but perhaps I want Verdialos to read this just the same.

Since the ritual had failed to kill me, I went on working for the Green priests. Floradazul made this less pleasant than it had been. Receiving my luck seemed to have turned her into a kitten again. Instead of sleeping most days and indulging in a rampage once a week, she rampaged all day long, every day. She hunted imaginary things all over and under my newly copied pages, smearing the ink; she fled from nonexistent monsters across the old manuscripts, scoring tens of pages with her claws and raising clouds of dust; she attacked the ankles of the clerks who came to collect my copies. After a week of this, I was obliged to leave her at home, where, as Cook and my family duly informed me, she pined for me. Cook said she pined; my family said she drove them to distraction.

I took less notice of this than I ought to have. I was sorry my cat was unhappy, but since my family was always complaining about something, I paid no attention to them.

On the next Tenth Day, though, I put her into the basket and took her to the Levar's Park, hoping to make her wear herself out chasing the squirrels. I thought of going to the Tiger's Eye and buying something for myself, and I couldn't take her there before I had somehow subdued her desire for destruction.

I could consider buying myself something at the Tiger's Eye because the Green priests now kept only half of the extremely generous wage they were paying me. Verdialos had explained that, first of all, my cat and I would probably live for another ten years, so the House would get its money; and, second, if I chose to sign this paper and that, the House could get my dowry out of my father as compensation for what I still owed them, should I die before I had paid it. He knew that this would please me very much. It almost soothed the sting of that "ten years more." I had a fine tangle of grudges against him by now, but the greatest was probably for his not telling me, when I yelled I could not wait long enough to learn magic, that I would have to wait almost that long for my cat to die.

Floradazul chased squirrels until I was tired, and delighted a number of wandering children. They were not dressed particularly well, and when the largest of them began casting covetous eyes upon her, I put her into the basket, gave them some coppers, and left in a hurry. She complained all the way from the Levar's Park to the fringes of the Canal District, when in desperation I stopped at a fruit stand and bought her a pear.

I should have peeled it before I opened the basket; she could not have withstood the smell. As it was, I opened the basket, cooing almost as foolishly as Jehane, and she sprang out and galloped away.

"Floradazul!" I shouted. "Stop!"

She knew what that meant, and she did, just before the feet of the camel that brooded over the trader's blanket next to the fruit stand. The trader had his back turned, and was pulling brilliant and fragile cloth from his pack. If she got into that, I would have to give him my dowry and the Green priests must learn to be less trusting.

"You stay!" I said.

Floradazul looked at me, sat meekly down, and swiped at the camel's right forefoot. The camel, without seeming to think much about it, kicked her. She didn't make a sound, but I heard something crack. She landed behind the fruit stand, before the tent of a woman selling uncut gemstones.

I thought I ran over, but the fruit vendor and two or three beggar-children were there before me. Floradazul looked vaguely irritated, as she would when you put a loop of wire around the door to the milk-box and she could not get into it. She made a heaving motion that got her nowhere, moved her front feet busily for a moment, and gave me her patient now-it's-your-turn look. I scratched the top of her head, and she began to purr.

"Her back is broken," said the gem woman.

"Don't cry, mistress," said a beggar-boy. I looked at the gem woman, but she was not crying. Neither were the two beggar-girls. The boy dug into his loincloth and handed me a little knife, the kind a lady would use to peel an apple, glittering-sharp. Floradazul purred on. I wished that a knife in my wrist or throat would accomplish the same purpose.

Behind me rose the voice of the fruit vendor. "I told you you didn't want to bring a camel here! It's bad for camels here. We had one shot right there not long ago."

"Looks to me," said the trader, nastily, "like it's bad for cats."

"You want me to do it?" said the boy.

"Lani, for mercy's sake," said a new voice, and someone put a hand on my head. I looked up into a face the color of orange-blossom honey. It was the healer who had taught Deleon and me so much. She did not seem to know me.

"Put your knife away," she said, took it from me and gave it back to the boy, who glowered. She looked at me with her black eyes. They saw too much, so I looked at the amulet at her throat.

"Shall I do it?" she asked. "Hold her head, if you like."

I put a hand under Floradazul's head, and she purred louder. The woman put one finger on my cat's nose. She wore two rings on that hand. She did not speak. The rings did not glow. Nothing happened except that Floradazul purred less, and a little less, and a little less, and stopped.

Nothing happened to me.

I felt in my skirt pocket for some money.

"You needn't," she said. "Or give it to Lani, for meaning well."

The boy said, "You won't be needing the collar now."

He was right, but the woman thumped him on the ear and said, "Don't give him a half-copper. Leave her alone, Lani."

The children made off, murmuring. The fruit vendor came up with my basket, and the woman put Floradazul's body into it, and I took it from them and walked away. I was trying to go in two directions at once: to Wizard's Row, and to the Avenue of Five Mice.

I went home. All the women in the family shrieked and wailed. Cook gave me a box to put my cat in, and Cinnamon dug a hole under the fig tree, and Isobel and Jehane and Livia and Gillo and Givanni stood around, the first three dripping and the second two looking silly, while I filled in the hole and put a good flat stone on top of it.

"Nissy, the Rannos's cat had kittens last month," said Givanni. "One of them is grey and white and two are black. I could—"

"What, and get your bowstrings all tangled up again?"

I sat in my room for several days, rehearsing what to say to Verdialos, except that it always foundered on the knowledge that this was not his fault. He had taken The Magician's advice about this matter, and The Magician had been wrong. Then I rehearsed what to say to The Magician, but that always foundered on the knowledge that if he knew I was looking for him, in a murderous frame of mind and with no intention of paying him anything, I would not be able to find him.

Finally, I thought that I might as well pay him. I had no

use for the money, unless to buy poison, and I could always get more from the Green priests. I took what I had and went hunting Wizard's Row. That I had found myself carrying Floradazul's empty basket downstairs with me did not make me like The Magician any better.

Wizard's Row was square and white in the morning sunshine. The shutters of Number 17 were closed. I stamped up the green walk, wondering where the yew tree was, and yanked at the tongue of the gargoyle.

"Where have you been?" it sang, and the door swung open.

So I had all the anger I had been saving for the gargoyle's questions to use on The Magician.

He was waiting for me in the hall, wearing red. His bracelets had been polished since I saw him last. In his right hand he held a black kitten, the unlovely kind with spiky fur sticking out in all directions. In his left hand he held a green collar with a silver buckle and three opals.

I thought I would choke before I got the words out. "By the holy, you monster, did you dig her up?"

"No," said The Magician, in an icy voice that quelled my anger in an instant, "and I advise that you not do so. Take your cat."

"My cat is dead, and you lied to me, or else you know nothing. Where did you get that collar?"

"It came with the kitten. Your kitten. Take her."

"That is not my kitten!"

"Look at it," said The Magician. "Call it."

I looked at the kitten. It was a most unattractive animal; it had a face like a fruit bat's. It sat bolt upright on The Magician's palm, looking unconcerned. I looked again. Any cat will sit upright and wrap its tail around its forepaws. Floradazul had always wrapped hers from left to right. So did this kitten. But Floradazul had also done what I never saw any other cat do: curl the tip of her tail up between the forepaws instead of wrapping both of them. So did this kitten.

"Floradazul," I croaked.

The kitten stood up and squeaked. The Magician put it down, and it bounded over with its foolish tail in the air, jumped as high as it could, and climbed the rest of the way, tucking its damp nose into my neck. I looked at The Magician. I was beyond feeling, and even in that moment, I remember, I wished this state would last.

"I thought you knew," said The Magician. "Cats have nine lives. I told you yours was in her first."

"Why did she come *here?*" This was not what I had meant to say.

"This is a center of power," said The Magician, in the tone of one who does not intend to explain further.

"But the cat's body died. Didn't you bind my luck to that? Are you sure you didn't bind it to the collar by mistake?"

"Entirely," said The Magician. "I could have bound your luck to its body. You did not ask me to. You asked me to bind it to the cat. The cat has nine lives. Therefore, your luck has nine lives. And therefore, so have you."

I considered his face. He did not sound completely certain, but I doubted he would tell me anything more. The kitten had begun to purr.

"I don't suppose you'd like a cat?"

"I have one."

He could stand there for days making similar answers, with the same quiet face. "Thank you for this late information," I said. "How much?"

The Magician bowed to me. "Consider this a part of the former service," he said, thus depriving me of the pleasure of throwing the money at him.

I went outside and stood in the dusty street. I wondered what I could say to Givanni, whose offer of a kitten I had refused. I wondered what I could say to Verdialos, who had offered me a mere ten years' servitude. Even if Floradazul never learned caution, I would have three times that with her.

I left Wizard's Row and took my cat home.

A Coincidence of Birth

by Megan Lindholm

THE GIRL SAT in the cool darkness, bony knees drawn up tight to her thin chest. Her eyes were closed. She drew long deep breaths in the steady cadence of sleep, but she had never felt more alert. About her in the darkness loomed countless casks, kegs, and dusty bottles. They held the potent wheat beer of Lenan on the western plains, Dragonsmoke from the Silverspine Mountains, and the many red vintages of Saltigos. Had she drunk them all, she could not have felt more intoxicated. Something burgeoned and grew inside her, struggling like a moth ripping out of its cocoon. This must be her day and her time, for luck was swelling in her, bubbling and begging to be harnessed. She was sure of it.

"Kookaloo!" There was the thud of the cellar door followed by the ponderous step of Daril. She could hear her foster mother breathing laboriously through her generous nose. "Kookaloo! What's keeping you? Those sailors want their beer now, not next week. They've a tide to catch. Kaloo!"

She tried to shut out the homey sounds, to stay within her bubble of belief, but she failed. With a sigh, the girl unfolded.

The elusive feeling had popped like a soap bubble on the daily wash. Kaloo stepped from behind the row of beer kegs, brushing cobwebs from her dark hair and bringing the filled pitcher. Daril gave a snort of impatience at the sight of the flattening foam. Snatching the pitcher, she gave it a fresh head. "And what was keeping you this time?"

"I'm sorry, Daril. I meant to hurry. But here in the dark and the cool and the silence, I felt something inside me, building up and rising like an incoming tide."

"Gut ache?" Daril said. "Drink some garwood tea. That'll make you pass whatever it is." She started up the stairs.

"Daril!" Kaloo was nearly speechless with disgust. "That's not what I meant!"

"Then what?" Daril paused on the steps and looked back in mild annoyance.

"I thought I felt my luck. You found me in the month of Meadows. If I were two months old then, I would have been born sometime in Buds. Maybe even today, at this hour. I keep having these . . . stirrings . . . inside me." Kaloo waved a hand helplessly, unable to describe what she had felt.

Daril paused on the steps to give her a fondly tolerant smile. "My little Kookaloo nestling. You could have been a tiny baby four months old, or a big whopper of an infant only a month along. You were so scrawny and weak when the sailor dragged you in, no one could tell. Besides. It's not your day that makes you feel that way, but your years. You'll be getting your woman's blood soon, and you'll start changing from a stick to an armful." She paused with a sudden speculative look. "It might not be too soon for you to be nibbling Worrynot. There's many a girl who thought she was too young to worry about such things, only to find her body knew more than she did. You know where it is; in a jar with the other herbs. Help yourself. Better safe than sorry."

Kaloo seethed silently at the bottom of the steps. "Woman's blood!" she sneered in an acid whisper as the cellar door thudded behind Daril. "That's what she's been saying to me since I was ten, whenever I felt good, whenever I felt bad." She glared down at the soft blouse that sagged limply over her thirteen-year-old ribs. She tightened the drawstring at the neck and retied it. She had asked Daril to stop making her blouses so ample, but the buxom mistress of the Mug and Anchor was sure that Kaloo would blossom any moment. The generous blouses and skirts that Daril turned out for her only made her feel more childish. As for Worrynot, Kaloo would probably never need the contraceptive. Who would want to lie with her? Even her face was plain. Black hair that curled the wrong ways, narrow black eyes, olive skin; like a dress cut from cheap cloth and sewn quickly, there was nothing to distinguish her from three-fourths of Liavek. The feeling of magic was gone. She was as sure now that today was not her time as earlier she had been certain it was.

"Kaloo!" Daril called again. She jerked from her musings and clattered up the wooden steps, back into the heat and noise of the serving room. In spite of the spring warmth, a full fire was burning on the hearth, and a servant was turning a spit of roasting meat over it. He was sweating at the task; Kaloo was glad it was not hers. Meats were cooked out in full view of the serving room, but the savory pot-boil that was the inn's reputation was kept safely bubbling back in the kitchen where its secrets could be preserved. That was where Daril's voice came from, and Kaloo brushed her way through the tables and patrons to answer.

As she passed the table closest to the kitchen door, she felt her arm snagged and she was suddenly lifted off her feet and deposited on a lap. "T'Nar, I am getting too big to be treated this way!" she protested.

T'Nar grinned, his gap-toothed pirate's smile like a fence in his whiskery face. "Actually, you are finally getting big enough to be treated this way. Why do you think I waited through years of damp diapers and skinned knees for you?"

She would have pulled T'Nar's beard for his rough teasing, but the serving room was full today. Too many sailors were turning to see what he had caught. So she only tugged free of him and gave him a smile she didn't need. "Daril calls me!" she explained and hurried off.

T'Nar was the one who had found her in a dusty ditch by the Levar's Highway. He had brought her to Daril, knowing that her youngest son had just married and moved away, saying, "Here's a little Kookaloo to fill the empty nest." The name of the wild songbird that left its eggs in other birds' nests had become her own. "With no more thought than they'd give to naming a kitten," she grumbled to herself.

"Kaloo!" The call blasted her ears as she stepped into the kitchen.

"I'm here," she said quietly, taking a furtive delight in watching Daril jump at her voice so close behind her.

"About time, too. Here's the basket, the coins are under the cloth in the bag. Don't lose them."

"It's Grinnel's turn to market!" Kaloo protested.

"He already went. And he already forgot cindra buds and spiny hearts. I'm to serve my pot-boil with no spiny hearts in it? I could have strangled him!"

"Why didn't you?" Kaloo grumbled softly to herself, but Daril picked it up.

"Well, if you'd rather take his place at turning the meats . . ."

"No!" Kaloo settled instantly. "I'll go."

"Then hurry. Don't go off in a dream and forget your errand. And hurry back, too. There'll be cleaning up to do before the dinner hour."

Kaloo picked up the basket and started for the door. Daril's voice, on a less distracted note, followed her. "And there's an extra half-copper in the bag. For a sweet. Time we started putting some meat on your bones."

Kaloo rolled her eyes and left. It was a balmy day and folk in the streets were taking their time. A harbor breeze nudged Kaloo up Park Boulevard. The Mug and Anchor was built close to the docks, so the tavern enjoyed the trade of every sailor too hungry to walk deeper into Liavek. And once they'd tasted Daril's pot-boil, they made it a regular port of call. On most days, Kaloo shared Daril's pride in that. But today it was just one more distraction that kept her from focusing on herself.

Ever since she had been old enough to wonder, she had pondered the question of why she had been left in a ditch to die. The last few years had brought an even more powerful question. On what day and at what hour had she been born? If she was ever to harness her magic, she had to know her luck time. And that was a thing no one could tell her.

Shops became more frequent as she entered the Merchant's Quarter. She slowed to enjoy the displays. As she passed the Tiger's Eye, four young rogues came boiling out of it, the crack of the owner's whip but a breath behind them. They rushed past her and on without a second glance. *See,* she told herself spitefully, *too plain even to attract trouble*. She shook her head and hurried the rest of the way up Park Boulevard to turn left on the Levar's Way. A half-dozen chipmunks, drawn by treat bowls left for Rikiki, scattered out of her path.

The Market was not crowded at this hour. Most folk preferred to shop in the cooler times of the day. Many of the cheaper stalls were unattended, their shades rolled down against the heat. But Daril never dealt with the cheaper merchants anyway. Kaloo went directly to Lexi's, where huge parasols and insect netting protected his produce. She selected cindra buds that crumbled easily between her fingers but did not crush into dry dust. And Lexi himself cut through a spiny heart to show her the starlike red pattern within the tuber. It was a good scarlet, and the spicy scent rose appealingly. Kaloo nodded and he filled her basket.

As she was turning to leave, Lexi gave an earthy exclamation of disgust. Kaloo whirled back in astonishment.

"Pardon, Kaloo." The merchant mopped at his second chin with a silk kerchief. "I meant no offense. But it's the third time this tendays that my stupid apprentice has gone off to make deliveries and left a parcel behind. Same customer, too! Look at this!" He gestured at a neatly tied package. "Those herbs were fresh picked this morning, and wrapped in damp cloths to keep them at their best. But by the time Roen gets back, they won't be fit to feed a bad-tempered camel. I'll lose my sale. I just hope he won't be offended," he added apprehensively.

"Is it on my way?" Kaloo knew she was being maneuvered.

"Well, perhaps it would be; or at most a block or two off your path. Oh, but I couldn't ask it of you!"

"You could, but you won't. You'd rather wait until I volunteered."

"Oh, you are such a good child! Don't lose that sweet temper as you grow! It warms my old heart, it does, to see that some young folk still help their elders! Be sure that Daril will hear of your courtesy from me!" Lexi tucked the parcel into her basket, and added a topping of two handsful of small sweet yellow plums. "To put a little flesh on your bones."

Kaloo nearly repented of her courtesy.

"It's to go to L'Fertti, the wizard," Lexi rattled on. "He has a little place right on the canal. If you turn left at the corner before the Tiger's Eye and go straight, you can't miss it. A little run-down to look at, but I always say, you can't judge a wizard by his dwelling."

Kaloo's ears had pricked up at the word "wizard," and she nearly missed the rest of his directions. When she had asked

Lexi to repeat them, she wandered from his shop, her eyes vacant and dreamy. A wizard. Her luck time must be near, for this to have transpired. Daril was always saying that a person's luck time brought quirks of fate, perhaps good, perhaps bad. Once Daril had fallen down the cellar steps on her luck day, cracking ribs. Another time, a new helper had spilled most of the pot-boil into the fire, nearly wiping out a heritage of cookery one hundred and fifty years old. And once, Kaloo thought wryly, a sailor had handed her a half-starved squalling baby, not only on her luck day but at her luck hour.

Kaloo hurried on, nibbling plums and shaking the sticky pits from her fingers into the street dust. Daril let her have no contact with folk who trained their magic. "It isn't for the likes of us," she had told Kaloo stoutly. "Let them dabble and take their chances with what isn't natural. Not us, my girl. We've a good life here, you and I. We've an inn to run, the best pot-boil in town, and a prime location. What need have we of magic? Let it do its mischief elsewhere."

Kaloo had always nodded dutifully, but felt that her heart beat to a different rhythm from the thump of mugs upon a table. There was a place inside her where power huddled and grew, longing for light and will to guide it.

Outside L'Fertti's door, she hesitated. She tightened the drawstring of her blouse again and shook out her skirts. She pushed her dark curls back from her face. No matter that the house was little more than a tumbledown shack on the edge of the canal. No matter that she had no idea what to say to him. Her luck had brought her this far; she'd trust it the rest of the way. She knocked smartly at the splintering door.

"Come in, already. You're late enough as it is!"

Kaloo pushed open the door. It sagged on its hinges, scraping across a worn stone floor. The small chamber revealed to her was neat and very sparsely furnished. Bare would also describe it. A little wooden table and two rickety chairs, a narrow couch with a straw mattress and three blankets folded at the foot of it, and, in fine contrast to the rest of the room's furnishings, a tall carved cabinet of some silky black wood. That was all. No one was there.

Kaloo ventured in hesitantly, and peered shyly into the next room. It was even smaller, but boasted a tiny hearth where the coals of a small fire glowed. L'Fertti swung his steaming kettle away from it and rose to scowl down at her.

L'Fertti was everything currently fashionable among wizards. He was tall, slightly stooped, grey-haired and bearded, and irascible. (He flattered himself that it all became him the better for being completely natural. He wasted none of his luck tampering with his appearance.) He knit his shaggy brows and peered down at Kaloo as he gruffly barked, "You're not Lexi's apprentice!"

"No, sir," Kaloo agreed readily. "Roen forgot your parcel and had already left upon his deliveries. Lexi knew I had to pass this way on my own way home, so he asked me to drop it off for him." She drew the parcel from her basket and offered it to him.

L'Fertti accepted it, ripping it open at once. "Well, you've done your good little deed, then. So go along. If you expected a half-copper from me for your trouble, forget it. And you can tell Roen for me that he wouldn't have had the piss scared out of him if he'd bothered to knock a little louder before he waltzed in here. Well, don't stand there like a stick! I've told you I don't have a half-copper to spare."

"But I do." The words leaped from Kaloo's mouth, and she stood gawking at her own boldness. But L'Fertti was not surprised.

"Need a potion, do you? Well, why didn't you say so? Just let me put these to simmer before their essence is lost completely."

He turned his back on her as he unwrapped the fresh herbs, pinched them into bits with his thick thumb nail, and stirred them into his kettle. He swung it back to the edge of the coals where it would simmer. He shot a look at Kaloo, who had drawn closer for a better look. "Stand back," he warned her. She retreated to watch in awe as his knuckly hands wove mystically over the brew. He rose with a sigh and a crackling of knee joints. Turning, he stumped past Kaloo to seat himself at the wobbly table. He waved curtly at the other chair and she joined him. He looked her over critically.

"I can guess why you've come. I'll be honest with you. I can do what you want, but it'd be better for you if you waited a few years and let your body catch up with you. Eat a little more and remember that the rose that blooms latest may have the sweetest scent. Knowing girls, I doubt if that changes your mind. Let's have your half-copper. I'll start you on a potion to be taken a spoonful a day. Come back when you run out.

May give you a few cramps, and don't expect it to taste good. . . ."

"It's not that!" Kaloo burst out indignantly. L'Fertti halted in surprise. "I want to know my luck time," Kaloo blurted into the silence. "Can you tell me that for a half-copper?"

L'Fertti was suspicious. "Why don't you ask your mother?" he snapped.

"I never knew her." Kaloo blushed as she explained her shame. "She abandoned me when I was a few months old. No one knows who she was or when I was born."

"I see," the wizard muttered to himself. "Let me see your hands."

The girl trustingly stretched her slender brown hands across the table to L'Fertti. He took them in both of his and closed his eyes to mere slits. Breathing stentoriously, he let his eyelids quiver and twitch. The girl sat breathless. But after L'Fertti had run his fingers across her palms and found the small scars and calluses of a working child, and skillfully appraised the sturdy cloth of her homemade skirt and noticed that the strap of her sandal needed mending, he pursed his lips sourly. If there was money to be made off this gull, it didn't show. He had no idea how to discover her luck time; no matter what he told her, she'd probably demand proof. Merchant stock. She'd know how to bargain; a hard one to con. But this was what he was reduced to. He took a deep breath and groaned softly in his throat. Satisfaction rose in him at the tremble it sent through her. He opened his eyes and leaned back in his chair panting.

"What is it?" the girl demanded breathlessly.

"It's not easy to explain," he said, stalling. "You must realize that your time of luck is not the simple thing that most people believe it to be. I am sure you know the basics of it: At the hours of your birth time each year, your luck is available to you. I am sure you know that exactly six months later, a wizard is vulnerable to the unlucky side of his magic. You may even know that a master wizard is able to tap into his luck for the few moments each day that correspond to his birth time." He took a breath and leaped into embroidery. "What you may not know is that each person's luck time is like a tide. It may be highest or lowest at certain months, but it ebbs and flows year around. From the coursing of your blood, I can tell that your luck time has not yet passed this year. But we are close to it." Her rapt nod showed him he had guessed well. "But what we must do is a ticklish undertaking, and will demand far more of my time than a half-copper can buy. If you could bring me, say, a half-copper a week, and let me check your blood coursing, I dare say we shall find your luck within a month or two."

"A . . . a half-copper is a dear thing to me," the child replied, embarrassed. "Is magic always so costly?"

He let her question go begging. "Have you nothing else of value you might wish to trade?"

"I . . . nothing." Her eyes dropped to her lap, then darted off to a bare corner of the room.

"I see. Well, a half-copper pays for this time, and be sure to come and see me again when you've another one."

"But I may not get one again until after my time is past! Please, isn't there some deal we can make? I mean, well, I can cook and clean. I can run errands. . . ."

L'Fertti had been shaking his head as he pocketed her coin. Abruptly he stopped. He stared at her shrewdly. Was he perhaps discarding the one good card his luck had dealt him lately? She was small enough to fit through a window. He studied her face. Thin, but good bones, and a flash of command in those eyes. Now, who did she remind him of? He dismissed it carelessly. "If I find a task for you, to pay for my magic, where would I find you?"

"Send a message to Kaloo at the Mug and Anchor," she replied eagerly. "But be subtle about it. My foster mother does not approve of my search."

"Subtlety is my specialty," he assured her. "Now hurry off before your own goods wilt in the heat. I've a potion to tend."

He listened to her thanks a dozen times before he could shoo her out the door. He went back to his kettle, stirring it slowly and thinking. It was no more than an herbal cure for the flux. His magical passes had been for Kaloo's benefit. Besides, folk paid more to buy the remedy from him, a wizard, than from a simple herbalist. So let them get what they paid for. He strained it into stoppered flasks and set them away on the shelves of the tall cabinet, frowning as he did so. That a wizard of his skills should be reduced to curing liver spots and diarrhea. Oh, how it rankled! He crossed hastily to his couch and stretched out upon it. His time of luck for the day, that small bit of magic left to him, was nearly here. He could feel it coming to a simmer. He closed his eyes and sent his luck questing.

Still there. The green-stoned earrings were shut up in a tiny box lined with velvet, locked securely in a wooden chest in Snake's shop. Damn and damn and damn. He would have a better chance of recovering them almost anywhere else. To burgle the Tiger's Eye was out of the question. He considered going in and asking Snake if she had any jade earrings; then, when he had them on the palm of his hand, he could tap into his magic invested in the green stone and . . . what? He tried to think of a magic that would get himself and the earring out of Snake's shop before that whip of hers could pop. But he knew his luck well. It was not a quick kind. His sorceries were limited to the slow and careful sort, the spells that, once wrought, were seldom undone.

His luck time passed and he sat up with a sigh. At least he still knew where the earring was. And he knew who to blame for it all, too. That sneaking Galida. He should have known her for a thief. But no, he had taken her in, spent all his coins on her soft sweet body, and awakened one morning to find himself worse than impoverished. Anything valuable and portable was gone. That included the earrings he had been wearing when he fell asleep beside her. Those clever, gentle hands of hers. The right earring he did not mind, for all that the green stone had cost him a nice bit of gold. But the left one: his magic. Only two months ago, he had spent all his birthday luck time investing his magic into that stone, to keep it safe and always close enough to tap. But then (and he wondered at his own foolishness), a brilliant idea came to him. He had worked a slow spell of ill-luck into the setting and the hoop of the earring, to vanquish any who might try to steal his magic. He must have been careless. For the spell had turned on its creator, bringing him a sticky-fingered lover to fleece him of his power. The only good luck he had had was that no one knew of it yet. If anyone found that it held his luck, they could destroy it on his midyear day, bankrupting his magic forever. He felt queasy at the thought. Spend his life mixing cures for gout and colic? It was more than he could bear.

Six anxious days were to pass before his luck time vigil was rewarded. On that day he found his earring lying in the palm of Snake's hand. Was she selling them to someone? No, that was Thyan, her assistant, leaning on the counter to peer over Snake's shoulder.

Snake turned the earrings over in her hand, examining them

both closely. But when Thyan reached for them, she snapped, "Don't touch! You've enough bad luck already!" Thyan gave a snort of disgust as Snake slapped them back in their box.

"I told you so!" she observed, not meekly.

Snake gave her a look that set her to polishing the counter. "Galida always did hide the truth in her lies. 'My mother's last gift to me, which bad luck forces me to sell.' I should have guessed it sooner," Snake observed regretfully.

"You should have," Thyan assented. Snake raised an eyebrow at her, then glared at the earrings. A sudden smile of wicked inspiration lit her face.

"What is it?" Thyan demanded.

"It's too bad the stones are valuable. I know just who deserves such a gift as this. Even if I'm wrong about the bad luck, the brass would turn his earlobes green."

(L'Fertti winced. Was the gold plating wearing off them so soon?)

Thyan's eyes widened; then she grinned. "I dare you," she challenged.

"He'd guess who sent them in a minute. He'd suspect a trap."

"Not if you did it right."

Snake didn't appear to hear her. Her eyes were roving the shop. "There!" she exclaimed suddenly. "Just the touch to let him have a turn at playing the fool." She strode across the shop to snip a lock of fair hair from an exotic doll, purported to be modeled on the national dress and features of the Farland folk. "So well do you plot; let's see you figure this out." She tucked the golden curl between the earrings in their box. Her grin became demonic. Thyan could not contain herself when Snake took up a bit of plain paper.

"Let me write the note!" she begged.

Snake leveled the pen at her. "You. Scoot! If this comes home to roost, I want it to land on me, not you. Did you finish that inventory of beads yet?"

"Snake!"

"Now."

But Thyan did not scoot. She dragged herself from the room with many a backward pout. Snake stared at the earrings for inspiration, then wrote with her left hand, "To the one who has magicked my heart with his dark eyes." Signing no name, she rolled the note and tucked it into the box.

The lid was snapped shut, and L'Fertti's vision went with it. He heard dimly the rustling of paper, then the sound of Snake hailing a street child. She spoke firmly.

"Count Dashif is expecting this parcel. Here, I will pay you for its delivery now. But before you think of running off with both coin and merchandise, I remind you that he is expecting it, and soon. Now listen. He wishes it most discreetly delivered. You are to pass it silently to the guard outside the Levar's palace. If he tries to detain you, say this: 'I will sully no lady's honor!' Only that, then run away. No, I don't know why. That is how the Count wishes it done, and I am not so stupid as to ask him questions. Are you? I didn't think so. Be off!"

Her voice faded. L'Fertti lay in a sweat, straining his magic after her, but his birth-time luck was gone. So she had passed the earrings on to Count Dashif. He wondered why. A remembrance of the Count's narrow black eyes and intense face assailed L'Fertti. The man had a most nasty reputation. No one knew exactly what he did for His Scarlet Eminence; smart people didn't ask, as long as Dashif didn't do it to them. Dashif was a walking arsenal, with the temper of an adder. L'Fertti's bad-luck spell was still working.

His mind swung into despair. Dashif would hate the earrings and never wear them. Then they would be locked up somewhere in the Levar's palace, hopelessly out of L'Fertti's reach, leaving him powerless for a year. A worse thought struck him. Dashif's own powers were rumored to be considerable. He would smell a trick in the gift. He would use his own luck to track the earrings back to L'Fertti, or he would sense the power invested in the stone, and destroy it!

L'Fertti rolled from his cot with a groan and headed for the small kitchen hearth and a cup of kaf to restore himself. But enroute, a mixture of inspiration and stubborn hope assailed him. He might have a chance, if Count Dashif harbored an ounce of human vanity in him. True, he was basing all his hopes on the chance of a coincidence, but what was magic but the manipulation of coincidence? Or so he had been taught at the Za-Drin Academy of Wizardry. True, it had been a cut-rate school and had barely existed long enough to teach him the basics of investiture. But it had been all his parents could afford, and high honor for a fishmonger's son to be accepted at all.

He thought fondly of his parents and the sacrifices they had made so he could attend the school. Briefly he wondered where they were and how they were doing now. Very briefly.

Kaloo could have wished for a more subtle summoning. Roen's face was white with awe. She took the little basket of sweet plums from his shaking hands as he whispered, "Remember the delivery you made for me? The one who received it sends these plums and says he would have your company again today, at just past midday."

The boy was visibly trembling as he backed away from the kitchen door. Kaloo bit into one of the plums thoughtfully as she stared after him. So she was summoned. But for what? She swallowed, the fruit suddenly sour in her mouth. Setting the basket down, she turned to Daril. The big innkeeper looked up from stirring the pot-boil.

"May I have an hour or two to myself today? The serving room is nearly empty."

Daril pursed her lips, as if tasting something both sweet and bitter. "I suppose you may," she sighed. Then, more gently, "You haven't forgotten the Worrynot?" At Kaloo's surprised look, Daril choked back a laugh. "Don't act so innocent. I don't need eyes in the back of my head to hear Roen whispering at the kitchen door, or see the flush on your cheeks. Now, don't get piqued. Go on, have your hour. I haven't forgotten when I was your age. But . . . be sure he's clean. And take your time about it. And if you do change your mind, tell him so. Don't . . ."

Kaloo let the door slam on the rest.

Kaloo arrived at L'Fertti's house out of breath. She had resisted the temptation to run, but she had hurried despite the heat. Daril's last words echoed in her mind. "If you change your mind, tell him so." It was the only valid bit of advice she had given. Well, and Kaloo would, if what L'Fertti proposed were too distressing. She shut her eyes, pushing away the old tales of disgusting and terrifying spell casting.

She knocked twice at the rickety door and then pushed in as his voice bade her. He was sitting at his splintery table, looking a bit surprised. "You've come early. Well, that's good."

"What will you ask me to do?" she demanded breathlessly.

"Nothing half so interesting as what you must be imagining," he replied with cynical amusement. "Sit down and stop fluttering. It's really very simple," he began. "Every day at about this time, we will stroll together through the Market for an hour or so. I will be acting like your aged uncle, and you will carry a basket for our little purchases. My appearance will be altered so that no one will know me."

"What about mine?" Kaloo cut in anxiously.

He looked at her with tolerant superiority. "My girl, a person could see you four times an hour and not remark on you. Perfect face for this work; very indistinguishable. Now, be quiet and listen. On one of our strolls, we will encounter Count Dashif. Not that we want him to notice us. He will be wearing some green-stoned earrings. When we are very close to him, I will work a small magic, causing the earrings to drop from his ears. You will retrieve them and run off into the crowd."

At the name Dashif, Kaloo had frozen. "No," she said simply when L'Fertti stopped. She rose to go. His knuckly hand detained her.

"Don't you wish to know your luck day and hour?"

"It sounds to me like we'd find my death day and hour. All know Count Dashif's reputation. He gives me the shivers. What about the Farmer's Market Massacre?"

"Rumors. There's no proof he was even there."

"And that poor camel?"

"Was just a camel. Besides, he won't have time to kill you. You snatch up the earrings and you're gone."

"I can't outrun his pistols," Kaloo said. "Sorry. It's not worth that much to me."

"Go on, then!" He gave her a disgusted push. "Look at you. I don't know why the idea crossed my mind. Now that I see you again, I realize that you lack the discipline to become a student of magic. No patience! No courage! Begone. I'd be crazy to accept you as a student."

Kaloo was halfway to the door. "Student?" she asked the graying wood. She spun around. "You mean you'd teach me? You'd show me how to invest my magic after we discovered my luck time?"

"I had been considering it."

"For just this one task?" Business sense, ingrained by years with Daril, came to the fore. "You're offering to tutor me for just this one task?"

L'Fertti hesitated fractionally. "After we do this one small task, we'd try you out on the training. I'd expect you to do small chores about the place here, cleaning up and whatnot, so I could keep your tuition low. But . . ." he hastily added at the look of dismay on Kaloo's face, "of course the first three lessons would be free. For helping me with the earrings."

Kaloo wet her lips. "When would we start?"

"As soon as we secured the earrings. A client of mine has seen them and longs to possess them, but the Count will not be parted from them. A simple matter."

"No." She eyed him closely and made her counteroffer. "We start today, and each day I walk with you in the Market, I get a lesson. Who knows how long it might be before we get a glimpse of Dashif wearing those particular earrings? It's purely a matter of coincidence."

L'Fertti frowned her down. "It is *not!* For a man to lose an earring is a random happening. For me to be following him, desiring his earrings, when he happens to lose both of them, that is magic. Don't you see? Coincidence is the Foundation of All Magic! That's your first lesson. Come, here's a basket. Let's take our stroll."

Kaloo was a bit disappointed when his disguise consisted of a broad-brimmed hat and a stained brown cloak. She swallowed it when he told her archly, "And another thing. Always conserve your magic. Never waste a spell where a lie or a simple deception will suffice."

But it was not on their first stroll, nor on their third, or even on the fifth that they met Dashif. Kaloo began to learn. She learned to wriggle the middle toes of her feet without the other toes budging. She learned patterns of breathing. Her hands grew steady as she tried to balance glass balls atop one another. She learned to look shy when Daril questioned her, and every other day to dump a little Worrynot into the fire.

She even learned to enjoy their slow strolls through the Market. She had thought that she knew it as well as the back of her hand, but L'Fertti introduced her to the dry and dusty shops that wizards frequented, and the strange herbs that one might purchase in them. He told her peculiar uses for ordinary cooking spices, and taught her more than he realized with his snippets of gossip about the folk they passed. Kaloo absorbed it all. She pushed away the knowledge that her lessons would end with her snatching of the earrings, for she would never have the money to pay even the lowest tuition. Her fear of

Dashif she pushed away as well. Magic had begun to seem a demanding but fascinating profession, until the day she caught a glimpse of a red linen cloak through the crowd.

She experienced a change of heart, unnerving in its intensity. Her hands were sweaty, her stomach cold. Something about Dashif repelled and fascinated her, drawing her to him as it terrified her. "Anyone but him," she whispered to L'Fertti, who appeared not to hear. His fingers tightened on her arm and she felt herself propelled through a crowd that seemed to magically melt out of their way.

Count Dashif was looking for someone. It was plain from his leisurely saunter and the way his eyes wandered over the milling people. His curly black hair was pushed back off his shoulders so the sun struck the dangling earrings and the vertical welts beneath his eyes. He paused to smile at fair-haired Selita of the rug booth, who went pale under her tan and vanished behind her wares. He gave an almost imperceptible shrug and strolled on.

"I've heard four different stories of how his face was marked," L'Fertti confided to Kaloo softly.

Kaloo was not interested in any of them. "He knows about us. L'Fertti, he's watching us. Let's get out of here!" Her frantic whisper had a hysterical edge.

"Don't be stupid!" the wizard growled. His brief puzzlement was being replaced by amazement. "He's trolling for blonds! I never would have believed it of him."

This cryptic remark was no comfort, and Kaloo nearly screamed as he maneuvered them ever closer to Dashif, until they were strolling along in his wake. She felt exposed, but the camouflage of the crowded market was effective. Dashif paid them no attention.

Kaloo peered sideways at L'Fertti, wondering what the delay was. His lips were mumbling in his beard, and his free hand made small, furtive passes. Nothing happened. The old man's magic wasn't working. Her mouth went dry and sweat stung her eyes. Why didn't he give up and get them both out of here?

But still they trailed along behind the whip-hand of His Scarlet Eminence. Kaloo began to feel she could not get her breath. Dizziness swept over her, and then a disorienting sense of being one with L'Fertti. She could sense the magic tingling in the hand that gripped her arm above her elbow. In the same instant, a jealous rage overtook her, and she wished Dashif every evil that could befall a man. Just as abruptly as her emotions had risen, they fell off.

So did everything else. Women shrieked and men roared in outrage as L'Fertti's spell of unfastening succeeded beyond his wildest expectations. The green earrings slipped from Dashif's ears. His white silk blouse flared suddenly open, baring a hirsute chest. He paid this no mind as the belt that supported his flintlocks came unbuckled as well. All around them, horses' cinches were dangling, women were scrabbling after bracelets and necklaces sliding from their bodies, not to mention garments artfully fashioned and tied that were now so many rectangles of slipping cloth. A City Guard stood astounded in the ringing hail of his chain mail dropping away from him in a shower of links. A flock of chickens, their legs trussed for the market, found themselves free and added their escape to the general confusion. L'Fertti dropped Kaloo's arm, hissed, "Get them!" and vanished into the crowd. He looked rattled.

Kaloo hesitated fractionally and then dove for the earrings. Her hand closed on one, and she sprang after the other that had landed to one side, nearly in an offering bowl of nuts for Rikiki. As she shot up, she almost struck foreheads with Dashif, who was struggling to fasten his belt while juggling his pistols. For an instant their eyes locked. Her heart jammed in her throat; the screams and curses of the crowd around her went unheard. Face to face, close enough to kiss or kill, they stood. His eyes held hers like a snake's hold a bird's. It took a long instant for her to realize he was as paralyzed by her visage as she was by his. Something . . . there was something there. She broke free of it at the same moment he did and sprang away, as much from his darting grip as to the other earring.

Her luck saved her. He was hampered by his loosened clothing. She had long grown used to dealing with hers. Just as her hand would have landed on the earring, however, a small brown chipmunk shot out of nowhere and snatched up the shining thing. Then it was gone, scampering up a post to spring onto the roof of a stall and disappear. She caught a glimpse of its brown body as it leaped to the next stall. She heard the Count's roar: "Stop that girl!" But most of the crowd was too busy refastening clothing or jewelry to obey, and the rest could not decide which girl he wanted caught. Kaloo writhed away, slipped down an alley between stalls, and was gone, her long legs stretched in a flat run. In one fist she gripped the earring.

"A chipmunk ate it?" L'Fertti glared at her suspiciously.

"Yes!" Kaloo was in no mood to be doubted. After eluding Count Dashif, she had taken a long, circuitous route to L'Fertti's house. Events had been falling into place in her mind. She felt angry and bold. "What's the matter? Is it the wrong one?"

She regretted the remark when his strong fingers closed tightly around her wrist. "If you have it, wench, you'd better turn it over to me now. If you've figured out what it is, then you know that you're close enough for me to use it."

"I don't have it!" she hissed, angry at the tears of pain that started in her eyes.

"Let's hope not!" He glared a moment longer, then dropped her wrist.

"You knew my luck time all along. You used me!" Kaloo flared at him, her anger so fierce she trembled in its grip.

"No, I did not!" the old man denied it. "I was as surprised as you when it happened. I had heard it was possible; rumor has it that the Gold priests were linked in just such a fashion, sharing their moments of luck. Evidently, we share the hour, but not the day. Today was your day. Your luck came and I accidentally tapped it, increasing two-fold the power of my little spell. A spell already made strong by my proximity to my invested object."

"It all just *happened* to benefit you, by coincidence," Kaloo said snidely.

L'Fertti looked at her with sudden speculation. "A bizarre chain of circumstances, and a fortuitous coincidence. Your magic will be very strong, once it's trained." He gave her a piercing look. Kaloo dropped her eyes before it. She knew that gleam from a thousand trips to the market. Daril had explained it to her. "When anyone looks at you like that," she had said, "it means you have something they want. Be cagey, then. It almost always means there's a profit to be turned." So Kaloo watched him through her lashes.

L'Fertti was suddenly sounding like her teacher again. "At that moment of magic you felt, did you have any recollection of your own birth? It's not uncommon. Some have even reported that during their first attempts at investiture, they were distracted by sharing the emotions their mothers felt at their births. What did you sense?"

"I . . . nothing." She shut her mouth with a snap. Whatever he was fishing for, he wasn't going to get it for free. Kaloo felt strangely possessive of those few shared moments. So her mother had hated Dashif. It was not an uncommon emotion in Liavek. And it was none of L'Fertti's business.

"I see. Well. Perhaps with more training. It was not as if you were actually attempting the magic this time." If he was disappointed, he covered it well. She watched him absently snap the earring back into his right ear. "You didn't happen to pick up any other jewelry, did you? There was a good bit of it lying about in the street when we were through."

"I'm not a thief!" Her words were sharp, but she felt a tingle down her spine. "We," he had said. It had been her luck, too, that had wrought that magnificent mess. Hers as much as his. But now her lessons were over. A thoughtful frown creased her forehead, and then she suddenly had to scowl blackly to keep the grin from her face. So that's what the wiley old codger was after—the use of her magic! She'd let him have it, of course. On her terms. She glanced up to find him watching her closely.

"Headache?" he asked solicitously. "Why don't you brew us some tea to ease it? We'll celebrate together. I'd still call our day a partial success, wouldn't you?"

"I suppose." Kaloo sighed. "At least you got one earring back. I'm sorry about the other one. And I'm afraid I don't much feel like celebrating. Maybe I'd better be going home."

"Now?" L'Fertti near yelped, then hastily cleared his throat. "You haven't had any tea yet! I can't send you off home with a headache. You sit still now, I'll make the tea. Don't go away!" He scuttled over to the kettle, smiling anxiously at her as he clattered for cups and herbs. Kaloo leaned her face into her hands, trying desperately to erase a grin.

"To my apprentice!" L'Fertti suggested the toast a few moments later as he poured steaming yhinroot tea into two cracked mugs.

But Kaloo only lifted a doleful face to his toast. "Not anymore," she reminded him. "I haven't a coin to go on with my lessons. Besides, I know my luck time. That's all I really wanted. After today, I know that investing my luck would probably just get me into trouble. You were right, L'Fertti. I was never cut out to study magic."

"No! I was wrong!" He spoke urgently. "You have a great future in magic. A marvelous future. Kaloo, you mustn't be discouraged now. You're my apprentice. For free."

She shook her head sadly, staring into her tea.

"Why not?" he asked coaxingly. He reached across the table to pat her hand. Tears brimmed the dark eyes she turned up to him.

"I'm afraid," she said simply. "I've heard stories about . . . things one must do to be an apprentice. You might ask me to . . . do something . . ." She let her voice trail off childishly.

"Oh, never!" He denied it warmly, squeezing her small, lax hand. "You'd never have to do anything that upset you. I promise. Why, you'd have as much say in what we did with our luck as I did."

"Do you mean that?" The relief in Kaloo's voice was pathetic.

"On my luck! I swear it!" he vowed fervently and hastily.

Kaloo's face changed. She leaned back in her chair, casually brushing the dark curls from her face. She smiled at him easily as she lifted her mug of tea. "Then let's drink to your *partner!*" she amended the toast, and felt a small satisfaction as he choked. "You still owe me a day's lesson," she reminded him curtly.

He nodded a brusque agreement to her deal. "I'll make it short," he snapped. "Ponder this and be humbled. Is magic our manipulation of coincidence, or is coincidence the magic manipulating us, for its own secret ends?"

"Short, but pithy!" Kaloo refused to be daunted. She set down her mug and gave him a smile. "I have to go. Yesterday Daril grumbled that delivering groceries isn't the only thing that Roen's slow about."

He stared blankly at her before he said, "Go, then. But come back tomorrow."

L'Fertti watched the narrow smile tip over her thin face, and then she was gone, slamming his door behind her. He eased back in his chair and let his own smile break out. She might be merchant raised, but he was fishmonger bred. Always let the customer walk away thinking she's driven a hard bargain, he reminded himself. Never let one know she's taken just what you wanted to sell her, at your price. Kaloo should have guessed that their moment of magical unity flowed both ways. He knew as much as she did; perhaps more. He wasn't an idealistic adolescent, who could look bare truth in the face, then deny it to herself. Maybe his luck was still riding around in a chipmunk's cheek, but he had Dashif's daughter in the palm of his hand.

Bound Things

by Will Shetterly

ONE SUNNY AFTERNOON in Buds, three wizards sat in a quiet room. The youngest, a small man with grim features, said, "You can handle this alone?"

The eldest was a very dark, very handsome man whose black goatee hung midway down his chest. He smiled and said, "Of course. After you do your part."

"There must be a reason," the youngest insisted, "why he is called The Magician."

The tallest, a woman who might have been a sister to the younger man, said, "Yes. Because he is vain. Because they do not know what magicians are in this uncivilized place. Because he is the most powerful of the village witches who live on that gaudy lane they call Wizard's Row."

The eldest laughed. "Don't underestimate him. Would we be here in Liavek, if he was weak?"

"Then why does he hide his name?"

The youngest said, "To keep us from gaining power over him?"

The woman sneered, then laughed. "If so, Liavekans are all superstitious savages! Do other magicians in Liavek hide their names or their parentage?"

"No," the eldest answered. "They are like most sorcerers.

They only conceal their birthdays and the vessels of their power."

Frowning, the woman said, "Then why does The Magician hide his name?"

"He does not," the eldest answered. "It is said his name is Trav."

"Trav?" the young man asked. "As in *trav?*" He almost barked the word; it meant "spider" in Tichenese. "Or *traav?*" Drawling its syllables, it meant "lefty" in Zhir. "Which hand does he favor?"

The eldest smiled at them both. "Does it matter?"

"No," the woman answered, returning his smile. "Not now."

Trav lay on his stomach on a carpet on the floor of his study and idly flipped through the most recent edition of the *Cat Street Crier*. A half-eaten biscuit sat on a green porcelain plate beside him, which interested a fat, shaggy black cat. Next to the plate was a cup of the same green porcelain, holding the dregs of some pale tea. On the small of his back was a sleeping silver-blue kitten.

Trav wore a long blue robe over tight black trousers, and his sandalled feet were crossed as he scratched the outside of his left ankle with his right foot. His only jewelry was a plain but heavy polished-brass bracelet on each wrist. His sandy hair was cropped close to his skull, his jaw was cleanly shaven, and his eyes were yellow, maybe brown, perhaps green. His face bore no more lines of age or experience than that of a pampered youth.

A voice filled the room like the striking of a gong. "Two prospective clients seek audience with you, O noble master."

The cat leaped away from the biscuit and fled guiltily out of the room; the kitten did not wake. Trav looked up from the *Crier* and said, "Who're you trying to impress, Gogo?"

"I shall ask their names as you request, O mighty Magician." Trav sighed, reached around to transfer the kitten from his back to a pillow, and received a swat for his effort. Gogo spoke again. "They are Sessi of Candlemaker's Street and her companion, the bold Sorel, O wise one."

He did not recognize either name, but he knew that Liavek grew faster than he could learn every person of consequence. He said, "Fine, Gogo. Let them in. And I don't care how rich they are, you needn't fawn so."

"I obey as always, O Magician of Magicians."

Trav sighed again, then stood. He set the cup and plate on a low ebony table by a wide wicker couch, popped the remaining fragment of biscuit into his mouth, glanced at the window which looked out on a sunny beach by a calm sea, and snapped his fingers. The scene beyond the window changed to the bright awnings of the Street of Scales. Hearing footsteps in the hall, Trav stepped to the door and, bowing low in the Tichenese manner, swung it wide.

The first thing he noticed was that the hall beyond was paved with glistening diamonds set in gold; Gogo was doing her best to impress these clients. The second thing he noticed were small, dirty feet which, he saw as his gaze traveled upwards, were attached to a small, dirty child. Her eyes were bright black beads beneath tangled hair, and her dress had been a sugar sack that still bore the imprint of the Gold Harbor Trading Company. The girl smiled shyly, saying, "Hello, Master Magician. Can you find my dolly?" In the palm of her outstretched hand was a very thin half-copper coin.

A boy, little taller than the girl though his gauntness and his swagger said he was twice her age, stood behind her. A silver knife was stuck through his sash as though he dared anyone to take it. He pulled a faded cloth cap from his head and said, "I came so's Sessi wouldn't get lost, Your Magiciancy."

Trav whispered, "Gogo . . ." The guardian did not answer. The children watched him with expectant eyes. "Your . . . dolly?" he said at last.

"Yes!" said the girl, beginning to cry. "My dolly!"

"Gogo . . ." Trav whispered again. When he saw that the boy studied him with his head cocked warily, Trav shrugged and said, "Enter."

Sorel took the girl's hand and led her into the room. "C'mon, Sessi. The Magician'll find your doll."

Trav bit his lip, then spoke carefully. "This isn't my usual sort of commission. You understand that, don't you?"

The girl nodded. "Yes. You'll find my dolly."

"That's not—"

"I got money. Lookit!" She thrust the copper coin at him. Her voice quavered as though more tears were imminent.

"That is a great deal of money," Trav said gently. "Still—"

The door from the hall opened, and a short woman with hair the color of brass stepped into the room. She was barefoot, and her tunic was a simple white garment, but her hair was elaborately coiffed and her copper-dark skin was very clean. "Trav . . ." she said. Her voice was husky, promising pleasure if he pleased her and trouble if he did not. Her eyes were as green as emeralds.

Trav glanced up. "Who's watching the front door, Gogo?"

"Didi, of course."

"Then who's watching the back?"

"No one's dared to go there in seventy-five years. And Didi's not so simple that he can't handle both."

"You want something? I'm in conference."

"No." Gogo smiled. Leaving, she added, "I'm glad you've agreed to help them." The door closed on her last word.

"Gogo!" Trav raced after her, but when he entered the hallway, it was quiet, shadowy, and empty. "I will never be rich," he whispered.

Gogo's voice rang in the hall like chimes. "Look again at the girl's coin, my wise master. And ask the boy to describe the doll, and how it was stolen."

Trav's eyes flicked wide. As he hurried back into the study, the children stared at him. "That's all we got," said Sorel. "Unless . . ." The boy's voice saddened as his fingers touched the hilt of his silver knife.

"No," Trav said. He took Sessi's half-copper piece and saw that it bore the stamp of Nevriath the Unlucky, the last ruler of S'Rian before Liavekan nomads came almost seven hundred years ago. Tel Jassil of the Street of Old Coins would pay a small fortune for such an antiquity, for His Scarlet Eminence, the Levar's Regent, would pay Jassil a larger one to add it to his collection. Trav allowed himself a tiny smile. "If Gogo thinks we've made a fine bargain, I could hardly alter it now." He nodded, and the coin disappeared from his fingers. "Tell me about this doll."

"It's my dolly," said Sessi. "Some bad men took it."

"The Titch took it," Sorel explained.

"The . . . Titch?"

"Yeah. The one that's got that big house on the Levar's Way, just past Temple Hill."

Trav stared, then laughed in delight. "The Tichenese ambassador?"

Sorel nodded.

"He stole a doll?"

Sessi sniffed, nodded, and said, "Bad old Titch."

"Not by himself," said Sorel.

"Of course not," said Trav. "There's a Tichenese saying: When others act for you, you pay for success; they pay for failure."

"Huh?"

"Who took the doll?"

The boy squinted nervously. "Some sailors. They snatched Sessi's doll, and she came and got me. I followed them to the Titch's house. I didn't actually see the head Titch. But that's where they went, the Titch's house, and they didn't come out again."

"And you didn't try to go in?"

"You know how well they guard that place?"

Trav nodded. "Describe the doll."

The boy looked at the girl, then said, "Well, it looks like a Titch, and it's about a foot long, and it's carved out of wood. Not very well carved, either. And it's got a little beard made of camel hair, but it was wearing a dress—"

"A long robe?" said Trav. "Golden, like the ambassador's? Or dark blue, with some silver trim?"

"Blue and silver, mostly."

"Gogo was right to admit you."

"What do you mean, your Magiciancy?" Sorel asked.

"Never mind." Trav stopped to face the girl. "Where did you find your dolly?"

She looked down, then whispered, "Sorel gave him to me."

"Oh?"

Sorel bit his lip. "Yeah. I didn't think anyone at the markets would want a Titch doll. 'Specially not a badly carved one."

"And where did you find it?"

"Um, I was in this house—"

The Magician's eyes narrowed, and he said, "I don't care that you stole it. Tell me from whom."

"Deremer Ledoro."

"On Pine Street? Dances at Tam's Palace?"

Sorel stared in surprise or fear. "How'd you know?"

"I'm The Magician. I'm amazed Deremer's home wasn't better guarded."

"It used to be. But all she's got now are a few locks on the windows and doors." Sorel shrugged. "Cheap ones."

"Yes," said Trav. "So someone suspected that Deremer's luck had been freed or stolen, and you were sent because you're dispensable."

"Because I'm good!"

"Did you find the S'Rian coin there?"

"I—"

"You want me to seek the doll?"

Sessi clutched Sorel's arm and said, "Yes!"

"Then tell me what I need to know."

Sorel glanced at Sessi. "The coin was in Deremer's house."

Trav nodded. "Thank you." He glanced at the ceiling. "I think we'll have refreshments now. And then one of my servants will call upon our ambassador from the north."

When Gogo entered with a tray of wooden mugs and a pitcher of pineapple juice, the children were sitting on the wicker couch facing The Magician. Trav sat on the corner of his desk, folding a sheet of paper into the shape of a bird. Several paper birds already flapped around the room, much to the annoyance of the black cat, which crouched beneath the desk, and to the delight of the kitten, which bounded into the air, swatting at the birds. Gogo glanced at Trav, who blushed and came to help her with the drinks.

"My," she said. "You are in a good mood."

The Magician shrugged, then laughed. "I've heard interesting news. Someone," he said, still grinning, "has been *very* careless."

Shortly thereafter, the two children emerged from 17 Wizard's Row. That day, the house was a white cottage that would not have been out of place on Kil Beach or Minnow Island, except perhaps for a tiny brass gargoyle's head set into the center of the front door. As the children left, the gargoyle called, "He said not to come back until tomorrow! So stay away until then! Or longer!"

Sessi whispered, "I liked the other one better."

Sorel said, "You mean that door-thing and the serving woman are the same?"

Sessi nodded. "'Cept somebody else is the door-thing, right now."

After an instant, Sorel said, "I knew that."

The tiny brass gargoyle snickered maliciously. The white

fence gate closed behind The Magician's clients. When they had left Wizard's Row, Number 17 opened again. A small balding man in the grey and blue of the Levar's Guard looked in either direction, then stepped toward the street.

"You needn't hurry back," the gargoyle said.

The balding man laughed. "I like the other one better, too." He strode briskly to One-Hand Lane, where a young woman waited by an empty footcab.

She glanced at his uniform and his flintlock pistol, and said, "Afternoon, Captain. Where to?"

He sat in the cab. "The Tichenese embassy. And don't spare the horses."

The woman frowned as she lifted the shafts to draw the cab away. "If I have to hear more jokes," she mumbled, "I expect a good tip."

The officer was silent for the rest of their trip. The footcab traveled north on Cat Street, passing the flatboats and barges that plied the river and the canals, and then passing the boats' destination: Fisher's Market, the Old Town Market. Hawkers shouted their wares with glee, except for one sad-faced fellow crying plaintively, "Camel stew! *Very* cheap!" and the crowd slowed their passage until they neared Temple Hill.

The homes along the Levar's Way to the west of Temple Circle were walled as though they were fortresses, to keep out invaders in forgotten times and thieves in the present. Two very dark women and a man stood before the iron gates of one, with their arms crossed and no weapons visible. They wore the blue and silver robes of the Guild of Power, which proclaimed them to be among Tichen's most skillful sorcerers.

The footcab stopped by the three foreigners. The Guard captain stepped down, counted out his fare in shiny coppers, and walked toward the spiked gate as the footcab hurried away. The tallest sorcerer blocked his way, smiled down at him, and said, "Does the Ambassador expect you?"

"No," the captain answered calmly. "But he would do well to see me, if he did not want the City General to inquire about his dealings with Deremer Ledoro."

The sorcerer's grin widened. "Come, Captain. We shall take you to the one you seek. You will surrender your pistol?"

"Of course."

The smaller woman accepted the weapon and sneered slightly. Two of the sorcerers, the man and the tall woman, stepped back for the captain to lead, so he took the cobblestone road into the embassy. The grounds beyond the granite wall were elaborately gardened in Tichenese fashion, with small, shaped trees and streams that ran over beds of colored pebbles. The embassy stood several hundred yards beyond the gate.

The captain glanced back at his escorts. Though the young man's face was somber, the tall woman smiled. Her teeth glistened like marble. She said, "Do you have doubts about your mission, Captain?"

"No," the Liàvekan answered quietly.

Both sorcerers extended their fingers toward the captain. "You should," the woman said, laughing as the captain disappeared.

Naked of clothing and jewelry, he stood on cold limestone before a wall of polished black rock. Something cast light from behind him, and as he turned, he heard a polite cough that said he was not alone.

A handsome, middle-aged man with Tichenese features stood five paces away. His goatee hung as low as his sternum, and his hair was worn in many long braids. His robe was almost entirely indigo, with only a thin piping of silver at the hem and on each sleeve. The man bowed low and said, "Greetings to you, Trav The Magician. Do not step from the place where you stand, or I must burn you until you are but ashes. That would be a waste, don't you think?"

"Rather," Trav answered cautiously. The lack of windows and the cool, moist air suggested they stood in an unfinished basement, probably beneath the embassy. His disguise of the little balding man had disappeared with his clothes, his freedom, and, he noted, all his carefully prepared protective spells. His skull felt naked. When he passed his hand over it, he learned that his hair had been taken, too.

"You needn't trouble yourself about the vessel of your power, Colleague Trav, whatever it might be. All that you wore is far, far more than three paces away from you." The sorcerer smiled gently. "I'm sorry about making you bald. I've never known anyone to successfully invest power in hair, but I take no chances with one of your skill. Please, accept this as a gesture of respect."

Trav shrugged, wondering what other precautions the Tichenese had taken, and sat cross-legged on the chilly floor. "Surely this is an excess of respect, Chiano Mefini."

"Oh!" The sorcerer pursed his lips in pleasure. "My fame precedes me?"

"Who doesn't know of the Guild of Power's Young Teacher, whom some say intends to replace the Old Teacher soon?"

"In this uncivilized city," said Mefini, laughing, "no one but Trav The Magician. I enjoy playing the ambassador."

"You do it well. Why've you troubled to lure me here?"

"Ah, you come to the point, Colleague Trav." Mefini patted his goatee, then said, "And since you do, I'll tell you honestly that another war between Liavek and Ka Zhir would insure that Tichen remains strong. Our Guild has done a few subtle things to hurry such a war, yet several of our agents have failed. We are not familiar with failure. When I suggested to the Old Teacher that Trav The Magician might have intervened, she laughed and said you were too concerned with your wealth and your safety to take sides. And then she suggested that I reassure myself." Mefini took a roll of yellowed parchment from his robe and opened it. "You recognize this?"

Trav studied the sigils. "Yes. The Scroll of Truth. You have much power, Chiano Mefini."

"Thank you." Mefini set the scroll carefully on the ground before Trav. "Place your hand upon it and swear on your luck and your life never to interfere in Tichenese matters. Then you may return to your house and your business."

"I don't suppose you'd accept my promise?" said Trav.

"I'm sorry. It must be the Scroll."

"I'd rather not."

"And I'd rather not kill you."

Trav nodded. "Good. Tell me, is the doll here?"

Mefini glanced at a dark corner perhaps ten feet away, where something small sat atop a crate. "Why?"

"Your ruse was well done." Trav propped his elbows behind him and leaned back as though he lay on the rug in his study. "I imagine you promised the boy a great deal of money to let you alter his memory for a few hours. Since he believed what he said, he couldn't give away your trap. Did you also bewitch the girl, so she believed she had owned the doll? Or did you fail to tell the boy why you had him burgle Deremer Ledoro's home, and he gave the doll to the girl as he said?"

"Does it matter?" Mefini asked.

"I suppose not," said Trav. "But you did have the boy burgle Ledoro's home."

"Yes." Mefini watched Trav as though he suspected there might be more to The Magician's speech than curiosity.

"I thought so," Trav said. "For me to believe his story, most of it had to be true. That was rather risky, Chiano Mefini." The shadows about The Magician seemed to grow blacker. Though his tone was casual, his eyes never left his captor's face.

"A risk worth taking," Mefini replied, smiling apologetically, "as you are now my prisoner." A hint of suspicion crept into his voice. "If you hope to regain your magic, I must confess that all your clothes and jewelry were sent into a volcano's womb. Whatever may have been the vessel of your luck, it is destroyed and you are powerless." Mefini coughed a command in Tichenese, and a ball of fire flared and died above Trav. As its ashes fell on Trav's naked form, Mefini said, "As you see, I am not. Tell what you think, Colleague Trav."

Trav laughed lightly. "I think that Deremer Ledoro seduced you in order to study Tichenese magic. She must have learned your weakness and stolen it. When Ledoro's luck was freed by a friend of mine, you learned she was powerless and sent the boy to take back your doll. And then you thought to use these events to lure me from my home."

Mefini frowned. "My weakness, you say? You think you know what the doll is?"

"You expected its description to intrigue me and doubted I would guess its purpose?" The Magician smiled gently. "You are old, Chiano Mefini, perhaps older than I. Magicians wonder about other magicians, especially those who live for many years. It is the Master's Conundrum, I believe you call it in Tichen, yes? A magician must invest birth luck every year, and it cannot be used for any purpose while it is being invested in a vessel. A magician may stay magically young throughout the year, but eventually, we all grow too old to survive the weight of our true age during those few hours of investiture. Yet a magician who binds birth luck to create a talisman to stay young forever will have no more magic to use. Such a magician with enemies or covetous friends will soon be dead by other means than age. Still, solutions are available, as both of us have found."

Mefini gestured sharply. "Go on."

"A magician loved you," Trav said, "a magician whom you convinced or forced to bind his or her luck into an object whose only purpose is to keep you alive." Trav leaned back further and crossed his legs in perfect ease. "The doll, of course. Rather embarrassing when your Liavekan dancing girl stole it, I imagine."

Mefini shrugged. "I have it back. No matter." Then he grinned. "I appreciate your wisdom, Trav The Magician, yet here you are, my prisoner. Your luck has been freed, all your spells have failed, and two of my students are searching the famous seventeen Wizard's Row at their leisure. But nothing shall be disturbed if you swear never to meddle in Tichenese matters." He pointed a ringed finger at the Scroll of Truth.

"I told you before," The Magician said carefully. "No."

"You have a rather foolish confidence, Colleague Trav."

"That's probably true. But let me tell you a story."

Mefini snorted, then smiled. "Very well, Colleague Trav. If you think it pertinent, I wish to hear it."

"Decide when I finish." Trav cleared his throat. "In 2947, while Liavek warred with Saltigos, there was a young Liavekan named Marik whose luck was such that he had learned the ill-luck periods of seven of the mightiest Saltigan wizards. He stole the vessels of their luck and destroyed each vessel during its owner's ill-luck period, thus freeing each wizard's luck for all time. The Saltigans, reasonably enough, believed Marik's death was vital to their cause. The leader of these Saltigans thought further, and decided that to strip Marik of his power and parade him before Liavek's walls might so dispirit the Liavekans that they would surrender. So the Saltigans hired three Tichenese sorcerers of your Guild to aid them. Perhaps some form of the tale has come down to you?"

"I almost recognize it," said Mefini. "Speak on."

"The three sorcerers studied the stars and the tides and the entrails of many rare animals, and then they got one of Marik's servants drunk and learned the time of Marik's birth. But they could not learn what vessel he used to keep his luck, so, at the hour when Marik's luck returned from its vessel to his body, the sorcerers used a spell to cast him naked into a prison of their choosing, much as you have done with me."

"Which is why you tell this story, I assume."

"Yes. Their purpose was different from yours, and they had

more time to prepare, or so I assume. You will not be insulted if I say that their prison was far cleverer than yours, Chiano Mefini?"

"Oh?" Mefini frowned.

"Indeed. They sent Marik to a place beyond our world where he floated in something like mist. His luck was within him then, full and powerful, yet there was nothing for him to invest it in, not even ground beneath him, and nothing for him to employ it upon. After the time of his birth had passed, the Tichenese sorcerers brought Marik back to our world."

Mefini raised his arms cautiously. "You are not saying we brought you here on your birthday? The odds of that are—"

Trav laughed. "No, Chiano Mefini. I swear it on my luck. I have not been telling you tales to lull you while I reinvested my magic."

"I see," Mefini said, though his shoulders were visibly stiff with tension. "Out of curiosity, Colleague Trav, was your luck in one of your bracelets? Wearing two is a common precaution."

"Not the bracelets," said Trav. "But let me finish my story. It is almost over."

"Very well."

"The sorcerers had complimented themselves on their cleverness as they called Marik back from that dimension of perfect emptiness. They had heard, of course, the rumor that a very rare individual could invest his luck in his own body, but they did not believe that was possible, no more than I believe it today. And so they imagined poor Marik would arrive magicless until his next birthday, ready for delivery to the Saltigans who would pay a premium for a service perfectly performed."

When Trav said no more, Mefini said, "And?"

Trav smiled. "And Marik appeared before them, as naked as he had been imprisoned, as naked as I am now. In his left fist, he held his severed right hand, the hand that he had cut from his arm with his birth magic and invested with his luck. They say Marik laughed as he slew his captors. Liavekans remember him as Marik One-Hand, and they still celebrate his birthday. The street near my house was named for him."

Mefini shuddered. "That's an ugly story. What's it have to do with us?"

"Much," said Trav, rising smoothly to his feet and pointing with his left hand at the crate where Mefini's doll lay. In the shadows, something like a large spider scuttled to the doll and embraced it. "You see," said Trav, bringing the stump of his right arm from behind his back, "I am Marik One-Hand, and I hold your life in my palm."

The two magicians stared at each other. The air in the basement seemed warmer and more humid than it had moments before. At last, Mefini set his hand on the Scroll of Truth and said sadly, "I swear to forfeit my life and my power if ever I meddle in the affairs of Liavek, or let anyone learn from me the secrets of Marik One-Hand, or use my knowledge in any way to harm Marik or Liavek. Will that suffice?"

"I could require more," Trav said. "But it will do."

"What of my students?"

Trav laughed. "My front door let them into a maze of mirrors. My cats have been amusing themselves by chasing your students through it for the past hour."

"Your cats?"

"Chaos and Disorder. They are a lioness and a tiger, at present."

"I . . . see." Mefini frowned. "Aren't the names redundant?"

"You have never kept cats." The Magician stepped to the crate where Mefini's doll was still in the severed hand's grip. As he fitted his right wrist to the hand, he glanced toward a door at the rear of the room and called, "Gogo!"

The door opened. Mefini's eyes grew wide in surprise as his students stumbled through it with two great cats snarling at their thighs. The hall beyond was brightly lit and seemed to be made of glowing diamonds set under glass. A short woman in a white tunic stood smiling in the doorway.

Trav told the cats, "That's enough," and they quit chasing the students in order to rub against his legs. "You can stop being affectionate; I'll feed you soon enough," he said. The cats continued, which almost made him fall several times as he carried Mefini's doll to the sorcerer. "It is hard to have cats and dignity," he said.

"I . . . suppose so," Mefini agreed, accepting the doll. The Magician's right wrist was ringed with a tiny scar, but otherwise appeared normal.

"Our powers didn't work in there!" one of the students gasped.

"No," Trav agreed. He glanced at Mefini. "I assume you'll be leaving Liavek soon?"

"Yes."

"Give my greetings to your colleagues in the Guild of Power."

"If I do, they'll guess that you were responsible for my leaving, no matter what I may or may not say."

"Yes," Trav said. "Farewell, Chiano Mefini." He stepped into the bright hall with his cats, and the short woman kissed him, saying, "Hi, Baldy," as the door swung shut.

Mefini and his students stared at the basement door for several minutes. At last, the tall woman said, "Shall I?"

Mefini nodded. The woman went to the door and cautiously opened it. The dusty stairs to their embassy lay beyond.

In the long hallway of many doors that was sometimes found in The Magician's house, Gogo said, "You know, you might as well have declared war on Tichen's sorcerers."

"Yes," Trav answered.

"Good. Just so you know. What'll you do when the children come tomorrow?"

"I doubt the boy'll return. When Mefini's memory spell fades, the boy'll go to the embassy for payment. Once he learns that the ambassador left suddenly for Tichen, he'll stay far away from Wizard's Row for some time, I suspect."

"And the girl?"

"I only agreed to *seek* the doll."

"Trav . . ."

"Maybe we can make her a doll that looks like the one she lost?"

"She lives on the city streets, you know. With no more friends than that boy, who will probably abandon her if he can think of no more schemes in which to use her."

"There is the Levar's Orphanage, Gogo."

"I was thinking of Tel Jassil on the Street of Old Coins. He's kind, and he has no children. If you made her adoption a part of the price for the S'Rian coin—"

"He'd pay me half its value, then!"

"Yes." She kissed him. "Poor Trav."

As they stepped into his study, he said, "I will never be rich."

Gogo laughed and put her arm about his waist. "But you'll live well."

The Fortune Maker

by Barry B. Longyear

It was the Thirteenth of Flowers. As he studied the tangle of yhinroot fibers at the bottom of his cup, Elmutt the garbage picker was thinking that there was something different about this day. It was more than Tavi being absent. The little troll always made himself scarce when Elmutt was in Almantia's presence. It was something else. There was something different about Elmutt.

"Elmutt?"

He looked up from his cup, not quite letting his gaze fall on Almantia's face. It was not that he found her face disagreeable. Quite the contrary. His eyes could not bear to tease his heart any further with the impossible.

"Elmutt? Will you answer me?" There was a note of impatience in her words. But it was the kind of note a parent plays for a beloved child. In his heart he felt something between anger and despair. Almantia was barely old enough to wed, and Elmutt was no child.

"My sorrow, good lady. My mind was wandering."

"They say that if one lets the mind wander, one might lose

it." She gestured with her hand at the loaf and pot. "I asked if you would care for some more tea."

He looked into her face. She had an uncommon fairness about her complexion and features. A kind of beauty Elmutt secretly suspected her grandfather, the wizard Yolik, must have created for her. No one, he thought, was ever that beautiful. How can she talk about tea? Can't she hear my heart dying?

"Yes, if it pleases you."

She talked as she poured the vaporous liquid from the pot into Elmutt's cup. "Do you remember the first time we had tea?"

"Yes. Three years ago today."

She grinned. "I'm surprised you remembered." She pointed at his cup. "Hurry, drink up before it gets cold."

Elmutt lifted the cup and sipped at the brew, the ribbons of sweet and bitter alternately caressing and flogging his tongue.

Of course he remembered. He had been picking among the infrequently visible refuse of Wizard's Row, Tavi nagging from his shoulder, searching for things that might aid him in breaking his luck. She had appeared before him, her delicate olive face a jewel in the setting of her white and silver gown and veil. Of course he remembered. The moment she appeared, Tavi had vanished. It had been the first time since he could remember that he had been free of the troll, not by the creature's choosing. Tavi was afraid of the wizard's granddaughter.

Almantia had said to him, "Picker, I have some cleaning and errands I want done. Could you use a few extra coppers?"

There was a terror in his heart. Instantly he loved her and, at the same time, forbade himself to feel his love. Such a love would be too easy a target for Tavi's scorn. It would be a ridiculous love—a woman of such station and an insect from Dung Alley? Ridiculous. A wizard and a lame garbage picker? Ridiculous. Existence had already placed upon his shoulders more weight than he could carry. Elmutt refused to carry the additional burden of being ridiculous.

He did the work that she wanted, and over the next three years she hired him many times to scrub steps, take away refuse, purchase things for her, deliver messages. But he never spent any of the coppers that she paid him. He could not bear the thought of parting with the coins, for Almantia had touched them.

When he had finished his errands that first day, she had invited him into her gold and white tiled kitchen for yhinroot tea. Taking tea together had become a regular ritual. He disliked yhinroot tea, but it was a small price to pay to be near her.

As they sipped from their cups she would talk to him, telling him of her magic studies, her hopes and her dreams. Sometimes she would fill the moment with idle gossip. At other times she would describe the seemingly endless parade of handsome, wealthy suitors that desired her, the gifts with which they showered her, the performances and ceremonies to which they brought her, every word both a treasure and a wound to the garbage picker.

Sometimes she would ask his advice about small things. Sometimes she would flirt with him, touching his face with her hand, winking at him, once even giving him a kiss on his cheek.

He raised his hand to his cheek where her lips had innocently touched it with eternal mischief. He heard her voice.

"Elmutt, you are not listening. Is something wrong? You look very strange."

He brought his thoughts back to the present and lowered his hand. "Again, my sorrow." He chanced a look at her face. Her brow carried a hint of genuine concern. His gaze touched her eyes and darted away in the fear that his own eyes might reveal his longing, his pain. He did not think he could survive her laughing at his love. He picked up his cup and pretended to be intensely interested in its contents.

"Elmutt, you aren't thinking of investing your luck, are you? I know you once entertained such a thought. I warned you about trying such a thing then."

Automatically he shook his head in the negative. "No, good lady. If one learned in magic, such as yourself, is not considered sufficiently prepared to attempt investiture, I would be a fool to try."

Her hand reached across the table and closed over his. "If you tried, Elmutt, you would sicken and die." Her hand withdrew as she laughed. "I would hate to lose my dear little picker."

He tossed down his tea, the scalding of his gullet nothing compared to the fire burning upon the back of his hand. He put down the cup and pushed himself up from his cushion. "I must be going, good lady. Will you need me tomorrow?"

She stood and began gathering the things from the table. "No. I will be away tomorrow, but come the day after and see."

"Very well. The day after tomorrow, then."

She turned from the basin stand and gave the picker a gentle look. "Be kind to yourself, Elmutt."

"I will. . . . My thanks."

He bowed out of the kitchen, the words choking him, and fled to the street as fast as his crippled leg would allow. Once outside he reached for his picker's bag, noticing that Tavi was not waiting for him. For the moment he would at least be spared his creature's abuse. Elmutt put the bag over his shoulder and looked back. Almantia's house had already vanished. The picker sighed and began the limp back to Dung Alley.

It was evening, the harsh, reedy sounds of the snake flutes mixing with the smells of spice and decay. As Elmutt entered the north end of Dung Alley he paused to let his gaze rest once more upon the Skull. Again, there was that strange feeling. It was not the helpless silent rage that usually choked him. It was different. Something much calmer, yet bearing more strength. A curious feeling.

He lowered his sack of pickings, still staring at the place that had been the closest thing to what he could ever call home. The building was not unusually tall for the city of Liavek. There were other structures much taller. Its four floors and spired roof, however, stood like a mast above the hovels lining the filth-strewn path in Old Town called Dung Alley. On the alley, they called the landmark Narkaan's Skull, referring both to the ancient god of ghosts and the gaping holes carved in the structure by weather, time, and vandals.

Viewed from the proper direction, it did look like a skull. The missing walls on the third and fourth floors formed the great gaping eye sockets and nose hole, the grinning teeth formed by a crumbling balcony. From any other angle the building looked to be nothing more than a ruin. From where Elmutt stood, it looked like a skull.

Beneath the structure was Ghaster the garbage picker's cellar. There he collected, cleaned, repaired, stored, displayed, and sold the minor treasures Elmutt gleaned from Liavek's waste. And there Ghaster would isolate himself and cancel the profit he had made by drinking an endless river of Dragonpiss.

Where there had once been fear of the old fat man there was now a numbness in Elmutt's heart.

Ghaster's cruelty was legend on Dung Alley. The story had often been told of the time when the picker's bond child, Elmutt, was three or four years old, standing at the top of the cellar's long flight of stone stairs. Ghaster had stood at the bottom of the stairs and had called to the boy to jump into his open arms. The boy had squealed with glee, jumped, and Ghaster had simply stepped out of the way, allowing Elmutt to crash to the stone floor. Those who witnessed the event heard Ghaster tell the boy, "That is to teach you never to trust anyone." The fall injured Elmutt's left leg, giving him the limp that he still carried.

Elmutt looked down at his crippled leg. It was the visible manifestation of one of the scars that he carried on his heart. But Ghaster at least was predictable. The beatings, the verbal assaults, the brief glimpses of a rapidly eroding humanity, were as familiar to Elmutt as the times of the sun, the moon, and the tides. As familiar as Tavi's taunts.

He thought of her. Almantia was much different.

He straightened as another scar on his heart opened, flooding him with shame, anger and pain. Elmutt held his hand to his cheek. She only kissed him in fun, because she was young, alive, and she found amusement in seeing the picker embarrassed. It was no more than that. It could never be more than that.

The image of Narkaan's Skull blurred and Elmutt realized that his eyes were filled with tears. Almantia's kiss hadn't embarrassed him. Her lips had shattered his heart.

"Move on, picker!"

He turned to his right, expecting to see Tavi. Instead he saw the hag, Cankera, standing amidst her evil-smelling piles of used clothing. "I have as much right to stand in this alley as anyone, hag."

She folded her fleshy arms and spat back at him. "I'll get no buyers with you stinking up the front of my stall. Move on, Worrynot's Humiliation!" Her cackle filled the alley, drawing the many eyes in their direction.

Elmutt swallowed his anger, put his bag over his shoulder and aimed his limp toward the Skull.

Worrynot's Humiliation.

Ghaster had titled him that, Elmutt's existence being graphic evidence of the esteemed contraceptive weed's fallibility. Sometimes Ghaster would goad him with the story of how he had acquired his bond child from the crone who had, in turn, picked the foundling out of the garbage behind Serena's Couch, a house of negotiable virtue at the south end of Rat's Alley. Elmutt would try at times to imagine his mother, the whore—

"There is only so much of this that any man can take," he whispered to himself.

That calm, strong feeling again invaded his pain. This time he recognized the feeling. Somewhere in the back of his head he had found the courage to make the decision. Tomorrow would be the Fourteenth of Flowers. Tomorrow he would attempt to change the luck that had steered him through sorrow ever since he could remember. He would invest his luck, or die trying. In the western sky, beyond the Hill of Temples and the Levar's palace, there were storm clouds building.

Outside it was raining into the blackness of the alley. In the cellar, Elmutt sat upon his pallet while Ghaster reclined upon his collection of greasy cushions, his perennial jug of Dragonpiss cradled in his arms. The shadows thrown by the two candles that burned between them made the mounds of bottles and cliffs of broken furniture shiver in the dark.

"Where is your little friend, Elmutt?"

"Do you mean Tavi?"

Ghaster snorted out a laugh. "What other friend do you have?"

"Tavi is no friend." He pointed a finger at Ghaster. "You cannot see him. How do you know Tavi isn't spitting into your precious bottle this instant?"

"I know." Ghaster took a swallow from his jug and replaced it upon the cushion as he wiped the back of his hand against his mouth. "I know because if Tavi were here, you two would be fighting. It is too serene here for Tavi to be present."

Elmutt slowly shook his head. "Tavi has been missing since before I entered Yolik's house this afternoon. Perhaps a dog ate him."

"You can always dream, Elmutt." After taking another swallow, Ghaster settled more deeply into his cushions. "Tell me your dream. Your other dream."

Elmutt ignored the request and closed his eyes as he leaned his back against a large wicker basket filled with junk.

"Tell me your dream."

Elmutt opened his eyes and glared at his master. "Why, Ghaster? So you can make fun of it again?"

"No, boy. I like to hear you tell it. It is a nice dream to listen to for one who sleeps in garbage."

Elmutt frowned. The fat, greasy man had often asked to hear what he called Elmutt's dream. Always, after hearing it, Ghaster would heap scorn and abuse on his bond child. There used to be beatings, as well. But Elmutt was now grown enough to kill his master, which he once proved as he terminated Ghaster's last whipping by beating his master senseless. For the first time, however, Elmutt saw that Ghaster was old. Very old, and sick. Elmutt also saw for the first time that Ghaster was not in love with his own life. His master had some pain of his own.

Elmutt shook his head. "I cannot bring myself to pity you, Ghaster."

The fat man laughed. "I do not want pity. Not from *you*." He took another swallow from his jug and lowered the container to his lap. He pointed a pudgy finger. "From you I want to hear the dream."

"It is not a dream. It is my plan."

"Yes, yes." Ghaster nodded, his face serious. "Go on."

Tomorrow evening he would attempt investiture. This might be, he thought, a good time to review it and see if there was anything left undone.

"My plan is to change my luck. From my birth, to the infliction of Tavi on my person, to my purchase by you, I have been at the mercy of a perverse fate. This can be changed. My plan is to place my fate under *my* control. During the time of birthday magic, I will perform the rite and invest my luck in a vessel. I will become a great wizard, and with my luck at my fingertips throughout the year, I will acquire the wealth to live in ease and splendor. I will have fine clothes, rich foods, servants, a beautiful and loving wife, the smell of clean air in my nostrils. I will have *power!* That, Ghaster, is my plan. Now it is your turn to try and spoil it."

Ghaster sat up on his cushions, his gaze fixed upon the flame of one of the candles. Instead of beginning his usual scornful review, however, the old garbage picker studied the flame for a moment, then lifted his gaze and studied Elmutt's face. "What day is it?"

"It is Windday."

"The date. What is the date?"

"It is the Thirteenth."

Ghaster frowned deeply as he sat forward and nodded. "And tomorrow is the Fourteenth, the day you think you were born. You have made a decision, haven't you? You are really going to try it?"

"Yes."

"That is the strangeness I saw in your face." The fat man shook his head. "It is so dangerous. If you are not successful, you will die. Don't you remember what happened to the shoemaker, Ulduss? His uncle was a magician, yet with that advantage he died."

"I know. However, my rotting master, only those who find life attractive fear death."

"Elmutt, learned magicians with many years of experience often fail at investiture."

"I know that as well. I am as prepared as I will ever be."

Ghaster leaned back against his cushions, took a swallow from his jug, and looked back at Elmutt. "How can you even be certain that the Fourteenth is your birthdate?"

"I have observed my luck. It is always bad, but on the Fourteenth of Flowers it becomes particularly bad. It was the Fourteenth of Flowers when you helped me to cripple my leg. You said it was in the middle of Flowers when you purchased me from the crone. It was that same date when I awakened to find that Tavi had chosen me as his victim. It was the Fourteenth—" Yes, he thought of the year before. It was the Fourteenth of Flowers when Almantia kissed me, destroying me.

Ghaster shrugged, seemingly not noticing the incompletion of Elmutt's words. "If it is not your birthdate, you will look like a fool. If it is your birthdate, it will be very dangerous. You will die. I am certain of it."

Elmutt replied more for his own benefit than for Ghaster's. "For years I have done errands for Yolik's granddaughter, and for the White priests. I have picked up much from their idle talk, from stolen glimpses of scripture, and from the refuse bins behind the temples and along Wizard's Row."

"It is still dangerous." Ghaster picked at a scab on his chin and smiled. "What will you use as a vessel?"

"The laws of magic say that I may invest my luck in anything that I choose. However, I would leave nothing to chance. There are discarded vessels. I know they will serve because they have served before. I have a great copper staff that once belonged to Yolik. He discarded it when he became too old and feeble to carry it, investing his luck instead in a ring. I have an iron mail cap that was once the vessel of the White priest Soldire, and the belt of woven brass that served as the luck vessel of the wizard Miena, until she became too fat to wear it."

Ghaster laughed out loud. "Ho, that is the way a true picker approaches investiture! There he is, people of Liavek! Clad in your garbage! The magician of muck! The wizard of waste!"

Ghaster's interest was deteriorating into scathing scorn. Elmutt turned away from his master and stretched out on his pallet. "Let me sleep, Ghaster."

"No, no!" A condescending tone crept into his voice. "Forgive me, Elmutt. My humor is out of place. See what I have brought you."

Elmutt kept his back turned to the old man. "Drink yourself to sleep and let me be."

"Elmutt, I have brought you yet another vessel. Here, look."

Elmutt turned his head. "What is it?"

The old man reached behind his cushions and pulled out a crooked brown shaft that was covered with fuzz, a busy clump of matted hair at one end. He threw it at Elmutt and collapsed on his cushions, laughing.

It landed at Elmutt's feet. It was a rotting tail amputated from some long forgotten camel. He kicked it back toward Ghaster.

"You are a pig. You are a cursed pig, Ghaster. Someday I will kill you." He turned his back on his master.

"What does Tavi say? Your little creature, Elmutt. What does *he* say?"

"Tavi doesn't know."

"You should find out what Tavi thinks. As much as you hate him, he is from ghostside and ought to know at least a little of such things."

Elmutt ignored the comment.

Ghaster took another drink, belched, and wiped one dirty hand across his face. "I know you hate me. Maybe you think I hate you. I don't, boy. Remember that."

Elmutt remained silent until the fat man drifted off to sleep. Once he heard his master's snores, he sat up and studied the shadows. Those shadows, the piles of refuse that threw them, the cellar, even Ghaster's sleeping hulk, had somehow become dearer to his eyes.

"It is true," he whispered. "This may be my last living night."

He heard a giggle and turned his head to his left. Sitting atop a pile of salvaged bricks, a creature no larger than a doll, but with a disproportionately large head, leered back. The face was lumpy with warts and was the color of mud.

"I wondered when you would show up, Tavi."

Another giggle. "You know you are not my only client, pitiful one. Do not be jealous. No, no, no, do not be *jealous!*" Tavi's voice was high-pitched, his speech rapid. "How was your crawl and grovel before the wizard's granddaughter, abused toady, hmmm?"

"Why didn't you stay away?"

The troll grabbed the stockinged toes of each foot with his hands and rocked back and forth upon his ample rear. "Why, me, why, my? Why, oh, why?" Tavi came to rest leaning forward. "I must watch you, I must. You fascinate me, you do, you do, you do. How much can Elmutt take before he takes his life, how much? And now I *know!* My, oh, yes, I know, I do, I do, I *do!*"

"I am not going to take my own life. Never."

"My, oh, my, a lie to Tavi? Tch, tch, tch." Tavi shook his head, still leering. "Naughty, naughty, *naughty.*"

"Go to sleep, you reeking gob of pus." Elmutt turned his back and stretched out upon his pallet.

The creature's face appeared in front of his. "Tavi knows, he does, yes. Tomorrow Elmutt kills himself, yes, yes?"

Elmutt pushed himself up upon an elbow. "Tomorrow I shall acquire the magic to turn you into a lump of dung. A *quiet* lump of dung. That is, if you don't foul th—" Elmutt's frown melted into a smile. "Thank you, Tavi."

The creature's eyebrows went up. "Thank Tavi? Thank Tavi? Why, oh, why?"

Elmutt settled his head upon his arm. "You reminded me of a detail that I have to take care of before my investiture, that's all."

"Detail? What detail, what?"

"You, little pestilence. You are the detail. Now crawl back to hell and let me sleep."

"Me? Me, what?"

Elmutt closed his eyes, his face smiling. As long as Tavi remained confused, perhaps he would remain silent. In the quiet of the storm from outside, Elmutt slept.

Early the next morning while Ghaster lay motionless upon his cushions, Elmutt walked through the rain, an oilcloth held over his head. From his perch upon Elmutt's shoulder, Tavi shivered.

"This is too early, this is. And too wet. Go back, Elmutt, go back."

Ignoring the troll, he turned right onto the Street of Mists, the rain coming from behind with such force that he had to lean backward against it to keep his footing.

Tavi shouted in Elmutt's ear. "Idiot!"

Elmutt stopped. "What is it?"

"You are so stupid, you are! It is raining, you see, you see?"

"If you don't like it, Tavi, you can get off now!"

The little creature sighed. "Why make your death so difficult, Elmutt, why? Take us out of the rain."

"I said you can get off. Go devil your other clients."

"Oh, pitiful one, it is your turn, it is."

"Bah!" Elmutt continued along the deserted street toward the north end of Rat's Alley. The shutters and doors of the Street of Mists were closed tightly against the storm. When the thunder rolled it seemed as though the very ground trembled. It is fitting, thought Elmutt. It is fitting that I would draw this kind of weather for my investiture.

Many of the investiture rituals could be conducted anywhere, indoors or out. The only ritual he knew by heart, however, required him to stand in the open atop the rise just off the Street of Trees. He felt the weight of the coins in the purse suspended beneath his dripping cloak. It contained every copper that he owned, including his wages from Almantia. He wondered if, at any price, he could hire dancers and musicians to perform in this muck.

He turned into Rat's Alley and noticed that the storm as well as the morning had drowned the notorious way's bright lights and gay sounds. One of many eternal puzzles played itself again in his head. Rat's Alley and Dung Alley were separated by only a few minutes of walking. Yet they were different worlds. Instead of drab hovels, on this part of Rat's Alley there were well maintained, if garish, structures providing a variety of services to satisfy every quirk and lust ever possessed by a person of wealth. The inhabitants made a speciality of parting the wealth from the wealthy, or as Tavi was wont to remark, "Rat's Alley. You will never find a more wretched hive of scum and villainy, good, good, *good!*"

Elmutt stopped beneath the sign of the ass's ass and tried the doors of Cheeky's, famed for delivering the minimum value at the maximum price. In addition to their questionable wine and solvent financial posture, Cheeky's employed some of the finest dancers and musicians in Old Town.

"It's locked."

"Perhaps, Elmutt, they noticed that it is raining, it is. May you learn from this establishment's example, you fool, you fool, you—"

"Be still!"

To his left through the rain he could make out another pedestrian struggling in his direction. It was an old woman wrapped in an oilskin cape and hood. "Ho, there!"

The woman stopped and Elmutt froze as he saw her arms move beneath her cape. The motion meant that at least a knife, or more likely a pistol or springdart, was aimed at his belly.

"What do you want?"

Elmutt bowed slightly, holding his oilcloth up from his face with one hand and holding his other hand out to his side with his empty palm facing the woman. "Forgive me, woman. But are any of the places with dancers open, do you know?"

Tavi clapped his hands and squealed, "Oh, I *love* dancers, I do, I do, I *do!*"

The woman's face assumed a sour expression as she held back her head to view the picker down her nose. "Youth today," she spat. "It is hardly light, and already you are on the debauch!"

Elmutt shook his head. "No, no, good woman. I need dancers and musicians for a ritual. I have come to see if I can hire some."

Tavi danced upon Elmutt's shoulder, still clapping his hands. "Dancers, oh, dancers! I *love* dancers!" The creature paused in midprance and turned his head toward Elmutt, a puzzled look upon his face. "Dancers, Elmutt? Dancers at your death? Why, why?"

The woman's eyebrows went up. "A ritual, is it?"

Tavi turned toward the woman and mocked, "A ritual, is

it? A ritual, is it?" Only Elmutt could hear the creature's taunts, and he refused to react.

"The old hag," hissed Tavi. "She has no weapon, Elmutt. She is only scratching her scabbed hide. A ritual, is it? A good lie, Elmutt. A *ritual*, poo!"

The woman shook her head, still keeping a wary eye upon the picker. "You should be on the Hill of Temples looking for ritual players."

"I cannot afford them."

She nodded with her head toward Cheeky's. "In back of the place. Try there. But they are too stupid to play a ritual. All they know is naked flesh and loud drums."

Again Tavi danced and clapped his hands. "Oh, I love, love, love naked flesh and loud drums, I do, I do, I *do!*"

Elmutt placed his outstretched palm against his forehead, bowing slightly. "My thanks, good woman." He turned away and headed for the walkway indicated by the woman. The path between Cheeky's and the next building was open to the sky and stank with a row of soggy, overflowing garbage barrels. Almost instinctively, Elmutt's gaze scanned the contents of the barrels. There was a wealth of bottles, most of them unbroken. Having them hidden from the alley meant that the proprietor of Cheeky's had contracted with professional garbagers. Ghaster would be pleased at this new source of supply. They would have to sneak in at night to avoid the garbagers—

Tavi tugged at his earlobe. "By this time tomorrow, Elmutt, you will either be too grand or too dead to be picking Cheeky's garbage, you will, you will."

Elmutt nodded and continued down the walkway. "Thank you, Tavi."

Tavi jumped up and down upon Elmutt's shoulder and shouted angrily, "Do *not* be thanking Tavi all the time! Not!" The creature's voice became sly. "Why you thank Tavi, why? Last night and now, why?"

"You do me favors, Tavi. That's why."

"Humph!"

As Elmutt knocked upon the only door that opened onto the walkway, the creature upon his shoulder stewed in hot confusion.

The man seated on the floor cushion leaned his elbow on a table and stroked his slick black beard. "A dancer, a drummer, and one on pipes, eh?" His name was Hidat.

Elmutt nodded from his cushion. "Yes. How much for an hour's performance?"

"When?"

"This evening, an hour after sunset."

The man shivered with projections of the rain outside. "Ten."

"Ten coppers?" Elmutt was surprised at Hidat's generosity.

The man laughed. "Ten *levars*."

"That's . . ." The figure swirled in Elmutt's head. "That's a *thousand* coppers! Too much. Too much for an hour's work." He began climbing to his feet, but Hidat gestured for him to remain seated.

"Do not be so eager to end the negotiations, Elmutt. Make a return offer."

"I think fifty coppers would be reasonable."

"Fifty!" Hidat shook his head. "I would not shame my clients with such an offer. If I told them I had hired them out for fifty coppers apiece, they would box my ears."

Elmutt decided to keep to himself that his offer of fifty coppers was for the entire performance. He had carefully counted his coins that morning. He had three hundred and two coppers, which included the nine that he had stolen from Ghaster.

Hidat leaned forward and gestured with his hand. "I can see no less than five hundred coppers apiece. Any less than that and I would lose my clients." Hidat studied Elmutt for a moment. "How much do you have? The truth, now."

"Three hundred and two." The words shamed him.

"You are wasting your time, Elmutt. But the worse, you waste *my* time." Again Hidat studied Elmutt. "What is this about? Speak."

"This evening I will attempt investiture."

Hidat's eyebrows climbed. "So?" He frowned. "What ritual do you plan to use?"

"From the White priests. I will use the White ritual."

Hidat smiled. "Then let me put your mind to rest, Elmutt. The Whites are a solemn lot. Their investiture ritual needs no performers. Even if you needed performers, my clients do not play rituals. I represent only entertainers."

Elmutt sighed as he rubbed his eyes. "I suppose there is little point in continuing." He lowered his hand. "But I *need* entertainers. I must have all of my concentration at my disposal during the ritual. All of it. And, I . . ." Elmutt shook his head. It is not a problem, he reminded himself, that can be understood without experience.

Hidat placed the tips of his fingers together. "And you, my poor Elmutt, are heavy with troll. You need entertainment to distract the creature while you make your attempt. Speak I the truth?"

"Yes. How . . ."

The man nodded around the room. "Where is it now?"

"It is a he. Tavi by name." Elmutt blushed. "As soon as we entered, Tavi jumped off my shoulder and ran through that door. I think he is trying for a peek at one of your dancers."

Hidat laughed until his eyes watered. "Ah, yes, Elmutt." He nodded and held out his hand as high-pitched screaming audible to both of them came from the back room. The screaming prompted another burst of laughter. "Here, give me your money. I have a dancer and a musician for you for three hundred and two coppers."

"I do not understand."

"I once had a troll, and the screaming you now hear is for a punishment administered upon your creature's posterior by Zayieri, my wife." Hidat grinned. "She is a Bhandaf. Are you familiar with the Bhandafs?"

Elmutt shook his head.

"An ancient tribe from far beyond the Silverspine. In the mountains they learn different ways of seeing. Trolls cannot make themselves invisible to a Bhandaf. Nor can the creatures escape from a Bhandaf. That is why I wed my Zayieri, to put my own troll out of the house. Take my advice, Elmutt. If you have a troll, marry a Bhandaf."

There were soft footsteps, and Elmutt saw Tavi coming into the room, his mouth down at the corners, his lumpy face black with anger, his hands gently holding his rear end. Behind him, wrapped in a dressing towel, was the tallest, most voluptuous woman that Elmutt had ever seen. Her hair was jet black and she had the eyes of a cat, deep and green.

She smiled and held her hand out toward Tavi. "This must be yours, strange sir. I caught the little beast while I was bathing."

Hidat rose and bowed toward his wife. "My love, this is Elmutt of Dung Alley. He comes seeking entertainment for his troll during the time of his attempt to invest his luck this evening." He faced Elmutt and held his hand out toward his wife. "I present Zayieri."

Elmutt stood and nodded, speechless. When he did find his tongue, he still had a question. "About the price, Hidat. For only three hundred and two coppers—"

"For that kingly sum, Elmutt, you shall have the most seductive dancer in all Liavek, my own Zayieri. And for a musician," he placed his hands against his breast and fluttered his eyelids, "well, modesty forbids."

"But—"

Zayieri walked to Elmutt's side and smiled down at him. Her eyes with their lens-shaped pupils were hypnotic. "If you are successful at investing your luck, you will remember us with kindness. The world can always use another magician who owes us a favor."

"And if I am not? If I die?"

Hidat stood next to him and clasped a strong brotherly hand upon Elmutt's shoulder. "We risk only a favor. You risk your life." His eyebrows went up as his face assumed a sly look. "But in case you lose your life and we lose the favor, we will keep your troll."

Elmutt laughed as Tavi hid behind his leg. "By the deep green waters, Hidat, you can have the creature now, and good riddance."

Zayieri shook her head, "It cannot be done. You must die before one can assume full power over your creature." Again she smiled. "Let Bhanda shine his face upon you in your quest. We would rather have the favor than the troll."

Tavi, still nursing his abused dignity, was mercifully silent during the entire walk through the rain back to the Skull. As Elmutt descended the cellar steps, Tavi hopped off his shoulder, climbed to the top of its mountain of salvaged bricks, and sulked.

Dim light from the alley filled the basement, and Elmutt noticed two small boys rummaging through Ghaster's wooden box of "valuables." Ghaster was still motionless on his cushions. Elmutt looked away from his master, anger contorting both his feaures and his words. "You boys!" The pair spied Elmutt and froze. "You boys, I am going to *kill* you!"

They split, going in opposite directions, Elmutt hard after

the one who fled to his right, behind Elmutt's pallet. The boy's neck almost within his grasp, Elmutt's crippled leg collapsed, sending him headlong into a pile of bottles. By the time he had extricated himself from the broken glass, the boys were gone.

The picker painfully limped to Ghaster's side. "You irresponsible pig! Do I cull the filth of this city so that you might give it away to any thief who wanders in here?" Although it cost him dearly, Elmutt reared up upon his crippled leg and delivered a swift kick to Ghaster's thigh. Again his leg collapsed, sending him to the earthen floor.

"You pig! You miserable, stinking, filthy, louse-ridden, drunken, worthless—" From his place on the floor, Elmutt saw that Ghaster still did not move. On his knees, he crawled to the old man's side.

"Ghaster?"

He reached out a hand and shook the old man's shoulder. Then he touched the icy coldness of Ghaster's hand. Elmutt released the hand and sat back on his ankles.

With only the sounds of the storm for company, he stared at his master for a long time, saying to him at last, "You are dead."

Tavi appeared behind Ghaster, sitting upon a cushion. The creature studied the old man. "There are no wounds. The Dragonpiss got him, it did." Tavi turned to look at Elmutt, the creature's face assuming a frown. "You have wished him dead a thousand times, Elmutt. Why do you cry, why?"

The young picker raised a hand and touched the tears on his cheek. "I am crying." He wiped the tears away with the back of his hand and sat surprised as they were replaced with fresh ones. "I don't know why." The beatings, the humiliations, the scathing words. Life with Ghaster had been an endless trial, and now the trial was over. Why was he crying?

Elmutt looked at the troll. "It should have been more. Ghaster and I. What we had should have been more. Now it can never be made right."

Tavi vanished and reappeared standing on Ghaster's belly, his head cocked in mock despair. "Poor Elmutt. You have spent all of your coppers upon the dancer and have nothing left to pay for your master's planting. Poor Ghaster. It is the city oven for him." The troll smacked his lips. "As fat as he is, Ghaster will baste himself, he will."

Elmutt pushed himself to his feet and dragged himself to his pallet where he began readying his things for the ritual. Tavi reappeared sitting atop the wicker basket. "I will stop your investiture, Elmutt."

"You cannot."

"I must. I won't be claimed by a Bhandaf, which is what happens to me if you die. And if I don't stop you, you will die."

Elmutt leveled his gaze upon the creature. "I may die, Tavi. But nothing will prevent me from trying; not you, not Ghaster's death, not the weather, not the Levar, not all of the wizards in Liavek, not all of the assembled ghosts of darkness, nor the host of demons from hell. *Nothing* can stop me!"

As a clap of thunder shook the dank cellar, Tavi scampered to the top of his mountain of bricks, frightened. He looked down at Elmutt beginning to polish Yolik's great copper staff. The young picker didn't pay the thunder any attention. He didn't even seem to hear it.

Just off the Street of Trees, high atop the grassy peak of Mystery Hill, lie the ruins of an ancient temple constructed by some long forgotten race. This ancient people built with great rough slabs of stone, the smallest of which weighed many tons. Legend had it that the builders of the temple were magic giants.

In the dark and rain, shaking at the cold and the roll of the thunder, Elmutt stood clad in his mail cap and brass belt, holding Yolik's copper staff. He could see lights in the distance marking the top of Temple Hill. Between the two hills was the Two-Copper Bazaar, at this hour nearly deserted. Looking toward the east, he could see the bright lights of Rat's Alley reflected from the remains of the old city wall. Backlighted by Rat's Alley's glow was the silhouette of Narkaan's Skull rising from the malevolent shadows of Dung Alley, the building's spires making it look like some sort of horned monstrosity reaching up from hell. Lightning illuminated the city for an instant, plunging it into darkness the next.

"When you start your chant, I will confuse you, I will." Tavi's voice was serious.

Elmutt turned in the direction of the Street of Trees. Two figures clad in oilskins were climbing toward them through the darkness. "That will be Hidat and Zayieri."

Tavi jumped up and down on Elmutt's shoulder and yanked

his collar. "Do you think your hired dancer will stop me from stopping you, Elmutt? Do you?"

Elmutt looked into the troll's face. "Listen, you corrupt little wart. Come power or death, this *is* the night I try. Unless you want to cry out the remainder of your existence under the power of a Bhandaf, you had better pray for my success."

Tavi clasped his hands together and knelt upon Elmutt's shoulder. "Please! *Please,* Elmutt. I know I haven't been as good to you as I should, and I can mend my ways, and I *will!* I will be good to you and mind my mouth. No more tricks, may I be gored by Narkaan's horns if I lie! I *promise!* Please don't try! *Please! Ple—*"

"Silence, troll." The voice was Zayieri's.

Elmutt turned and faced the pair. "There is a place against the west wall of the ruin where there is an alcove. You can keep dry there."

Hidat nodded. The musician's robe bulged with the things he carried beneath it. "Good." He gestured with his head at the night sky. "This is a good night to invest your luck, Elmutt. There are many spirits in the air."

Tavi began to protest, but as he saw Zayieri's left eyebrow go up, the troll clamped his lips together. Zayieri smiled, nodded her approval and looked toward the west wall of the ruin. "Where is the alcove you spoke of, Elmutt?"

"Follow me." Elmutt walked across the darkness of the weedy court, Hidat and Zayieri close behind. As he reached the alcove, he faced Tavi. The creature's eyes were bugged to the point where one might reasonably fear an explosion. Tavi closed his eyes and again knelt, his hands clasped together, his lips silently forming the word "Please."

Elmutt watched as Hidat placed his belongings on the floor of the alcove and lit the wick of a lamp, warming the interior with a yellow glow. As Zayieri removed her oilskin cape and hood, revealing her flowing costume, Hidat sat on the floor behind the lamp and placed a combination drum and timberbell instrument between his knees.

"You are too fat!" Tavi screamed at the dancer. She simply smiled as Tavi continued. "You cannot tempt me, Bhandaf! You are fat and ugly! I will not watch! No I won't!"

Hidat's skilled fingers began tapping out a seductive rhythm. Elmutt watched as Tavi clamped his hands over his ears to keep out the sound of the drum. Just when it looked as though the troll would resist the efforts to distract it, he opened his right eye slightly to take a peek at the dancer. In seconds it was as though Tavi had been hypnotized. The troll swayed on Elmutt's shoulder, his arms limp, his eyes unblinking.

Elmutt turned to nod his thanks to Zayieri. In less than a second it was as though Elmutt, too, had been hypnotized. The dancer had removed her gown and was dancing in her imagination. Elmutt knew that there was something that he should be doing, but for the life of him he couldn't remember what it was. His vision, his mind, was filled with the image of the dancer as she performed moves that made snakes look awkward.

"Ritual," gasped Elmutt, forcing himself to look away. "The ritual." He tried to concentrate, thinking that it would be just his luck to have Zayieri's performance break his concentration instead of Tavi's. Leaning the copper staff against his shoulder, he held his palms to his ears, blocking out most of Hidat's drumming. To drive the image of Zayieri out of his mind, he stared at the spires of Narkaan's Skull and thought of Almantia. Then he thought of Ghaster and Dung Alley. He thought of the life his luck had driven him through. Pain. Despair. Emptiness.

As his mind cleared, he felt a tremble in his spine and a chill sweeping over his body. This must be the beginning, he thought. The beginning of the labor that birthed me. Until that labor ends, I *can* change my luck.

There was a strange, exhilarating aroma upon the night air. He gripped the copper staff, moistened his lips, and began to speak the words he had learned from the White priests.

"Nathaan-ra ee, Eeatra. Nathaan-ra ee, Doe. Leave me, my fate, my chance, my future. Withdraw from my being and rest in this." He held up the copper staff to the night sky. "By the laws of Sarrow, by the pain of Rujo, by the lust of Yane, by the anger of Narkaan! Rest here! Rest here! Rest *here! Nathaan-ra ee, Eeatra! Nathaan-ra ee, Doe!"*

He frowned as the cold rain trickled down his arm into his sleeve. Nibbling at his lower lip, he wondered if the Fourteenth of Flowers was in truth his birthdate. He muttered beneath his breath, "Not only will I look the fool, but what shall I tell Hidat and Zayieri?"

If he remained alive, they could not claim the troll. But he would have no powers with which to grant their favor. Did that mean Hidat would press for full payment for the performance?

"It would be just my luck to walk away from this with nothing more than the price of a bill I can never pay."

Tavi. Tavi would wallow in Elmutt's failure, Elmutt's foolishness. He could almost hear the troll's wicked laughter. He looked to his shoulder, but the creature was gone. Turning further around, he saw Tavi before the alcove swaying to the beat of Hidat's drum. He closed his eyes and turned his face back toward Dung Alley and the Skull.

"By Narkaan's beard, no!" he swore. "This *is* the night! Now *is* the time!"

He straightened the arm holding the staff, pushing it higher into the sky.

"Nathaan-ra ee, Eeatra. Nathaaaaaaaaaaaaaaaaaaaaaaa—"

In the same instant, Elmutt realized that lightning had reached down and touched Yolik's copper staff, and that he was dead. The roof of hell opened beneath his feet as blackness covered the universe.

Without sound, without color, strange faces passed before him. The faces had no bodies, no expression, but were alive. They passed as though he did not exist. He opened his mouth to call them, to scream, but silence was his voice.

A face he recognized, Ghaster, passed by him, followed by the image of Soldire, the White priest whose abuse Elmutt had withstood for the years it had taken him to piece together the White ritual of investiture. Tavi's face followed. Hidat's, Zayieri's, Almantia's, Cankera's and all the faces of Dung Alley.

There was a cellar deeper and darker than Ghaster's. It was piled with an infinite number of trash mountains. Ghaster sat there cleaning a bottle. His master looked at him and smiled. "Welcome home, Elmutt." Ghaster held out a dirty hand toward a straw pallet. "I have saved you a place."

Elmutt screamed, "No, nooooo! No—"

"No!"

There was a hissing in his ears. He felt the rain upon his face, the hard ground against his back. The rain was cold; the ground very warm. He opened his eyes. The gleaming wet stones of the Giant's Temple stared down at him. "I am alive."

Elmutt gingerly flexed a muscle or two and pushed himself to a sitting position. He trembled as he gave a dazed look around the court. Hidat's lamp still burned in the alcove, but the drummer, the dancer, and the troll were nowhere to be seen. The ground around him was misty with steam. He turned to his right and saw the source of the steam. There was a glowing gold puddle of molten copper. Yolik's staff, or more correctly, the remains of the wizard's vessel. As the rain touched it, it sizzled and cooled, rapidly changing to red, then black.

He looked at the hand that had been holding the staff. It twitched, but was not burned or scarred. "I am alive!" He swayed to his feet, exultation filling his heart. "It worked! I am alive! I have invested my luck!"

He paused in midcavort. "Where . . . *where* is my luck?" The copper staff could not be the vessel. It had been destroyed. He placed his hands upon his head to feel for Soldire's mail cap, but it was gone. When he again looked at his hands in the glow from the alcove, he saw that they were covered with rust. He reached for Miena's brass belt, but it too was gone. Looking down, he could see the glint of the belt's pieces next to his feet.

"Elmutt?"

He looked around to find the source of the voice. "Yes? Who is there?"

A face peeked out from behind one of the temple's vertical stone slabs. It was Zayieri. "Elmutt, you are alive."

"Evidently." He began patting his pockets, wondering where he had invested his luck. The dancer rushed to the alcove, donned her oilskins, and approached the garbage picker.

"You were struck by a great bolt of lightning. I was certain you must be dead." She turned and called into the darkness. "Hidat! Come out, my husband! Elmutt lives!" She turned back to Elmutt. "What are your powers? They must be magnificent! What can you do?"

Elmutt shook his head as Hidat emerged from behind another stone slab. "I don't know. I can't even be certain what finally became my vessel. The staff is nothing but a lump, my cap has turned to powder, and you can see what remains of the brass belt." He kicked at the pieces with his toe.

Hidat approached and stopped next to Zayieri, his wary gaze upon Elmutt. "You must try your powers."

"I must, first, find my luck."

Hidat shook his head. "Later. Just keep with you what you have right now and you will be safe. You can determine which article it is by elimination, once you know what you can do. Try your powers."

Elmutt looked up and saw Tavi sitting atop the temple ruin above the alcove. He glanced at Hidat and Zayieri. "What should I try first?"

The musician held out his hands. "You are the one who studied magic, not I."

"Very well. I shall conjure fire." Elmutt held his arms out to his sides, parallel to the ground, and muttered the incantation enslaving Daak, the demon stoker of the Devil's Furnace. The incantation completed, Elmutt pointed his finger at the ground between himself and Hidat.

Hidat waited for a moment. "I don't see anything."

The garbage picker rubbed his chin and frowned. "It isn't conjuring fire, that's for certain." He noticed that Tavi had come down from above the alcove and was now standing in the court. Elmutt nodded at Hidat and Zayieri. "Levitation."

There was the incantation to Wheer, the bellows pumper for Karris, god of the winds. The incantation completed, Elmutt gestured with his hands for Zayieri to rise. She remained firmly upon the ground while what little wind there was died out. Tavi moved a little closer.

Zayieri glanced at her husband and turned back to Elmutt. "Perhaps you can read minds, tell fortunes, create illusions or spells."

"I'll see." Elmutt shook his head. "I find it difficult to believe that an investiture of such power could produce nothing." He assumed a pose, closed his eyes, and tried to see into Hidat's mind. He opened his eyes.

Hidat nodded. "Well?"

"Either you are completely empty-headed, Hidat, or reading minds is not one of my powers." And neither could he see fortunes, or create illusions, or make spells.

With each failure, Tavi moved ever closer until with the final failure, the troll was again seated upon Elmutt's shoulder. As Elmutt slumped dejectedly in his wet clothing, Tavi leered at him. "Card tricks, Elmutt!" The troll clapped his hands. "Perhaps you can do card tricks! I *like* card tricks." As Elmutt glared at the troll, Tavi rolled off his shoulder, laughing. "The Wizard of Dung Alley! Show us how you can fall off a log, Wizard!"

The garbage picker glanced at Hidat, then guiltily cast down his gaze. "Nothing. I have no powers. Somehow I will pay you the balance for the performance. Somehow—" He turned to go but was stopped by Zayieri's touch upon his arm. "I will pay. I promise."

The dancer stood with her face very close to Elmutt's. "Perhaps it is a sufficient miracle that you survived the lightning. I think it is more. I see something in you, Elmutt. A difference. I cannot tell what the difference is, but it is there. You must be patient until you find out what it is."

Elmutt shook his head. "No. The only difference is that I have never before made quite this big a fool of myself."

Hidat placed his hand upon Elmutt's shoulder. "My boy, Zayieri is a Bhandaf. Bhandafs see differently than you or I. Have faith and forget paying us with money. We will wait for the favor."

"You may have to wait a long time." Elmutt again shook his head, turned, and began trudging through the dark toward the Street of Trees. Behind him, Tavi cackled.

"Wait, Wizard! Pick a card, any card, any card at all! Ah, hah hah! See, the Wizard conjures *mud,* he does! And rain! And dark! He can conjure dark once a night! Ah, hah hah haaaah!"

Elmutt paid little attention to the troll's ridicule. Inside he was telling himself things of a much harsher nature. Once he reached the street he turned his feet east and limped in the direction of Dung Alley and Ghaster's cellar.

The rooster's crowing the next morning found Elmutt and his sack again on the back streets of Old Town, Tavi upon his shoulder, picking among the rubbish. "Your humility is admirable, Wizard, it is. To think that such a powerful magician as yourself would stoop to crawling through the glop and slime of Liavek as if nothing had changed. It is a marvel, it is. No one can say that your power has gone to your head. My, my, I do think—"

"Be silent, Tavi."

The creature laughed as it jumped up and down on Elmutt's shoulder. "Oh, my, mighty Wizard! Have I offended thee? What horror will you inflict upon me for my punishment? Aaaaaargh!" Tavi rolled off and bounced upon the cobblestones of the Street of Scales. "The horror! The horror! The great Wizard of Dung Alley has turned me *into a troll!* Aaaaaaaarrrggh!"

Elmutt turned the corner onto Wizard's Row. Almantia had said to see her that morning. In exchange for the pain of being near her, there would be a few coppers. Despite what Hidat and Zayieri had said, Elmutt wanted to pay the balance he owed. It was a goal. The only goal he had remaining. It was something with which to fill his days—to stave off the despair that he knew would take his life if he allowed himself to feel it. His picker's bag was already near to full. His finds that day promised to reduce his debt by ten or fifteen coppers. That in addition to what Almantia would pay him would give him a start.

He looked up from the gutter to see the buildings. The grand houses of Wizard's Row seemed to mock him. "Look at us, Elmutt! Look at what you will never be; look at where you can only pick garbage! Look at yourself, Wizard of Dung Alley!"

He glanced at his shoulder. Tavi was back on his perch. "Ah, me, Wizard. If the feeble tricksters that live here only knew the vast powers of He Who Picks Among Them."

Elmutt paused as Yolik's house came into full view. There were litters and bearers, carriages and drivers crowding the street. On the steps and walk were men, women, and children garbed in finery, laughing, happily greeting each other. It is probably a party or celebration, thought Elmutt. Almantia would hire him at a good wage to help the menials. He closed his eyes, thinking that his heart could not bear to hear any of this laughter and heartiness from rich people, in addition to viewing Almantia's forbidden beauty.

"Elmutt!"

He heard his name called. The voice was her's. "Elmutt!"

He opened his eyes. She stood in the doorway of her grandfather's house wearing a filmy gown of pale blue. She was waving at him. He let a ragged breath escape as he began walking toward her. Tavi snapped his fingers. "This be where Tavi gets off, Wizard. Tavi will find you later, he will, he will." The troll slid off the back of Elmutt's shoulder and vanished. Almantia worked her way through her guests, and as the garbage picker reached Yolik's gate, she met him there.

"Yes, good lady?"

She smiled, her face radiant. "My dear little picker, you

have come just in time. I can promise you thirty coppers for helping today, and I have such good news. Can you guess what it is?"

"Good lady, I am no mind reader."

She didn't notice the bitterness in his words, but prattled on. "Do you remember me telling you about one of my beaus, Brice Abnabas? Do you?"

Elmutt shook his head. There were so many, how could his memory sort out a single admirer from the herd? "My sorrow, good lady, I cannot."

"He owns five great sailing ships. Of course, I didn't know that until yesterday. He was only a ship's mate when I knew him years ago, but he is back!" She smiled and placed her hand upon Elmutt's sleeve. "He asked my grandfather for my hand, and today we are to be wed. . . ."

Elmutt's heart stopped beating. Her words and the chatter of the other guests faded into a numb miasma of meaningless sound. All he could think of was escape, to seek the fetid security of Dung Alley. It was no more than he should have expected. A garbage picker and Yolik's granddaughter! Ridiculous!

Perhaps, he thought . . . perhaps the Fifteenth is my birthday. It certainly looks like today is a day of especially rotten luck. He reached out and held onto the gate for support.

". . . it is such a rush because Brice must leave on the evening tide and I am to go with him. There are so many things to do." Her words paused as her eyes studied Elmutt's face. The slightest of frowns marred her perfect forehead. "Is something wrong, Elmutt?"

"It's just that your news is so sudden." He felt light-headed. "I feel a little ill, good lady. I must go."

"So soon? Rula Verune is one of the guests, Elmutt. She is a fine physician. Shall I call her?"

"Please do not bother, good lady. I will recover as soon as I can get some rest."

"Are you certain? It would be no trouble, and I do value my little picker."

"Please, no." He released the gate and stood up. "My best wishes to you and your . . ." Another wave of dizziness swept over him. "Your husband."

"Oh, Elmutt, I am *so* happy. What do you think will happen? Will I always be this happy?"

A strange heat shot through his heart. "I hope so, good lady. I must go now."

"If you're certain you'll be all right." She took his hands in hers and kissed his cheek. "Thank you for being a friend, Elmutt. Be kind to yourself."

He couldn't remember leaving her. He saw none of the streets and houses as he walked. He did not hear the cries of the merchants or of the animals in the Two-Copper Bazaar. He simply walked without direction, without purpose, until a great tiredness came over him. Then, he stopped where he was and stood weaving, the heels of his hands dug into his eyes. He pulled his hands away and looked at his empty palms. He had forgotten his bag.

"It must still be next to Yolik's gate," he whispered. For the life of him he could not imagine going back there to retrieve his bag and its contents.

"Well, if it isn't the Great Wizard of Dung Alley!"

He realized he was standing at the north end of the alley. He turned. The voice belonged to the hag, Cankera. Her toothless mouth laughed at him.

"One of these days, old hag, your mouth will cost you."

"Will it now, Wizard?" she screeched. Again she laughed, her husband Mortice's cackle from the back of the stall joining in. Joining in as well were the several residents of the alley whose attention had been attracted by the exchange. Elmutt's face burned.

Cankera clasped her hands together and bowed in mock respect. "Oh, powerful one, you must tell me my fortune! Will I become rich? Will I exchange my worn-out piece of a husband for a handsome virile young thing? Oh, *please,* Great Wizard of Dung, what does the future hold in store for me?"

A roar of laughter surrounded Elmutt. He faced the hag, his fists at his sides. The alley became silent as that strange heat again shot through his heart. "Hag, may you—"

He watched as her eyes burst and tentacles snaked from the woman's eye sockets and ears. As she screamed, her skin erupted into boils and weeping pustules. A black clawed thing reached out from beneath her skirt and bit through her ankle, sending her toppling over into her stall. More tentacles came from her nose and mouth, flailing her, choking her, ripping off her arms, tearing her head from her bleeding body. The pieces of her, along with the things that had come from her, began to smoke. There was a bright flash. When the smoke in the stall cleared, there was nothing left of the hag except a memory and a handful of ashes.

Stunned, Elmutt turned from the stall. The people of the alley were motionless, as though frozen in that instant of time. They stared at him. Their eyes were filled with terror. As they began to back away from him, a painful wail came from the stall. Elmutt turned and saw Cankera's husband, Mortice, helplessly waving his hands at the ashed remains of his wife.

"Oh! Look at what you've done! Oh, woman, you had the dragon's mouth on you, and you stank!" Mortice looked up at Elmutt, tears filling his eyes. "She was everything horrible, Elmutt. But she did not deserve to die. Bring her back! Bring her back, I say!" The observers in the alley, who fear had edged away, were drawn back by anger.

Elmutt shook his head. "I didn't, I couldn't, I can't . . ."

"This is murder," muttered a voice from the alley.

"Someone should call the Guard," muttered another.

Mortice stepped forward and grabbed Elmutt's collar. "Bring her back, monster!"

All the garbage picker could do was to stand there helplessly absorbing the accusations. Mortice, his anger dissolving into grief, released Elmutt's collar. Still he looked at the picker. "What is to become of me? Now that you have taken my old woman, what will become of me? Do you have a fortune in your bag of vengeance for me?"

Elmutt spoke as the heat once more shot through his heart, the words pitifully dry and small in his throat. "It will be all right, Mortice. You will see. It will be all right."

Mortice's eyebrows went up in surprise, then came down in a glare of hate. *"All right!"* The alley observers, now a crowd, rumbled with the reflection of Mortice's outrage. Mortice held out his hands to the crowd. "I have murdered your wife, Mortice! I turned her into a horrible pain-filled crawling thing before her pieces were consumed with hell fire, Mortice! I have taken away your reason for living, Mortice! But, says Elmutt, it will be all right, Mortice! It will be *all right!"*

By this time the crowd had lost its fear and was quite capable of acquiring and administering a length of rope to satisfy its sense of justice. But they quieted as they watched a quizzical look come upon Mortice's face. He nodded at the street once and looked at Elmutt. "She *was* a spiteful old bitch, wasn't she?" Mortice snickered and shook his head. "Life with her was a continuous tongue-lashing from dawn to dusk." He rubbed his chin and nodded. "And she never let me have any of the coppers that *both* of us earned." He placed a hand on Elmutt's shoulder. "Ungrateful fool that I am, you do me this good turn, Elmutt, and I spit in your face. Can you ever forgive me?"

Embarrassed, Elmutt looked at the faces in the crowd. He read the same thing in every face. Elmutt had said it would be all right, and now it was. The picker shook his head and backed away from Mortice. "There is nothing to forgive. I am sorry. I am so sorry."

He ran through the crowd toward the safety of Ghaster's cellar. Just before he entered the doorway that would take him down the stone stairs, he looked back toward Cankera's stall. The crowd buzzed with talk and exclamations of wonder. At the edge of the crowd, silently looking at Elmutt, was a dark figure clad in a white hooded robe, the robe of a White priest.

Sickness filling his heart, Elmutt scurried down the steps and hid in the cellar's darkness.

That night Elmutt sat alone amidst the salvage in the cellar, with only Cankera's nightmare for company. Again and again he replayed the horror in his mind, trying to remember exactly what had happened. When the dawn light crept down the cellar stairs, he had sorted out enough to accept that what had happened to Cankera was exactly what his heart had wished upon her. He had not told her fortune. It was bitter upon his tongue.

"I *made* the hag's fortune." She was mean, cruel, and ugly, and Elmutt hated her. He shook his head in guilt-embroidered despair. "She did not deserve to die." A thousand times that night he had wished and prayed for things to go back the way they had been; that the hag would reappear in her stall, mouth and all. A thousand times he failed. He looked up. "Is this my gift, then? Is this my power? A limitless capacity for irrevocable evil?"

The murk above him revealed the edge of a horrible truth. He had not only ended the hag's passage through this life. In addition, what had happened to her had revealed to everyone on the alley what Elmutt carried in his most secret heart. Cankera's death had thrown the evidence for his judgment as a worthy or worthless man upon the public way, for anyone to see. They had seen his hate. They had judged him for it.

There was still more. He had told Mortice that it would be all right, and now it was. At least it was all right with Mortice. That, too, had been in his heart. But he had not made it all right with Cankera, or with himself. All he had done was to stop Mortice from blaming him for the crime that he had committed. That act, too, was a judgment upon himself, revealing to everyone who and what he was.

Upon the cushions where Ghaster used to recline in unwashed splendor there was now a much crueler resident. It was a leather pouch bulging with coppers. Mortice had dropped it by to express some small part of the gratitude he felt toward Elmutt. The garbage picker could not escape that the gratitude expressed had been planted in Mortice's heart by Elmutt's desperate desire to evade responsibility for what he had done. "My power is a more burdensome thing than having no power at all." Another instance of Elmutt's luck, he reflected.

He frowned as a thought presented itself. "If I can make futures for others, can I do the same for myself?" Power, wealth, fame, fine foods, a glorious house, the parades of noble and wealthy persons coming before him for favors.

He wished for these things. When he had completed his attempt, he was still Elmutt the garbage picker, sitting in the gloom of Ghaster's cellar. "Elmutt's luck remains intact."

He looked again at Mortice's bag of coppers. It could make for a comfortable living, being a contract killer. He covered his eyes and huddled on his pallet, the universe too small a container for his shame.

There was a sound: footsteps. Elmutt did not remove his hand from his eyes. If it was Mortice with another bag of gratitude, he could not bear to face him. If it was a thief after Mortice's coppers, or a killer after the garbage picker's life, it would be good riddance to either or both as far as Elmutt was concerned.

"You are the one called Elmutt?" The voice was deep and powerful. Elmutt stayed as he was. "Look at me, boy!"

At the command, Elmutt lowered his hands. Before him stood the White priest he had seen standing in the alley the evening before. The priest's eyes were black and set deeply beneath bushy black brows. On his right cheek, only partially covered by a closely cropped beard, was a long crooked scar. Now that he had Elmutt's attention, the priest glanced around for something upon which to sit. Disgust curled the man's lips. He spread the fingers of his right hand and held his arm forward, holding his palm toward the cellar's earthen floor. Elmutt started as a satin-upholstered throne of gold appeared. The priest lowered himself into it, crossed his legs, and fixed his gaze on the garbage picker. "I am Geth Dys, Vavasor, priest of the Church of Truth and an advisor to Her Magnificence, the Levar."

Elmutt issued a bitter laugh and held a hand to his own breast. "My humble establishment is honored by your presence, Master Geth Dys. I am Elmutt, cripple, garbage picker, and murderer of the hag Cankera."

"You are insolent."

Elmutt again covered his eyes. "And you are where you are not wanted, priest. Either do your destruction or be gone. I want no conversation."

There was a strained silence. Elmutt looked up and angrily waved his hands at Geth Dys. "Go! Go! Leave me and my garbage!" He pointed at the golden throne. "And take your illusion with you!"

Geth Dys slowly brought the fingers of his left hand together into a fist. As he did so, an ominous black cloud formed over his head. The priest leaned back in his throne and smiled. "You are a mouthy creature, Elmutt. You killed someone last evening because of her mouth, didn't you? However, I am inclined to be more lenient."

Elmutt's jaw was locked with fear. To hide his fright, the picker folded his arms and glared at Geth Dys.

"Now that I have your undivided attention, picker, I would confirm my knowledge of a few recent events. On the night of the Fourteenth you attempted investiture?" Geth Dys raised his black brows. Elmutt gave a curt nod.

"And you were struck by lightning?" Again Elmutt nodded.

Geth Dys stroked his beard and nodded in return. "What you cannot do has been a joke in the streets ever since. I have seen something of what you *can* do. In your pitiful ignorance, do you have any understanding at all concerning your powers?"

"Not a great degree of understanding."

The priest thought for a long moment, his forehead creased in a frown of decision. The decision made, he nodded and spoke. "In the most ancient writings known to my sect, *The Book of Oblivion,* there is mentioned a White priest named Xaviat Nihl who was what they then called a *juriet,* a fortune maker. By wishing it, Xaviat could create a person's future. One limitation upon his ability was that the seeker of the fortune had to ask Xaviat for his future, much like you would do with a fortune teller. He couldn't simply create unrequested realities. In addition, the form of the request presented further limitations. Specific requests severely narrowed the aspects of future reality that he could alter. General requests, such as 'What will my future be?' made the remainder of the seeker's realities subject to Xaviat's wishes. Do you understand?"

Elmutt sat motionless. Geth Dys opened the fingers of his left hand and the black cloud vanished. Elmutt shook his head. "What do you want of me?"

"Do you understand what I have told you?"

"I suppose, but—"

"Very well. Are you familiar at all with the beliefs of the Church of Truth?"

"A little. I have done errands at the White Temple."

"Good. As I said, the story comes from an ancient writing. As nearly as I can place it, Xaviat Nihl lived and practiced his art over two thousand years ago. Ever since, the White priests have sought another with similar powers. The search is such an ancient one that many of the Whites believe Xaviat and his powers to be nothing more than legend." Geth Dys pointed at Elmutt. "I believe you to have this power."

Elmutt shook his head as he moistened his lips. "My head did not wish the woman dead. I swear it."

"Your heart did, just as your heart took the opportunity to avoid the blame by creating a new attitude for the hag's husband. And they did ask for what they received."

Elmutt thought back. Cankera's mock request: *Oh, please, Great Wizard of Dung, what does the future hold in store for me?* But Mortice had not asked him for a future, in jest or otherwise. He thought again, trying to remember. *What is to become of me? Now that you have taken my old woman, what will become of me?*

Elmutt looked sadly at the priest. "Neither of them knew what they asked for."

"It is written that one should be careful when praying. One might receive that for which one asks." Geth Dys waved a hand in a depreciating gesture. "A matter of complete irrelevance." He placed the hand upon the throne's armrest. "I am here for another purpose."

"What purpose?"

The priest stared into Elmutt's eyes and raised both hands. "What you will see now, only your heart will remember."

There was Elmutt picking among the garbage,
There was a baby in the garbage behind Serena's Couch,
There was an old man dying in the garbage in the Merchant's Quarter,
There was a young man picking garbage in the Merchant's Quarter,
There was a baby being sold to a garbage picker named Radneh,
There was an old man dying in the garbage of the Canal District,
There was . . .

"Reality is a prison; an endless succession of births, deaths, and rebirths. The only escape from reality is to destroy it. It is the secret of the magicians of the Church of Truth that we, the White priests, seek this destruction and the secrets and powers that will make possible this destruction. You, Elmutt, may have such a power. You might have the power to free us all from this prison, and to end your own trek through infinite refuse.

"To make this future, you must wish for it with every particle of your being. To do that, you must believe, as the White priests believe, and you must know yourself. Become one of us and one with us. Become a priest of the Church of Truth. Consider."

The cellar came into focus. Geth Dys still sat upon his golden throne. The priest looked as though he expected some kind of response, but Elmutt couldn't remember the question—if there had been a question. "What would you have me do, Master Geth Dys?"

The priest stood and the throne vanished. "Come to the Levar's palace at noon today and present yourself and your name to the guard at the Eastern Gate." Geth Dys turned and pointed at the bag of coppers on Ghaster's cushions. The bag rose in the air, flew toward Elmutt, and thumped into his lap. "Purchase something respectable to wear. You shall be meeting Her Magnificence, the Levar."

Elmutt touched the bag and looked up, but Geth Dys had vanished.

"I see you've been busy since last I saw thee, you have."

Atop the brick pile sat Tavi. "A murder, a visiting vavasor, and soon to be presented to Her Magnificence, Tazli Ifino iv Larwin, the Levar, the Mad Child of Liavek. My, my, but we are getting up in the world, we are."

Elmutt climbed to his feet. "Where have you been?"

Tavi laughed. "Oh, Tavi had to make certain that you could not turn *him* into a tentacled wonder as you did to that poor old woman, may her soul rest in Narkaan's tender claws. Be certain that Tavi will never ask you for his fortune. No, no." The troll leaned in Elmutt's direction, a sly look on his face. "With the Levar under your power, Elmutt, and Tavi upon your shoulder advising you, just think of the chaos we can cause, we can."

As Tavi prattled on about how they could wreak havoc upon the world for fun and profit, Elmutt studied the creature. For the first time he asked himself if Tavi was an independent being or a creature created by his own hate and despair. There was no answer. He looked at the morning light upon the cellar stairs. Hooking Mortice's bag of coppers onto his belt, he headed for the alley. Tavi appeared on his left shoulder.

"Where do we go, fortune maker, where?"

"In a few hours it will be noon. Before then I must purchase new clothing." He paused, wondering if the vessel of his magic was composed of some article of his clothing. And why, he asked of himself, why can I not create my own future? Why can I not wish myself a new reality?

Tavi fell into silence for a moment, vanished, then reappeared garbed in purple suit and slippers with a bright yellow cape. "Tavi has completed his shopping, he has. Tavi will shame the palace trolls. Do you like?"

"It's fine, Tavi, except for the hood."

The troll frowned. "There is no hood, Elmutt."

"That is what I mean. You need a hood to hide your ugly face."

Tavi grinned slyly at the picker. "Your mood is excellent for the evil we will cause at the Levar's court today, it is." The troll fell into silence as it giddily contemplated death and destruction.

As Elmutt came to the top of the stairs and turned south toward the Street of Rain, he resolved to find out from Geth Dys the next time they met why he could not work his magic upon himself. As the picker passed by them, the people of the alley avoided looking in his direction.

Later, as he rapidly walked the Avenue of the Moon around the south of Mystery Hill, it gnawed at him that the power he had achieved had produced little more than fear. Fear from the people on the alley, his own fear and shame of his darker self, and in addition, the attention of the magician–priest, Geth Dys, who frightened him. Perhaps this power, he thought, is not the answer. On the other hand, perhaps I simply do not have *enough* power. His association with Geth Dys might be the way toward increasing his power, however much the scarred priest frightened him. And there was the Levar.

It was said in the streets and markets that the young girl, Tazli, Levar of Liavek, was mad. The demons that plagued her made her a creature of whims. She might make one's fortune or seal one in a barrel full of snakes with equal consideration and compassion.

As the Avenue of the Moon opened onto the Two-Copper Bazaar, revealing merchants and traders spreading their carpets and wares among the few early morning shoppers, Elmutt paused. He would not search for his clothing here. No Two-Copper hawker would be selling things fit to wear at the Levar's palace. Instead, he would examine the wares of the famous tailors in the Merchant's Quarter. He had picked through Merchant's Quarter garbage long enough to know which tailors sold names and which tailors sold fine value.

Still, he paused. From where he stood he could look above the activity of the Bazaar and see the buildings atop Temple Hill. The Levar's palace was hidden by the crest of the hill, but facing the same court was the Temple of the White priests. He could see the back of the temple and wondered at his sudden, curious desire to know what the White priests knew, to become one of them. He looked at his left shoulder just in time to see Tavi, a scared look upon his face, vanish. Elmutt frowned for a moment, then put it out of his mind. Whatever had frightened his creature was Tavi's problem, not his.

An enclosed litter-chair born by eight servants entered the Bazaar plaza from Merchant's Way. The servants were heavily muscled and garbed in uniform suits of gleaming tan leather and white linen. What there was of a crowd instinctively parted for the litter-bearers, the Tichenese bowing with his arms at his sides, the Zhir with both of his hands to his forehead, the Liavekan holding but one hand to his forehead. Regardless of the origin, this was respect. The kind of respect the picker craved.

The silken window curtains of the chair were drawn. Elmutt nodded. This was indeed the kind of finery he desired. Perhaps Geth Dys and the Levar would be the means through which he could attain such a station. As did everyone else within view of the bearers, Elmutt tried to catch a glimpse of the personage behind the curtains. As the bearers passed by on their way across the plaza to Bazaar Street and the Levar's Highway, the curtain on Elmutt's side pulled back slightly, revealing one eye of the dark figure behind it. Elmutt bowed after the manner of those from Liavek, his gaze fixed on the chair's window.

The curtain drew back further, revealing the twisted, warted face of a hideous crone. She held up a gnarled hand and motioned in Elmutt's direction. Her mouth opened but what she said could not be heard. At a call from one of their number, the bearers came to a halt. One of the pair carrying the right rear released his share of the carrying pole, walked forward and pulled shut the curtain. The bearer turned, placed his hands on his hips and glared at Elmutt. The picker completed his bow and continued on his way. He had no desire to tangle with the bearer, and even less desire to talk with the crone, however high her station.

Shortly after noon, Elmutt stood in an anteroom just off the Levar's audience chamber with a finger stuck between his new collar and his neck. The shirt of crisp linen and lace chafed, the coat and trousers of deep blue velvet were uncomfortably warm, and the slippers of stiff black leather hurt his feet. Another goal achieved, fine clothing, and another achievement that measured something short of expectation. There, too, he was standing in a luxuriously appointed room of maroon, grey, and gold, he had the smell of gently scented air in his nostrils, and by the standards of the alley, he was wealthy. In a manner of speaking, he was also respected. As the litter bearers had traveled through the crowd toward Fountain Court and the palace's eastern gate, the citizens had parted for him, their heads bowed in respect. However, it was all wrong; all less than it should have been.

He didn't like being in that room, smelling that air. Despite his fine clothes and the grandeur of his arrival, he felt like a spot of mud on a new, white carpet. When the people on the streets had bowed toward him, he knew they were bowing toward his chair and his suit.

What made him even more uncomfortable as he waited in the anteroom was contemplating how he had acquired the clothes. Mistress Rhina's shop on the corner of Gold and Thimble streets was the only establishment that had a complete suit of adequate fit and sufficient quality ready to wear. The suit had been ordered by Obone, eldest son of the Margrave of Rookhurst. Unfortunately for Mistress Rhina, Obone had come in second in a duel before paying his bill, the suit remaining on display ever since. Those who could afford such woven grandeur preferred their attire to be made specifically for them.

Elmutt negotiated for the suit, Mistress Rhina barely tolerating his less-than-common appearance. Mortice's entire pouch of coppers, however, was far short of the tailor's most generous price. Elmutt, devoid of more honorable options, posited to the good woman that it would be in her best interest if she gave him the suit at a price he could pay.

She laughed at him and asked what would happen to her. In a moment her shop was hung with rags, the floor covered with fresh garbage and at least a dozen confused Dung Alley rats.

Not only did he get the suit at no charge, but the good Mistress Rhina threw in a bath, haircut, shave, shoes, stockings, and undergarments as well. In addition, she ordered the litter chair and bearers for him and paid his way to the palace's eastern gate. Elmutt had arrived in style, true. However, he wore his suit like an aura of personal guilt. To get what he wanted he had driven the tailor to the limits of hysterical distraction, not to mention upsetting the rats.

"If she just hadn't laughed at me," he muttered. The thought removed not one particle of the guilt he carried, even though he had returned her shop to its original state, minus the articles on his back, and had sent the rats back to the alley, somewhat more confused. Murderer and extortionist, the picker named himself. I wonder what new skills this experience with the Levar will require?

"Good sir?"

Elmutt faced the door to see a servant clad in black and scarlet bowing in the doorway. "Yes?"

"I may present you to the Levar now."

"Where is Master Geth Dys?"

"He is with Her Magnificence."

Elmutt's fright climbed to dizzy heights. "I thought I . . . I mean, I wanted to speak to Geth Dys before seeing the Levar. I don't know what I am supposed to do."

The servant straightened, a pained expression on his aging face. "I am not in possession of this knowledge myself, good sir. If you would follow me, please?" The servant turned.

Elmutt followed in the servant's footsteps through the Grand Hall, each step toward the huge doors at the end of the hall seemingly another step closer to an undefined noose. As they approached the doors, two grey-uniformed stalwarts of the Levar's Guard opened them, revealing the interior of the Levar's Court.

The room was long, the wide tiled center completely empty. Four courses of stairs led to a higher level that surrounded the first, in addition to supporting the forest of columns that, in turn, supported the vaulted ceiling. The room was devoid of decoration or furniture save for the massive gilt throne occupying the center of the upper level opposite the huge doors. Standing to the right of the throne was the White priest, Geth Dys. Sitting upon the throne, her feet on a stool, was a little girl.

Elmutt was confused. The girl could be no older than eleven or twelve years. The Levar? He began to ask the servant, but before the first word escaped his mouth the girl turned her head from Geth Dys and looked in his direction. She was so far away that he could not make out her expression. The chamber was otherwise deserted.

As they came to the edge of the course of stairs, the servant stopped, causing Elmutt to bump into him. "I'm terribly sorry—"

"Your Magnificence," shouted the servant, "I present Elmutt, uh, Elmutt of the City of Liavek."

The girl giggled. "Elmutt Elmutt?"

The servant's face soon matched his scarlet trousers. "Just one Elmutt, Your Magnificence."

She motioned with her hand. "Bring him here, Togus. Be quick about it, then you may go back to spying for His Scarlet Eminence."

The servant's face achieved an even brighter shade of red. However, Elmutt thought he saw a hint of a smile on the White priest's face. Her Magnificence, the Levar, did not smile at all, even when she giggled. Elmutt hadn't thought faces that grim appeared on little girls any place other than Dung Alley.

As he limped behind the blushing servant, down the steps and across the sunken level, the Levar's image became clearer. She was a thin girl, her face a study in unhappy angles. Her complexion was fairer than average, but this seemed to be less a matter of heritage than of health. Her eyes were dark and expressionless, her hair black and cut short. On her head she wore a simple tiara of silver that gleamed in contrast to the black film of her gown.

The servant pulled Elmutt to a stop at the foot of the stairs to the throne level, bowed deeply, then turned and left the chamber, the huge doors closing quietly behind him.

Tazli Ifino iv Larwin, Levar of Liavek, kept an unblinking gaze on the garbage picker. "Geth Dys," she said, "this one is crippled."

The White priest nodded. "Yes, Your Magnificence."

"Leave us."

"Yes, Your Magnificence." Geth Dys bowed deeply, his hands at his sides, turned, and exited through a door behind and to the right of the throne. The Levar continued to stare at Elmutt after the door had closed. The chamber was as silent as death.

"Well?"

Elmutt tried to swallow, but his dry tongue became stuck in his throat. He attempted a badly executed bow of deep respect and wobbled back to a standing position. His lame leg was killing him.

The girl's eyes became hooded as a sneer crossed her mouth. "You are pitiful."

"Yes, Your Magnificence," croaked Elmutt.

She pushed with her feet, causing the stool before her throne to move in the direction of the stairs. "Sit there."

As best he could, Elmutt scurried up the stairs and sat on the stool, looking up at the girl. With the weight off it, the pain in his leg eased. "My thanks, Your Magnificence."

She sighed as though she were terribly bored. "Well, get on with it."

Attempting and failing at yet another swallow, Elmutt closed his eyes. "With what, Your Magnificence?" He opened his eyes to see that hers had, at last, acquired some expression: that of surprise.

"You do not know why you are here?"

"No, Your Magnificence."

She leaned her head against the throne's backrest, her dark-eyed gaze again upon him. After completing her study she pointed. "Those are not your usual clothes."

"No, Your Magnificence."

She nodded once. "What do you do, Elmutt of Liavek?"

"I . . . I am but a picker of garbage, Your Magnificence."

"Explain."

"I search through the things others discard, looking for things that I can clean and repair. I then take these things and sell them."

The Levar nodded. "I envy you." She closed her eyes, hence she failed to note Elmutt's raised brow and hanging jaw. "Geth Dys says that you have a rare power. A power to make fortunes."

"I seem to, Your—"

"I would have you make mine, garbage picker. What must be done?"

Elmutt's expression turned to one of horror. "No, Your Magnificence!" He knelt before her, his hands clasped before him. "I beg you not to have me do this! I *beg* you!" She simply stared at him with those unblinking eyes. He lowered his hands a bit and moistened his lips. "Your Magnificence, I have very little control over my power. I do not know either its strength or its limits. I could cause horrible harm. It is not my mind that controls the kind of fortune one receives, but my heart. I am discovering that I do not know my heart and the monsters that lurk there. Please spare me this."

She glanced to her left. "Geth Dys explained all of this." She suddenly looked back at him. "What do you think of me?"

"I?"

"There is no one else in my court chamber, picker. Tell me, and if you lie I will have your tongue torn out."

All Elmutt could think of was the perfection, regularity, and infinite nature of his luck. What does a garbage picker think about his world's ruler? "Your Magnificence, I have never thought of you before. This chamber is in a different world."

"I am mad, picker. You have heard that in your world, haven't you? She is *insane!*" She rolled her eyes and made smacking sounds with her lips. She stopped her performance, again fixing Elmutt with her stare. "What do you think of that?

What do you think—what do you believe—when you hear them say I am mad?"

Elmutt shook his head. "I do not know. How can I judge such a thing? I am—"

He felt her frighteningly strong grasp close over his clasped hands. "What do you *believe*, picker? In your most secret heart, what do you believe?"

He watched her hand on his for a second and looked up into her eyes. "I believe . . . I believe that you are very unhappy."

She held his hands more tightly. He thought he detected the glisten of tears in her eyes. "Do you hate me, picker? Do you wish me any harm?"

"No, Your Magnificence. No, but I cannot be certain. How can one be certain of such a thing?"

She released his hands and again leaned back in her throne, her eyes looking up. "There is a very stupid corporal of my Guard who once told me that a soldier always looks forward to change. Whatever the change might be, it has to be an improvement." She looked back down at the garbage picker. "To him it was a joke. To me it is not. What should I do?"

Elmutt closed his eyes, bowed his head and searched the dark corners of his heart for any little hate or resentment that might be hiding there for the girl. He could find nothing. He did find, however, the pain of his own life reflected in the Levar's face. He couldn't imagine why a Levar should find life to be the same burden that a garbage picker carried, but in truth this is what he believed about the girl. At least, that is what he *believed* he believed. He opened his eyes and struggled up off of his knees.

"You simply need to ask, Your Magnificence. Ask me for your fortune."

"What will be my fortune tomorrow, Elmutt? What will be tomorrow for me?"

The strange heat shot through Elmutt's breast. He looked wanly at the Levar. "Tomorrow, Your Magnificence, will be what my heart wished for you." He held his hands out to his sides. "But I have no idea what that will be." He held his hands together in front of him. "I am sort of new at this."

She made a hardly audible snap with her fingers. Immediately the huge doors to the chamber opened. "Picker," she snapped.

"Yes, Your Magnificence?"

"Until I find out what tomorrow will be for me, you will remain in the palace under guard." She waved her hand in dismissal. Elmutt bowed deeply, his hand to his forehead. When he stood he felt a presence behind him. He turned and facing him were four rather large soldiers of the Levar's Guard. As they marched out of the chamber, Elmutt gimped along as best he could in the center of their formation, convinced that his eyes had seen sunlight for the last time.

As dungeons go, Elmutt's guarded apartment in the palace overlooking Fountain Court was luxurious. It was certainly superior to Ghaster's cellar, and the roast pig with all of its trimmings that he had consumed that evening was the best meal he could ever remember eating. In fact, Obone's suit did not appear to take the possibility of gluttony into account. As the hour approached midnight, Elmutt still sat with his trousers unbuttoned and his jacket open as he watched the night. His surroundings were too dear to waste on sleep.

A thousand times he had searched his heart and had finally convinced himself that, if not good, the fortune he had made for the girl would at least cause her no harm. He began to imagine the possibilities, given that the fortune did turn out well for the Levar, especially if the girl kept asking for her futures one day at a time. In such a case he would always be needed at the palace. He had just congratulated himself on coming a long way from Dung Alley when he heard a tiny voice.

"The food and appointments are adequate, Elmutt, but why the armed minions outside your door, why?"

Elmutt looked to his right and saw Tavi, still in his purple outfit, reclining upon a golden cushion, gnawing on a grape. "I knew something would come to spoil it for me, you little beast. Crawl back beneath your rock."

"Why did the Levar want to see you?"

Elmutt looked back at the darkening square. Units of the Scarlet Guard, protectors of the Red Temple, were formally changing posts amidst shouted orders and drum beats. "She asked me to make her fortune."

The creature laughed. "Ho, and what kind of crawling thing rules Liavek now? Tazli the Tarantula? The Lobster of Liavek? It must have been very special, it must."

"You do not understand, Tavi. The Levar asked for a fortune

limited to tomorrow. We will have to wait to see what happens."

"Elmutt, what did you wish upon the mad brat?"

The picker felt the heat come to his face. The Levar was unhappy, not mad. And she was a young girl as well as his ruler, not a brat. He frowned as his feelings for the girl became apparent. What then had he wished for her? He slowly shook his head. "I do not know."

"With the reptiles hidden in your heart, pitiful one, I think we can depend on deliciously horrific results." The troll paused, continuing with a much quieter voice. "Geth Dys wouldn't have had you come here otherwise."

Elmutt sat up. "He advises the Levar. Obviously he hoped to do Her Magnificence a good deed."

The troll cackled. "In truth, Elmutt, you are fit for nothing more complicated than picking garbage."

Elmutt stood, buttoned his trousers, and faced Tavi. "Explain yourself!"

The creature reached for another grape. "It is so burdensome to peel one's own grapes." A mock sigh of despair, then Tavi leered at Elmutt. "Geth Dys is a White priest. You know something of their faith: that business with the endless births and rebirths. That is their public face. What you obviously don't know is their secret. I overheard Geth Dys when he planted it in you back in Ghaster's cellar. The Whites seek the destruction of reality. That is their secret mission; what they believe to be the path to ultimate freedom. Why do you think the priest had you make the Levar's fortune?"

"To destroy . . . Her Magnificence is but a part of reality. Even if I did my worst to her, it would only be a part of reality."

The troll shrugged as he popped the peeled grape into his mouth. "Darken the corner where you are." After swallowing the fruit, the creature observed, "As religions go, the Whites seem to have the opportunity for more fun."

"If you consider destruction fun."

"I do, I *do!*"

Elmutt again looked from the window at the night shrouded court. On the other side of the fountain, the White Temple loomed like a nightmare. If you destroy enough pieces of reality, reality itself will eventually be destroyed. He closed and rubbed his eyes. Does the White priest count upon my secret heart to destroy the Levar? Am I indeed engaged in a contract killing?

The new guard posted, the scarlet soldiers of the Red Temple stood motionless at their stations. If this is true, thought the picker, then the deed is already done. It is past midnight. This is tomorrow.

His creature asleep upon the cushion, Elmutt continued watching the square. Hours later the Scarlet Guard changed posts once more. Before they changed posts again, the morning sun was behind the White Temple, touching the waters high atop the court's fountain.

Outside the doors of the apartment there was a sharp voice issuing commands, measured footsteps moving away. Elmutt faced the door, his throat again dry. Tavi was missing from his cushion.

The door opened, revealing another scarlet and black clad servant. The fellow bowed and announced, "Master Elmutt, I present Her Magnificence, the Levar." The servant stepped aside as Elmutt doubled over into a deep bow, his gaze fixed on the carpet.

"Leave us." He heard the door close and again the Levar's voice. "Stand, Elmutt."

The picker straightened to see the girl. He almost didn't recognize her. Her face was soft, radiant, her mouth in a pretty smile. She wore a bright yellow gown and tiny pink flowers in her hair. Her dark eyes sparkled. A mock frown crossed her face. "Would you keep your Levar standing, garbage picker?"

Speechless, Elmutt again bowed. Without rising from his bow, he stumbled over to a chair and faced it toward the girl. "Please," he croaked.

She laughed and seated herself in the chair as the picker moved to stand in front of her, still bowing. "I ordered you to stand, picker. Why do you disobey me?"

Elmutt came out of his bow, the color drained from his face. "Your Magnificence, I . . ."

She waved him into silence. She sat staring at him for a moment, then she spoke. "Did you hear how the servant addressed you?"

Elmutt shook his head. "No, Your Mag—"

"*Master* Elmutt. That is what he called you. *Master*. I have made you a vavasor to show my appreciation for the fortune that you made me. What lands do you hold? I would make your title hereditary with lands."

"I am but a garbage picker, Your Magnificence."

"Where do you live?"

"Dung Alley, Your Magnificence."

The Levar frowned and rubbed her chin. "That will never do: the Vavasor of Dung Alley. That will never do. I will speak with the City General and have the alley renamed. If it is an alley, it would be too narrow to call a street." She nodded. "Fortune Way. That will be its name, and you are Elmutt, Vavasor of Fortune Way." She sat back, smiling. "Well?"

"I am, er, very honored, Your Magnificence." He put from his mind for the moment the disagreeable reaction of the alley toughs he knew who had unknowingly become his vassals. "Magnificence, what was the fortune I made for you, if . . . if I may be so bold as to ask."

The Levar looked puzzled for a moment, her gaze toward the window. She looked at her new vavasor as the puzzlement left her face. "Happiness. This day I am happy. Nothing more." Again she looked puzzled. "In words it sounds like such a small thing, happiness. However, it is more than all the wizards of Liavek could do for me." She placed her hand over her heart. "In here it is the fortune of fortunes, Elmutt." Tears came to her eyes. "The fortune of fortunes," she whispered.

Elmutt watched as the Levar laughed and wiped the tears from her cheeks. Perhaps, thought the Vavasor of Fortune Way, perhaps there is more to my secret heart than Tavi's reptiles. Perhaps I am not quite the loathsome creature Geth Dys counted upon me being.

"Again, my fortune, Elmutt. What will you make for my fortune tomorrow?"

Elmutt felt the glow in his heart and smiled confidently as he bowed toward the Levar. "It is done, Your Magnificence."

She stood as the door opened. "You will remain here with me in the palace, Elmutt. I cannot afford to let you get too far away from me."

"Yes, Your Magnificence. Thank you."

She left the apartment and Elmutt stood, a strange pride in his gut. I am not, he told himself, a complete monster. There is some good in me.

The door remained open and in stepped Geth Dys. Elmutt caught himself beginning a bow, reminding himself just in time that he too was a vavasor. He grinned at the White priest. "Good morning, Geth Dys."

The priest cracked the slightest of smiles. "Yes, it does seem to be an unusually good morning for a number of persons in the palace."

Elmutt felt a different kind of heat in his heart. "Geth Dys, where is the destruction you would have had me inflict upon that little girl?"

The priest looked surprised for an instant. He nodded as his face resumed its usual expression. "Of course, you have a troll. It never crossed my mind. I misread that." He reached out and closed the door to Elmutt's apartment. Turning back, the priest seated himself in the chair recently vacated by the Levar. Geth Dys nodded again. "I admit I misread you, too, Elmutt."

"Then my creature spoke the truth when he told me what you would have had me do? Destroy my corner of existence."

"It was an honest mistake. It is a cruel thing that a fortune maker cannot make his own fortune. Existence has always been your enemy. And you react to cruelty magnificently."

"That is something I would ask you, Geth Dys. Why can't I make my own fortune?"

"The laws of magic make it impossible to work magic on one's vessel of luck. A fortune maker *is* the vessel of his own luck. Hence, you cannot work your magic upon yourself. Unfortunate."

Elmutt pointed at the priest. "What did you mean by what you said: my reaction to cruelty? Why did you think I would be such a certain agent of destruction?"

The priest raised his brows. "After what I saw you do to the woman, I thought—"

"Cankera?" Elmutt dismissed the evidence with a wave of his hand. "I hated the hag. Everyone hates someone. But you, Geth Dys, counted on me to hate the world and everything in it. Why?"

Geth Dys read Elmutt's eyes for a moment, the hint of a smile on his lips. "I was referring to the wizard's granddaughter, Almantia. What I saw you do to her."

Elmutt felt desperate life draining from his veins. "Almantia?"

The priest placed his elbows on the chair's armrests and touched his fingertips together. "I was one of Yolik's wedding guests, except that there was no wedding. It seems that the shipowner, Brice, values Almantia's beauty above her other qualities."

"What do you mean?"

"You know my meaning."

Elmutt remembered: . . . *the feel of her hand upon his arm, the sight of her face glowing with joy and anticipation.*

"Oh, Elmutt, I am so *happy. What do you think will happen? Will I always be this happy?"*

A strange heat shot through his heart. . . .

"What . . ." Elmutt could hardly breathe. "Geth Dys, tell me, I beg you. What happened?"

"It seems that shortly before the ceremony was to take place, the bride-to-be conversed over Yolik's gate with a shabby, unhappy-looking gutter rat. Shortly afterward, Almantia's beauty began to fade. Her posture became stooped, her body twisted. Her face became narrow, her eyes receded into wrinkled sockets, her nose became hooked, and she acquired quite the most astounding dose of black-headed warts it has ever been my privilege to witness."

Elmutt covered his face with his hands. "No. Please, no."

"You see, Elmutt, I read the mind of that gutter rat as he stood there at the gate. The woman he did that to was the woman he loved more than life itself. And a spell of such power! Yolik himself could do nothing." Geth Dys leaned forward and stabbed at his chest with his thumb. *"I* could do nothing. It had to have been more than a mere magician's spell. It had to be the work of a fortune maker." The priest lowered his hand and leaned back in the chair. "I went after you and caught up just before you made the fortunes of the hag and her mate on Dung Alley. As I said, my mistake was an honest one. From the available evidence, how could I have concluded that your heart contained anything other than destruction?"

Elmutt shook his head. "Almantia? What has happened to her? Where is she? Does she . . . is she still . . ."

"To the best of my knowledge she is alive. Yolik had her sent deep into the Silverspine seeking the Bhandafs and a reversal of what he imagines to be her spell."

"The east . . ." Elmutt thought back. In the Two-Copper Bazaar the day before, Tavi vanishing in fright for no apparent reason, the litter-chair with its eight bearers. The drawn window curtains . . .

The curtain drew back further, revealing the twisted, warted face of a hideous crone. She held up a gnarled hand and motioned in Elmutt's direction. Her mouth opened but what she said could not be heard.

The bearers were headed toward the Levar's Highway. . . .

Geth Dys pushed himself to his feet. "If you could search

for her and find her, and then get her to ask you for her fortune, I suppose you could restore her beauty. Perhaps you could even create a future that would force her to be your wife." The White priest grinned. "Think about that, Elmutt, as you sit here day after day under the Levar's cruel confinement. Perhaps you can achieve a slight resentment against the one who would keep you here against your will. Understand that Almantia is under no mere spell. She is living her present; the present that you wished upon her. No magician, sorcerer, or Bhandaf spirit doctor can alter her condition. All that can be done is to cloud her mind, making her blind to the horror that she has become."

"Geth Dys, what of another fortune maker? Another fortune maker could—"

"No." The priest smiled. "You are the only fortune maker to come along for over two thousand years, Elmutt. There are no others." Geth Dys opened the door. "Think upon what I have said when next the Levar would have you make her fortune." The priest left the apartment, closing the door behind him.

Elmutt stared at the closed door for a long time. He had no doubt that if he could have made his own fortune at that moment, his death would be such as to make Cankera's end seem like a peaceful passing to a better land.

"Oh, woe! Oh, woe!"

Tavi appeared on the floor, rapidly pacing in a circle, his gaze downcast, his tiny hands pulling at his hair. Elmutt felt like killing the creature. He did not make the attempt, since through many prior investigations he had learned that he could not. There were two other reasons as well. First, the wish of death in his heart shamed him. It was just such a thing that had taken Almantia's beauty. Second, he realized that the troll's words were not mocking him. Tavi was agonizing in earnest.

"Speak, Tavi. What pains you?"

The troll waved his hands in the air and came to a stop facing Elmutt, his right hand scratching his chin, his face wrought in deep thought. "The White priest will be our ruin, Elmutt. He is too clever for *our* own good." He pointed a finger at Elmutt. "By Narkaan's knees, he would have you do your worst to the Levar!"

"I thought that is what you wanted, Tavi."

Again the troll's arms waved in the air. "Fool! Do you not see that the result of making the Levar's future a horror would end in your own death? If the Levar couldn't order up your nightmare, you can count on the Regent, a *Red* priest, to dish up disaster." Tavi shook his head. "Most likely, a very slow and *very* painful death!"

"Again, Tavi, I would think that end would be the kind of entertainment that would set your tiny warted toes a-tapping and your black little heart all aglow."

Tavi placed his hands on his hips. "We need solutions right now, Margrave of Muck, not sarcasm!" The troll folded its arms and glared at Elmutt. "If you die, the Bhandaf dancer will get me. Do you understand now?"

"Oh, yes." Elmutt thought of Zayieri. In another moment the course he must follow stretched before him. "We must escape, Tavi."

The troll clasped his hands behind his back and resumed pacing. "How? There is a guard outside your door, and more guards throughout the palace. They have all been warned by Geth Dys not to give you any opening to use your power. We can be certain that none of those uniformed lumps will ever ask you for a fortune."

The garbage picker managed a slight smile. "Perhaps, Tavi. However *you* might convince one of them to ask me for a fortune."

"Me? How could I?"

"You underestimate how seductive you can be, Tavi."

Guard Private Mandar Lann stood confidently at his noon post in front of the fortune maker's apartments, reviewing his orders. If the fortune maker wanted to go anywhere within the palace grounds, he was permitted, but could go only under escort. If the fortune maker should make an attempt to escape, Mandar would call out the remainder of the guard and restrain him bodily.

The White priest had stressed the importance of never saying any phrase that could be construed in any manner as a request for his fortune. No casual statements, such as, What of it, What will happen, and the like. Especially, he was not to let temptations of wealth or station seduce him into asking for a fortune in exchange for turning his back. Master Geth Dys had said that he had carefully picked the ones who were to stand guard upon the fortune maker. They were all fairly well off financially, and they were loyal soldiers—men and women of trust and honor with comfortably secure futures should they earn the gratitude of the White priest. It was a particular reflection upon Mandar's worth, and the recognition of that worth, to have been given this task. The guard was allowing his chest to inflate with pride when he heard a tiny voice.

"You are Mandar Lann?"

The guard frowned and looked around. "Eh? Who goes there?" He could see no one. Ignoring his ceremonial short sword, Mandar pulled his pistol from its holster and looked again. "Show yourself!"

"Down here."

Mandar looked down to see a tiny creature in a purple suit and yellow cape standing before him. The creature's ugly large head sported a mouth curled into an even uglier leer. "Eh? What *are* you?"

"You are Mandar Lann, soldier of the Levar's Guard?"

"Aye," Mandar responded warily. "What of it?"

"I am your troll. My name is Tavi."

"What!? My *what?*"

The troll's eyebrows went up as he held out his hand. "Now, Mandar, don't go making a big fuss. Each troll must be inflicted upon someone, and I have been assigned to you. You'll just make yourself crazy buzzing your head wondering why you. Simply accept your fate, and it will go easier for you." The leer widened. "A *little* easier."

The guard felt the cold sweat beading over his entire body. "There must be some mistake, creature—"

"Tavi."

"There must be some mistake, Tavi. I am a good man. A *good* man."

The troll blew on his fingernails and buffed them on the chest of his purple jacket. "And?"

"I am a *good man!* A true and loyal soldier, faithful to my church and my sovereign, thrifty, honest, reverent, kind to the elderly, helpful to the poor . . . nice to small animals—"

"Nevertheless," interrupted the troll, "I am yours." The troll reached up and placed a handprint in the center of Mandar's highly polished brass buckle. "Inspections in ranks are going to be much more exciting for you."

Mandar looked in horror at the handprint. Quickly pulling a cloth from inside his blouse, he polished the print from the buckle. "You can't do this to me—" By the time he had finished with the buckle, Mandar saw the troll scratching the polish on his boots with its fingernails. Mandar jumped back, away from the troll, raising his pistol. "No!"

The troll held out his hand, palm up, and a suspiciously oozy brown gob appeared upon it. "You certainly keep your uniform immaculate, Mandar."

"Take a step toward me, troll, and I will fire! I warn you!"

The creature moved toward him and the guard pulled the trigger. When the smoke cleared and the echoes concluded their circuit of the palace, Mandar looked in horror to see the troll still standing, unscathed. The troll was looking with amusement at the huge scar the guard's pistol had made in the Levar's polished marble floor. The troll leered again at Mandar. "Yes, yes, this *will* be an interesting assignment."

Mandar felt light-headed, and even more so when he noticed that the brown gob was no longer on the troll's hand. He hesitantly glanced at the front of his trousers and almost fainted. As the sound of approaching footsteps came from the Grand Hall, Mandar dropped his pistol, clasped his hands, and sank to his knees. "I have been everything good that a man can be. I do not deserve a troll!"

Tavi vanished and reappeared on the guard's left shoulder. "I can help you there, Mandar. You seem to be under the impression that reality is fair. I am pleased to be able to clear up this matter for you. It isn't." The troll pointed the fingertips of both hands toward his own breast. "I rest my case."

Mandar, still on his knees, his eyes closed, shook his head and wailed. "What can I do? Great Sarrow, what can I do?" The footsteps and shouts of a guard came closer.

"I suppose, Mandar, that there is only one thing that you can do."

The guard opened his eyes and looked at the troll. Tavi was reclining on the guard's shoulder, raised up on one elbow, his legs crossed. "What can I do? Please, creature, what can I do?"

A door opened and Mandar looked up to see the fortune maker standing in front of him. The guard looked back at the troll. The creature was pointing at the fortune maker with a gnarled thumb. "Ask him."

"What . . ." Mandar moistened his lips, swallowed, and hung his head. ". . . will be my fortune?"

The hallway was quiet and deserted, the marble floor unblemished. Mandar stood at his post, frowning. He looked down and confirmed that his uniform was in its usual immaculate condition. He unholstered his pistol, examined it, and confirmed that it was cleaned and loaded. He replaced the pistol in its holster and scratched his head. Something was bothering him, but he had no idea what it was. He looked down again and saw a tiny handprint in the center of his polished belt buckle. Quickly he pulled a cloth from inside his blouse and buffed away the mark. As he replaced the cloth he reviewed the orders he had gotten from the White priest, pleased at the honor of being selected for this important task.

"I can make you your fortune. That is my power."

Zayieri and Hidat sat upon their cushions. The dancer stared at Elmutt with her cat eyes. The troll was silently seated on the picker's shoulder. "And you would have us come with you to the land of the Bhandafs to find Yolik's granddaughter?"

Elmutt looked down at his hands on the table. "You would be a great help to me there, Zayieri. I have no knowledge of the Bhandafs and am ignorant of their ways. But more important than that, I need to know my heart. Should I have an opportunity to remake Almantia's fortune, I must do so free of anger, hate, jealousy, revenge, greed . . . all those things which now rest there." He looked up at her. "Before I make your fortune, and Hidat's, I need to do this. There are great risks, otherwise."

The dancer looked at the musician. "My husband?"

Hidat did not return the look. "You know I cannot go with you. Not to the land of the Bhandafs. Old Ogume would have me mutilated and put to death." Hidat looked at Elmutt, his lips touched by a bitter smile. "Ogume is Zayieri's father. He is a very powerful spirit doctor. I am not a Bhandaf; I only love one. Ogume disapproves." He turned his head toward his wife. "He would disfigure you, then cast you out."

Zayieri reached out and placed a gentle hand on Hidat's forearm. "My husband, our fortune could be to remove this pain between my father and yourself; between us and my people. We could live among the Bhandafs again, our land and position restored."

Hidat leveled his gaze at Elmutt. "We could, if the picker can learn his heart and gain control of his power." The musician glanced down at the table and watched as his fingers drummed there for a moment. The fingers stopped. Hidat took a deep breath, letting the air escape from his lungs slowly. He nodded and held out his hand to the picker. "Very well. We will take you to the land of the Bhandafs. I will arrange for the transportation and provisions."

Elmutt clasped the musician's hand. "I am so grateful, Hidat. To both of you."

Hidat smiled. "Keep in mind, Elmutt, that in associating yourself with the pair of us, whatever we receive at Ogume's pleasure will be shared by you. That is the law."

Elmutt felt Tavi pulling at his ear. He turned and looked at the troll. "What of me?" whispered Tavi.

The picker looked at the dancer, his eyebrows raised. Zayieri smiled warmly at the troll. "Tavi, if Elmutt should die in the land of the Bhandafs, you will not become mine. You will belong to an entire tribe, any individual of which can see and catch you, all of whom believe that trolls are hell demons, and that torturing hell demons brings one further into Bhanda's favor. In the land of the Bhandafs, Tavi, I suggest you devote your every effort toward keeping Elmutt alive."

The picker looked at his troll, and Tavi's face was no longer the color of mud, but was instead the color of ashes.

Beginning late that afternoon, and for the next twelve days, the tiny caravan of three camels followed the Levar's Highway east toward the city-state of Saltigos. On the twelfth day, just before reaching the city, they turned their mounts north into the evergreen forests of the Silverspine Mountains. In the forest the travelers would at times catch glimpses of the hideously ugly mountain folk that lived there, but they would jump from the tree branches, extend their membranes, and be gone among the trees shortly after seeing that one of the travelers was a Bhandaf.

The nights were spent by fires with Hidat's drum sounding a quiet beat and Elmutt sleeping with his head nestled between Zayieri's breasts, her arms wrapped around him, her lips whispering into his ear, the picker unconsciously answering her with slurred words and silent tears. At first this bothered Elmutt, thinking that Hidat would certainly take offense. Both of them assured the picker that this was the Bhandaf way of teaching him his heart.

And he was learning his heart. It was mostly good, the blemishes acquired as defenses against a life and existence of want and pain. It was a strong heart, too. Nothing less could have survived the pain, and the greater measure of the pain he had inflicted upon himself. Among many examples was Ghaster. The old man had said the words, but Elmutt had chosen to be hurt by them. His master had administered the beatings, but his bond child had chosen to stand there and take them, hoping that his welts would somehow please the unpleasable. He had even turned his love into pain.

He had learned that there was love in his heart, and not just a small measure. There was the love, of course, for Almantia. But love too for Zayieri and Hidat. Love for the little girl who carried the Levar's mantle. Even love for Ghaster. Even love for Tavi. What was the most incredible, and the hardest to find, was the love he had for Elmutt the garbage picker.

When he understood it, he shook his head in wonder. All of the things he had desired—the power, the friends, the possessions, the titles—were false lodestones, attempting desperately to attract the one thing of which he had an abundance: love. Love of self, and love of works. He found that his work had not degraded him; he had degraded his work. He had been a good—no, a *great*—garbage picker. He could see finds where others were blind, he could repair what others believed to be unrepairable, he could hold in his mind thousands of details concerning who threw out what at what time of the year or week, and he could make a profit at it. More than that was being his own master, the open sky above his head, the rich sights, tastes, and sounds of the city for a workplace, the countless interesting persons he knew, and the countless more he had yet to meet. But he had taken the joy out of all of it by telling himself that it was not enough. In the same manner, he had taken the joy out of his entire life.

As the caravan reached the crest of a pass that in the language of the Bhandafs was named Forbidden Way, despite the rows of skulls flanking the opening, Elmutt felt a strange peace within his breast. It was strange because it was a peace that had never before existed.

At night, in the pass:

"Zayieri, what if that which the White priests believe is true?"

"What do they believe?"

"That I am condemned to an endless cycle of births and

rebirths. That the only way to escape is to destroy reality itself."

The dancer looked at Elmutt with puzzled eyes. "There are worse things, Elmutt, than being condemned to immortality."

"Not if it is endless pain."

"True. But what if it is endless happiness? With each birth you get anew the choice between pain and happiness. If you choose happiness, your joy will go on forever. Most of us call this heaven. Why would you want to destroy that?"

The morning they reached the fertile bottom of the Valley of Bhanda, there was a single outstanding badness in his heart. It was not guilt over the hag. There was nothing he could do about Cankera's death. He could not change the past. For that same reason he had accepted his past with Ghaster and let go of what might have been. There was the guilt about how he had acquired his velvet suit. He had put that to rest when he determined to make restitution to the tailor. But still there was the badness of Almantia testing in his heart.

It was still a confusion: guilt for what he had done to her, knowing that making amends by restoring her full beauty would again place her out of his reach, grief at this certain loss, the desire to manipulate her future, shame at the thought. These were the things on his mind as he heard a shout, then an army of voices raised in a spine-vibrating cry.

"Hidat!" he called, Tavi's arms wrapped about his neck. "What is that?"

The musician held up his hand for silence. Before his hand came down they were surrounded by great black feline beasts ridden by springdart-wielding men and women who were clad in skins and red battle paint. All of the riders had the eyes of the cat. One of the warriors reached up and grabbed the reins from Hidat's hands. He grinned, displaying startlingly white teeth.

"Jhaas, Hidat! Jhaas! Re cagthgat te, tyah!"

Elmutt did not need a translator to understand the warrior's sentiment. It fairly radiated from his pores.

"At last, Hidat! At last! We have you now!"

More hands reached out, taking the reins from Zayieri and Elmutt. Weapons and voices upraised, backed up by the howls of the huge cats, it was difficult for Elmutt to hang onto his new sense of serenity, and he didn't.

• • •

They were taken to a stronghold within a city such as Elmutt had never before seen. The buildings were magnificent despite being made from stone and beaten earth. The largest of these, high atop a barren hill of naked rock with a view commanding the valley, was where they were taken. Deep within its bowels was a huge circular room illuminated by the flames of the pit that occupied the room's center. Six warriors stood behind Elmutt, Zayieri, and Hidat, while a seventh warrior held Tavi by the scruff of his neck. They faced the firepit.

Across the pit on the opposite side of the room rose an imposing idol, blackened by the flames that kept the smells of charcoal and crisped flesh in the air. Below the neck, the idol was carved into a huge cat, much like the ones ridden by the Bhandaf warriors who had captured them. Where there should have been a head, however, there was a terrifying tangle of at least a hundred living snakes, their bodies rising from the giant cat's neck, their black mouths issuing a chorus of quiet hisses.

Standing before the idol was a tall figure wearing the head of one of the same black cats. He was clad in robes of black fur. As he held his hands out in front of him, an enormous head of flames formed just above the pit, obscuring the view of the idol and the spirit doctor. The head of flames opened its eyes and spoke. The words were Bhandaf, and they shook the stones.

"Te, Zayieri, Hidat. Re cogh peh dyad!"

Zayieri took a step forward, bent over, and spat into the flames. As the flames died, so almost did Elmutt. Tavi had fainted. There was a murmur of shock from the warriors guarding them and from the Bhandafs gathered around the walls.

Zayieri shouted "Ogume, this is your daughter, not one from the other side of the Forbidden Way. Place your illusions aside and let us talk."

The cat man on the other side of the pit growled angrily, "Speak not the language from beyond the Forbidden in your father's temple!"

Zayieri held her hand out toward Elmutt. "My companion does not understand the words in Bhandaf."

"Hah!" The spirit doctor removed his mask and handed it to an assistant as he stormed around the edge of the pit, coming to a halt facing Elmutt. "Is this the new thing in your bed, Zayieri? I am not surprised at the ways you picked up beyond the Forbidden." Ogume glanced at Hidat and hissed, "I at least thought you to be a man!"

Hidat lunged at the spirit doctor but was restrained by the two warriors who guarded him. Zayieri stood between her husband and her father, facing Ogume. "Your mind rots with the evil it carries, my father. Hidat is my husband. I have no other bed. We have brought Elmutt of Liavek here upon his own request."

Ogume faced Elmutt. "Speak!"

"I . . . er . . . uh—"

"What language is this?"

"I, uh, do not know what to say, good sir."

The spirit doctor held his head back and looked down his nose as though he were examining an insect whose extermination was long past due. "My daughter and this man she wed will be consumed by the pit fires and your own bleached skull will join the ranks outside the Forbidden Way as the price of your visit. I would think your reason to be an important one."

"Oh, woe. Oh, woe!" wailed a tiny voice.

Ogume turned to his right and looked down at Tavi dangling from the end of the warrior's arm. "A troll? A fat little thing, too." He shook a finger at Tavi. "Take note, hell demon. We shall have that fat flailed off of you before night!"

"Oh, woe! Oh, woe!"

The spirit doctor faced Elmutt. "Now speak. Why have you come?"

"I seek the granddaughter of Yolik, wizard of Liavek. She was sent to the land of the Bhandafs by her grandfather to have a spirit doctor attempt to break the spell that has trapped her."

Ogume's cat-eyed gaze was unblinking. "She is here. Is that information worth three lives?"

"I have come to break the spell."

"You?" Ogume laughed and turned to wave his hand at a darkened arch beyond the pit. *"Goth vyad! Almantia nepri."* He backed out of Elmutt's view as a Bhandaf girl-child assisted a stooped, black-robed figure in their direction. Elmutt knew it was Almantia. The knowledge tore at his heart as he watched her struggle. Her head was completely covered by the hood of her robe, hiding her face. She pulled the child to a halt a few paces away. Ogume pointed down at his feet and ordered the child, *"Hys, nepri!"*

The child pulled the misshapen figure until it stood before Elmutt. The figure kept its head turned away from the travelers. Ogume pulled her until she faced the picker. With his right hand the spirit doctor drew back her hood, revealing her face.

"This is the woman you seek. She was a great beauty of only seventeen years, I have been told. Break that spell, Magician of Liavek."

The universe was filled with the hideous sight of Almantia's face, her eyes, the tears that flowed from them, the responsibility of it all. Her lips trembled, but she said nothing.

Ogume released her and folded his arms. "Bhanda does not want this spell broken. I have seen this for two days. Not all of the powers of this temple can change a single wart. What can *you* do?"

Elmutt pulled his arms free from those who held them and reached out to the crone. He took her hands in his, stared into her eyes for a moment longer, then drew her toward him. He held her tightly, one hand against the back of her head, his lips next to her ear.

"Almantia," he whispered, "you cannot forgive me for doing this to you, and I was the one. I was the one. I loved you and you didn't know. When you told me about the one you loved, my heart . . . But let me restore you to the way you were before. All you must do is ask me for your fortune. But you must limit it. Otherwise my heart, which still loves you, would force your tomorrows into a path that would shame me. Say only this: What will be my beauty? Say it."

He heard a whisper in his ear and felt the heat flash through his heart. For a moment longer he held her, knowing as he opened his arms that she would be gone forever.

Her hair was mussed, her eyes dazed, but she was again as beautiful as before. Her eyelids closed and she sank against Ogume. The spirit doctor, shocked at the transformation of the woman and startled at the sudden weight against him, lowered Almantia to the stones of the floor. Zayieri knelt next to her and placed a hand over Almantia's eyes. She looked back at Elmutt. "There is nothing to fear. She only sleeps." Zayieri moved her gaze from Elmutt to her father.

Ogume looked shaken. His gaze moved from his daughter to Hidat to Elmutt and back to Zayieri. Although glistening with tears, his eyes and voice were hard. "Forgive me, my daughter. It is the law. It is not my law, but Bhanda's." He gestured with his head toward her guards and the ones holding Elmutt and Hidat.

They were all dragged to the edge of the pit. Ogume, looking old and broken, stood before his daughter, his words coming hard. "You have gone beyond the Forbidden; it is tabu. You have wed one from beyond the Forbidden; it is tabu. You have come back; the law must be obeyed."

The spirit doctor glanced down, turned, and stood before Hidat. He looked into the musician's eyes. "You are from beyond the Forbidden; to be here is tabu. You have wed one of our daughters; it is tabu. You have . . . you have come back; the law must be obeyed."

He stood before Elmutt. As the spirit doctor talked, Elmutt searched his heart and studied Ogume, seeing not hate or cruelty, but the pain and love the old man had for his daughter, for his son-in-law, even the respect he had for a garbage picker from Dung Alley. "Young man, you have a great power. It is a treasure that you have squandered for a woman's beauty. May it be worth it to you. You are from beyond the Forbidden; to be here is tabu. You are here; the law must be obeyed, and the law is fire."

Elmutt smiled and asked, "Why?"

"Why?" Ogume frowned. "Why? The law is from Bhanda."

"What would happen if you didn't obey the law?"

The spirit doctor looked outraged. "Not obey the law! What would happen if we did not obey the law? Why . . ."

As a familiar heat glowed within Elmutt's breast, Ogume pondered the question. The more he pondered, the wider became his smile.

Elmutt left the Valley of Bhanda before Almantia awakened.

Hidat and Zayieri, comfortably established in Ogume's home, had wished him well upon his journey back to Liavek, and had invited him to return someday to see their fine home that they had already started building. Someday, perhaps, the fortune maker replied, and invited them all to visit him. Now that the Forbidden Way was no longer forbidden, a traveling Bhandaf might need a guide sometime. Along the way to Liavek, Elmutt met a traveler and swapped his fine suit of blue velvet for the traveler's more comfortable, if rougher, wear.

Elmutt carried with him a gift of magic from Ogume. The spirit doctor had cast Elmutt's future and had read much trouble for him from the Levar and her Guard as a result of his absence. Even at that moment, the White priest was filling the young girl's head with poison and her life with misery. Elmutt explained to Ogume why the Levar wanted him and the spirit doctor had given him an artifact of great power that would accomplish for the Levar the same thing.

They were only words, and words in Bhandaf at that. However, as Elmutt read the words, they made for him the future he would have wished for himself. In translation, the artifact read:

Yesterday was,
Tomorrow might be,
Today is.
I will cherish it.

Ogume's magic worked and Elmutt, Vavasor of Fortune Way, returned to picking garbage, and it was his festival. With his health, the open sky above him, and all of the people of Liavek for potential friends, he was a man of means. The people liked to see him come by, not just because they might alter their fortunes by asking for it, but because it made one feel good to be in his presence. He was a superlative garbage picker.

A few of the friends who visit him are Bhandafs, and they come away with tales of a depressed troll. The creature is not depressed, it seems, simply because its victim is always happy. There is more to it. All the troll needs to do to make himself happy is to ask the garbage picker for such a future. And the garbage picker is willing. However, the troll remembers too well the things he did to the picker in the past and is afraid that the picker's secret heart might contain one or two leftover bad turns. With all of his greedy dreams dangling before him, yet not being able to work up enough courage to trust the one who could grant his wishes, the creature remains depressed. The most delightful form of troll torture the Bhandafs had ever seen.

Some say that the garbage picker's fine home was restored to its former grandeur through his pickings' profits, but his loyal vassals along Fortune Way know differently. You see, if you should go to his home, once called Narkaan's Skull, to have him make you a future, you will be standing upon a fine carpet among expensive furniture and tapestries at the same time that Master Elmutt offers a joke about the squalor in which he lives. If you would ask his wife, she would explain to you that Elmutt refuses to give himself airs, believing that to live the way he always had lived is better for his character. Therefore, the magnificence you see, Elmutt sees as Ghaster's cellar. No one really knows what the place looks like. It's an illusion. After all, his wife is the granddaughter of a wizard. They seem to like it that way.

APPENDIX ONE

A Tourist's Guide to Liavek in the Year 3317

Contents

1. *Liavek*

Liavek, a trading city of perhaps 300,000 people, is located on the Sea of Luck. An excellent harbor occurring near the mouth of the Cat River encouraged the Liavekans to develop a fleet of merchant ships, and then a fleet of warships to protect their trade routes.

The city is composed of thousands of different quarters, each with its own style. The more notable neighborhoods include the Canal District, a very old but newly fashionable area for successful merchants and artists; the Levar's Park, a large public park with fine restaurants and strolling entertainers; the Merchant's Quarter, location of the city's largest market, called simply the Market; the Fountain of the Three Temples, once known as the Fountain of the Five Temples; and the docks, primarily warehouses and shipping offices of gaily painted wood that bustle with Liavek's trade during the day.

Liavek's Old Town is almost a city to itself—a city of rogues, artists, the very poor, the eccentric wealthy. Here are the Two-Copper Bazaar, a small market that does not close for nights or holidays, and Rat's Alley, famous for its disreputable entertainment. The more daring of the wealthy will spend an evening at Cheeky's, known for good dancers, bad wine, and exorbitant bills. The *very* daring visit the Big Tree, a sailors' tavern where theft can be less subtle than at Cheeky's. Not far from Rat's Alley is the Street of Trees, an ancient avenue that dates from S'Rian times. Wizard's Row, when it can be found, is on the edge of Old Town, between Bregas Street and the Street of Scales, terminating at Cheap Street and Healer's Street, and intersected by One-Hand Lane.

In the hills beyond Liavek's walls are farms, plantations, and the second homes of the very wealthy. Both tropical forest and swamps lie to the southwest. To the northeast are the foothills of the Silverspine Mountains. All these fall under Liavek's law. Traveling overland to the north takes one through farmland and savanna until reaching the Great Waste. At Waste's Edge is a village known as Trader's Town, the beginning of the most common route across the desert to the rich, distant city of TICHEN.

2. Citizens

Liavekans are a dark-skinned people of medium height who tend to have brown or black hair, though auburn and sand-colored hair is not uncommon. Liavek, being a cosmopolitan city, is inhabited by many peoples. All inhabitants over the age of fourteen are considered citizens, excepting bond servants, who acquire citizenship when their bond ends.

Men and women are equals at all levels of Liavekan society. This may be due to the Tichenese discovery some eight hundred years ago that the dried leaves of the plant now called **Worry-not,** when chewed every forty-eight hours, are an effective and inexpensive contraceptive for both men and women. Visitors to Liavek are often amused that Houses of Pleasure are easily identified by windowboxes filled with beautiful blooms, and among them are the unassuming pale blue flowers of Worrynot.

3. History

Dated from the legendary founding of TICHEN, Liavek was settled in 2619 by nomadic tribes who had lived among the Tichenese for several generations, until they were driven from Tichen. The town of **S'Rian** existed on the hills overlooking Liavek's harbor, but its inhabitants, a slightly smaller, slightly darker people than the present Liavekans, were conquered and much of S'Rian was destroyed.

The next several hundred years were ones of slow growth and many minor wars with the nearest coastal city, Saltigos. The Liavekan colony of Hrothvek was founded, and Liavek began its expansion across the Cat River into New Town. The last Saltigan war ended in 2948. Saltigos has since been, in name, an independent city-state, though its Chancellor has always been a relative or a nominee of the Levar. In the absence of a direct heir, the Chancellor of Saltigos generally succeeds to the Levar's throne. Hrothvek is also, in name, an independent ally of Liavek, though its ruler is a Chancellor of Liavek.

Following the acquisition of Saltigos, Liavek entered into a long period of competition with KA ZHIR, the major trade city across the Sea of Luck. This eventually led to war, which ended in 3298 with Liavek the stronger.

4. Social structure and government

Liavek's hereditary ruler is the Levar, a title that translates to "the luck of the people" in Old Liavekan. The present Levar is Tazli Ifino iv Larwin, who will come of age in 3320. Her present Regent is His Scarlet Eminence, Resh, the First Priest of the FAITH OF THE TWIN FORCES.

Liavek's nobility are composed of chancellors, margraves, counts and countesses, and vavasors. Much of the governing is done by a group of eleven nobles and eleven merchants known as the Levar's Council, whose decisions require the Levar's sanction. The noble members are chosen by Liavek's chancellors, who may sit on the Council or appoint a representative. Merchant members of the Council are elected every five years by the members of the Merchant's Society.

Nobles are all those who are acknowledged offspring of a noble parent or who are adopted by nobility, though titles and lands usually go to a single heir. Merchants are all those who pay the annual dues of fifty levars to the Merchant's Society.

Beneath the merchants are the independent traders, who pay ten levars yearly to the Merchant's Society, followed by skilled craftspeople, unskilled workers, and indentured servants. Though Liavek once permitted slavery and made much profit from trading in slaves, slavery has been banned for over sixty years.

5. Law and law enforcement

In Liavek, laws almost solely concern property. Penalties are harsh, beginning with flogging or a day of public confinement tied to a post in Fool's Square, and progressing through branding, death, and mutilation. Imprisonment is thought unusually cruel, fit only for kidnappers, rapists, and counterfeiters of Liavekan currency. Such people are exiled to Crab Isle.

Duels are illegal, but are generally ignored by the law. Traditionally, duels must be agreed to by both parties in the presence of four disinterested witnesses, two chosen by each participant, and a healer must attend the duel.

The Levar's Guard is also the City Guard. Guards are well paid, and therefore less susceptible to bribery than comparable forces in other cities. Guards are known by their grey vests and pants. Badges of rank are sewn onto the left shoulder, and higher officers are identified by a blue sash or cape.

All citizens have the right of trial within twenty-four hours of accusation. Three judges are chosen from older citizens who have been recognized by the Society of Judges. One is chosen by the accuser, one by the defendant, and one by the Society of Judges. If these three cannot come to an agreement, the accused is freed. Retrial is permitted once if new evidence is found.

6. *Language and greeting customs*

Liavek's heritage is most evident in its language. Properly a Tichenese dialect, Liavekan is so thickly accented with the sounds of southern languages such as Old Saltigan, Zhir, and S'Rian, and so richly spiced with words for things that are unique to the south and the sea, that it is unintelligible to the modern Tichenese.

The forms of greeting in Liavek are an unamalgamated mixture of several traditions. The Tichenese bow with their arms at their sides; the depth of the bow and how long it is held indicate the degree of respect. The Zhir (and, long ago, the S'Rians and the Saltigans) place both hands to their foreheads.

In Liavek, the bow is used mostly by those whose ancestors were the conquering Liavekans and is therefore appropriate in Court. The hand gesture is favored by those descended from S'Rian or emigrated from the south, and is more often used casually. However, the Liavekan gesture is done with a single hand, and certain subtleties have crept in. The number of fingers touched to the forehead and the length of time they're held there indicate the degree of respect or formality intended. Uncommon usage has extra impact: a friend might thank you by pressing both palms to his forehead; an enemy might insult you by touching one finger to his forehead and grinning while holding it there.

7. *Clothing*

As the climate is warm, clothing tends to be loose or lightweight. Modesty is not a dictum of the society, but the sun demands certain precautions be made by the fair-skinned. Sandals are the usual footwear, though light shoes and short boots are sometimes worn. As the nights can be cool, jackets, capes, and other forms of outerwear are common, though these are usually of linen, cotton, silk, or lightweight wool to protect the wearer from the daytime sun as well as the cool night.

8. Weaponry

Single shot muskets and pistols sometimes supplement the wealthy soldier's equipment. These are generally matchlocks or wheellocks, for flintlocks are rare. The harbor, ships, and city walls are guarded with cannon, catapults, and arbalests. Officers and the wealthy frequently carry pistols, though swords are considered more appropriate for dueling and are generally more dependable. Swords tend to be sabers or rapiers, though short swords are favored by sailors.

9. Transportation and communications

Horses belong to the wealthy, donkeys or camels to the middle classes. Oxen and water buffalo are common draft animals. Taxis tend to be human-drawn two-wheeled carts called footcabs, and polemen serve the canal district.

A primitive postal system is evolving, both within Liavek and in other cities, and post horses are stationed along the Levar's Highway for royal use. There is also a thriving "scandal sheet" or "half-copper rag" business that provides news, gossip, lies, fiction, reviews, and essays to any who care to buy from street hawkers. These are usually four or eight page newspapers, sometimes illustrated with woodblock prints.

10. Money

The basic monetary unit is the levar, a small round gold coin. The five-levar gold coin is larger and five-sided. The ten-levar piece is thicker than the five, and ten-sided. Silver pieces are half-levars, quarter-levars, and tenth-levars. Copper coins are, prosaically, two-coppers, one-coppers, and half-coppers. One hundred coppers equals a levar. Five levars will feed and house a family of four to six people living moderately for a month; a half-copper will buy a mug of ale or a couple of apples.

11. Food and drink

The plains to the west produce a seemingly endless supply of grain, beef, pork, mutton, and domestic fowl. Due to the distances involved, vast underground granaries have been built along the Farmer's Highway so livestock will not lose too much weight on the trek to Liavek. These granaries are of immense strategic and economic importance.

A variety of game birds are caught in the salt marsh to the south, as well as exotic seafood, particularly crustaceans ranging from tiny marsh crabs no larger than a thumbnail to something resembling a giant sea-going cockroach that weighs as much as forty pounds. The mountains of the Silverspine provide their share of produce. In the foothills are ancient vineyards, higher are olive groves and, still higher, is the domain of crag sheep, prized for the difficulty of their hunting as much as for their meat.

The sea provides Liavek with its people's favorite food. Fresh raw shellfish in the spring, dried salt fish for long journeys, healthful sea grasses to flavor soups and stews, and the meats of uncountable sea dwellers all form the heart of Liavek's cuisine. Perhaps the only staple of Liavekan dining that cannot be found near Liavek is kaf, the strong, hot drink brewed from beans imported by the Zhir or the traders of GOLD HARBOR.

Perhaps the most distinctive Liavekan dish is the pot-boil. At its lowliest, a pot-boil is a long-simmered soup of fish or meat or fowl, but in Liavek, it has become an art. More than one establishment has had pots in continuous operation for over four hundred years. High on the craggy face of Snowhome is a monastery rumored to have tended a pot-boil for two thousand years.

Alcoholic beverages range from the wheat beer of the western plains to the red wines from Saltigos and the foothills of the Silverspine. Several tiny mountain villages distill Dragonsmoke from barley that is malted and cooked slowly over peat fires. Less skilled distillers, in an effort to duplicate this, produce a cheap, potent liquor often called Dragonpiss.

12. The calendar and holidays

The Liavekan calendar was taken from TICHEN, with twelve months of thirty days to the year (Snow, Rain, Wind, Buds, Flowers, Meadows, Reaping, Heat, Fruit, Wine, Fog, and Frost) and five days of Festival, which begins the year on the winter solstice. Every four years is the Grand Festival, which has six days.

The week of five days consists of Sunday, Moonday, Windday, Rainday, and Luckday. For some workers, the week is divided into four days of work and one of freedom, though others work eight days and take two days off. Tenth Day is an unofficial holiday for almost everyone.

During major holidays, such as the Levar's birthday (which is always celebrated on the summer solstice), almost all work ceases, except in such establishments as those in the Levar's Park, the better restaurants in the Canal District, and all other businesses that ordinarily operate twenty-four hours a day. At such times, Wizard's Row can never be found.

13. Gods

There are uncountable beings who are either gods or demons or neither, depending on one's faith. Many of these beings favor a particular people or locale. Some will come when summoned, some will not. It may be that some are created by their summoner in the act of summoning.

Rikiki is a small blue chipmunk who will sometimes grant tiny favors in ways one least expects, in return for nuts and much patient explanation. Though not presently worshiped by any organized group, Rikiki may have been a god of S'Rian. Many Liavekans leave bowls of nuts "for Rikiki," particularly on holidays.

14. Religion

Perhaps the largest, and certainly the most conspicuous, religion is the **Faith of the Twin Forces,** or the Red Faith. The Red priests believe that fate is decided by weighing the many tiny choices one makes in one's life. Their leader is His Scarlet Eminence, Resh, the First Priest.

While "good" is to be preferred when following the Red faith, the worst mistake that Red adherents can make is to divide their actions between extremes of good and evil. The Reds believe that in the afterlife one is treated according to one's behavior in the world. For example, those who alternated between torturing small children and saving the lives of wounded animals will be torn apart throughout eternity by the two conflicting forces of the universe. The way to avoid this is to center one's acts around a standard. A common center for such activity is self-survival, since survival is usually thought morally neutral. Good deeds are sought since they ensure a certain degree of better treatment in the afterlife, but after an unusual good deed (such as saving a child), one should perform other deeds of intermediate goodness (such as giving food to a beggar) before continuing life as usual.

The Red priests function largely as counselors: "What shall I do, O scarlet one, so that the conflict between the person I am and the deed I must do (have done) will not destroy me?" An effective priest knows exactly how "good" or "evil" a person is, and knows how to counsel that person in behaving consistently with his or her present self, with a secondary goal of weaning that person to a path of "good." A professional thief who finds a lost child will not get the same advice as a doctor.

The Book of the Twin Forces is the most commonly known collection of the writings of the Red Faith.

The Scarlet Guard is a mercenary force almost as large as the Levar's Guard. The duty of the Scarlet Guard is almost exclusively to protect the wealthy temples and monasteries of the Red priesthood, though they have come to supplement the Levar's Guard in the palace since His Scarlet Eminence became Regent.

The Black Faith, or the **Kin of One Path,** believe in an Absolute Goodness, and that only by always choosing honesty can one achieve a heaven that is kept for those who are truly good. They also believe that contact with evil or with compromise will corrupt, so their order is primarily a monastic one. Their temples are open one day a week for instructing any who come seeking truth. They are led by a council of five elders.

The White Faith, or the **Church of Truth,** sees the universe and all promises of heaven as cruel lies, and seeks to accept or escape an endless cycle of rebirth. These "anti-Illusionists" believe that the only choice worth considering is that of self-interest. They do not hire guards, for all White priests are magicians. Most White priests carry a device of string and wood called a Sharibi puzzle attached to their belts. *The Book of Oblivion* is the most ancient collection of writings of the Church of Truth.

The Pardoners, a sect of mendicant priests who will intercede with any god on anyone's behalf, have a modest hostel in Liavek. Most people like them but consider them a little crazy; few actively disapprove of them. They are the jacks-of-all-trades of the priesthoods, and often come from those who left or were cast out of other faiths.

The Way of Herself is more a path to enlightenment than a belief in a deity. "Herself" refers to the teacher-saint who founded the religion. Practitioners of the Way kill only out of need. Food is considered good reason, but gluttony, especially overindulgence in meat, is contrary to the Way. Self-defense is also considered good reason.

Whenever practitioners draw or are offered water, they pour a libation onto the soil to symbolize the principle that anything given to the earth returns multiplied. Other humans also rate good treatment according to the Way. It encourages sensitivity, patience, and kindness toward believers and nonbelievers.

The Green priests, or **The House of Responsible Life,** are an order of suicides, and an offshoot of an older and more sinister church that concerned itself largely with death. The original Green priests had preferred to kill others; the first members of the new order applied the old order's collection of exquisite, exotic, or painful methods to themselves.

The Green Order has a formidable bureaucracy to delay, give advice to, or screen out altogether those candidates who hope to escape their legitimate responsibilities, or who have otherwise unworthy motives for suicide, or whose families are likely to raise a fuss. The order thus finds itself being the only organized body in Liavek that attempts to prevent suicide.

15. Tichen

The Tichenese Empire has reached its greatest geographic expansion, extending to mountains in the west, the Great Waste in the south, the ocean in the east, and the ice lands in the north. Tichen is famed for its schools, which are governed by centuries of tradition, and its crafts. It is the largest city in the known world. Though Tichen has been conquered several times in its distant past, its conquerors have always been absorbed into Tichen's culture.

Tichenese are, for the most part, a very dark people with wiry hair and broad noses. Their navy is not very good, but their army is immense, so none of the southern cities openly play pirate with Tichenese vessels.

16. Ka Zhir

The city of Ka Zhir, located across the Sea of Luck, is Liavek's primary trade rival. The Zhir are related to the S'Rians, and so are slightly smaller and slightly darker than most Liavekans. Their speech is more guttural. Ka Zhir controls much of the kaf, sugar, copper, and woodworking trade from the lands around it, which are noted for jungles and volcanoes. Slavery is permitted in Ka Zhir. The ruler of Ka Zhir is King Thelm; his heir is his eldest son, Prince Jeng.

17. Gold Harbor

Gold Harbor is a trading town near the mouth of the Sea of Luck. There is almost no such thing as a typical resident of Gold Harbor; though the town is smaller than Liavek, it's even more racially and culturally mixed. It occupies an important strategic position, since it is halfway between KA ZHIR and Liavek-controlled Saltigos, and its neutrality is a pivotal point in the uneasy peace between the two nations. Gold Harbor is governed by a Mayor who is elected by Gold Harbor's wealthier merchants.

18. Ombaya

The little inland nation of Ombaya is located to the southwest of Liavek. Its people are as dark as the Tichenese, but very tall and slender. Ombaya is governed by a benevolent matriarchy, and the dominant religion is the Way of Herself. The tenets of the Way are demonstrated to good effect on the farms of Ombaya, which produce huge yields of vegetables, fruits, and grains—and the poultry is almost beyond belief.

Ombaya also follows the Way in its defense posture. It is a peaceful, neutral nation, but if threatened, it destroys its enemy in the most merciful fashion possible.

19. The Farlands

"Farlands" is the Liavekan name for the continent across the ocean where paler folk live. One of its more important countries is **Acrivain,** and there are a few Acrivannish exiles in Liavek, generally called Farlanders or, even less politely though perhaps not maliciously, "ghosts" by the Liavekans.

20. Other sapient beings

The **Kil,** or the sea folk, are mammals, not amphibians. The Kil are tall, and most of their skin is covered with a reddish brown pelt. Their hands and feet are webbed, and their faces are very broad, with deepset eyes and wide, almost flat, noses. Mating between human and Kil results in a sterile child. The Kil pity these halfbreeds, who have less skill in the water than sea folk do.

The Kil, when trading with humans, use their race and their sex as a last name. A male Kil is *a'Kil,* a female, *i'Kil.* Though the Kil have warred with humans, they have never warred with Liavek. Kil Island is forever theirs by treaty, and they seem to accept the encroachment of humanity along Kil Coast.

The **mountain folk** live high in the Silverspine. They have a name for themselves, but it is so long and so hard to pronounce that no human has yet successfully memorized it. Their hands and feet are very strong, with long, clawed digits. They are almost unstoppable climbers, and a membrane stretching from arm to torso on both sides enables them to leap and glide downward for short distances. They are astonishingly ugly by human standards, wrinkled, leathery, hairless, and grayish. They are mammals. Their language is rich and subtle, and their highest art is storytelling. The mountain people are shy and fierce, and humanity has only begun to learn about them. It may be possible for a human/mountain folk interbreeding to produce offspring, but that may never be tested, given how unsavory each race finds the other.

Trolls are possibly mythical beings that choose an unwilling companion to torment, generally until the victim's death. It is said that only the victim can see and hear the troll, though some say it can make itself visible to whomever it chooses. Many people in Liavek do not believe in trolls, though "May you be ridden by a troll" is a common curse. It is rumored that cats and a few other animals might be able to see trolls, who may therefore avoid people who have such pets.

The **Bhandafs** are a fierce and independent people who may or may not be human. Their eyes are inhumanly catlike. Whether this is the result of genetics, or magic, remains to be learned.

Appendix Two

A Magician's Primer

Everyone born in the world has an attribute commonly called one's "luck," one's "magic," or, in Tichenese fashion, one's "power." This magic manifests itself on birthdays, and then only for so long as one's mother was in labor. During this birthday luck period, one's fortune will be unusual, either good or bad in tiny, quirky, often unnoticeable ways. It is customary for people who are content with their lives to stay indoors during their birthdays in hope of avoiding situations where a freak of chance may intervene in their fate. Except for birthdays, this luck period is a minor matter for the average person. For anyone who wishes to be a magician, it is crucial.

During the birthday luck period, it is possible to perform magic. It is not, however, easy. The study of magic requires years of practice, which cannot be achieved to any significant degree during the few hours each year of an individual's birthday luck. The solution is to transfer the essence of one's magic (one's "luck") from one's physical self into another thing or being. Then, so long as one is within three paces of the vessel containing one's luck, one can practice magic throughout the year. This transference, called *investiture,* can only be done during the birthday luck period.

Investiture is extremely difficult for novices. If a would-be wizard can't invest birth magic into a vessel before the birthday luck period ends, the luck is freed and the person sickens, and within a few days, dies. Therefore, magicians study the theory of investiture for years and practice tiny magics during their birthday luck periods until they are ready to attempt investiture. If the transference is successful, the serious practical study and eventual mastery of magic may begin.

A consequence of investiture is that a magician's luck is more predictable than that of other people, being slightly benevolent during the magician's natal anniversary and slightly malevolent for an equal period six months later on the midyear day. Every birthday, the magician's magic leaves the vessel in which it has been placed and returns to the magician's body for renewal. The magician must then reinvest it before the period of birthday magic ends. If this is not done, the magician will be without magic for the next year.

If the vessel of a magician's luck is lost or stolen, it may be destroyed by the magician's enemies during the ill luck hours of the magician's midyear day, thus destroying the magician's luck forever. The magician whose luck has been destroyed invariably sickens, but having already been weaned from luck, will usually recover, no longer subject to the yearly whims of fate—and no longer able to practice magic. If the vessel of luck is destroyed at any time other than the midyear period, the luck will merely be freed from its vessel to return to the magician's body at the magician's next birthday.

Master magicians who lose the vessel of their magic or who choose to spend a year without investing their power have one advantage over their nonmagical fellows. Being familiar with the use of magic, they can still use magic in very tiny ways during the five or ten minutes each day that correspond to the moment of their birth. But the magicians whose luck was destroyed during their ill luck hours and the magicians who chose to bind their magic (see below) cannot draw on this "birth moment" magic.

There are many schools of magic, each holding that it is best for learning the nature and use of magic. Though the schools vary in many ways, the following facts remain true:

1. It takes years to master magic, even after successful investiture of luck.

2. No magician can use magic if the vessel of magic is not

within three paces, excepting master magicians, who can do very tiny magics without their luck nearby during the five to ten minutes of each day that correspond to their birth.

3. Magic must be invested outside of the magician's body. If the vessel of magic enters the magician's body (if an invested ring is swallowed or an invested sword pierces its owner), the luck is freed.

4. Magic can only be invested in a unified thing. If that thing is significantly altered, the magic is freed. If this happens during the magician's midyear hours, the luck is destroyed.

5. Magic can be invested in a living thing, but at great risk. Death of a living vessel invariably frees the magician's luck.

6. No magician can do magic directly on his or her vessel of luck, as it is the magician's source of magic (or perhaps it is the magician's link to the source of magic; opinions vary).

7. Only acts of an immediate nature can be done directly with words or gestures by a master magician. These include such things as levitation, mind reading, fortune-telling, conjuring fire, creating simple illusions, etc.

8. Major spells must be done through ritual. The key to ritual magic would seem to be the creation of an appropriate mood, and faith in the act being undertaken. Many magicians create their own rituals, which often involve the use of arts such as painting, doll making, and storytelling to aid in defining the desired result.

9. As magicians cannot create something from nothing, and as no magician's spell can last longer than a year (when luck returns to the magician's body), magical artifacts are rare. Only a major magician can create one, during the time of that magician's birthday luck, by permanently investing an object with magic, leaving the magician forever magicless. This process is called *binding*, to distinguish it from the temporary investiture. A magical artifact is almost impossible to destroy, and its destruction means the physical dissolution of its creator. However, the creator's death will not affect the artifact's existence.

Magical artifacts may be used by anyone who knows their secret, but they never have more than one magical function, for the process of binding demands intense focus of will.

Appendix Three

Liavek: A Creation Myth

Know, my Excellencies, that there is a world beyond ours where magic is not bound to the laws of luck, where magic may not exist at all, and if it does, that world's inhabitants know little of it. In this world, seven writers gathered together, and these are their names: Pamela Dean, Nathan Bucklin, Steven Brust, Patricia Wrede, Kara Dalkey, Emma Bull, and Will Shetterly. They lived in a city named Minneapolis, and when they first gathered, their names were not known as those of writers, for none of their work had ever been published.

Because their world seemed deficient in magic, several of these writers created other worlds, and they would invite friends together on a weekend evening to have adventures in these imaginary worlds. The friends would take the parts of individuals in the world. The creator would direct their adventures and act the part of any additional characters that might be necessary for the entertainment, which was akin to a game and to an improvised play. The name of Patricia Wrede's world was Lyra, and Kara Dalkey's was Vesta, and Steven Brust's was Dragaera, but those realms take no part in my story (though in other tales, they are mighty lands, indeed). What is important is that they existed, and provoked Will Shetterly to create a world named Liavek.

Ah, you listen more closely! But this is not what you expect, for that Liavek was the faintest shadow of ours. Two adventures were enacted there. Will Shetterly was The Magician, Rikiki, the Levar, Rusty, and Stone. Emma Bull was Snake. Steven Brust, Patricia Wrede, and Kara Dalkey were adventurers who have not been seen since those games. Pamela Dean was audience, prompter of ideas, and baker of cookies. Still, this is a thread, it is not the tale. For the second adventure in that dim Liavek was the last, and Liavek was all but forgotten.

Now, to return to the first thread: Patricia Wrede sold her first novel, *Shadow Magic,* soon after these writers gathered together, and then *Daughter of Witches, The Seven Towers, Talking to Dragons,* and *The Harp of Imach Thyssel.* Steven Brust sold his first, *Jhereg,* and then *Yendi* and *To Reign in Hell.* Will Shetterly sold *Cats Have No Lord,* and Emma Bull sold "Rending Dark" to *Sword and Sorceress.* When Terri Windling, the editor who had bought all of their novels so far, received Pamela Dean's *The Secret Country,* and Kara Dalkey's as-yet-unpublished novel she decided to set these writers to a task. She asked them to create an anthology in which all the stories occurred in the same place and time. But they were too few to fill such an anthology, so she bade them invite writers whose work they knew and respected to complete the volume.

The first part of the task was to build a world in which many writers might play, and so the two threads of this tale finally intertwine. The writers had all created literary worlds of their own for the sake of their fiction. Confronted with the task of creating yet another world, they remembered Liavek, and that it had hardly been used, and so it was adopted for their purpose.

As for the other writers invited to this anthology, they were known to the group only by their works. Gene Wolfe was recommended by his masterwork, the four books that compose *The Book of the New Sun.* Nancy Kress was known by her delightful first novel, *The Prince of Morning Bells;* her second, *The Golden Grove,* had not then been published. Megan Lindholm's credentials were *Harpy's Flight* and a gripping short story in *Amazons,* for *The Windsingers* and *The Limbreth Gate* had yet to appear. Barry B. Longyear had written *Circus World,*

You are the key to the entire story

SWORDQUEST™

Enter the magical realm of SWORDQUEST™—where every hero you've ever wanted to be or know lives at the call of your imagination. Written by Bill Fawcett, a life-long gaming enthusiast, the SWORDQUEST™ novels are also challenging games. Instead of just reading the exciting adventures, you decide when to use your magic, when to fight, when to run, and who should live or die!

__0-441-69715-1 **Quest for the Unicorn's Horn** $2.95

__0-441-69709-7 **Quest for the Dragon's Eye** $2.95

Prices may be slightly higher in Canada.

Available at your local bookstore or return this form to:

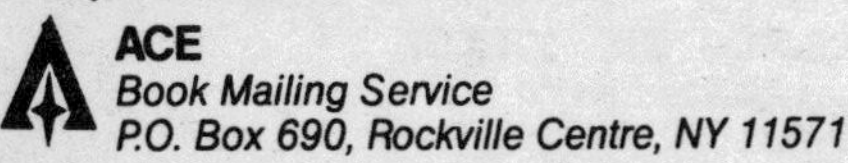

Please send me the titles checked above. I enclose ______. Include 75¢ for postage and handling if one book is ordered; 25¢ per book for two or more not to exceed $1.75. California, Illinois, New York and Tennessee residents please add sales tax.

NAME________________________________

ADDRESS________________________________

CITY________________ STATE/ZIP________________

(Allow six weeks for delivery.) SWORD

MURDER, MAYHEM, SKULDUGGERY..
...AND A CAST OF CHARACTERS YOU'LL NEVER FORGET!

TM

EDITED BY

ROBERT LYNN ASPRIN and LYNN ABBEY

FANTASTICAL ADVENTURES

One Thumb, the crooked bartender at the Vulgar Unicorn...*Enas Yorl*, magician and shape changer ...*Jubal*, ex-gladiator and crime lord...*Lythande the Star-browed*, master swordsman and would-be wizard...these are just a few of the players you will meet in a mystical place called Sanctuary. This is *Thieves' World*. Enter with care.

__80583-3	THIEVES' WORLD	$2.95
__79580-3	TALES FROM THE VULGAR UNICORN	$2.95
__76031-7	SHADOWS OF SANCTUARY	$2.95
__78712-6	STORM SEASON	$2.95
__22550-0	THE FACE OF CHAOS	$2.95
__80594-9	WINGS OF OMEN	$2.95

Prices may be slightly higher in Canada.

Available at your local bookstore or return this form to:

ACE SCIENCE FICTION
Book Mailing Service
P.O. Box 690, Rockville Centre, NY 11571

Please send me the titles checked above. I enclose ______. Include 75¢ for postage and handling if one book is ordered; 25¢ per book for two or more not to exceed $1.75. California, Illinois, New York and Tennessee residents please add sales tax.

NAME_______________

ADDRESS_______________

CITY_______________ STATE/ZIP_______________

(allow six weeks for delivery)

SF 2